Praise for Tiffany Baker's

Mercy Snow

"Tiffany Baker excels at creating offbeat characters with big hearts who live in difficult circumstances. Nineteen-year-old Mercy is unforgettable as she ekes out a living in the harshest of circumstances while caring for a young sister and battling the town's wrath. This third great novel, following *The Little Giant of Aberdeen County* and *The Gilly Salt Sisters*, clinches Baker's place on the 'must-read' list."

—*Minneapolis Star Tribune*

"Baker is masterful at creating elegantly flawed characters who are both believably ordinary and extraordinary."

—*Family Circle*

"I was completely swept away in this gothic tale of three women linked by secrets, some long buried, some far more recent. From the opening scene to the final page, Tiffany Baker kept me entranced in a novel so richly atmospheric that when I closed the cover, I was sure I could smell the paper mill on my clothes and hair, and hear the churn of the filthy Androscoggin River outside my door. MERCY SNOW is a testament to the dark power of secrets; a power that can bind us together, or drive us apart."

—Jennifer McMahon, author of
The One I Left Behind and *Island of Lost Girls*

"Baker deftly balances personal grievances with broader concerns about pollution, economic justice, and corporate responsibility in small-town America." —*San Jose Mercury News*

"Strength and quiet beauty mark Baker's writing...Her style perfectly suits the mood, time, and place of this tale. Though it tells an old story that extends back at least to Shirley Jackson's 'The Lottery,' MERCY SNOW provides an authentic universe of damaged souls and a fantastical heroine."

—Anita Shreve, *Washington Post*

"[MERCY SNOW] limns tensions between two disparate families in Titan Falls, NH, while adding the dark, gothic feel of a decades-old mystery. When a terrible bus crash threatens to expose a secret, the mill owner's wife decides that she can protect herself only by driving out the on-the-margins Snow family. But young Mercy Snow heartily resists efforts to blame the crash on her troublesome brother. Then a crumbling skeleton is uncovered near the crash site, and the narrative goes into high gear."

—*Library Journal*

"Tiffany Baker's raw and powerful writing almost reads like a screenplay in its simplicity, suspense, and dialogue that jumps off the page... The town, the woods, the river, the blood of humans and beasts: they're all characters in Baker's novel, as important as any of its living women. That's what makes her writing so gripping. It's an experience that haunts long after the final page has been turned."

—*Toronto Star*

Mercy Snow

Also by Tiffany Baker

The Gilly Salt Sisters

The Little Giant of Aberdeen County

Mercy Snow

A Novel

TIFFANY BAKER

GRAND CENTRAL
PUBLISHING

NEW YORK BOSTON

This book is a work of fiction. Names, characters, places, and incidents are the product of the author's imagination or are used fictitiously. Any resemblance to actual events, locales, or persons, living or dead, is coincidental.

Grand Central Publishing
Hachette Book Group
1290 Avenue of the Americas
New York, NY 10104

www.HachetteBookGroup.com

Printed in the United States of America

RRD-C

Originally published in hardcover by Hachette Book Group.

First trade edition: January 2015
10 9 8 7 6 5 4 3 2

Grand Central Publishing is a division of Hachette Book Group, Inc.
The Grand Central Publishing name and logo are trademarks of Hachette Book Group, Inc.

The Hachette Speakers Bureau provides a wide range of authors for speaking events. To find out more, go to www.hachettespeakersbureau.com or call (866) 376-6591.

The publisher is not responsible for websites (or their content) that are not owned by the publisher.

Library of Congress Cataloging-in-Publication Data

Baker, Tiffany.
Mercy Snow : a novel / Tiffany Baker. — First edition.
pages cm
ISBN 978-1-4555-1273-7 (hardcover) — ISBN 978-1-4555-1274-4 (ebook)
1. Families—New England—Fiction. 2. Family secrets—Fiction. 3. City and town life—New England—Fiction. 4. Domestic fiction. I. Title.
PS3602.A5887M47 2014
813'.6—dc23

2012051304

ISBN 978-1-4555-1275-1 (pbk.)

For Ned

Grief teaches the steadiest minds to waver.

—Sophocles, *Antigone*

Mercy Snow

Prologue

It was the beginning of winter, and except for the drone of the St. Bartholomew youth group's bus, Devil's Slide Road was empty, dark, and icy, the result of a late-November freeze. The children on the bus were either sleepy after the outing to the movie theater in Berlin, New Hampshire, or hyped up and distracted by the antics of their friends. The alert ones gathered in a noisy cluster at the back of the ancient yellow bus, the boys shoving and teasing, girls giggling. Up at the very front, eighteen-year-old Suzie Flyte sat by herself, staring silently out the grimy window at the prickly expanse of pines, birches, and oaks she knew was there but couldn't see.

In one fist she clutched a single red woolen mitten. She had lost the other one somewhere on the excursion—probably in front of the theater, when she'd taken them off for an illicit smoke—but when she'd looked after the movie ended, she didn't find it. She closed her fingers tight around the remaining mitt, her lips flattened in annoyance. She was the daughter of a mill man. She knew not to lose what little was given her. She knew even better not to let someone else take it.

But then she had taken something herself tonight—taken it back at least, which maybe wasn't the same thing, especially since it hadn't been for her own benefit. She licked her lips and blinked in the nocturnal gloom of the bus. From the back she could feel the puzzled gaze of her childhood friend Nate seeking her out, but she refused to turn to meet his eyes. She would talk to him when they got back to Titan Falls, when they were standing again on familiar ground, although after what she had unintentionally witnessed in Berlin, Suzie was no longer sure if where she was going and where she had been were one and the same. She used to think so. Now she wasn't so certain. She was just riding along here in the middle of the quandary she suddenly found herself in, on this muddy excuse for a road, bounded by trees on one side and a steep ravine on the other.

She squinted as the bus's spindly wipers passed across the blurry windshield, watching as Fergus, the driver, downshifted and then gripped the steering wheel tighter. An evil S-curve with a tilt was coming up, and the snub nose of the bus was leaning into the curve now, Fergus's cue to start pumping the brakes slow and gentle before switching to the accelerator. Suzie braced herself against the bus seat, waiting for the centrifugal pull of the turn, but it never came.

Instead a set of high beams illuminated the bus from behind, ricocheting off the rearview mirror, blinding Suzie. She blinked and watched as Fergus groped for the wobbly gearshift, but before his hand could connect, they were once again plunged into darkness as the vehicle that had been behind the bus tried to pass inside the curve, forcing Fergus closer to the ravine. Suzie gasped as she turned her head and realized who must be driving and that she was very likely the only one who had. Fergus let out an indignant half stutter as the bus fishtailed, then teetered, and finally began to roll.

The instant of great disaster, it is often said, is an elongated one, as if in witnessing its own demise the human mind is wont to wind the moment out long and then longer still. *God from God, light from light,* Suzie dutifully recited every Sunday in one of the plain pews of St. Bartholomew's Church, chin tucked against her neck, hands folded in front of her, but until this very instant, in this confusion of the bus's free fall, she had never known what the words meant. Now, in a terrible rush, she divined the lesson: God or man, you were only as good as what you begat on this earth.

Far ahead of them on the road, the indifferent sputtering of a truck could be heard, vanishing slowly around the bends. Suzie barely registered the noise as the bus plunged toward the bottom of the ravine. Her focus lay solely with the boy behind her. *You are not your father,* she thought, pushing the idea toward him, as if it were a sentient thing he would be able to scoop up to his chest and cradle. *You are so much more.*

God from God. Light from light. In the end it was all one and the same. But this illumination was brief for Suzie—a mere flash, as is all revelation. Before it had faded, the bus hit bottom, Suzie's vision exploded into a kaleidoscope of dancing glass, and she slipped into darkness, taking everything she had just gleaned with her.

Chapter One

At the time of the accident in the mid-1990s, when the area's string of paper towns first began to wither and die, Titan Falls wasn't yet a hollowed-out settlement stuck at the wrong end of nowhere, but it wasn't a far cry from that either. While it was true that the sulfurous, stinking waters of the Androscoggin were running much clearer than they had decades before, the village was still only just full enough of wood pulp, buzz saws, and good honest muscle to be barely tipped to the correct side of profitable. Now and then it struck June McAllister—the mill owner's wife—that Titan Falls was nothing more than a drunken jumble of timber and human grit, an accidental collision of industry and nature, but she was careful never to voice that thought out loud, especially not to her husband and most especially not to the other mill wives. To them she appeared to believe in the singularity of the town's fate with the same blind assurance her fingers took on during the sewing circle she hosted. At first, June had found the custom archaic, a throwback to her mother-in-law's time, but, as with everything else in her life, she soon learned that personal will was no match for force of habit where the women of Titan Falls were concerned.

"The Lord giveth and the Lord taketh away," she found herself chirping week after week, doling out advice like she was serving up neat pats of iced butter. It was an old wives' saying she'd often heard growing up and had hoped by now to have escaped. The ladies around her would pause, then shrug and bob their heads. One of them might snip a thread from her pile of sewing with a bare front tooth. Another would slide a new row of stitches across the cool steel of a knitting needle. It was fine and well for June McAllister to sit there and orate in her own house, of course. The Lord *did* give and then take away. The problem—and the truth that none of them ever dared to utter—was that in a town like Titan Falls, smeared up flush along the river and frequently pummeled by it, it was often difficult to tell which was which.

It wasn't that the other women didn't like June (although in truth they didn't), it was just that they didn't trust her very much. She wasn't, after all, a natural-born daughter of the place. Instead she'd struggled to become one over twenty years of marriage to Cal, the fourth-generation owner of the Titan Paper Mill and, really, the sole lifeblood of the town. At first, as a scholarship girl fresh out of the ranks of Smith College and totally unfamiliar with the mores and means of the North Woods, June had found the geography of Titan Falls shocking in its stony glory. She'd been raised in a shaky-jointed, not-very-prosperous town on the Gulf Coast of Florida. The architecture of June's childhood had been sandy and loose-slatted, all tin roofs and concrete blocks, peeling shutters and slow-twirling ceiling fans. The smell of sea salt had corroded everything all the time, clattering insects had made the sticky air vibrate, and colors were either vibrant and urgent—bougainvillea, birds-of-paradise opening on their stalks—or buffeted and past their prime.

Until Smith, June hadn't known that air could turn so crisp

it was like getting a first kiss, that a tree could burst into the color of fire and then change again into a skeleton of itself and then yet again, in the spring, haze into unexpected blossoms. She learned to drink tea hot from a silver pot instead of sweet and iced, saved up for and bought herself a camel-hair coat, and dreamed of becoming a literature professor so that she would never, ever have to leave this new and glorious world of leaded windows, mahogany library shelves, needlepoint cushions, and cathedral towers.

And then she met Cal on a weekend jaunt to Boston. She was at a house party hosted by her roommate, Janey, who knew Cal's best friend from summers spent on Nantucket.

"He's a senior at Dartmouth, and I hear he's a mill man," Janey had whispered in her parents' well-appointed living room, eyeing Cal's chiseled jaw and strong shoulders with appreciation as she handed June a warm beer. At first June had misunderstood. Her heart had skipped to think that finally, after almost two and a half years up north, she was meeting another soul like her, another working stiff accepted into this rarefied world of college and summer houses but yet not of it.

"No, silly," Janey had said with a laugh, correcting June. "His family *owns* the mill." One of the very oldest in the East, it turned out, and June's cheeks had flamed like the autumn trees around her. She spilled some of her beer onto her skirt, but Cal didn't seem to notice, or if he did, he liked what he saw.

"Hello," he said, stepping right up to her and cupping her thin hand in his generous palm. "You're Janey's roommate at Smith, aren't you? What are you studying?"

"Literature," June had answered without hesitation, and Cal had nodded thoughtfully. She held her breath, waiting to see what he would say.

"You know, Whitman wrote *Leaves of Grass* on paper made by my family's mill."

June gaped at him. It had never occurred to her to consider the physical provenances of the works she pored over day after day. That this wide-necked, blue-eyed boy would be able to lay such casual claim to what June considered mythic amazed her. When he offered to fetch a second drink for her, she let him, and when he asked, one year later, for her hand, she said yes right away, egged on by her girlfriends, who assured her that she was trading up—books for real life, an unfinished education for a giddy leap up the social ladder.

But Titan Falls, it turned out, was nothing like the New England of Smith or, indeed, of the literature she'd studied so ardently and written so many essays about: the blooming lilac bushes of Whitman, the pin-straight woods of Thoreau. Instead the world of Titan Falls reminded her a little of her old life in Florida, but on a much vaster scale. If she went five minutes out of town in three directions, she found herself enveloped by a swath of forest so great it was like stepping out of time. The river cut along the fourth face of the village, forming a line of currents, sludge, and rogue logs. June learned quickly that in Titan Falls the wilderness was a bounty, yes, but that it could also turn around and swallow a man whole in a heartbeat.

The Androscoggin, June also discovered over time, came with its own problematic history. It was a long-troubled stretch of water, beautiful on the surface but poisoned underneath, like a ruined woman who'd kept up her face but let the rest of herself fall to hell. Sulfur dioxide still escaped from the mills, and in the summer the town sometimes had to put out bubblers to aerate the water enough to keep the fish alive. In spite of that, clumps of algae continued to bloom like roses every August, spreading a tangy phosphate odor across the back of June's tongue. During her first year in Titan Falls, she'd found the stench overwhelming, but her mother-in-law, Hetty, had assured her that she would get used to it.

"This is nothing. When *I* was a bride," she said, twisting her dented wedding ring for emphasis, a ring so worn that June pitied her for it, little imagining the coming stretch of years that would rub her own ring to dullness, "we used to say the river was too thick to paddle and too thin to plow. Mud would turn yellow, and the paint on all the houses would peel. Kids used to bounce quarters off the scum that floated down here." Her expression soured. "Now we're so regulated, fish can barely piss in the river. Not that it stops the damn town from blaming the mill for every last thing. You'll find that out, too."

Hetty died from liver cancer a short year after June was married, and a heart attack claimed Henry, Cal's father, soon after, and though June never said so, she often wondered how much the pollution from the river had to do with their demises, just as she wondered if it was the cause for the occasional flotillas of dead trout that popped up or even the babies sometimes born in the area with stunted fingers, cleft palates, or tongues so stubbed they couldn't suck their mothers' milk. When she found out that she would be unable to bear any more children after the birth of her son, Nate, she spent hours pacing along the banks of the waterway, staring at the swirling muck, a misgiving building inside her that she knew she could never voice.

For that was part of the deal she'd made by coming to live in Titan Falls—a private bargain she'd struck in the deep tissue of her heart. As long as the town spared her its eternal suspicion and took her in as one of its own, she vowed, she would turn a blind eye to the soot clinging to roots of the place. She would do as her mother-in-law suggested and ignore the little details of decay that snagged along the corners of her gaze, letting the dark surface of the river ripple in peace, the way it had for generations.

Over time June proved to be an apt pupil of Titan Falls. Even the other women couldn't begrudge her that. In a blizzard her pantry was the best stocked, and she was always ready to share. She possessed a whole cupboard of muffin tins molded for various holidays: bunnies for Easter, trees and stars for Christmas, jack-o'-lanterns for Halloween. Following in Hetty's civic footsteps, June oversaw improvements to the library, handpicking the leather chairs and the globed reading lights as if she were outfitting a fancy gentleman's club. On the Fourth of July, she helped festoon the tiny main street in patriotic bunting before handing out ice cream with the other Acorn Association ladies.

The parts of Titan Falls to which she couldn't turn a blind eye, she simply avoided. The derelict mill cottages, for instance, down by the river, where her son used to love to play in the summer when teenagers weren't carousing in them. The mill itself, since it was a largely male domain except for Gracie, Cal's phlegmatic secretary, and the quiet woman who came in on Friday night to clean the office. And most of all, the old homestead out on Devil's Slide Road, where the river folded back in a crook and stewed in such foulness that no one was very surprised when a lone woman named Gert Snow went missing out there in the early 1950s.

As a very young child, gossip had it, Gert had been waspish and sour-faced, but as a young woman she'd grown into a great beauty—so lovely, in fact, that it was rumored she'd even turned the acquisitive eye of Henry McAllister. Fire broke out in the family home and killed her parents during the great drought of '42, when the river stank so hard that all the silverware in town tarnished overnight and even the flies out that way dropped dead. People said Gert survived the disaster out of pure spite. Some folks even suggested she might have been the one to light the blaze, but absolutely everyone agreed that the girl's behavior after the tragedy was not right. Instead of accepting the baskets of vittles and wares people left for her on the edge of Devil's Slide Road, Gert hurled them into the ravine with curses, then proceeded to build herself a shack barely fit for livestock. She stalked the woods of her family land with a rifle and perfect aim, bringing back the corpses of deer and hares, skinning them and leaving their remains hanging in the trees as a warning to intruders. The chimney of the little smokehouse, untouched by the conflagration, belched at all hours of the day and night, and people assumed that Gert must be living on the hardest foods imaginable: smoked jerky, roots, and the bitter berries of the North Woods.

A halfhearted search party tramped up and down Devil's Slide Road when she disappeared a decade later, but not much effort was made and she was never found. In truth, no one would even have known how to bury the likes of Gert. Since she was godless to her guts, it wouldn't have been right to mix her bones up with the town's good Protestant ones. The other Snows had always been laid to rest elsewhere by their kin—no one was sure where—but there wasn't a soul left in the immediate family to do that now, and no need anyway. The townsfolk simply bowed their heads that week at prayer and then let a slow tide of moss and rot pull the empty shack back down to the earth for the next twenty years, when a distant relative of Gert's, a man named Pruitt, showed up to claim the place. People tended to drive slow past the Snow stretch, even in all sorts of weather, and they were wise. The river cut a notch deep down to the bottom of a ravine there, and the mud oozed a peculiar yellow color. "Brimstone," the locals called it, and knew enough to take it easy on those patches.

"Let the river lie," was Hetty's advice on the matter the first time June asked about Gert's history, shortly after her marriage. When June pointed out that she'd been talking about a woman and not the Androscoggin, Hetty simply smiled. "In Titan Falls," she said, "everything begins and ends with the damn river. You'll see. If you're smart, my dear, you'll stay clean out of all of it."

Cal had put it another way. "What you don't know can't hurt you," he'd said, and for many years—right up until the crash that changed everything—June chose to believe this.

She was mixing the batter for a cranberry cake on the evening when it happened. Thanksgiving was tomorrow, and the recipe was one of the deceased Hetty's holiday specials, a combination of sweet and sour that perfectly recalled her disposition. Later it would occur to June that perhaps this casual whisking and stirring was what ended up muddling her future, but eventually she decided that couldn't possibly be. After all, providence wasn't something you could stick a spoon into and mix to your own devices. If it were, June would have done so long ago. Any woman in Titan Falls would have.

She was alone. Cal was leaving straight from the mill for the lake cabin, where they always spent Thanksgiving if the road wasn't snowed in yet. She was supposed to wait for her seventeen-year-old son, Nate, to return from a trip with the church youth group to the movies in Berlin, then head out to the cabin with him, where she would finish baking her cake, infusing the air with a bittersweet haze before she finally slept. All around her on the counter, neatly boxed, were the trappings for their holiday feast—the plump turkey, legs folded like those of a portly gentleman taking his ease, a sack of dusty yams, a bag of marshmallows, and a stalk of brussels sprouts. Two cans of pumpkin. A tin of lard. Cream and pearl onions and white bread already cubed and mixed with sage for the stuffing. June could name the contents with her eyes closed. Too much for three people, and certainly too much for June to load into the car with no help, but tradition called.

She ran her hands over her hips, ruing how square they were growing. Nothing helped. Every year there was just the littlest bit more of her. June's mother had been a wide-set woman, too, and it was one of the things June had sworn she wouldn't repeat in her life, even if it required ever-increasing severity. She baked cakes and cookies. She grilled steaks, and she creamed potatoes, and she buttered bowls of peas, but she rarely ate any of it. Maybe that was why, more and more frequently, she felt like an observer when it came to her own life.

In the earlier years of their marriage, Cal used to come home early from the mill and help her carry the Thanksgiving items out to the car, fitting boxes in the trunk like he was doing a puzzle, laughing and trying to grab June's hips when she swished past him for another load. But that was before—back when Nate was still in elementary school, when the mill could barely keep up with orders, and most definitely before Cal returned from a business weekend in Boston with another woman's bra rolled inside one of his dirty shirts.

Although it was five years ago now, June could still close her eyes and see the black scrap of a thing like she was peering through a freshly washed pane of glass. It had been lacy and so cheaply made that June hadn't even had to ask if the woman was someone Cal was serious about. When she confronted him, Cal had admitted everything and then promised it wouldn't happen again. And it hadn't either, as far as June could tell. Still, ever since then it seemed as if Cal had come back to her in body but not completely in spirit. Normally it didn't bother June—much. Marriages cooled. Their strings loosened and stretched, like the sagging plastic straps on old lawn furniture. It didn't mean you had to rush off and buy a whole new set. Until tonight, in fact, June hadn't even thought of that other woman.

The phone rang. June jumped and wiped a smear of flour off her forearm and then very slowly laid down the rubber spatula she was holding. The back of her neck stiffened, and the little hairs on her forearms stood up. She glanced out the window. The evening had gotten genuinely nasty. When it was icy and wet out like this, when the dark started to come early and the days grew short, evening calls were never very welcome things.

"Hello?" Just as she feared, through a terrible cloud of static, she heard the gruff voice of Abel Goode, the sheriff. "Abel," she said, untying her apron and trying to keep herself calm. "What can I do for you?"

She and Cal received calls all the time from Abel—some of them serious, some of them less so. Titan Falls had never had a proper mayor. Instead it relied on generations of McAllister men and their wives to function as de facto arbiters of the town's disasters, windfalls, and disagreements. The phone might ring at midnight—indeed did on many occasions—and Cal would be summoned to help break up a bar fight, or negotiate a round of gambling gone bad, or help someone haul a drunk friend out of the river: men's business, always, matters of blood, whiskey, money, and fists. The stickier details of town life—the pain of childbearing, for example, or the ways you could feed five children on one mill man's salary, the consequences of early widowhoods and pregnancies—were left to the women to solve with common gossip and tight purse strings.

The line crackled as June forced herself to concentrate. It turned out that this time Abel wasn't saying anything good. "June, I don't know how to tell you this, but there's been an accident with the St. Bart's youth-group bus. It's plunged off Devil's Slide Road. You'd best come quick."

All June could do was form an empty balloon of noise, an ineffective syllable sent heavenward. She closed her eyes. No one ever got close to the edge of Devil's Slide Road unless it was someone who deliberately wanted to take the long way down, but surely that couldn't be the case with Fergus Bell, who'd been driving the youth group's bus for thirty years and who could make those slippery turns with one hand roped to his chest.

June felt the backs of her knees start to buckle, but Abel barked an order. "June, listen. I'm taking care of Nate. Call Cal."

The command strengthened her resolve. She drew in a fortifying breath. Now was truly not the time for panic. "Yes, of course. I'll do it right away." She hung up and dialed the mill, her fingers moving from rote memory, but the phone simply rang again and again, maddening as a single note struck over and over on a piano, not even going to the answering machine. June replaced the receiver, frustrated.

She gathered her coat and hat, leaving the cake batter a sticky mess in its bowl. She thought about trying Cal one more time but knew it would be useless. He must already be on his way to the lake cabin. People would be expecting him—broad-chested and bossy as a bull—to arrive at the accident scene, his shirtsleeves rolled to the task, his rumbling voice giving orders in the night, but she was going to have to do. Maybe it was even for the best. After all, in Titan Falls sorrow usually did end up being women's work.

It was cold on the road when June arrived—cold enough to freeze the treacherous mud from yellow to brown, cold enough to mute the usual hooting of the owls. She parked as close to the accident scene as she dared and climbed out of her car, peering down into the ravine where the river flowed and where she could see the ancient bus smashed on its side, its windows blown out, part of its roof dented, its back end sunk in the river's icy water. In front of her, lit by panicked bursts of flashlights and too-bright ambulance sirens, paramedics scurried and bustled. They slipped and grunted as they ferried first-aid boxes, stretchers, and lanterns over to the lip of the gully, taking deep breaths and descending into the blackness like reluctant divers entering a toxic sea.

"Nate!" June cried into the pandemonium, praying he wasn't one of the children being brought up on a stretcher or, worse, left behind in the half-deluged bus. "Nate!" Where *was* he?

"Mom." Out of the darkness, Nate suddenly appeared beside her with a tartan blanket wrapped around his shoulders and a piece of gauze taped over a bloody notch above his left eye. He was walking—slowly, but still on his own power—and he appeared severely chilled. He had the beginning of a shiner, but otherwise he was fine, June saw, blessedly, wonderfully fine.

"He's the best of both of us," Cal had been fond of claiming in the early days of Nate's infancy, when parenthood had still been a fresh bruise for him and June, leaving the two of them tender in spots they weren't accustomed to yet. They would hang over

Nate's crib as he drifted off to sleep, watching his tiny chest rise and fall.

"He's the best of *everything*," June would answer back, and she still felt this way. By all rights Nate should have been off at prep school like his father and his grandfather before him, but June had been unwilling to end his childhood so soon, and Cal, who was happy to save the exorbitant tuition, reluctantly agreed to break tradition and let Nate attend the local high school. "As long as he keeps up his grades," Cal had warned, glowering. "He has to do that. McAllister men go to Dartmouth. End of story."

Other seventeen-year-old boys sulked and stole beers from their parents' refrigerators. They slouched over bowls of cereal in the morning and listened to cacophonous rock music. They wore dirty blue jeans and smelly shirts, impregnated girls, and crashed cars. But not Nate. Even during adolescence he had remained tidy in his personal habits, studious without being nerdy, well reasoned, and polite.

In any other boy, such goodness might take a turn to treacle, June recognized, but Nate was too much his father's son for that. Without even trying—certainly without June's help and without much of his father's either, who was always at the mill, always fretting over the endless business of grinding wood into pulp—he seemed to have absorbed the unwritten rules of male conduct to perfection. On the football field, he slapped his teammates' backs and told filthy jokes, with teachers he was able to distinguish himself without getting called a suck-up, and when it came to girls, he always seemed to have a date if he needed one, even though June suspected that his soul secretly belonged to Suzie Flyte, just two weeks older than him and his devoted childhood friend.

Closer than playmates, Nate and Suzie had grown up almost

as cousins. They'd had the chicken pox together, and learned to swim at the same time, and had run away from home to a fort they'd made out of one of the old worker cabins behind the mill. So far there had never been any indications that Suzie reciprocated Nate's affection, but the thought that one day the girl might declare her love always gave June a bittersweet pang. She didn't mind sharing her son, but she wasn't quite ready to lose him for good yet.

She folded as much of Nate as she could into her arms now, trying to collect all of him against her. *It's okay,* she reassured herself. *He's okay.* The bargain she'd made with the river all those years ago had apparently held. June had never once crossed it, and it hadn't crossed her back. But that didn't mean she couldn't question the gift. She straightened her arms. "What happened?"

Nate appeared dazed. "I don't know. There was a car behind us or something, and then the bus jerked, and then I don't remember much. Just that we rolled and then slid until we hit the water."

June brushed her fingers over the cut on Nate's forehead. "Are you sure you're okay?"

"I'm fine. The paramedics checked me out."

"What about Suzie?" June peered around her, trying to find the girl in the confusion.

Nate frowned and slid his eyes away from his mother's. "I don't know. We weren't sitting together."

June wrinkled her brow. That was odd. She opened her mouth to press Nate for more information when she saw something that stopped her tongue cold. Two of the paramedics were struggling up the incline with the slender body of a teenage girl slung between them, a single red mitten dangling from one of her coat pockets, her long silvery hair wet from the river.

"Oh, my God," June choked, turning her face into the chest of Abel Goode, who'd silently materialized beside her. The brilliant scarlet of the wet wool vibrated behind her closed eyes. She knew that color well.

"She's the second-to-last one," the stouter of the two paramedics puffed to Abel on the edge of the ridge. "Just got the driver to deal with now. He has a heartbeat going on and not much else."

Beside her, June could feel Nate go stiff. "Is Suzie...?" He trailed off. June could understand his not wanting to finish the sentence.

She did it for him. "What's the condition of that girl there?"

The paramedic bowed his head. In the glare of the ambulance's lights, June could see how thin he was, as if he himself formed the dividing line between life and death. "I'm real sorry."

June reached out to take Nate's hand, but he moved it away from her and said nothing. Abel filled the silence. "Jesus. I'm sorry as hell about all this, son."

"What *happened*?" June asked.

Abel's mouth withered into a knot of distaste. "Looks like one of those new Snows just arrived out on the old homestead—namely the boy, Zeke. We found his truck a little ways up there." Abel gestured into the night. "He plowed into a tree on the bank side of the road." The sheriff inched his arm to the left a little, indicating a different arc of road, and furrowed his considerable brow. "The thing is"—he dropped his arm—"there's *another* set of tracks coming from that direction, too." He shook his head. "I don't know. It's a mess out there." He hesitated—never a good sign in a man as resolute as Abel. "There's one other complication. Not even a complication, really, but I guess you ought to know. In the mayhem of everything tonight, we think we somehow managed to uncover Gert Snow's remains. There." He pointed. "Just a ways up from the crash."

June considered this information. After Gert's disappearance the Snow place had stood empty for twenty-some years until Pruitt had put down his boots in the 1970s and lived in much the same seclusion as had his ancestor. When he'd died recently, the town had breathed a sigh of relief, looking forward to some peace, only to have a whole new clot of his relatives show up. The discovery of Gert's remains would no doubt make Abel's investigation into the crash much harder, since Snows had a reputation for being elusive on the best of days and downright shady on the rest of them.

June bit her lip, wishing she could summon Cal, but he was probably already at the cabin, and anyway, in their twenty-odd years of marriage, beckoning him was something she'd never managed very well. Instead she'd done all the bending in the relationship, giving up city life for tiny Titan Falls, sacrificing her dream of graduate school for wifehood, letting him be when he declined to answer his damn phone. She turned her attention back to Abel. At least he was here in front of her right now, when she needed him. She decided to ignore the issue of Gert and focus on the more immediate panic of the crash. "You arrested Zeke Snow, right?"

Abel shook his head. "Tried to. I sent my deputy, Johnny Stenton, out to the old place, but when he got there, Zeke was gone. Not a soul to be found." He eyed the dark mud uneasily. "Don't worry, Junie. On a stretch of road like this, it's passing tough to get to the bottom of things, but we'll be hunting that boy down."

In front of June, the paramedics slammed their ambulance doors and flicked their sirens to life, spraying salt and dirt in their wake as they departed. The commotion made her shudder and draw her scarf closer around her throat as she tried to expunge the image of Suzie's limp arms and that sodden red mitten. Suzie's mother had borne three boys before Suzie, and then, finally, along had come a daughter. *My compensation*, Dena always called her to the other ladies in the sewing circle, stitching up pair after pair of torn boy trousers, her recompense, she liked to say, after years of balled-up sweat socks and fart jokes and jeans pockets that arrived in the laundry filled with dirt, stones, and sometimes living worms.

Back in September, Dena had arrived at the sewing circle with the intention of making Suzie a little something. "I don't know what yet," she'd said, sighing, "just something to catch her fancy." Then her eye had fallen on the ball of red yarn nestled in the sewing basket that sat near June's feet. "That's pretty. Is it from Hazel? It's such a color, isn't it? I never saw anything like it from her before. I wonder how she got it so *red*?"

June had laid her embroidery in her lap. The wool was a long-forgotten offering from Hazel Bell, who raised sheep in a valley at the end of town, but in truth there was something about the sulky richness of the color that had always offended June. She handed it to Dena with relief. "Take it."

"Oh, I couldn't. Are you sure?" But already Dena was drawing out a pair of knitting needles.

"Absolutely." To be honest, June had never been sure just what to make of that gift from Hazel, whom half the ladies in Titan Falls feared and the other half just didn't trust. Among all of Hazel's peculiarities, maybe her biggest was the makeshift graveyard she'd created in a disused sugar bush on her property after her only son had died. Whenever a woman in town lost a child, Hazel would put a stone out in the wood. "Sugar babies," the ladies called them, and June could never quite tell if the term was a fond one or not. Personally, she thought it was all superstitious poppycock, and she frequently said so, but the women of Titan Falls were stubborn in their histories and not inclined to change their minds, no matter what June barked, and this, too, was another bargain she had no choice but to honor. June might not have had the ears of the ladies in her sewing circle a hundred percent of the time, but neither did she share the brunt of their burdens. Nor did she want to. No one would.

June had returned to her embroidery, feeling vaguely guilty, like she did the time Mr. Collins had given her change for a twenty in the hardware after she'd only given him a ten, and she didn't tell him. There hadn't been any good reason for it, but June had taken the money anyway just to see if she could. All that afternoon a fizz of guilt had bubbled in the middle of her, electrifying her and terrifying her in equal measure, until finally, hours later, she'd snuck back into the store and left the difference on the counter when Mr. Collins wasn't looking. With Dena she suspected she ought to mention how glad she was to be rid of the red ball of wool, but a mean kernel inside her thrilled to see the other woman so happy with what was essentially a cast-off. She sighed and reached out for Dena's knitting needles. She needed to be a little nice. Their children were the best of friends, after all. "May I? I'll teach you the new pattern I learned last week. You slip two stitches after the knit. Here, you try."

Across the road now, June saw that Dena had collapsed into a heap on herself, her head bent over her knees, the frayed edges of her coat splayed in the yellow mud. A concerned knot of mill wives was gathered around her, some of them stroking Dena's hair, some of them glancing at one another and shaking their heads. June put a foot forward to join them but stopped, arrested by the fact that she had no idea what she should possibly say to Dena in this moment. Relations had been cool between them ever since Cal had gone and fired Dena's husband for drunkenness on the mill floor.

"He was higher than a loon. I just can't have it," Cal explained to June over dinner the night of the incident. "Insurance on the place is through the roof, and you know I've got those state inspectors riding my ass about water quality every damn minute. Costs are way up. If Fred falls and smacks his head or cuts one of his fool arms off—or someone else's arm—he'll take us all down."

"What if you got him some help? What if he took some time off?"

Cal had simply stared at her, his knife and fork crossed on his plate like a pair of deadly military sabers. "You still don't get it, do you?"

June's stomach had dropped a little. "Get what?"

"That there are no second chances in a mill. Don't you know that by now?" He'd stomped away to his office then, leaving June to face his empty plate alone at the table. She gathered together the dish and the silver, rolling up her husband's still-pristine napkin, uncrossing his knife and fork. No second chances. She knew that truth better than anyone. All the women in Titan Falls did. Men might go and slice off legs or crush entire arms in a spectacular fall of logs, but it was the females who wound up carrying that missing weight for the rest of their natural days.

There was something else as well. Even though she was two decades out of college, married, and mistress of the town, June had never been able to wholly shake the feeling of being a scholarship girl, conscious always that she was the product of someone else's largesse, that she needed to perform or face permanent exile, that, for her, good enough wasn't. Of all the people in the world to whom Cal needn't have pointed out the unreliable frailty of second chances, it was his wife.

The tangle of women stared expectantly at June from across the road. They were waiting, she knew, for her to join their cluster of grief, keen with them, and run her fingers through the dank tangles of Dena's hair. They were waiting for her to come and say just the right thing. Instead June found herself remaining fast where she was, immobile and undecided. She pulled her coat around her ribs like she was drawing curtains to keep the light off something precious.

Dottie Billings stumped over to her, her eyes questioning. She reached out and took June by the elbow. "I believe Dena could use a shoulder right about now." Dot was a big woman, with hamlike upper arms and hips that could nudge a stuck boulder free, but her crochet work was so delicate that it looked as if insects had spun it. Last year, when June had come down with the flu so badly she couldn't stand up, Dottie had been the one to deliver pot after pot of steaming-hot soup to her door until she felt better. "Time to put that bad business with Fred aside," Dot proclaimed now—the voice of calm sense, the voice June knew *she* should be.

Still June hesitated. There were three things that women in Titan Falls never turned their backs on: the river, a man in drink, and another woman in need. Down in the ravine, narrowed by rock and hill, she could hear the Androscoggin gurgling like a cat licking its paws after a kill. June felt a drop of sweat bead on her chest, deep under her clothing. If the river were a live thing, she would have sworn it was pleased with itself at that moment.

"June?" The corners of Dottie's mouth curved down like weighted fishhooks.

June took a faltering step backward, toward her car, where Nate was waiting bundled up, a living package she was lucky to have. What could June say to Dena, really, that would make any of this any better? Anything she did would be wrong, she saw, while she still had Nate safe and warm by her side and while Fred was still locked out of the mill and stuck down the wet end of a bottle. Dena was the kind of woman, June knew, who didn't just keep score of the injustices in her life but settled them hard and fast, the way she stitched seams closed, knotting them extra tight at the ends. June had never learned to knot her thread with the same quick ferocity. She'd never had to. She turned her head away from Dottie, her cheeks flaming. "I'm sorry," she whispered, a burning beginning to rise in her belly.

Dottie's mouth fell open as her capable hands traveled to her hips. "What in holy hell is wrong with you?"

Instead of answering, June turned and fled. Low down in the ravine, the babble of the river rose up to follow and taunt her, telling her things she didn't want to hear.

Chapter Two

The newest set of Snows had arrived on the outskirts of Titan Falls at the end of October. Right away there was a whiskey-fueled debate in town about them. "Back-to-nature misfits," Archie Lincoln scoffed at the steel-topped bar of Lucky's Tavern, his belly sticking out and his toes turned even further, but Frank Billings disagreed. "They're *backwoods*, not back-to-nature, Arch. There's a difference, you know."

"Not in Titan Falls," Arch retorted, and, like always, he had a point.

There were three of them altogether: an older brother and his sister, both in their late teen years or early twenties, both long-haired and tangled in every aspect from their clothing to the loose-hipped way they walked, and a small child the villagers took some time to determine was a girl.

The town had had problems with vagrants in the area in the past. During the Vietnam years, draft dodgers would scoot up north on their way to the border, and even now, decades later, the occasional drugged-out vanload of washouts from summer music festivals would still pull in, erect filthy tents made from quilts and sheets, and proceed to do laundry in the river. Their children were snot-nosed and decked in bells and rags, and the adults engaged in unconventional sexual arrangements that didn't seem appealing to anyone local. There were fewer of these lost souls now, but pockets of them still remained, their cosmic freewheeling and lack of boundaries testing the working mettle of the town.

While he'd been alive, Pruitt Snow had run the interlopers off, and for that service alone the town tolerated him. To him the homestead was nothing more than a remnant of distant kin, an unwanted swoop of woods and dirt inconvenienced by the muddy thoroughfare that ran parallel to it, a place he'd once or twice heard tell of and never desired to inhabit, which was why, after all the trouble with his wife, after Arlene had sent him spinning into the trees with a busted jaw, half his tongue sliced open, and a promise to cut off something worse if she ever saw him again, Pruitt figured it was the last place she would ever come looking for him, and he was almost right. He and Arlene suffered through a brief reunion that resulted in the birth of Hannah, their youngest child, and then Arlene had taken off in the dead of the night, offspring in tow, and Pruitt had returned to Titan Falls.

Why Pruitt had chosen to stay for good the second time, no one knew. He mostly kept to himself, shacking up in the homestead's old smokehouse, killing for food, and working the very odd job on a lumber site or at one of the many failing mills up and down the river. As he aged, he grew shifty-eyed, rotten-toothed, and meaner-tempered than a coiled snake, but Titan Falls grew used to him. Better the devil you knew, the people said—the same thing they told themselves whenever they had to settle for less, which turned out to be more often than not.

June's only face-to-face experience with Pruitt came shortly after his first arrival. She and Cal had been married for two years—long enough for her to feel the strangeness and unease of having a new Snow in residence but not quite enough time for her to feel like a native of the place herself.

"I heard he's the heir to a lost lumber fortune," Alice Lincoln whispered excitedly during June's weekly coffee and sewing circle, her needle flashing like a canny eye.

"Don't be ridiculous," Margie Wall drawled back. "He's clearly no such thing. I bet he's just some shell-shocked leftover from 'Nam. Maybe the Vietcong had him or something. We just don't know." The women fell silent. That was the point. They *didn't* know. If Hetty had been alive, June mused, tugging on a piece of thread, she would have dug down to the bottom of the whole story with the brisk authority and teeth-gritting efficiency that had been her trademark. June looked up to find the other women blinking at her expectantly, like deer contemplating a new species of shrub.

"Fine," she sighed, laying aside her stitchwork. "Let's go see for ourselves."

Led by June, the women formed a flotilla of condiments and concern and then marched upon the old homestead bearing baskets of blueberry muffins, trays of scalloped potatoes set with cream, and a blanket they'd stitched in rounds together. June wore a brightly checked apron over a pleated skirt, sturdy shoes, and she'd knotted her frizzed hair up out of the way of the heat and temptation.

Pruitt received them with the calm equanimity of a dictator, standing in front of the tipsy old smokehouse he'd patched up, thumbs hooked through the belt loops of his filthy dungarees, a broad hat tipped low over his forehead. "Well, now," he drawled, and every single one of the wives shivered a little. Pruitt's voice sounded like it had spiders crawling in it, a fact he seemed to intuit and use to his advantage. Generally, as soon as he started talking, people immediately wished for him to zip his lips, and in this way he'd mostly been able to pass among men with little friction or bother. Women, however, were a different matter.

Because she was married to Cal, June was the one to step forward, keeping her arms clamped tight to her sides. It was August, and steaming. She hoped sweat wasn't marring the underarms of her dress. Down in the ravine, the stink of the river roiled and insinuated itself into the already heavy air, but June was growing used to it. The paper rolls came out of the mill as clean and white as freshly bleached bedsheets, but it was a dark magic that made that happen, one June knew the townspeople paid for with this stench, not to mention with the odd child born twisted or cleft, with shoals of fish they didn't dare to eat at the wrong time of year.

The Snow place was cursed—everyone in Titan Falls knew that much, even June. The problem, June suspected, wasn't the land but the river. No one in his or her right mind would want to camp downstream from the mill and its attending swirl of not-entirely-legal effluvia. Pulp slurry and broken logs, eddies of acid—all of it floated loosely away from the chutes of the Titan Paper Mill and collected here in the elbow under Devil's Slide Road. If the town, which sat just above the mill, couldn't escape the stink of what went on all up and down two states' worth of the Androscoggin, June couldn't imagine what life right next to it in the ravine must be like. No wonder disease and ruin always seemed to stalk the Snows.

June nodded at the basket in her hands. "We brought you some food."

Pruitt didn't move to take it, so June set it down halfway

between the two of them, resisting the urge to reach up and plug her nose. Really, the river was terribly ripe out here. The other ladies followed June's lead and laid their gifts next to her basket, smearing the weft of the blanket with grime and streaking the napkins that wrapped the loaves of bread.

Again the chill of Pruitt's voice crawled up and down June's spine. "What's all this for?" He didn't call them "ladies" as the other men in town did, June noticed. He didn't call them anything at all, and this absence of decorum unsettled her the way a fox at the bottom of a tree might startle the birds nesting above. The wives tightened into the comfort of one another and inched away from Pruitt.

June was beginning to realize that their visit was a mistake. The smokehouse door had a rusted horseshoe nailed over it, she saw—an ironic sign of hopefulness on a structure already so past its prime. She wondered if Gert had nailed it there before her disappearance or if it was the more recent work of Pruitt, and then she wondered if Pruitt had heard any of the stories about Gert.

Even now, more than twenty years after her disappearance, there was still a running discussion between the men at Lucky's Tavern about what had really happened to Gert Snow. Half the bar believed she was as dead as a stone somewhere out in the anonymity of the woods or food for the fish down at the base of the falls, but whether by an act of God or the lowly hand of man, no one could exactly agree. There was a vague, unspoken pact among the drinkers that none of them would dwell too heavily on *who* might have dispatched Gert, for in a town as tightly woven as Titan Falls a prick of gossip could go only so far before it would shred too much of the common fabric. The optimists maintained that Gert wasn't deceased at all but had escaped in the nick of time for good reason. Maybe she'd been ratting out the mill to state water inspectors. Maybe she'd bedded the wrong man. The why wasn't so important. It was far more fun to imagine the where. She'd crossed the river, the men said, and had gone to work in a logging camp two towns over. She was working in food service, or as an ancient, saggy-titted stripper, or living as a man, driving a cab. She was everywhere and nowhere at once.

Pruitt watched June wondering, leveling his flat gaze at her and her alone, as if he knew everything about her, even though June had never spoken to him before in her life. She colored and turned her cheek. Cal didn't look at her like this, and June was suddenly glad for it. She drew her belly in toward her backbone and took a fortifying breath. "We won't trouble you again."

"I'm sure you won't."

June couldn't tell if the expression on Pruitt's face was sorrow or triumph as her flock departed in an affronted mass. Only she hung back, anchored by an unease that was thickening by the minute, like gelatin setting in a bowl. "What are you really doing in our town?" she whispered.

Pruitt sneered, but at the same time his eyes glittered for the barest moment with a sheen of what nearly passed for sadness. "Keeping secrets."

June cocked her head, listening to the fickle gurgle of the river below them. "The waters here have plenty."

"They're not the only thing that does." He said it so low that June almost believed he hadn't uttered anything. She eyed Pruitt, but he was staring at an invisible point just over her left shoulder. The conversation was finished.

"Well, there's a man you can tell doesn't know the first thing about women," sniffed Margie as soon as June returned to the station wagon. Margie's face was radiant with sweat. The front of her dress was damp, her lips loose and parted. She was a woman, June thought, who leaked secrets like curds seeped whey.

June slammed the driver's-side door hard and threw the engine into gear. A new Caddy, bought even though the mill owed a backlog in pay because, Cal insisted, the trappings of success would surely engender more. "Oh, he knows plenty," June spit. She just wasn't sure what. Truth be told, she wasn't certain she *wanted* to know either. She drove home in silence with her teeth gritted, feeling more and more like her late mother-in-law with each passing mile. She never told Cal about the encounter, and over the years she forgot all about it until Pruitt's death and the subsequent arrival of his estranged children picked the skin off that wound and left it as exposed as the tattoos she sometimes glimpsed etched onto the mill workers' backs—fiery, fanged creatures posed with wild eyes and claws drawn, yet trapped forever in the pale of human flesh.

For as long as Pruitt's eldest daughter, Mercy Snow, could ever remember, the color green had signified the rough hue of North Woods living—not just vast acres of spruce, maple, and fir but also the shade of rot trimmed off weeks-old vegetables, the tint of fiddlehead ferns plucked and fried with an onion in the spring, and the shine of algae slicking fallen logs. When Mercy ate, she tasted green in the bile of the deer livers her older brother hunted and in the tang of the copper of their kettle. When she slept, she dreamed in green, and when she looked in the mirror, Mercy could see how the verdancy of her life had bled into her skin, her hair, and even her eyes, making her appear aged before her time.

But she wasn't old. Quite the opposite. She was only nineteen, still baby-cheeked from certain angles. Backwoods mud hadn't yet muted everything in her, but almost. Her newly dead mother and her mother's mother before her had been famous among the North Woods loggers and hunters for their healing touches, their ability to close a wound with a hunk of moss and a firm squeeze, or to cure a case of the whiskey shakes with the press of three fingers on a man's throat. Mercy supposed she must have inherited at least a smidgeon of these gifts, but so far they were proving to be like everything else in her life: threadbare to the point of invisibility, not in working order, and as late as her older brother Zeke's last paycheck.

They'd come to Titan Falls in search of Pruitt, their long-lost father, but had found him dead, too, making the three of them official orphans, their legacy a plot of land that didn't feel anywhere close to home. The terrain was slanty, choked with poison ivy, and full of unexpected hollows and drops. Right from the beginning, Mercy had a dread of it, with its Tilt-A-Whirl hollows and the river waiting down at the bottom of the ravine like a snake's open throat. Mercy couldn't swim.

"No Snow woman ever could," Arlene had once explained to her. "We're bound body and soul to the earth." In return for that loyalty, Arlene was privy to a cache of secret riches, a cornucopia of antidotes and cures that bloomed right under her feet. From Arlene, Mercy had learned that a crush of mallow soothed and evened broken skin, that chicory made cold blood run hot, and that hemp leaves eased the mind. She'd been taught that the fat rendered from a white-tailed doe could grant a barren woman birth and that a squirrel's tail, severed and bound with flaxen twine, could ward off bad dreams. But nothing good ever came from water, running or still. Even Mercy's wild baby sister, Hannah, exercised caution around the springs and creeks that dotted the North Woods, planting her boots square before she dipped a bucket.

Hannah wasn't fooled by the ravine below them either. "If this place is supposed to be so great, why didn't anybody else want it?" she grumbled the day Mercy steered the caravan from the crumbling logging roads of Maine onto the smoother interstate into New Hampshire, and finally onto Devil's Slide Road itself, the vehicle teetering and skidding on the ugly yellow mud. Zeke was ahead of them, driving the barely better truck. All their worldly goods rattled along on uncertain wheels. Lord help them, Mercy thought, if any of them dared to stop spinning. It had been only a bare month since Arlene's death, and there were times when Mercy missed her so badly she thought the ache might crack her teeth in half, but she tried to hide that sorrow from Hannah. She shifted now, wincing as the engine made another bone-crunching grind. She prayed that the transmission would hold out for just a few hundred yards longer. "Beggars can't be choosers. Think of this as a fresh start. It'll be good for us."

Hannah bounced in the passenger seat. "What will there be for us to do when we get there?" They made their money wandering—doing seasonal work, foraging for fungi in the right season, picking apples in the fall, pulling in at logging sites, always moving on before they wore out the sweetness of their short welcome. They were down to the last five twenties in the old coffee can Mercy used as a makeshift bank, a fact she hadn't yet told her two siblings and that made the walls of her stomach cramp.

Mercy tried to put on a smile and sound reassuring. "Things will be different. You'll see. We're planting roots now. Everything's going to be great." She put her foot down harder on the gas, and the RV's engine sputtered and whined, as if even it recognized a lie when it heard one and felt bound by honor to protest.

When they arrived at the clearing, however, Mercy's heart sank. She barely remembered the place, but the impressions she did have of it were all bad. Mercy had only been days old when Arlene had left Pruitt the first time, Mercy and Zeke bundled on her chest like a pair of rabbits, and eleven when they tracked him down to Titan Falls for the briefest of reunions. Mercy could still recall the brass belt buckle Pruitt used to wear and how he would swing it when he got drunk or angry, and she knew that for Zeke—who'd taken the brunt of Pruitt's rages—the memory must be even sharper. Before he met his father, he'd been a happy-go-lucky, gap-toothed boy. Afterward it was as if something inside of him had been irrevocably rearranged, like a box of dishes dropped, shattered, and then shelved for good. He retreated into days of silence. His reading—never good—dwindled down to the level of a very young child, as if by giving up the complicated world of words he could find a deeper, more dependable layer of the universe where things were simple to understand.

Zeke pulled the truck into the clearing and let the engine sputter and die. He climbed out, peering around him, as wary as the deer he went after during the fall. "Where is he?"

Mercy stalked over to the smokehouse—the only structure standing on the place, albeit wonky as a jack-in-the-box—and tapped on the door. When there was no answer, she opened it and stuck her head inside. Dust particles stirred to life and floated in a kaleidoscope of neglect, but nothing else moved. A trio of iron hooks barbed out of the ceiling, patches of black were burned onto the foundation's cinder block, and a rusty cot stood in the far corner, its blankets stripped and folded, but there were no signs of life. Mercy closed the door again, her brow furrowed. "He's not here. Doesn't look like he's been for a while either. Guess we're on our own."

Zeke folded his arms in front of him. "That's fine. Better than fine." His chest expanded, and Mercy realized how carefully he'd been breathing up until now.

They didn't grieve when they learned two days later that Pruitt had been found dead in the woods by some townsmen. Hannah had never met her father, and Mercy and Zeke only wished they'd been so lucky.

"So we get a fresh start," Mercy murmured, laying her head on her brother's shoulder. "How about that?"

Zeke didn't respond, and Mercy didn't half blame him, for she knew as well as he did that there was no such thing as a brand-new start for the likes of them. There was only starting over.

The morning of the accident on Devil's Slide Road, Mercy heated a pot of coffee on the camper's wheezing stove and rummaged for the last of something to eat, feeling about as crotchety and sag-hipped as a girl her age could. She sat grumbling on the "banquette," the fancy word Arlene had liked to use for "bench," as if, Mercy thought, the walls around them weren't really dinged aluminum and the light on the table didn't come from a stinking pot of kerosene.

Eventually Zeke came banging through the door, letting in a blast of cold. He courted the chill and preferred to sleep out in the smokehouse on Pruitt's old cot. Mercy, however, was still wary of that space. If there was anywhere on the property that was haunted by Pruitt, she thought, it would definitely be the smokehouse. She wondered if Zeke chose to bunk there in spite of that fact or precisely because of it, battling his demons in the dark, where no one but a ghost of a man could see him.

"Best fetch a tank of propane when you head over to Berlin," Mercy said, sliding a bowl of stale food-bank cereal over to him, though what he'd buy the gas with, she didn't know. Even the change in the coffee can was scant.

Every morning Zeke disappeared in the wheezing truck to hunt for work, but sometimes, Mercy suspected, he simply slipped into the woods, where he felt most comfortable and could at least track some game for a few hours. Mercy couldn't really fault her brother for that. Hell, there were days when she wanted nothing more than to vanish, too, but someone had to make sure they had clothes on their backs, figure out a way to make expired cans of tuna and stale rice taste like something better, and generally keep Hannah alive.

More and more, Mercy missed her mother. Arlene had been their glue. In addition to a talent for healing, Arlene had possessed other, far more practical gifts. She could track a squirrel through the brush and skin it so fast it barely had time to bleed. She knew the dark and loamy spots where morels and oyster mushrooms sprouted in lush colonies. And most important of all, she'd owned the gift of flight, sensing when to pack up and hit the road before the long arm of the law could reach out and tap them on the shoulders. Or at least she had until that arm caught Zeke six months ago now and popped him in jail for something that wasn't his fault. It had thrown all of them for a loop, stopping them in their tracks, forcing them to circle the imprisoned Zeke like unsettled planets, just waiting until he got out and they could hit the road again.

Mercy didn't like to think about the incident, but sometimes the memories pierced the fragile skin of her days anyway, like a new hole in her jeans exposing a patch of flesh underneath. When Zeke caught her floundering in those recollections, teeth tearing at one of her ragged cuticles, her brow furrowed, he would give her a secret gesture from their childhood—a finger under the chin that meant *Eyes up, head up.* It was the way he'd taught her to sit in a blind, finger ready to pull the trigger, her shoulders relaxed, her back straight and strong. It was the way she should always be in the woods, she knew, but wasn't, which was why a pair of hunters had grabbed her on that dusky evening half a year ago, when she was coming back from a spring with a bucket. Mercy still flinched whenever she remembered the wet feel of their breaths sliding down her neck and on her bared stomach, their teeth on her shoulders. What they did to her was bad, but she couldn't imagine how it would have ended if Zeke hadn't come along, fists flying, and told her to get up and run.

She never saw what Zeke did to the two men, but she knew it was serious enough that one of them would never walk right again. Zeke was arrested that same night and sentenced for battery and assault. No one in the area believed his story about protecting his sister over the word of two locals.

"Let me say what happened," Mercy pleaded, but Zeke had refused to entertain the idea.

"What they would do to you... it would be worse than what went down with those men. It would be like it happening twice, and it would hurt more the second time around. Keep your mouth shut, Mercy. Trust me."

When Zeke was finally released from prison, he exited leaner in his stomach and thighs and chiseled in his jaw, an effect heightened by the scruff of beard he'd kept and the buzz cut he was still growing out. He'd come back different inside, too, Mercy had noticed. It didn't matter now if he was out shooting in the woods or scanning a crowded bar for lit-up women—it seemed that everything had become a kind of hunt to him.

Never a drinker before, he started occasionally losing himself in a bottle or two, although now that they had Hannah to look after, he'd sworn to Mercy that he would stay away from the stuff, especially after the brawl he'd gotten into at Lucky's Tavern their first week in Titan Falls. Over the occupancy of a barstool of all things, at least ostensibly. The real reason, Mercy suspected, was the death of Pruitt, but when it came to that subject, Zeke was as cool and secretive as a rock buried under snow. She knew that something sat frozen at the center of him, yet all she could see of it on the surface was a white suggestion, nothing but shadow and innuendo.

The only time he'd let his opinion of Pruitt slip was the night of that bar fight. "He was a bastard, right?" he'd rasped, tipping himself into the RV long after dark with a bloody nose and a swollen jaw before doubling over in a coughing fit, holding his ribs, which were probably bruised and maybe even broken. He'd come out of jail with a wheeze in his lungs that wouldn't respond to any of Mercy's remedies, and Lord only knew what she would do to fix these new injuries. They couldn't afford a doctor, and Arlene had died before Mercy could learn enough about healing from her. She needed her brother whole and strong, the way she remembered him before jail, not heaped in a drunken pile. She reached out for Zeke's hand and took his fingers in hers. She kept her voice low so Hannah, asleep in the loft of the RV, couldn't hear, and she whispered fiercely into his ear. "Yes, he was a bastard."

Zeke's head lolled against Mercy's chest. His eyes filmed over with grief. "God, I hope I'm nothing like him."

Mercy gripped his hand for dear life. "No. You're nothing like him. At least not if you don't want to be."

Now Zeke stayed away from anything alcoholic and mostly avoided Titan Falls unless he was looking for work—always stone-cold sober, his hands folded in front of him, hat clenched tight in his fingers as if to prove that he could hold things in check—but it didn't help. The town had labeled him a ne'er-do-well, a chip off the dead block of Pruitt, and they closed their doors on him hard.

To make it up to Mercy and Hannah, Zeke was being extra solicitous, almost courtly. He brought Hannah a collection of rabbit pelts he'd skinned and dried, and he promised that when there were enough, he would sew her a cloak with a hood. He wouldn't let Mercy lift anything heavier than a flour sack, and when he chopped wood, he sang all the bluegrass ballads Arlene used to love, one by one, until his voice gave out and grew as rough as the wood chips by his feet. But there were still moments when Mercy saw an unfamiliar rage bubble up in him, and those instants scared her, for just as her time in the woods with those two men was a memory she wished to keep to herself, as stagnant and singular as a puddle drying up on asphalt, she knew that Zeke also had pockets of similar disquiet that wouldn't evaporate in him either, and she prayed every morning that he would make it through one more day without those waters breaking.

"Where's he going?" Hannah climbed down from the loft of the RV and began gobbling the bowl of cereal that Mercy had set out for her. Outside, the engine of their old truck shook to life like a reluctant dog being roused to herd. In the months since Arlene's death, Hannah had become particularly attuned to Zeke's comings and goings. She reminded Mercy of a miniature weather vane, always spinning in the wind.

Mercy cleared Hannah's bowl and rinsed it, regretting that she couldn't offer her another helping. "Berlin." She turned to see Hannah making a beeline for the door. Before she could reach it, Mercy caught her by the collar and sat her down hard. "Where do you think you're headed off to?" Though she knew full well. Hannah had an insatiable curiosity about the smokehouse, a place that Mercy still found unsettling in the extreme. "That thing's bound to be chock-full of snakes, spiders, or both. You stay in here."

"All the snakes are sleeping for the season." Hannah crossed her arms and pouted, though she had a point. The ground was chilly as a widow's heart. But Mercy had other reasons for holding her little sister back. She knew too well what could happen to a girl alone in the dark of the trees, and it was something she was determined that Hannah would never experience.

And maybe Hannah wouldn't have to either, Mercy half hoped. She herself had recently found work with a woman named Hazel Bell, who kept sheep. Maybe Zeke would nab something soon, too. And maybe then they would settle in better. Zeke would find a way to change his reputation in town. Mercy would no longer feel the need to fall asleep with a knife stuck under her pillow.

And maybe hogs would sparkle and fly.

Hannah, sensing her older sister's apprehension, moved in for the kill, pestering Mercy with a subject she wouldn't drop. "Am I really going to get to go to school?" She leaned her scrawny body forward, all big ears and skinned knees, her teeth crowding together in the front of her mouth.

Mercy eyed her sourly. She'd known only a couple of schools

off and on throughout her own childhood, and she hadn't thought much of them. "We'll see. You say that like it's a good thing."

"Oh, it is." Hannah clutched her fists to her bony chest. "It *is*."

"Hush." Mercy turned around and put a hand on her half sister's shoulder. Hannah was literally a gift from heaven, but honestly, everything about the child was a mystery. Unlike Zeke, words were Hannah's biggest problem. She never shut her mouth when she should, and when she wasn't talking, she was reading or picking up some fancy words off the radio. The first thing she did whenever they pulled into a new campsite or town was find the nearest library, and the second thing she went and found was the closest school. "You're *supposed* to be sending me," she would harangue Arlene. "It's the law."

Mercy sighed now. Hannah knew far too much and not nearly enough for an eight-year-old, and it drove Mercy crazy. She'd never planned to have to mother anyone—she still needed her own mother—but the love she felt for Hannah was as simple and huge as the sun rising in the sky every morning, a phenomenon so primal and necessary that she knew she would die without it.

"Here." Mercy fumbled in one of the cloth bags bundled near her feet. "Put on your hat. It's extra cold in here today." It was Hannah's favorite one, a ridiculous swirl of rainbow colors topped with a pom-pom. They'd gotten it for fifty cents in a secondhand store. "Zeke needs to get us more propane."

"You off to work?"

Mercy bundled herself into one of Zeke's old jackets. It broke her heart leaving Hannah alone, but what choice did she have? A handful of twenties in the coffee can wasn't going to get them through the coming winter.

"Yup. Off to take care of the sheep." She didn't want to be late. It was a half mile into town, and Mercy had another mile to go on foot after that.

Hannah's face lit up. "Can I come see them, too?"

Mercy rubbed a hand over Hannah's delicate shoulder blades, which stuck out of her back like hopeful little nubs. They were Mercy's favorite part of her sister. "I'm afraid not. Not this time anyway. How about this? If you promise not to talk to *anyone*, I'll drop you at the library. At least you'll be warm."

Hannah sulked her way into her parka. There was a new tear at the elbow, Mercy saw. She couldn't believe how rough Hannah was on cloth. "I'd rather see the sheep."

Mercy bit her lip. "I know, but maybe let's wait. Nothing terrible ever came from that." *Nothing wonderful either*, she thought as they clattered down the RV steps into the cold, but given the life they were leading, she didn't feel like she needed to point that truth out.

Chapter Three

Over the slow course of years, Hazel Bell would lose sight of why or how Mercy Snow first landed in Titan Falls, but when she thought about it, it seemed that the girl had sneaked up on her the same way keeping sheep did: out of plain nowhere and without Hazel's permission, a necessary evil, or maybe a blessing in disguise, though, really, Hazel suspected, the difference between the two was about as small as the pulpy space squeezed between the walls of the devil's own heart.

When it came to honest company, there was nothing like a flock of Shetlands, in Hazel's opinion, and honest animals needed honest people to care for them. Sheep were trusting creatures, susceptible to everything from thievery to coyotes to hoof disease, and while this made them placid and easy as pie to corral, by the time Hazel met Mercy, she was starting to have her days when she resented having to think of every little thing all the damn time. More often than not, she was finding herself in a state of blind worry. Would the ewe with the spot of black near her tail produce white offspring or speckled? Would the ram with the broken horn be bullied to kingdom come by his brothers? Poor Fergus would come home from a long day of driving buses or tow trucks wanting his recliner and a hot plate right quick, and Hazel would just about natter his ear off. "What do you think?" she'd stew. "Should I put paper and straw down in the barn or wood chips? The paper turned straight to mash last year, remember? But I'm worried those chips might combust."

There was only so much gab a man could handle, even an extremely patient specimen like Fergus, and finally, after two long months of Hazel's rising anxiety, it got to be where he'd plain had enough. "You need a hand," he told his wife the night she started in on the wood chips. "Your knees are giving out. Your back hurts. It's time to get someone."

Fergus never wanted sheep in the first place, Hazel knew, but the man was nothing if not a soft touch. One blustery spring night ten years ago, he was called to a towing job down near the Franconia Notch, and when he stomped back in to their front room, still shaking the March wet off his coat, Hazel saw that he was holding a dirty towel all bundled up. It worried her whenever he was out in the weather. "What the Sam Hill—" she started to say, but before she could finish the words, Fergus unfolded a corner and showed her what he'd brought. It was an orphaned Shetland, hours old, all legs and bleat, its white wool marred by a single black spot.

He slid the creature right onto Hazel's lap. "The farmer doesn't want it. Said he was going to let nature take its course if I wasn't interested."

Hazel eyed the stony March clouds piling on the horizon, then the lamb, and felt such a clamping around her heart that it was as if the Almighty himself had shoved his fist down her throat and given her soul a squeeze. She started to protest—what did she want with a barnyard animal when she didn't even have a barn?—but the little beast skittered its hooves around her thighs, then looked up at her, and that was that. Hazel was a goner. The fact was, the lamb needed her and she needed it. "Well, don't just stand there," she growled at Fergus. "Go fetch a box or something."

"Yes, ma'am." Fergus tried to put on his hangdog look, but Hazel could see a sneaky half smile dancing around the corners of his mouth, and she knew she'd been had. *Fine,* she thought. Sheep it would be, then.

Sheep turned out to be her salvation.

The real reason Fergus brought that sorry animal into her life, Hazel realized full well, wasn't wholly to do with her tender heart. In actual fact, it had more to do with her broken one. It wasn't Fergus's fault, though, this flaw of Hazel's. She'd warned him before they got married that she had a crack running right down the middle of her soul and that over time it would very likely only get worse, and in this she turned out to be correct.

Simply put, Hazel had been born with a shaky foundation. Orphaned at birth, she'd been found fifty years earlier laid out naked and blue on the banks of the Androscoggin. It was a rare but not totally uncommon occurrence at the time. Lots of girls back then got themselves in trouble and couldn't fix it, and some of the poor wretches made the decision to let the elements do their work. In Hazel's case mankind interfered, specifically an itinerant Portuguese logger who gave her over to the Duncan Home for Girls in Gorham while she was still wet behind the ears. There she was brought up right quick. The place wasn't bad, but it was hard on a body. Hazel and the other girls always had just enough and not a thread more to their names: two pairs of woolen stockings kept going with strategic darning and cut down to socks when they outgrew them, an itchy hemp pinafore that Hazel couldn't stain if she tried, and a rickety cot she learned to crimp her bones into as they stretched. She wasn't sorry to leave when she turned seventeen and wasn't unhappy either when she heard that the place shut down a few years later, right after she met and married Fergus.

Fergus had enough gentleness in him to make up for a whole world of sorrow, and right from the beginning he did just that for Hazel. They saved their money, Fergus from his driving and Hazel from odd jobs cleaning or waitressing in local diners, and they eventually bought a place outside Titan Falls in the pocket of a grassy valley where life was good.

Much as she wanted to, Hazel couldn't find it in herself ever wholly to leave the river or the woods where she'd been discovered. Maybe because the Androscoggin had spawned her—or was the closest thing she would ever know to what had—it both repelled and attracted her. When she went too far away from it, she grew anxious and irritable, feeling she was missing something, and when she traveled too close, she grew panicked and afraid. So she compromised, setting up house with Fergus near enough to Titan Falls that the mineral smell of the mud drifted faintly in the air during the muggy summer months but otherwise kept a respectable distance.

For a good long while, Hazel managed to forget that she was a soul who'd been put on the earth untethered. She bore a son and tended a garden of sweet peas and roses right outside her kitchen, but the river played its tricks and orphaned her all over again. When Rory was two, he passed away from a hard-sucking blood cancer. Hazel didn't want much to do with life after that—any of it—and she knew in her marrow that most mothers would feel the same. To be a mother, after all, was to know the most perfect fullness on earth followed by the most terrible emptiness. Even with healthy children, you were always losing them a little, Hazel figured, right from the moment the cord was cut and you heard that first cry. With Rory it just happened faster and more painfully, catching her by surprise.

She puzzled the town by refusing to bury her son in the tiny cemetery adjacent to St. Bart's, overlooking the Androscoggin. Instead she convinced Fergus to lay their boy to rest in the sugar bush at the end of their little valley, surrounded by trees, cradled by nothing but good black earth.

In spite of that, though, she couldn't shake the feeling that the damn river, insolent in its foulness, capped by the belching smokestack of the Titan Mill, had somehow stolen her child, and Hazel was nothing if not obdurate. She would be a monkey's butt if she was going to give Rory over to the Androscoggin for all eternity. Fergus, knowing the futility of resisting his wife's opinions, dug a deep hole under one of the maples and marked the spot with a crude granite block he carved himself. When a woman in town gave birth to a stillborn a few months later, Hazel added a second stone out near Rory's, for remembrance, she said. Soon another stone was placed as another child died in a car accident, and then another when an infant succumbed to cot death, until a small unofficial graveyard of the unconsecrated grew upon the spot, feeding the trees with unrealized sweetness.

For the next decade, as the stones in the sugar bush slowly increased, Hazel foundered. She let her garden sink to weeds. She respectfully declined to attend St. Bart's with Fergus. The townswomen, horrified by the graveyard that Hazel was curating at the end of her valley, kept their distance, choosing to take their chances with the river. None of it mattered to Hazel. Nothing at all mattered to her, in fact, until the night that Fergus walked in the door with that lamb. It was the first thing since Rory that Hazel cared about the end of. Without her, Hazel saw, the creature would die, and she didn't have the energy to go through that misery again, not even with a stupid bleating sheep. So she roused herself, fed it by hand, kept it warm by the stove, and when it was ready, Hazel got it a mate. Two Shetlands became four, and four became ten, until she had built herself a little family in fleece, all of it blessedly white except for two spotted ewes, which Hazel kept anyway because she of all people knew that nothing on this godforsaken earth was ever perfect no matter how much she wished it might be so.

There were three basic choices with sheep: fleece, meat, or milk, and after a long, hard think, Hazel chose fleece. It turned out to be the correct one, because she didn't have the heart for butchery or the patience to wait for cheese to age, and except for that pair of spotted rogues her babies produced beautiful ecru wool, perfect for spinning and dyeing.

Hazel's coming to color was the second half of her revival, but she arrived at it slowly, the same way she took to husbandry. The first time Aggie, the shearer, visited, Hazel didn't have the foggiest clue what to do with the raggedy pelts he stacked in front of the house at the end of his time. When she said so, he stared at her with his mouth cricked open, showing all the stumps of his teeth. "Why, you skirt them, woman, and wash them, and go from there. These can be whatever you want them to be." And that was when Hazel first understood that she'd been given much more than wool. She'd been granted the stuff of life.

She began her experiments in dyeing with the shade of black, because ever since Rory's death that was what had filled her heart. When summer arrived, she took herself out gathering up and down the swath of her valley, returning with her arms full of sumac branches. Then she fetched an old pot, boiled a batch of the leaves, and watched with satisfaction as the alum-soaked skeins she'd spun turned a sickly gray and then a dusky black. She lifted them out, staining her fingertips, and hung the wool to dry off the side of the porch.

When the cornflowers bloomed later in the season, they lightened Hazel's mood to blue, and she added drips and dots of cerulean to the black smears on the porch railing. Dandelion roots gave her brown, lichen and lilac provided a dulled gold and orange, and lily-of-the-valley produced a toxic green quite suited to her general interior mood. Slowly the railings and boards of the porch splattered, then smudged, then erupted in the muddy rainbow of her grief.

For all that, Hazel only ever made the color red one single time, with the most peculiar result. First she edged up to the shade with pink (roses mixed with the tips of lavender) and purple (pulped huckleberries), then danced around it with a peachy brown leached from the branches of a weeping willow tree. She wasn't sure yet if she was ready to let red—the happy buzz of paper valentines and velvet Christmas bows—back into her soul.

But you couldn't have a parade without the horns, Hazel told herself. And so, on the hottest day of that summer, she walked past the sugar bush and past the cluster of graves—one or two more of them every year—gathering chokecherry branches by the armful. Then she came home and stoked a fire on the old woodstove. She soaked the last three skeins of her homespun yarn in alum, waiting to sink the wool in the vat until the berries in the old nicked pot were oozing from fury and heat. The fiber bloomed to blush, then grew winey, then burst into the color of flame. She stared at the spectrum of dyed and dried yarn piled along the porch and bit her nails raw, because what she saw before her was an awful truth: All the colors of the rainbow weren't going to bring her Rory back.

She considered burning the whole mess of color she'd created, but that just seemed melodramatic and a waste, and if there was anything Hazel couldn't abide, it was a waste. So she did the next-best thing she knew. She decided to try accepting what life had given her. She laced up her boots, gathered her wool, and set off into town.

"Why, Hazel. How kind! What's this all about?" June McAllister answered her door in a blue apron starched to military rigidity, the ruffles on it ironed to razor sharpness. Hazel handed over the basket full of yarn balls, all neatly wound and prettily arranged, the scarlet one hidden down at the bottom. June's house often smelled of cooking, and that day the air swirled with the scents of lemons, cinnamon, and sugar. In the front hall, Hazel could see a baseball glove and a pair of little boy's sneakers.

June folded her hands dutifully at her waist. She was known for always welcoming callers politely if not a hundred percent warmly. "Would you like to come in? I have iced tea."

Hazel shook her head. There was something about June McAllister that Hazel had never really cottoned to—and it wasn't because she hailed from some fancy college, which was Fergus's theory. There was something else about June that Hazel couldn't quite put her finger on, and that was odd, since everything June did was perfect. Maybe that was simply it. In Titan Falls there was no reason to try that hard.

"I can't," Hazel said. "I just wanted you to have some samples. I'm going to be selling wool, hand-spun and hand-dyed. Come on out when it suits you."

June ran one of her polished fingertips over the blue ball of yarn. "This is lovely. I bet you'll be swimming in business before too long. I'll make sure I get the word out."

That's what I'm counting on, Hazel thought, but she kept that thought shoved under her hat. "Thank you so much. And you take care of that boy of yours."

June's face briefly lit up, and this made Hazel like her a little better. "Oh, I will. They grow up so fast, don't they?" And then her smile faded a bit.

Hazel's heart squeezed with that sentence—she wouldn't lie. She nodded. "Yes, they sure do." Before June could detect the stirrings of sympathy, Hazel turned and set off down the porch steps cursing. What had she been thinking? Giving away that basket of yarn hadn't done a single thing to ease her grief. But at least she had company. The stones in the sugar bush were testimony to that—a hardened alphabet of grief spelled out on the ground—and what they said was simple. Everyone lost something once, no matter how beloved. There was nothing you could do. And thus a sorrow to one mother was a sorrow to all in this mill-pounded town, where the dead never really did go away but lingered, their woolen strings tangled up in everybody, knotted and frayed, impossible to snip no matter how hard you damn well tried.

For a decade Hazel handled the sheep just fine mostly on her own, but by the time of the accident the work was taking a toll on her. She was fifty, after all. Her knees weren't what they used to be, and there were days her back pained her so bad she would have let a demon dance on it if she thought it would help.

Once Fergus determined that Hazel needed to get help in

with the sheep, he didn't let the notion go until she agreed to follow through on his plan. Obviously he had a boy in mind for the job. A strapping high-school lad would do, he concluded, someone a bit like who Rory might have been. A youth who could work after school, or maybe even a fellow who couldn't score a job in the mill but needed cash all the same. Hazel thought they should be fair about the opportunity. She would, she decided, place an ad in the *Titan Press*.

Sitting at her kitchen table, she chose her words with care. *"Wanted, a strong back for strong work,"* she wrote. *"Good with animals, trustworthy, flexible. Outdoor labor involved. Felons need not apply."* A week went by, then two, and no one called. Hazel couldn't understand it. She reworked her phrasing, removing the part about felons and adding in a promise for decent pay, but the telephone line stayed dead. Finally, at the end of October, on a frosty day that boded no good at all in Hazel's mind, a flurry of footsteps crossed her porch.

"It's about damn time," she grumbled, pulling on a cardigan and stumping to the front door to see what the winds had thrown her way. She was disappointed to find a compact, black-haired girl standing at the door clutching a copy of the *Press* with Hazel's advertisement circled in red.

"Hello, ma'am. I'm here about the job. I'm Mercy Snow." She stuck out her hand.

Hazel declined to take it. "I don't need a girl." She folded her arms across her chest and tucked her chin.

She tried to close the door, but before she could, Mercy's skinny arm shot out and stopped her. "Hold on. What's the work, exactly? Your ad don't say."

Hazel leveled her gaze. "Sheep."

"*Your* sheep."

Not only was the girl stubborn, but Hazel was starting to think she was stupid, too. "Well, obviously."

"But *you're* female."

Hazel couldn't argue that perceptive detail. She sniffed. "What did you say your name was again?"

The girl's voice came out a little quieter. "Mercy Snow, ma'am."

"You related to that late scoundrel Pruitt?"

The girl hung her head and stayed silent, and Hazel didn't blame her there. If she were related to Pruitt Snow, she'd bow low, too. The man had been a disgrace, living out on that old place on the edge of the Devil's Slide Road, poaching whatever he could put in his belly, and drinking himself stupid.

As for Pruitt's children, Hazel had heard that the feckless boy had a record and time under his belt, but she didn't know much about this sister of his. *And don't want to know either*, she thought, trying to close the door again. "I'm sorry," she said, "but you're really not who I'm looking for."

The girl was surprisingly strong. Before Hazel could stop her, she'd stuck her foot between door and jamb. "Why not let me work today and see how it goes? I'll do it for free."

Hazel considered. "Nothing's ever free."

"So pay me if you want." The girl shrugged, but underneath the hard glaze of her eyes Hazel could see a slick of need. She ran all the rumors about Pruitt through her mind again. Several stories immediately sprang to her imagination, none of them very comforting.

On the other hand, the girl looked strong enough, and beggars couldn't be choosers. It's not like there was a team of young men thundering across her porch for the work. "Fine," Hazel finally said, swinging open the door a fraction of an inch wider, wondering who exactly was helping whom. "I'll give you one morning. If my sheep take to you, you can stay."

"Oh, they will." Mercy scraped her boots carefully on the mat before crossing the threshold, trailing the scents of pine sap and bacon grease into Hazel's clean hall. "You don't need to worry about that, ma'am. Animals are just fine with me, I always find." Her face clouded for a moment, and her eyes grew dark. "Folks are more often the problem."

Hazel sighed and closed the door quick before the girl could drag in the wind, flies, or something worse. "Folks mostly are."

All through that November, Mercy delivered herself to Hazel's doorstep early and lingered for the ostensible purpose of work, but the real reason she loitered on Hazel's farm was for the company. Out in the barn, the Shetlands were constantly bleating and stammering over one another, and up above them a colony of starlings lived in the rafters and could set up a ruckus of their own. There was sound going on inside the house, too—the gentle hum of Hazel's spinning wheel, the wheezing gasp of the vacuum that Mercy offered to run at the ends of her shifts, Hazel rattling sudsy spoons and forks in a sink full of dishes. Sounds that reminded Mercy that in spite of Arlene's death, life was going on all around her and that it was fine; she could let her shoulders relax and her mind wander a spell the way she was never able to when she was looking after Hannah.

There was one spot at Hazel's, however, that ran a chill up Mercy's nerves the single time she saw it. Down at the end of the valley, where the pastureland narrowed and the forest took over, hidden under a bare canopy of trees, there was a smattering of stones, some of them roughly carved, some of them still jagged.

They weren't large, but there were too many of them to be natural. Mercy rounded them twice before she found the stone with Rory's name on it and a third time before she realized she was standing in a sugar bush—unused for quite some time by the looks of it. She paused for a moment, painfully aware that she was caught in a twin bower of sorts, bones spreading under the earth even as branches closed above it, and decided it would be a very good idea never to tell Hazel she had trespassed on the spot.

Tonight there was a cold snap whipping in the air, and Mercy was thinking about food. She and Hazel had just finished making sure the sheep were locked securely in the barn, that they had water and enough feed, that none of the rams were fixing to fight. "Margie Wall swore to Fergus that she saw a gray wolf out by Bretton Woods the other week," Hazel said as they wound their way back to the house, her breath steaming into the night air. It made a spirited cloud to rival the size of her whole head. "Skinny thing. Quick, too, but I think she's full of it. Margie Wall will say anything to bend somebody's ear her way."

Mercy thought about that. The green sway of the forest was the most familiar thing in the world to her, but at the same time it was full of leafy mysteries better left alone. Mercy knew that there were some things in the trees you didn't want to have to answer for.

As they clattered into the kitchen, Mercy saw that Hazel had set a plump turkey out on the draining board to defrost. Thanksgiving was tomorrow. Mercy stared at the bird, picturing the spread Hazel would no doubt conjure up, and her mouth watered. The Snows' celebration was always more of a paper-napkin-and-beer affair. Zeke had come home the other day toting an extra sack from the food bank and had proceeded to slam the wares one by one on the RV's single chipped counter: a can of cranberry sauce, a can of corn pone, and two tins of green beans. Combined with the venison he'd shot the day before, it would be a passable enough holiday, better than some they'd had, especially if Mercy could rustle up something fresh—it didn't matter what to her—just something with some fiber in it and no tang of metal aftertaste.

She had an urge to make things nice for Hannah for a change. And maybe a real holiday would start to loosen some of the tighter angles of Zeke, prying him open and bringing back the daydreaming boy Mercy remembered from childhood.

A woman's magazine sat on Hazel's kitchen counter. The cover featured a sumptuous Thanksgiving feast laid out on a farmhouse table much like Hazel's. In the background a fire roared in a brick fireplace, casting an appetizing glow on the bourbon-glazed turkey (according to the caption), green-bean succotash, and cranberry chutney. As quietly as she could, Mercy flipped through the pages and ripped out the recipe for the green beans, folded it, and slipped it into her pocket. There was no chance she would ever be able to reproduce anything like what it offered, of course, but she liked the idea of carrying the promise around anyway. It was like having a lucky penny or a road map to some other existence. Hannah had her pilfered library books for that, and Zeke had the hours he spent in the woods, but the only thing Mercy could rely on for transcendence was the coil of her own soft innards. She was never full of the things she wished to be.

"Fergus will drive you home when he returns," Hazel said, coming up behind her. "He ought to be back any second. Archie was going to drop him by from town when Fergus was done with the youth-group run over to Berlin. Fergus likes to leave me a vehicle, even though he knows I won't drive at night."

Mercy closed the magazine to hide the scar of torn pages. "Okay." She stuck a guilty hand over her pocket. She didn't like the dark either. She knew all too well what lurked once the sun went down.

"Here." Hazel tossed a skein of yarn at her and kicked out a chair in her direction. "Wind this." Mercy ran the wool through her fingers. The color was an orange so zesty she was tempted to lick it. She sat down and started balling up the fiber. So far Hazel hadn't let her much near the uncombed fleeces or yarns. She said she was still learning what kind of touch Mercy had. Hazel sat down in an opposite chair and watched as Mercy's fingers worked the wool.

The jangle of the phone broke up the puddle of still air spread between them. Hazel sighed heavily and rose to her feet, pushing hard against her thighs with the heels of her hands. She always moved stiffly in the evenings, Mercy had noticed, as bandy-legged as her Shetlands.

"What?" Hazel didn't so much speak as bark on the phone. "What do you mean? How do you not know?" There was a pause, and then she rasped, "Yes, of course. I'm on my way."

The orange wool in Mercy's hands flashed too bright all of a sudden, the color of alerts and alarms. "Hazel?"

Hazel's hands were shaking. She couldn't have wound wool if she wanted to. "Do you know how to drive?"

Mercy nodded. "Yes. Of course." Anything after the monstrous RV and Zeke's death trap of a truck would no doubt handle as smoothly as a limousine.

Hazel snapped Mercy her sedan keys. "That was Abel Goode. He said there's been an accident and Fergus is hurt. Go start the car. You're coming with me."

Chaos greeted Mercy and Hazel in the waiting room of the Heritage Pines ER. Even the light in the place was calamitous, Mercy thought, flooding into every nook and cranny, chasing the shadows of death back under the floorboards for a little while longer.

Hazel pushed her way up to the reception desk and rapped her knuckles on it. "My husband," she demanded in her gravel-dust voice. "Where'd they take him? Fergus Bell."

Hazel seemed preternaturally calm to Mercy, who always itched on the rare occasions when she stepped anywhere institutional and never knew what to say. Around her, knots of panicked parents tapped their feet or just sat, silent and grim. Normally the Heritage Pines ER was a sedate place, even when full. Chainsaw accidents weren't unknown, of course, and there were always car accidents, sports injuries, and little kids who shoved peas up their noses, but never all at once.

A fresh pair of ambulances squealed up outside. Mercy could see through the sliding glass doors that the news was not good in one of the vehicles. The first team of paramedics was already bursting out of its rig, shouting out codes and confusing acronyms to the waiting doctors, pushing a boy on a stretcher, but for the second set of paramedics there was no such hurry. They pulled their stretcher out of the back, but the girl on it was too still and too completely covered to suggest any chance of recovery. Mercy watched as they momentarily drew back the sheet for the doctors and conferred in hushed voices. She took a step forward and then stopped.

The girl had been beautiful. There was no doubt of that,

even in spite of the bloody contusion where her hairline met her forehead. Her hair, Mercy saw, was drying to the color of clean straw. Already her skin had lost the color of life, taking on the waxy sheen of the dead. The paramedics had strapped her arms down by her sides. On her chest someone had laid a bright red mitten, knit in a chevron pattern. Mercy wondered where the other one had gone.

Hazel reappeared at Mercy's side as a group of nurses wheeled the girl away. Hazel stared after her for a moment with her hand over her mouth, but if she knew who the girl was, she didn't say. "They'll take us back now. I'd like it if you'd come, if that's okay. I don't..." She trailed off, then cleared her throat. "They say he's alive, but in bad shape. I don't know if it's the kind of thing I want to see alone."

"Sure." Mercy squeezed Hazel's hand. If there was anything she was good for, she knew, it was beholding the kinds of things most people would rather not.

They made their way to one of the individual rooms on the far side of the ER. That right there was a bad sign. Those rooms were reserved for serious cases. They stopped at the third door. Mercy tiptoed up and peered in. The privacy curtain hadn't been pulled closed, and she could see Fergus laid out on the bed, unconscious from the looks of it and not breathing on his own. Two doctors seized Hazel and began trying to explain his condition to her. Mercy caught their words midstream.

"...a chance he's injured the brain stem."

"...no apparent cognitive awareness."

"...we'll run tests, obviously, but does he have a living will?"

Hazel's growl cut them off. "I'm not letting you shut those machines down."

A silence ensued before the first doctor spoke. "Mrs. Bell. You should prepare yourself for the possibility that your husband may be in a persistent vegetative state."

Hazel's reply was as good as a slap. "You gentlemen do your jobs and I'll let the good Lord do his."

Just then the younger of the two doctors glanced up and spied Mercy lingering in the doorway. He scowled and, without further warning, twitched the curtain across the door. Mercy took the hint and backed out the doorway toward the nursing station. The staff was abuzz with the circumstances of the accident.

"Maybe they'll put up a guardrail on that stretch of road now," the charge nurse sniffed. "It's a death trap."

A much younger nurse sighed. "Jimmy in rig two told me that the bus only rolled off the road like that because of another car. Some dude in a pickup. Drunk, probably. They found the truck crashed into a tree a little ways from the scene, and I guess they went out to make an arrest. An ex-con from Titan Falls. Name of Snow, or something like that." Mercy let out an involuntary gasp, and the charge nurse looked up and frowned.

"The night before a holiday no less," a third nurse injected. "It's terrible. Little kids and everything."

The charge nurse was more direct. Her voice flew to Mercy's ear like a wasp with its stinger cocked. "I hope they punish the bastard who did this. I mean it. Someone should pay for this. Someone really should."

Mercy needed fresh air. She made a beeline for the waiting room and the front doors. As she passed through them, she shivered. Even when she left the woods, it seemed, she was never really out of them.

Chapter Four

June and Nate didn't speak in the car after the accident. It really was brutally cold, the night so absolute and dark it smothered like a hangman's hood. June, completely shaken by the events of the evening, drove as if she were narrowly escaping some unseen danger—a lurking wolf maybe, its yellow eyes plotting, or contact with some poisonous species of spider.

Nate gazed out the black passenger window, and June knew without asking that he, too, was picturing the still form of Suzie on the stretcher, the blob of her red mitten falling out of her pocket like the heart of a gutted fish. June put her foot down and drove a little faster even. She couldn't erase that image from her son's mind (or indeed her own), but she could take him somewhere safe. It was lucky, then, that they were headed to the lake cabin—the safest place June could think of. It sat ten miles west of Titan Falls—not so far that driving to it was any kind of trial, but wild enough that the press of woods around it always felt dark and dangerous to June, and never more so than tonight, when something terrible, something no one could take back or put right, really had happened.

Cal's great-grandfather had hewed the cabin's logs himself and thrown up the frame using hand tools and the famous McAllister gumption, but he'd gone overboard and the place had ended up turning into more of a bunker than a true house, fortified against bears, snowdrifts, and the passage of time itself. An enormous, rough-cut porch overlooked the egg-shaped lake and the scrappy dock, while inside, the cavelike rooms offered respite from high summer's humidity and vague clouds of biting insects. In the summer, though, when the house was opened up, the character of it completely changed. It became the kind of place where people felt comfortable walking dripping wet into the kitchen, grabbing a cold one from the fridge, and slamming the screen door on their way out. In fact, there was a line of water stains dotted across the living-room floor from generations of McAllisters doing just that.

Like all the other McAllisters before them, Cal, Nate, and June spent their summer evenings crouched over an ancient, tattered Monopoly board. They ate beef franks and potato chips at lunch and grilled steaks for dinner, hung their faded swimsuits on specified hooks on the cabin's back wall, and they'd been using the same clutch of gnarled fishing tackle since before Nate was born. Every year, on the first day of summer, even if it was smack-dab in the middle of the week, the three of them would bump down the dirt road, unlock the front door, and flick on the kitchen's overhead light, holding their breath and hoping it didn't spark. If the snow held off enough, they used the cabin one last time for Thanksgiving and then performed the whole arrival routine in reverse, layering sheets over the threadbare couch and sagging armchairs, fixing the latches on the shutters, and, finally, snapping off the murderous kitchen light.

During the thick of winter, the cabin sat unused, hunkering under snowdrifts and ice. Unless a person chose to ski or snowshoe in, the little dirt lane that ran around the lake was impassable, and in the early spring even skis couldn't plow through the mud, never mind whole automobile tires. Over the course of the season, bands of snowmobile drivers occasionally congregated on the house's porch, scattering cigarette butts and beer cans, but, daunted by the cabin's fortresslike exterior, they never tested the windows or doors. With the furniture covered and all the sporting equipment put away, the cabin was as bland and lifeless as a boulder, and that was its genius. When it was time to walk away, the McAllisters could do so with complete confidence, forgetting all about it until summer.

As June pulled up to the house now, she saw with relief that Cal had in fact arrived and parked crooked across the drive as usual. He simply must have been en route when she'd phoned the mill and tried his cell. All her worries had been for nothing. She pictured him passing down the long mill hallway and out into the night, stretching his arms overhead and wrapping his scarf tighter around his throat, fishing in his corduroy pockets for his car keys. Familiar actions performed in the familiar and careworn geography of their life together. He had no idea how close the accident had come to stealing Nate and erasing the whole map of everything that mattered.

She cursed as she tried to maneuver her own car close enough so she and Nate wouldn't have to tramp too far in the dark, stumbling over branches and clods of mud. All that summer she'd been bugging Cal to do something about the cabin's so-called drive—to pave it, or at least spread some gravel, but things at the mill had been awful lately, and Cal was never in the mood for spending what he didn't have to. Orders had plunged, jobs were all going overseas, and recently several parts on the kraft converter, the machine at the very heart of the mill, had broken. Just yesterday Cal had come home, poured himself a double scotch, and bent over his drink with his fingers thrust in his hair, an old habit when he was thinking too hard about matters with no clear answers.

"I should upgrade the equipment," he'd moaned, "but with what? I've got payroll to worry about."

June had stepped behind him and squeezed his shoulders, which were still as broad and strong as the day she met him on that college weekend in Boston. Right from the start, Cal had reminded her of nothing so much as a tree. He was physically solid, yes, tall and tapering through his hips, but more than that, to June he'd seemed *rooted*, completely planted in the life of Titan Falls in a way she envied. Even now, after twenty years of marriage, it still felt almost like a trick that he was hers along with everything else—the churning mill, the gabled house with its neat rows of windows and decorative trim, the front pew at St. Bart's, a new car leased every two years, a slot waiting for Nate at Dartmouth, just because he was a McAllister. She was safe, and she'd let nothing—not even that damn fling he'd had—take that away from her.

"It will be fine," she'd told him, massaging his shoulders, rubbing hard, down to the bone, the only way to get the kinks out of a man of Cal's size. "You'll see. Anyway, the river's so much cleaner these days, and that has to be a good thing."

Cal had pushed her hands off his shoulders then and looked at her like she was stupid. But June's attempts at reassurance didn't come from ignorance. If anything, they came from knowing *too* much and wishing against wishing that it weren't so. Cal blinked at her, then turned his gaze away and told her something she already knew, a damning trace of pity lacing his voice. "It's still the same water, June. It's a dirty old river. All the rules in the world aren't going to change that."

As June stumbled out of her car now, she noticed something strange about Cal's sedan. Like hers, it was splattered with mud from the lake road, the tires caked, but—she squinted and peered closer—there were also yellow mud splatters along the shiny red paint. She paused in the dark, confused. There was only one road in a fifty-mile radius with mud that color, and Cal's car had been clean that morning, June remembered. So when had he been on Devil's Slide Road?

"Mom?" Nate stumbled up behind her, and June snapped back to her senses. It was the first time he'd spoken since they left the accident, and she was tempted to reach out and hug her son, to prolong this moment between the two of them, but Nate shifted uneasily, and so she spared him and tugged her glove off, reaching for the cold lock of the cabin's front door, already anticipating the relief she would feel once she told Cal about the accident.

Just then she felt one of Nate's bare hands take hers. Her son's nearly grown fingers were surprisingly strong. The November air prickled against her cheeks, and the press of the brass doorknob was a shock of cold against her palm. *I haven't lost him yet*, she reassured herself, and immediately wondered whom she meant: Cal or Nate, father or son. Before she could formulate an answer, the door groaned and budged, and she and Nate tumbled into the darkened front hall, where they were rewarded with an olfactory flood of pine shelving, musty sofa cushions, and lemon disinfectant, a complicated mix of rot and clean that suggested that no matter how hard June tried with the place, no matter how good her best intentions, something was always going to escape her. Something would always linger.

Inside, Cal was reclined in the dark on the sagging couch with a glass of scotch, his legs crossed on top of the nicked coffee table, a small fire blazing in the hearth in front of him. He didn't look up when the door banged open, but this didn't surprise June. It had been like this between them of late, as if she were a ghost whose presence he'd grown bored of. As June and Nate crossed the kitchen, Cal lifted his head. He frowned and shifted his bulk. "Do you want me to go and get the boxes?"

June snapped on the light. The obligatory shower of sparks shot out of the fixture and electrified the room. Cal blinked, putting a hand up to shield his eyes. "I was avoiding that."

June's voice came out sharper than she intended. "Nate, why don't you go upstairs?" She expected him to argue or protest, at the very least to want his father to gather him close and squeeze his thickening shoulders, but Nate didn't even make eye contact with his father.

"Okay," he mumbled, and slipped past his parents to the sleeping loft like a shadow trying to escape the sun.

Now June had Cal's full attention. They'd been married long enough that he could sense her moods the way old sailors could feel drops in barometric pressure without instruments. He put his sweating tumbler on the table and waited. For a moment June held her breath, hoping he would call Nate back and ask what was wrong, but he didn't. An unfamiliar wave of rage washed through her then, leaving her gummy in the knees, brittle in her bones, feeling older than her years.

A marriage doesn't run like the lousy mill! she had the urge to shout at Cal. It wasn't a whirring room of cogs and wheels, or like the pulping machines he switched on and off at his will. Nothing was so simple. But of course these thoughts were unfair. June was simply angry that Cal didn't know anything about the night's incidents yet, and he didn't know because she hadn't told him. She almost didn't want to. It was terrible, but as long as she held the knowledge of the accident bundled tight to her chest, it could be as if it hadn't happened at all. The moment she spoke of it, though, that spell would be broken. Time would race to catch up with itself and leave her stuck here, standing in the living room of the cabin, her son's best friend dead, her husband a mystery. She blinked away tears and cleared her throat. "There's been an accident."

Cal furrowed his brow, confused. "What?"

"Fergus went off Devil's Slide Road. He was unresponsive when they found him, but alive. Abel told me he thinks it was that Snow boy. They found his truck crashed a little way from the scene." June paused. There was no good way to say the next part, about Suzie. She licked her dry lips. "There's something else you should know. Suzie Flyte. She's... passed."

Cal froze. In spite of all his bad qualities—the ones June had only seemed to be focusing on lately—she could always count on him to act calm and supremely competent in any crisis. But not tonight. He seemed genuinely rattled, sweat beading along his hairline, his eyes shifty. He picked up his glass in distress, but it was empty. "Oh, my God. Are you sure?"

How very like Cal, June thought, to demand certitude, even in—maybe *especially* in—the face of a tragedy, as if bad things could happen only with his permission. She frowned. The yellow mud on Cal's car was bothering her. He shifted, and his face sank into shadow. More than anything, June wished to see his expression at that moment. Lately he never seemed to face her.

"Were you at the mill for the whole day today?"

Cal remained in the shadow. "Jesus, June. What has that got to do with anything?"

Before, when he'd cheated and she'd caught him, he'd at least admitted it. Looking at the bearish hang of his shoulders, June wondered if Cal's current posture denoted grief, or guilt, or, more likely, a mixture of both. Inside, she knew she was still the same scholarship girl she'd been in college—a faithful reader at heart. She believed in providence and in denouements, though maybe no longer in happy endings.

Lately she had been plagued with dreams about her Florida youth, floating in her sleep in a palette of moss greens and scrubbed pinks, her throat closing in the sticky air. She always woke violently after these incidents, jerked back to the straight lines of her brass bed, the sky outside her window a rebuke in iron gray or antiseptic blue, depending on the season. She'd been rerooted entirely by free will, she reminded herself. She'd chosen to pace her life by the rush of the Androscoggin and the noise of the mill. Instead of her now-deceased mother, she had Nate and Cal to look after, and without them she would have nothing. She blinked back tears. "I can't get it out of my head. What if Nate had been the one? What would we ever do?"

Cal's gaze drifted out the darkened window. He looked as if he'd seen something he couldn't explain, though the only thing reflected was his own image. "I don't know," he confessed.

June waited for him to say something—anything—else, but he didn't. "Let's just stay here tonight. I don't want to go back to town yet." Usually Cal made these kinds of decisions, but he remained silent. June pictured all the food she'd left sitting on the counter—the plugs of yams, the cake batter dripping out of its bowl in viscous streaks. Not that any of them would feel like eating tomorrow. Mourning and feasting didn't go hand in hand.

Cal had risen. June knew he was going to see Nate, to reassure himself that he was safe. He paused at the foot of the worn wooden stairs, the banister perennially cockeyed. "Did you say they caught that Snow boy?"

How very like Cal to want justice at the earliest opportunity. But then June supposed you had to be that way when you had a whole town of men depending on you. Sometimes she thought Cal would make the better sheriff. Abel always saw too many sides of the equation, but maybe that, too, was an asset in a lawman. Maybe you had to think like a criminal in order to outsmart one. "Abel sent Johnny Stenton out to the Snow place, but no one was there. They're looking for the boy." She stretched out a hand in the room's darkness. She ought to tell Cal about the discovery of Gert's bones, she knew, the same way Abel had told her—as an aside, almost as an afterthought. There was something unsettling about the unearthing of those remains. Gert hadn't been good news during her lifetime, and June suspected she'd be even less so now. She took a quick breath. "On top of everything, Abel and his men found the bones of Gert Snow tonight. By accident. After all this time, she was buried right there on the edge of the ravine."

Cal looked grim at this additional information, but he didn't remark on it. Years of juggling accidents and near accidents, booms and busts and equipment failures at the mill had made him circumspect in the face of disasters large and small. He was not a man to let emotion rule or distract him. Rather he tended to hoard the measures of his sentiments, clutching them tight to his belly the way a hungry man guarded two fistfuls of food. "Are you coming up?"

June considered. The bedroom would be cold, the sheets stiff and dry. Cal's body would be reassuring ballast under the covers, a counterweight to keep her tethered. But she wasn't ready for sleep. Not yet. "Soon."

"Spread the ashes out before coming up." Cal's feet were heavy on the stairs.

"Of course." She always did. She always would. But fire wasn't the real danger, June thought, not compared to the filaments of a life—her life—a little too loosely woven, its threads starting to show the kinds of holes she was worried she'd never be able to mend.

Nestled in the loft of the cabin, where he'd been sleeping since he was a toddler, Nate lay inert and fully clothed under a pile of scratchy wool blankets. Downstairs he could hear his parents' low murmuring back and forth—his mother's voice a quiver of contralto, his father's the rumbling, steady bass that vibrated through every memory Nate possessed.

He reached up and ran his fingers over the bandaged gash on his forehead, pressing until he felt the ache deep down in his skull. If he could just keep the pain present, he thought, if he could stay in the chaotic moment of free fall, the bus tipping into darkness and then bumping down the ravine, he might figure out what had happened. He didn't mean the actual accident itself. There was no explaining that. All Nate could remember was a bright set of headlights filling the bus from behind, then a vicious swerving, and finally the terrible and elongated sensation of teetering on the edge of a precipice. It was the events before that, all the way back to the movie theater in Berlin, that Nate couldn't square.

On the way to Berlin, Suzie had sat with him the way she always did, her long, jean-encased thigh pressed against his, her bony shoulder poking his bicep. It was nice. They hadn't sat that way for a while. They were too old for the youth group, but Fergus had let them come along tonight anyway, just so they could get out of Titan Falls for a spell. The movie even seemed like it might be good. But Suzie had been preoccupied and quiet. She didn't nudge Nate with the point of her elbow and ask if he'd heard any filthy jokes lately. She didn't roll her eyes and snort when he described the touchdown he'd thrown in the last football game. She didn't even snap her gum.

Maybe, Nate thought, *she's worried about her dad*. His own father had fired Mr. Flyte, Nate knew. One day, he was all too aware, he would also be expected to make decisions like that, potentially dismissing and bossing boys he'd known all his life, boys he'd bled for on the athletic field, boys he wanted to be like but wasn't quite, not with a mill to his name. And every day he would work surrounded by thousands of pieces of blank paper, each one a small fate he could choose to blacken if he wanted or keep pure, sending it out into the wider world like an unfinished prayer for someone else to complete. It was a freedom Nate envied. All the pages of his life were already thoroughly inked with the soot and grease of the mill, his future written for him.

His breath had fogged the bus window, muddling his thoughts. The bus lurched over a pothole, and Suzie fell against him, her body a familiar and comforting weight but with curves now instead of little-girl angles. An electric jolt buzzed along Nate's ribs and spine, but if Suzie felt it, too, she didn't show it. Instead she squeezed the red mittens she was holding and straightened herself back up, making herself separate again. A lump formed in Nate's throat. *Maybe*, he thought, *she's in love with someone I don't know about.*

She was antsy during the movie, sighing a lot and jiggling her legs, crossing and uncrossing her ankles. Finally she stood up and threw her coat around her shoulders. "I'm going outside for a smoke," she whispered.

Nate sat alone in the dark, missing her. The fact of her empty seat bothered him, as did Suzie's newish habit of cigarettes and her apparent amnesia when it came to any of their old jokes. He glanced behind him, willing her to come drifting back down the aisle, but she didn't. He waited another heartbeat, then another, and then at last stumbled over legs and knees in the dark, apologizing as he passed. If Suzie wasn't going to come to him, he'd go to her. He wasn't a smoker, but he was willing to start if it meant he could share something with her again.

In the lobby he blinked from the sudden light, even though the overheads were dim. Through the glass panels of the building's front doors, he saw the blur of Suzie's brown plaid coat coming back inside, the sweep of her yellow hair. As if pulled by a beacon, he sailed toward her.

"What are you doing?" She scowled when she spotted him and glanced quickly over her shoulder. The sky outside had darkened, and the street had dimmed into a palette of industrial uncertainties, the many boarded-up buildings question marks. Once a city in these parts decided to die, you simply had to let it.

"I just came to find you." Nate began to step across the lobby toward her, but she quickly closed the space between them. Through the cloudy doors, Nate saw a figure who reminded him of his father. A man in a camel-hair coat, about the same height, and walking with a matching impatient hitch in his step. Nate watched as he bent down to the pavement, then straightened and disappeared from view. Nate squinted, but whoever it was had gone, leaving Nate to doubt he'd seen anyone at all. Once again he wondered if Suzie had a secret boyfriend. "Who was that?"

Her blue eyes darkened. "Who was who?" Too late, Nate remembered that she'd never been the kind of girl who required rescuing. He blushed, and Suzie jumped on his discomfort. "Oh, for heaven's sake, Nate. Go sit back down in the theater. I have to go to the bathroom. I'll be there in a minute." Nate wanted to prove his fidelity by waiting, but he didn't want to seem like a creep, so he'd skulked back into the dark theater, bumped over knees again, and settled himself in his seat, trying to slow his breathing, trying to pretend that his heart didn't feel as big and bruised as an old banana.

He waited, but she didn't sit with him—not for the rest of the film and not on the bus either. She let him board first, and then she took a seat right behind Fergus up in the front, leaving Nate to stew alone in a backseat, occasionally catching glimpses of her hair as she flicked stray pieces over her shoulders. What could she be thinking about alone up there? he wondered. She was clutching only one of her red mittens, he noticed, and he wished he'd noticed earlier when she'd dropped its mate so he could play the hero and return it now. She was fond of them, he knew. Her mother almost never gave her anything special. And her father...well, he was a worse story altogether. From years of childhood escapades over at the Flyte house, Nate knew that Fred kept a bottle of rye in the broken freezer in his garage. He knew that dinner conversation around the Flyte table often consisted of Fred's fists pounding the wood in a drunken rage, and he knew that the bruises Suzie said she got from clambering through the woods sometimes came from much closer to home.

Up ahead of him, Suzie's profile was hidden by rows of children's and teenagers' heads, their hair electrified with the cold air or covered by hats decorated with pom-poms and tassels. Half of those hats were probably made under the hawkish gaze of his mother, Nate reflected, the yarn looped right under her eye during her sewing circle. Nothing in Titan Falls happened without his parents knowing about it, and this, he felt, was both a blessing and a curse.

Only with Suzie had he ever felt a kind of parity. He knew everything about her: her shoe size, her favorite flavor of ice cream, what she had nightmares about. Surely he would sense if she was in love with someone. He would guess with whom. The bus wobbled over yet another pothole, and Nate jerked sideways, but this time all that his shoulder and ribs met with was empty air. No Suzie to crash into. He stared out the window at the black swath of trees that straggled along the lip of Devil's Slide Road, their outlines barely visible. One day they might be turned to paper.

Just then a blinding set of headlights filled the bus from the rear. He turned to face the source of the light, but the other vehicle—a dark blur—was trying to pass them now, plunging the end of the bus into blackness. Nate held his breath, waiting to see if the light would catch Suzie's face and reveal whatever she was hiding, but before it could reach her, there was a violent jerking, then an ominous wobble, and then just falling. A drop that he survived but Suzie didn't.

Nate rolled onto his back and blinked at the knotty-pine ceiling, worlds colliding in his mind. He closed his eyes and tried to sleep, but it was useless. Suzie was everywhere and nowhere at once, like the imprint of a president's head on a coin. Nate could flip it a hundred times, he knew, and there she'd be, a memory he would never be able to ignore.

On the stairs he heard a volley of heavy approaching footsteps. His father, coming to check on him, to breathe the mill's grease-laden air straight back into his only child's lungs if that's what it was going to take. He would be allowed to grieve only so long, Nate knew, before he would be told to lift his chin and chest, to brace himself and walk like a real man.

The door opened, letting in a single slant of light, pointed as a saber. Nate suffered it, lying as still as he could, his eyes closed, his breath stilled. Then the door closed and the light disappeared. Nate waited for his father's footsteps to ebb before he crept back down to look for his mother.

Alone in the cabin's living room, June pulled out her knitting—a baby blanket she was working on for Stella Farnsworth—before she remembered that she'd left the pattern for the project in Cal's car after church last Sunday. She'd been sharing it with Alice during the church coffee hour, the two of them cooing over the promise of a new infant in town. She hesitated, reluctant to go back out into the cold night when, really, all this could wait until morning.

It took her a moment to find Cal's jacket in the mudroom. It wasn't on the peg where he normally left it but thrown crosswise over a heap of unused rubber boots in the opposite corner of the room. June let out a wifely *tsk* of annoyance and fished in the closest pocket for the car keys. She shoved her feet into the closest pair of black rubber boots, threw Cal's coat around her shoulders, and flung open the door to the howling misery of the weather.

Shivering, she darted out into the dark where Cal's car sat still streaked with that unsettling mud. She unlocked the passenger-side door and fumbled around in the pocket for the pattern, illuminated by the weak interior bulb. Just as her fingers touched paper, however, she froze, for the mud she'd spotted on the outside of the car *was* definitely yellow up close, and it was fresh. June blew out a punch of air and considered what she was seeing. She pulled herself out of the car and shut the door, returning the scene to darkness.

That might have been the end of it, but once inside again, June stamped her feet to get the snow off and stuck her hand in Cal's coat pocket to return the keys. This time, however, her fingers encountered something soft, what felt like a length of crumpled yarn. Puzzled, she pulled whatever it was out into the light and then froze, her vision narrowed to a single point as she saw that she was holding Suzie Flyte's other mitten.

June would have known it anywhere, not just from the color—the insolent red of chokecherries—but also from the diamonds of cable knitted into the fabric, a pattern her own fingers had demonstrated to Dena. She extended a hand to steady herself and then, just as she'd done a hundred times before, she stepped out of her boots, shrugged off Cal's coat, and walked into the kitchen with the mitten, trying to think. There had been so many people milling around at the accident scene—police and rescue workers, distraught parents—but certainly not Cal, for how would that even have been possible? He was waiting in the cabin when she and Nate had arrived. And yet here was Suzie's mitten laid out on the scratched kitchen counter, the wool puckered from where it had gotten wet, the shape of Suzie's graceful fingers still crimped into the yarn.

I need a drink, June thought. Where had Cal stashed the scotch? She began banging through the cupboards faster and faster, unconcerned with the noise she was making, grateful for it, really, because as long as there was a steady thumping to pay attention to, she didn't have to think about Suzie's mitten sitting on the counter and the yellow mud streaks on Cal's car, and what those things might mean.

"Mom?"

June whirled around, smashing the side of her hip into the corner of the counter and letting out a yelp. Nate was crossing the living room wearing a sweater she'd made him for Christmas last year, the wool pilled down the front. She hadn't heard him come downstairs.

"Yes?" Without thinking, she shoved the mitten into the back of the nearest drawer and hoped Nate wouldn't notice. It was a drawer no one but June ever bothered with, filled with the detritus of summer: capless pens, inconvenient lengths of dirty string, warped paper clips, and orphaned buttons. One day, she was always vowing, she would sort it all out. Now she was glad for its confusion.

"What are you doing?"

June smoothed her slacks, wincing as her fingers touched the spot on her leg that she'd just bruised. "Oh, nothing. Looking for something I left here last August."

Nate shoved his hands in his pockets. His face was puffy and red, and his nose was running. *He looks so much like his father,* June thought, regarding her son's strong chin and the wide plane of his forehead, his honey-blond hair. He had always been more like her in temperament, though, reflective, measured, careful about his future. She had an urge to run her palm over his head, to cup his cheeks, but Nate was already edging back toward the stairs, his gaze sliding back to his feet. "I just came down to say I love you. I'll see you and Dad in the morning."

"Okay," June said to the empty spot he left behind him. "Sleep tight." The same incantation she'd always bestowed upon him in the same singsong lilt. But nothing was the same anymore, she knew, nor would it be, not with Suzie's dirty mitten shoved in the back of that solitary drawer, lost to the light, as treacherous as a single yellow footprint dusted under new-fallen snow.

Chapter Five

The moon was up high, peeking over the clouds and the trees, when Mercy finally extracted herself from the hospital. Hazel had planted herself fast as a weed by Fergus's side and told Mercy to take her car for the night. Though Mercy tried to refuse, she was secretly grateful for the favor, since her body longed for sleep the way a hungry man's stomach demanded food.

She didn't think Hazel had heard the news yet that it was Zeke who'd caused the crash. Otherwise Hazel surely wouldn't have loaned her the car. She wouldn't have put her powdery arms around Mercy and squeezed good-bye, whispering her thanks. She wouldn't have given Mercy the key to her house and begged her to look in on the sheep in the morning. Those sheep were family to Hazel, and good people didn't put their families in the path of trouble if they didn't have to, Mercy was all too aware.

In the forest Arlene had blended in as naturally as bluebells in spring, but in a town folks would get one look at her and the rope of grizzled hair tossed over her shoulder and they'd set their lips and pick up their feet. This used to make her laugh. "If I'm the scariest they've seen, then they sure haven't seen much," she used to crow, straightening the knife attached to her belt, and in these moments Mercy always used to feel a surge of pride in her mother, who knew how to snare a bird so that it would be waiting fresh with the morning dew, who could draw fire out of two rocks and make a blade of grass sing between her fat thumbs.

Remembering all this, Mercy almost developed the courage to blurt out to Hazel what she'd heard at the nurses' station about Zeke and the accident. She wanted to, but her throat choked up like a stream jammed with stones, and the words stuck inside her, swirling indefinitely. What would she say anyway? An apology, maybe. *I'm sorrier than sorry.* Followed by an explanation of what Zeke had once done for her, how he'd taken care of a pair of men in the woods who'd hurt her and then paid the price for it. How, after jail and losing Arlene, he wasn't really himself anymore. Hadn't Hazel buried her own son? She must know all about the razor teeth of grief, Mercy reflected—how if you weren't careful, they'd scrape you raw, eating up your flesh before going for the far more delicious meat in the middle of your bones.

Instead she suffered Hazel's embrace in silence, guilt making her arms stiff and her back a ridge of stone. She couldn't remember the last time another woman besides her mother had embraced her, and the too-sudden proximity made loss fresh all over again for Mercy. Would Hazel rebuke her tomorrow, curse her, or simply close the door in her face with the gentlest and firmest of clicks? Mercy wondered.

"I have to go," she said. "My little sister…" She trailed off. The less she said about Hannah, the better. She hoped to God that when the sheriff had come for Zeke, Hannah had had the good sense to hide the way Mercy had taught her. She wasn't declared Hannah's legal guardian, and she had an abiding fear that one look around their filthy RV would be enough to send

Hannah to foster care. These occasions were times when Hannah's love of reading came in handy. It kept her quiet for one thing, but, more than that, the fairy tales and folk yarns Hannah so loved provided easy bait for her imagination.

"You know they'll take you away if they find you," Mercy would tell her. "Exactly like the witch in one of those stories of yours. And just because a man wears a star, that doesn't mean he's any good. You have to look at what's underneath, and to do that you have to look without being seen. Do you understand?" And Hannah always nodded and said she did.

Mercy sure hoped so now. She patted Hazel's shoulder one last time. "I'll bring you some things from your house, if you want."

Hazel sniffled. "That would do kindly." Mercy turned away. Such a small thing in the face of such a great wrong, but it was all she had to give. *I would do anything*, she thought, stepping into the glare of the hospital hallway, *to put things right*.

If she were smart, she'd head home, find Hannah, fire up the RV, and get the hell out of Titan Falls. Maybe Zeke was already in custody. Or, likelier, the more complicated scenario by far, he'd taken off, hell-bound not to return to jail. Either way, Zeke had made this mess, and he could damn well lie in it. It was none of Mercy's doing.

Except family didn't work like that when you'd spent your life rattling through the backwoods, the hard woods. In that geography what was past and what was present were one and the same. Crime and punishment danced ever close on the heels of brotherly love, and Mercy, so help her, was tied fist to palm to her older brother and to Hannah whether she liked it or not. It was the very last vow she'd made to Arlene, and she'd rather be tarred a black sinner than go back on that word now.

Would. Should. Could. In the long run, those words led to no end of trouble if you chose to use them.

Mercy wasn't going anywhere.

When Mercy finally parked Hazel's car on the edge of Devil's Slide Road and crept down the skinny path to the clearing where the camper was parked, she saw that Zeke's truck was indeed missing. A kerosene lantern flickered in the RV's window, elongating Hannah's delicate silhouette.

"What the heck do you think you're doing?" Mercy growled, banging into the sardine-can space, stomping what snow she could off her wet boots. She moved the lantern to a corner. "The window's lit up like a damn Christmas tree."

Hannah hustled over with a ratty towel for Mercy to squeeze the frost out of her hair with. Her eyes were too big in her face, and her hands were shaking a little. "It's okay. All the lawmen are gone now. They came looking for Zeke, but he took off when he heard them coming, and I hid in the trees and kept away, just like you taught me to."

Mercy's heart skipped a beat. "Zeke came back here?" It flat out didn't make any sense. If he'd gone and knocked Fergus's bus into the ravine, wouldn't he have tried to get as far away from it as he could, even if he'd had to leave his truck? But then who could ever explain what Zeke did? "Was he sober?"

"His nose was bleeding, and he was holding one of his shoulders crooked, but he didn't stink like drink."

"What happened?"

Hannah's teeth were still chattering a little. "I don't know. I overheard the police talking about some bones they found and a school bus falling down into the ravine, but Zeke didn't say nothing about any of that when he came in. He was just cussing up a blue streak because he said he'd smashed the truck and now what were we going to do for wheels?"

"Hannah, look at me. Are you sure that's everything that happened? He didn't say anything about the bus?" Mercy knelt down and put her hands on her sister's shoulders.

"I'm sure."

Mercy sat back on her heels. The one thing her brother had never been was a liar. "How did he seem when the boys turned up looking for him?" It was what Arlene had always called law enforcement. *The boys.* As if they were a band of friendly relations. Because once you knew one, you knew them all, Arlene liked to say.

Hannah pursed her lips. "He didn't stick around when he heard them coming. He just lit out, and so did I." So maybe he *was* guilty, Mercy thought. Maybe he just hadn't wanted to scare Hannah.

Just then, however, Mercy spied Zeke's jackknife laid on the dinette's counter. Dented and worn, the handle was bone, carved in relief with the antlered head of a stag. Arlene had given it to him on his fifteenth birthday, and except for prison he was never parted from the piece. Mercy picked it up. "He didn't take his knife." She tightened her fingers around the bone, comforted by the sure way it fit her hand, hollow to hollow, curve to curve. She opened her palm and dropped the blade back onto the counter, then closed her eyes, picturing her brother running fast through the woods, his hat half pulled over his eyes. Underneath its brim those eyes would be alert as twin moons, and on his belt an empty space sat where the knife used to rest.

When she opened her own eyes, Mercy saw that Hannah had taken off her sweater and that welts were blooming up and down her arms. She scratched at them without complaining, and this fact suddenly broke Mercy's heart. She went to fetch a tin of salve that Arlene had taught her to make, a mixture of beeswax and chamomile, clean-smelling and soothing, and then took one of her sister's needle-thin arms in her hand. So slight, but also surprisingly strong, like a green switch cut from a willow. "Let me see. Don't scratch."

"It's from the ghost that haunts around here," Hannah said matter-of-factly as Mercy capped the salve. "She's real mad about something."

"Don't be silly, Hannah. That's just another one of your stories."

Hannah, once she believed in something, was not easy to dissuade. "There is *so* a ghost. I told you. They found her bones tonight. She wants something from us, Mer. I just don't know what."

Mercy twitched the curtains. "You keep out of that whole business. We're not here to delve into ancient town history. It's nothing to do with us. Anyway, they're going to be up in our lives enough as it is, what with this accident and Zeke running off. Leave it."

Hannah pouted. "But Zeke didn't *do* nothing. We get all the trouble," she said, mournful and slow. "It just sticks to our sides."

Mercy almost burst out laughing. Hannah, with her tousled hair and huge eyes, sounded and looked like a kitten complaining in the rain, only things weren't funny. Mercy was bone tired, damp, and there were precious few hours left until dawn. Tomorrow was Thanksgiving. Now, *that* was a joke. Mercy still had the pilfered page she'd ripped from Hazel's cooking magazine folded in her pocket, but she saw now how stupid she'd been to think that she could ever re-create anything from that world in this one. She fisted her hands on her hips. "Let's go to bed now."

Somewhere in the darkness, an owl let out a scream—a wet and panicked noise like a woman drowning. Mercy shut the curtains tighter on it. When the weather got good enough, she would have to remember to give them a good wash and an airing. She watched as Hannah began to climb up to the sleeping loft. "Why are you so sure Zeke's innocent?"

Hannah's head wobbled on her frail neck as she echoed Mercy's earlier thoughts. "He may be a box of fury, but he's not a liar."

Mercy looked at the dented cans of corn pone and green beans lined on the kitchenette counter next to Zeke's knife. When she and Zeke were little, anything could make him mad, but the one thing that could do it fastest was being blamed for something he didn't do. Mercy remembered the time he got whipped for stealing eggs from a farmer's henhouse. A few days later, when the man caught a fox and tried to apologize, Zeke wouldn't even look at him. He still hated eggs to this day.

Hannah achieved the loft. Her disembodied voice floated down, a mere suggestion in the dark. "A road's an open book. Mama always said that, remember? Anything can happen on it, and who would ever know?"

Mercy stripped down to her T-shirt and long underwear and settled herself beneath her thick quilt. Across from her the knife gleamed, its sheen still visible in the dark, and she wondered just how long it would be before Zeke returned for it. To be a Snow, after all, was to keep things close. She pictured Zeke slumbering somewhere in the vast woods surrounding them, the knowledge of his crimes bundled tight in his heart, and then pondered Hannah and the library books she collected from town to town. There was whatever had happened to Zeke in jail and the memories that Mercy carried of what happened to little girls in the woods, wolves or no.

One secret at a time, she thought, punching her jacket into a pillowlike shape and laying down her head. Not everything in a forest desired to be dragged to light, she knew, but just because you couldn't see a creature, that didn't mean it wasn't there. It just meant you'd better be twice as careful where you chose to walk.

June woke in the cabin far later than she meant to, well after Cal and Nate, and when she came down into the kitchen, they were both there, Nate silent as the grave with a plate of eggs and Cal making a pot of coffee. June tensed as he opened the drawer next to the one with Suzie's mitten—he was looking for the coffee filters—and exhaled as he crossed the kitchen to another cupboard. "They're on the third shelf," she said, going over to help him, her hip butting up against his. She cursed herself for not getting rid of the thing last night.

She wanted to ask Cal right now, right here, just how he'd come to have the mitten, but Nate was behind them, alternately brooding and watchful. June thought she could handle whatever Cal's explanation might be—maybe even the fact of his lying about it—but she wasn't sure Nate would be able to square himself with a betrayal like that. Much as they argued lately, Cal was still his father, and Nate hadn't left childhood all the way behind yet.

Outside, it had begun to snow, the flakes dizzying down in a confused flurry, gentle at first and then faster. During her freshman year at Smith, June had run outside every time a burst of winter weather started, spreading her arms wide and tipping her face up to the sky to feel the crystals kiss her forehead and cheeks. Her friends had teased her, but June hadn't cared. She was baptizing herself, being reborn as a New England co-ed, a girl who wore circle pins and cheered at football games and quoted Whitman, not one who ate gator, fended off her mother's bad boyfriends, and only wore shoes when she had to.

It had been twenty-odd years since June had stood in the dizzying swirl of being two people at once, the one you let people see and the one you kept buttoned close to your chest. With the mystery of Suzie's mitten shut up in the drawer, she was both horrified and surprised to remember how exciting it was—that sense of boundless possibility. In the monotony of married life, June sometimes forgot that she'd become who she wanted to be after all, even if she'd had to drop some of her dreams along the way. She looked at the drawer where the mitten resided, and she suddenly knew: She was not about to let a scrap of red yarn undo her life's work.

Cal gave up on the coffee and joined Nate at the table, where he had his own plate of eggs waiting. How similar they were, June thought, father and son, both left-handed, both averse to jam on their toast, both shot through with the famous McAllister stubbornness. They ate without speaking, heads down, avoiding eye contact. The night's catastrophe had made them careful with each other, June saw, though she couldn't tell yet if this was a good thing or not.

After breakfast Cal helped her wash and dry the plates, the egg pan, and the butter knives. June let him, saying nothing about the mitten and nothing about the mud streaked on his car. She watched as he pulled the winter sheets over the faded couch and chairs, closed the shutters, and piled the cooled ashes from the fireplace into a metal bucket. He didn't move like a man with a secret, but he was capable of them, she remembered, thinking back to the horrible afternoon when she'd found that strange lacy scrap of a bra hidden in his shirt.

"Here." She handed him his coat, watching with interest as he shrugged on the garment. She noted—she was almost sure—a slight awkwardness when he plunged his hands into his pockets. First his square fingers patted the jacket's exterior pockets—one, then the other—and then they fluttered to the pocket hidden in the lining. He glanced up, his face dark.

June watched him, her hand on the front doorknob. Nate was waiting for her in her car. "I noticed last night there was a hole in one of your pockets, so I patched it up," she lied. She was glad for the cool air licking down her bare neck. She'd stripped the beds and unplugged every appliance. All they had to do was close the door. The secret of the mitten would be safe until late spring, when she could return to burn it or bury it for good. By then everything would be back to normal.

June's heart pounded as Cal gave her a probing look and then stepped through the door. Suddenly she was desperate to get back to Titan Falls, where she would mend the hole in his pocket for real. If there wasn't one there, she'd make one and then fix it. Some rips, she thought, you could manage to repair, providing you were quick with your thread, but there were others not worth bothering over. The real trick to holding two things together, June was coming to see, wasn't how tightly they were bound but how well. Sometimes a loose thread was a saving grace.

Chapter Six

Time slowed and warped in a hospital. Hazel remembered this from Rory's illness—how a minute could stretch itself out like a whole damn day and then how the instant of death itself tricked you, sneaking up and stealing your loved one so fast you couldn't believe it had really happened. In that vein, Thanksgiving passed without Hazel's caring one fig. Maybe the turkey had defrosted and rotted on the counter. Or maybe Mercy had wrapped it up and hauled it out to her place—Hazel didn't know, and she didn't rightly care. Hours turned to days, and all the while Fergus hovered between the here and now and the hereafter, his brain occasionally beeping out a blitz of activity but otherwise unresponsive. He was breathing on his own. His heart was pumping. Fluids were going in and out of him, but he simply wouldn't wake up.

Hazel knew without a doubt that the man she'd wed and to whom she'd given over the better part of her life was in there somewhere, but the doctors didn't seem partial to her belief. If his situation didn't improve, they kept warning her, she was going to have to make a difficult decision. Was she prepared for such an event? they wanted to know. A fool question she didn't see fit to answer. Of course she wasn't ready. Who in her right mind would be?

Visitors from town came and departed, but Hazel didn't talk to any of them, and finally the nurses starting asking people to stay away. Wherever Fergus was—some icy, dark place—Hazel wished to be there, too, and so she clutched his hand, closed her eyes, and hour after hour hunkered down with him, praying for a miracle.

The only soul she allowed near her was Mercy, who arrived daily with updates on the sheep and the state of the farm. Fergus might have stopped in his tracks for the time being, but the rest of life didn't work that way, Hazel knew. Of course she'd heard the news about Zeke supposedly causing the accident and being on the run, but the situation was complicated. For one thing, it was breeding season for the sheep, and if matters weren't managed right in that arena, Hazel would end up paying for it later. Each afternoon she waited for Mercy's arrival, pouncing on her with furious questions, throwing all the living she wasn't doing at the girl's feet. "Is the big ram eating the littler one's share? He can be an awful bully, and you can't let that happen. Did you pen the white ewe with the black ears in with the big ram? In a week or so, it will be time to bring them all into the barn for the season. You think you're up to the task?"

Mercy responded to Hazel's demands with resigned calm and few words. "Yes, ma'am. All done. The feeding's going fine." Then she'd stare gawp-mouthed at the shrouded figure of Fergus, her lips working themselves around the silent apologies Hazel imagined she must want to get out and never did, whether from pride or fear, Hazel couldn't determine. It didn't matter anyway. What was done was done. There was no putting that bus back up on the road, no turning back the clock. All her married life, Hazel had worried about her man driving that icy stretch of road, and now that her blackest fear had come to pass, she was almost very close to being actually relieved. The worst had happened, and she would no longer need to live with the dread of wondering.

When the nurses found out that Mercy's brother was wanted for the crash and was on the run, they fell into a flurry of indignation. "You don't have to receive her, you know," the little blond nurse told Hazel, her nose twitching as she watched Mercy's scrawny shoulders disappear down the hall. "I wouldn't."

Hazel hesitated. She hadn't been out to the crash site, but Mercy had, and she described a scene of confusion: panicked divots of footprints leading everywhere, stray bits of metal, the hollow scoop of earth where they'd reportedly found Gert Snow's long-lost bones, much to everyone's uneasy astonishment.

Gert's disappearance was a story that had always haunted Hazel. It seemed wrong to her that a woman so allegedly rooted to a spot of earth would have left it in such an open-ended way. Now it turned out Gert had been there the whole time, and Hazel wasn't sure she considered that idea any more comforting. No, not at all. She sighed. Any way you sliced it, the Snows—all of them—were double helpings of nuisance and trouble. Still, Hazel found herself praying that Mercy was different, and it bothered her in the extreme, this unaccustomed little sun of optimism burning away inside her. When she replied to the nurse's concerns about Mercy, her voice came out far gruffer than she meant it to. "The girl says her brother didn't do it."

The nurse scoffed. "My brother's in law enforcement down in Concord, and that's what all the lowlifers say, honey. None of them ever did it."

Hazel picked up her spindle. "You don't understand. I need her help with my animals. There are so few people I trust." But there was more to it than that. The terrible truth was that Hazel half enjoyed the guilty way Mercy skirted around Fergus and his machines. It gratified her to watch Mercy's head snap to eager attention when she gave the girl instructions, for it meant that there was someone else in the world who wanted Fergus to get well even more than she did.

The nurse wrapped a blood-pressure cuff around Fergus's unmoving arm. Her nostrils flared again. "You're a more forgiving woman than I am."

Hazel worried her spindle between her fingers, coaxing out inch after inch of yarn, the pile of fleece growing thinner and thinner on her lap. Maybe it took an accident to uncover something that had been there all along. Maybe that's what that nurse was trying to say. Hazel stared at the wooden tool in her hand. She hadn't been paying attention. She'd reached the end of the thread, she saw, and now had nothing to do. Somehow, without even knowing it, she'd come around full circle, empty-handed, right back to the same damn place she'd started.

After death there was still always some kind of life. It was the unofficial dogma of Titan Falls—a creed long ago arrived at not out of civic hope or optimism but simple practicality. When a man was churned to bone in a mill accident or simply wore his skin clean out, when a wife turned her toes up to the sky and closed her eyes for good, there was always someone left behind: snotty-nosed children not yet out of diapers, twin sisters or brothers who'd never married, sometimes just a dog—long in the tooth and matted, perpetually hungry—but always someone. The women of Titan Falls recognized this. Of the many things they did well, they excelled at carving order out of mess. They rose at dawn to smooth the wrinkles from threadbare sheets and scrub the black off kettles, to sort odd socks and wrap the day's sandwiches in squares of waxed paper. Because life required attention to the little details, they knew. Because sometimes those small things were all a woman had.

Three days after the accident, Stella Farnsworth sat in the comfort of June's parlor, like a cat preening its fur. Twenty years old, Stella was a recent bride and expecting her first child in April. To June she seemed still to be half child—twig-limbed and doe-eyed—but so far she'd approached her pregnancy with a hypnotic calm.

"Oh, Paul already put the crib together," she said, giggling and waving her hand when June asked if she needed any furniture. "It took him half the night, but he got there in the end. He's started in on painting the nursery now. Apple green, we chose, because we don't know if the Nugget here"—she lightly touched her belly—"is a boy or a girl."

June thought back to her own expectant days, when Cal had taken one look at the crib's instruction sheet and then called Tom Plimpton, the mill foreman, to come and sort out the whole thing. "He can fix the pulp screens in ten minutes flat," Cal reasoned, staring at the diagrams of instructions. "He ought to be able to figure this out."

Now, sitting surrounded by the women of Titan Falls, June wondered if maybe she'd skipped some important step of wifehood. She'd made sure everything in her domestic life had always gone so seamlessly, so easily, just as Nate's crib had been assembled without one wrong step but also without any of the laughter or the shared intimacy that small failures created between couples.

Soon, as June hoped it would, gossip began to flow. "What do you think it means that they've gone and located poor Gert Snow after all this time?" Alice Lincoln started in, her eyes goggling. "Isn't it just the strangest thing?"

Dottie waved one of her meaty hands. "Never mind that. It's the living we ought to be focused on. I hear that the Flytes are down to the bone in their savings. I don't know what will happen now with the funeral expenses." The women darted little accusatory glances at June, as if it were *her* fault that Fred Flyte was an incurable souse and a piss-poor provider.

Alice laid down the pillowcase she was needlepointing and turned to face June full-on. "Have you been to see them yet?" Alice's husband handled the incoming logs at the mill. She'd had a daughter of her own on the bus, a ten-year-old who'd escaped with a broken wrist and a bracing new fear of the dark.

Dottie glared at her. "That's a terrible idea, Alice. If you were stuck in Dena's shoes, would *you* want to speak with June right now?"

Alice bowed her head and slid her eyes away from Dot. "No. I guess not."

Dottie shifted her considerable bulk. "I didn't think so."

June wondered at Dot's change of heart. "Have *you* been to see her?"

Dot fixed her with her gaze and sniffed. "She's not in a good way."

"I heard that Snow boy was in some previous trouble in Maine," Margie Wall broke in, trying to change the subject a bit. Everyone knew that the mill was teetering on the edge of another round of layoffs. That wasn't technically June's fault, but it was hard not to hold it against her all the same. "That's what Abel said, at least. I heard the little bastard was drunk when the bus went down but that no one can find him."

June picked at the stitches she'd looped onto her knitting needle. With the women of Titan Falls, there were always two sides to things, she knew, never more. The good and the bad. The black and the white. The innocent and the damned. June's mother-in-law had taught her that lesson right off the bat, and, once dispensed, Hetty's advice had not been optional. If June didn't take it, Hetty would hound her until she submitted. It was a skill that came in handy during gatherings like these. "Ten to one if they don't go and charge Zeke with murder," she said now, dropping a conversational pebble to see what kind of ripple it made. Not the sort she was expecting.

"But it was an accident!" Stella cried.

This was worrying. June hadn't expected to hear sympathy for the Snows. "The court won't see things his way when they catch him, I can guarantee."

Stella cleared her throat. "I'm just saying, I don't think the crash was intentional. Those Snows are awful, but I can't believe they would go and deliberately hurt the Good Lord's children."

Pregnancy was making Stella soft in her head, June thought. She wrapped a tail of yarn around her knitting project. It wouldn't do for the whole damn town to go tender on any of the Snows just now, not with Suzie Flyte's funeral right around the corner and Abel still looking for Zeke and that mitten sitting in the cabin's drawer. The story of the crash was going to have to go the right way, and if she had to, June would make it. Once she'd been very good at that kind of thing. Once she'd written her own better ending. "Justice has to be served." She tried to say it gently, as if she truly lamented this state of affairs. "What kind of world would it be if it weren't?"

That stumped Stella. She rolled up her needlework and opened the lid of her sewing basket. Her top lip was set in a stubborn curl. "What kind of world would it be without the benefit of the doubt?"

Dot came to the rescue. "That's no way to talk, Stella. We're all women of faith here."

Just then the front door slammed and Nate walked past the open door of the parlor into the kitchen without saying hello. The women started gathering their loose threads and patterns, shoving fabric scraps into bags and shrugging on coats. The sewing circle was over. The next time they met, they all thought but no one said, they'd be gathered together under the rafters of St. Bart's to bury Suzie. Maybe Zeke would be caught by then and his bail would be set. Dena would have to pull herself together, and Cal would once again lead the town in resuming its normal routine. Hopefully, the mill would keep churning out its white rolls of paper and the river would run clean. No one would ever know about the mitten in the drawer at the cabin—a little scrap of Suzie stuck behind on earth, all but forgotten.

One by one, the women approached and kissed June on the cheek and thanked her for her hospitality. Margie Wall asked for her marble-cake recipe. Stella said she had a few questions about the upcoming Winter Carnival. None of them noticed the tremor in June's fingers as she attended to the door or the way she bit the corner of her bottom lip, and none of them guessed, as she waved them into the darkening afternoon, that she was carrying, folded and tucked under the starched bib of her apron, a pinpricked length of dread stained a deep, unsettling scarlet.

It was strange in Hazel's house without her. The air smelled of dust and pine, and the only sound was the grating of the clock on the sitting room's mantel. Every time she came, Mercy checked it to make sure it was wound, then let herself into the kitchen, where the cupboards were stocked with all manner of good things to eat: noodles and bags of creamy rice, packets of powdered onion soup, canisters of apple tea. All of it free for the taking. Mercy thought of Hannah, growing so fast that her pants were short around her ankles, but she quickly pushed the thought of stealing out of her mind. The Snow name was low enough as it was. Instead Mercy took any spoiled food out of the fridge, then took the sack out to the row of metal rubbish bins lined up behind the house. Fergus used to haul everything to the dump twice a month, but now Mercy supposed that she would take over that job for Hazel. She'd do it gladly if it meant bringing Fergus back to life.

Telling Hazel what the police believed about Zeke had been the hardest thing so far. Mercy had been terrified that Hazel would fire her on the spot, and then what would she do to put food on the table for Hannah? But Hazel had surprised her by not reacting at all.

"I know all of this," she'd said from the chair placed next to Fergus. Her head had been tipped back and her eyes were shut, so Mercy couldn't tell what she was thinking. Up close, the bare skin on her neck was veined and papery like an insect wing, a thing both delicate and deceptively strong. "I've already heard. Now, here's what I need you to do for the sheep..."

Hazel's refusal to discuss Zeke was a frank relief. Every day since then, every hour she was in Hazel's presence, Mercy had tried to think of a way to say thank you, but Hazel was having none of it. And so Mercy was doing what she could to make it up to Hazel. She owed her more than she could ever say, she knew. Hazel was the first person Mercy could remember who'd opened her home to her, and Mercy was surprised to find how quickly she'd grown to count on the little comforts of stable domesticity, things no one else would think to notice, perhaps, but which touched her to the quick: a calendar with cats on it hung in the kitchen, to-do lists pegged on the fridge, a wall of photographs showing the progression of years—Hazel's face starting off thin and smooth, then plumping and creasing—houseplants grown lush and lazy. Bits and pieces like this, Arlene had always dictated, would just drag them down on the road. Better to stay anonymous and uncommitted. For the first time, Mercy had begun to wonder at everything she and especially Hannah were missing.

In Hazel's bedroom Mercy slid open dresser drawers and found clean socks and underwear, then fished a fresh pair of dungarees and a crisp shirt out of the wardrobe. The garments hung in patient order, placeholders for the absent couple, Fergus's shirts nestled next to Hazel's, work-worn trousers folded over the hangers' neat halves, Fergus's one suit zipped in a dusty plastic cover. If he passed away, would Hazel bury him in it? How wrong to go down into the ground in something you'd never really worn, Mercy thought. Surely the earth should receive you the way you'd really been in your life. It's what they had done for Arlene—dug a grave deep in the woods and tumbled her into it wrapped in a dried deerskin and wearing her favorite black hat. But civilization had its own customs. Town folks, Arlene had always told them, buried their dead right under their feet, stomping on the bones as if that would ensure the departed remained that way.

Mercy shivered and closed the closet door. Fergus wasn't going to die. She had to believe that. She pictured him in his hospital bed, shrouded in white, tubes and wires shooting out of him like tentacles. If only he would get better, he might be able to say what had really happened. Arlene would have known how to do it. She would have gone straight into the forest, plucked an assortment of flowers and buds, and made a miracle. But that was just wishful thinking on her part, Mercy knew. In the end even her mother hadn't held sway over the whims of life and death. Her own passing had proved that. No, if Mercy was going to sort out the mess of the crash, she was going to have to rely on her wits, not magic. She shoved Hazel's spare clothing into a duffel bag she found in the bottom drawer of the bureau. Problem was, she *wasn't* her mother. These days she wasn't even herself. She zipped the bag and left the bedroom.

Considering everything, maybe that was all to the good.

Some backwoods girls had a way with water. Give them a forked stick and a beat of time and they'd strike you a spring. Some had a feel for granite seams or knowing where game was hiding, but Hannah had always had an ear for bones. Deer carcasses whispered tales to her of tall grass and buzzing flies, dog bones growled tired and low, and bird skeletons twittered. But human frames were the trickiest. They swirled with echoes of laments or vibrated with unfinished business. They never brought good tidings. It wasn't until she encountered Gert Snow's remains, however, that Hannah learned just how tricky the dead could be.

Hannah sensed the bones within her first five minutes on the Snow place, and as soon as she was able, she'd gone exploring, walking half a mile up the road to find them. *Help me,* they pleaded from their resting place, a bump of earth jutting out just at the beginning of the descent into the ravine, guarded by the delicate trunk of a bent white birch. Hannah approached it, drawn to the peculiarity of a bowed tree growing in a forest of razor-straight sticks. It was an empty, unfinished shape, she thought—half a heart, the curve of a broken cup. Curious, Hannah reached out to touch the milky bark but stopped, the hairs on her arms prickling, goose bumps shivering up and down her skin. She listened with her whole body.

The bones were loud. They fizzed with leftover fury, as electric under the earth as live wires, humming with information. They were of a woman who had died with her heart cracked in two, Hannah deduced. *Please,* the bones begged, but before Hannah could bend down to them, to put her mouth to the earth and answer back, Mercy sneaked up behind her. "I thought I warned you not to go wandering," she barked. "I had to track you all the way out here like a dog. Now, come on back to the rig. You need to get cleaned."

"There's something down there," Hannah had said, pointing at the birch.

Mercy didn't show a whisker of interest. She glanced around at the trees, then flicked her gaze down the ravine, swatting at a late-season fly. "There's lots of things around here. And I'll bet half of them are hiding in your hair. Now, come on back and let me comb you."

Reluctantly, Hannah had allowed herself to be trotted back to the RV, casting a worried stare over her shoulder. She'd stood by plenty of times while her sister and brother had gutted game, and she'd skinned and flayed enough rabbit and squirrel herself to know that you didn't turn one of God's creatures inside out—beastly or otherwise—and not expect some corresponding shift in the universe. Sometimes retribution arrived large in the form of a storm or a terrible illness, and sometimes it crept in small. A broken dish. A jammed gun. A blown tire. But that was the price of life. A body needed to eat. Arlene had taught them that first and foremost. Hunger called to be filled, she'd told them, just never for free.

As soon as she heard about the crash, Hannah became certain that the skeleton was lurking behind the whole business of it, for it seemed clear to her that anyone with bones that loud wouldn't be the kind of soul to let the great beyond interfere with plans for a long-awaited reckoning.

The morning after the accident, Abel and his men returned to investigate the wreck and its environs in daylight. Hannah, crouching upwind in a prickly holly thicket, held her breath as Abel's shepherd dog made straight for the birch where they had found the bones. Even from where she was hiding, Hannah could make out a clean length of white angled in the rocky loam. Abel sighed and spoke to his deputy, who was fiddling with the radio hooked to his belt. "Looks like we're going to need some more digging equipment. I'm betting anything we just found Gert Snow. Who else would be buried out here?"

"Gert Snow? Really? Then, I figure a plain old shovel will do."

Gert Snow. Hannah mouthed the syllables silently. Finally a name to go with the seething spirit. Someone from her own family, from way back. She whispered the letters again, this time her voice coming out as a tiny rasp, almost imperceptible, a moth wing scraping a leaf. Before the two lawmen could spot her, she took off into the woods.

That night the ravine's wind blew sideways through the trees, redistributing the snow in unusual shapes. Hannah woke to the ghostly forms of snow rabbits, horses caught in mid-gallop, even a man. The forms quivered in the breeze, assuming their contours for only a moment before shifting once again into something else entirely, gone but for Hannah's witness.

She tiptoed down the RV loft's ladder and silently eased herself into her boots and parka. Mercy had come home late again and was still wrapped like a pig in a blanket in Arlene's old quilt, just the dark ends of her hair fraying out the top. Holding her breath, Hannah squeaked the RV door open and shut it fast behind her, slipping down the metal steps and high-stepping through the snowdrifts to the smokehouse.

Mercy had warned her time and again to stay out of that place, but Hannah loved the little hut with its crooked roof and slanty walls and its ancient odors of rendered fat and burned spruce logs. Over the door there was a rusty horseshoe nailed up for luck. Mercy had gone inside to investigate when they'd arrived, but there hadn't been much of Pruitt left to clean up after. Whoever had found his body had also apparently made off with most of his worldly goods, not that he'd owned much. Besides the trio of rusted iron hooks that were bolted to the rafters, there was a sagging army cot and a rough shelf of minor treasures Hannah liked to tinker with: a dented copper kettle, a length of wire knotted into a figure eight, a smattering of greenish pennies, and a funny kind of button she'd found in a tin can rolled under the cot. She took it out and inspected it now. It was two buttons, really, joined together by a little silver chain, and on the face of each one there was a letter *M*. She ran her finger over the points and wondered why on earth Pruitt would have had something so polished and sleek in his possession, especially since his name started with *P*.

But today something was different in the smokehouse. Hannah noticed immediately. She tiptoed closer to the shelf, blinking, and there it was: a twist of yellow yarn. Hannah lifted it, and a row of thin wooden stars dangled and danced, some of them stained dark, some clearly whittled from the green wood cradled at the heart of a young tree. She smiled and tied the bauble around her neck, pleased with the way the stars fanned across her, decorating her. There was only one person she knew who would have left her something like this, and if he had, it surely meant that Zeke was fine and well.

Mercy, however, was not as delighted with the trinket. She spied it as soon as Hannah entered the camper and stripped off her parka. "What is that?" She pulled at the neck of Hannah's sweater.

Hannah jerked away from her sister's sharp fingers. Now she was glad she hadn't tied the funny button onto the yarn, too, as she'd been tempted to do. Instead she'd left it back in the smokehouse, nestled in the can. "I found it outside." That wasn't a total lie. "I think the ghost left it for me. I see her sometimes, in the snow."

Mercy whipped around to face the counter. "There's no ghost, and you know it."

Hannah tossed her braid.

Mercy took a breath and knelt down in front of her sister. "It's very important you tell me the truth. Have you been out in the smokehouse?"

Hannah bit her lip, then nodded.

"And that's where you got this?" Another nod. Mercy sucked her teeth and sat back on her haunches.

Hannah fingered one of the stars on the necklace as Mercy approached her with a pair of rusty scissors. She took a step away, but Mercy was too fast. She caught her little sister by the collar and, before Hannah could say boo, snipped the yarn from around her neck, pocketing the trinket, stars and all. Now Hannah was very glad she'd left the funny silver button in the smokehouse.

Mercy waved the scissors to make her point. "Gert Snow didn't leave this. You and I both know that. Zeke did." Mercy patted her pocket. "And while we're on that subject, you need to keep your nose out of that whole Gert situation. Hazel told me that the reason people hated our father had something to do with Gert. Probably Pruitt knew something about her death, and if he did, I'm guessing it wasn't anything good. So drop it."

Hannah folded her arms across her chest and stuck out her chin. "What's going to happen to Zeke?"

Mercy laid the scissors on the counter and considered. "There are lots of folks out looking for him, so I need to make sure I find him first." She fixed Hannah with a flat stare. "If anyone asks, you ain't seen him, you ain't heard from him, you don't even know him. He's as good as dead. Got it?"

Hannah pouted. "How's it going with Fergus Bell? Do you think you can get him to wake up?" Even in a snit, Hannah could be persistent as a deerfly. "Do you think he remembers anything? And what if he *doesn't* come back to his senses?"

Hannah always was able to articulate a conundrum as clear as morning—a simultaneous gift and plague. Across the RV, Mercy spied the book of Greek myths Hannah had stolen from one of her libraries and went to pick it up. "Don't worry, little pickle. Why don't you come here and read me something out of this?" She opened to a page with a picture of a winged goddess on it. *"Athena,"* the caption said. *"Goddess of wisdom. Goddess of war."* Mercy ran her fingers over the drawing, wishing it could speak. Maybe it would have some answers for her.

Even before prison Zeke had far preferred the company of trees to that of men. Only in a forest could he breathe deep, all the way down to the bottoms of his lungs. Only among the trees did he feel a true ease and connection with the world, what he supposed other men found in church or in the arms of women they said they adored.

Zeke had only ever loved Arlene and his two sisters. Not in *that* way, of course—though they'd once come across a family where that had appeared to be the case—but in the manner it counted, where he would die for them without a second thought, or go to prison for that matter. Zeke had never been around so many men as he had during his time in jail, and he'd hated every minute of it. He'd slept crammed into his bunk, his bulky cellmate tossing and turning on the mattress above him, mashing the springs. He ate elbow to elbow with men who stank like old meat and sometimes like blood, showered hip to hip in a line with them, worked silently in the steam of the laundry with them, loading and unloading the big round machines, his ears filled with the insufferable roar of the dryers.

It took him weeks after his release to get rid of that sound, a constant grumble in his inner ear that made it impossible for him to hunt or even navigate brush in the same unthinking way he used to, with all his senses, like one of the animals he was tracking. It was ironic, he thought, that in prison he'd finally become fully human and found that it was a disaster. Everything he did felt too deliberate and decided. With every branch he broke underfoot, with every bush he accidentally set aquiver, Zeke was made painfully aware that he was never again going to be the boy he once was. And this, he realized, was the real genius of incarceration—not the time you did behind bars, which eventually ended, but the extension of the sentence afterward into everything you did.

Maybe it was for this reason he found himself drifting into Lucky's Tavern after he and his sisters had arrived in Titan Falls and learned that Pruitt had passed away. Instead of finding the long-missed connection to his father that he could almost not even admit to craving, Zeke had gone and done the next-best thing: sought trouble. Lucky's, it turned out, wasn't too different from prison. The men there, especially the ones who had congregated that particular evening with their shoulders hunched over doubles of gin or rye, wearing boots worn to the shank, could also talk with their stares, and it was a language Zeke now spoke fluently.

But he'd been sober as a judge the night of the accident, and that was what made everything so frustrating. After getting the shit beat out of him at Lucky's, Zeke had walked the straight and narrow just like he'd promised Mercy he would, and even though his mouth watered more often than not for the quick burn of a shot, he ignored it. Mercy mixed some weird concoction for him when the craving got really bad—something that tasted like juniper and cinnamon—and it gave him the strength to stay dry for a few more hours.

He'd spent the entire day wandering around Berlin and its outskirts. He almost landed a job in a body shop, but when he admitted to the owner that he was an ex-con, the man's face turned to granite. "I've been held up three times," he said, shooing Zeke out the door. "You don't want the kind of handout I'll give you, son. Don't show your face here again."

By evening his legs and feet hurt so bad he thought his bones might have finally given up and decided to crack, collapsing him from the inside out like an empty building packed for demolition. The truck, when he found it again, was parked in front of a bar. He hadn't noticed in the morning, when the establishment had still been closed, but now, in the thickening dark of a town he didn't know, the cheery red script of the neon sign and the sounds of music coming from inside were almost too much to resist. He closed his eyes and let himself imagine the surgical whiff a shot of tequila would provide or the fizz of a cold beer sliding down his throat, the bubbles energizing him, going straight to his head. He stuck a fist in his dungaree pocket to feel for any change or the chance of a dollar or two, but there was nothing. He sighed and opened his eyes.

In the space of a few moments, evening had ceded to night. The temperature had dropped, and snow flurries danced and swirled in the air. Mesmerized, Zeke threw his head back and jigged along with them, illuminated by the glow of the tavern's neon sign. Across the street the entrance to the town's movie theater blazed. A pretty blond teenager in red mittens came out, fished in her coat pocket, then slipped into the alley next to the theater and lit a cigarette. Zeke cocked his head. She looked familiar, but he couldn't place her.

If he hadn't been watching the girl, he might never have seen the couple coming around the corner. The man was tall. His hair was too slick and cheeks too well shaved to belong to anyone but a man of means. Zeke squinted through the snow, not fully trusting his eyes, but it really was Cal McAllister, the owner of the Titan Paper Mill. Even if you clung onto the very edge of Titan Falls like Zeke and his sisters, you couldn't live there and not know the man. In fact, Zeke knew him very well. Last month Zeke had approached the foreman at the mill to ask about work, but the encounter hadn't gone well, for he turned out to be one of the souls who'd beaten him purple at Lucky's. Cal himself had ended up coming onto the floor and throwing Zeke out of the mill with the stern warning that if he saw that boy's sorry ass hanging around again, he'd set dogs on him. Not wanting trouble now, Zeke stumbled into the street shadows, automatically reverting to the hunch-shouldered stance he used in the woods. When he wanted to, he could be damn near invisible. And given what was unfolding in front of him, Zeke suddenly thought going low-visibility might be a very good idea.

The woman with Cal was peroxided and big-breasted and very, very pretty in lots of red lipstick and bright earrings, but by no stretch of the imagination was she his wife. As they came around the corner, she laughed and said something in an accent that Zeke didn't catch, then giggled again as Cal reached under her coat and squeezed her buttocks while he drew her into the alley where they wouldn't be seen. The fun didn't last long, though, as Cal saw that the alley was occupied, and then by whom.

Zeke watched as Cal left his companion in the dark and grimly marched the blond girl back to the front of the movie theater by the elbow. "What do you want?" he was saying, and the girl wrenched her arm free and practically snarled at him. Zeke tipped his head, unwilling to move too much and give away his location, but he thought he could make out the words "my father." He swayed and put a hand out onto the sooty bricks next to him for balance. The world tipped and lurched in a hundred snowflakes, and Zeke's stomach danced with them. He hadn't eaten since the morning, and his head felt like a balloon, much lighter than the rest of him.

When he looked up again, Cal was standing alone in front of the theater. At his feet one of the girl's blood red mittens nestled in the snow, dropped and forgotten. Zeke watched as Cal bent over and considered it, then slipped it into the pocket of his camel-hair overcoat. He glanced about him, then stepped around the corner to fetch the woman he'd left waiting in the alley.

"Not tonight, Bryga," Zeke heard. "I have to get back. I told you it was a stupid idea to meet here like this. Tomorrow's Thanksgiving, for Christ's sake." With a final pat on the woman's ample rear, he left her shivering alone, her earrings quivering and flashing in the shadows.

Zeke had seen enough, he decided. Besides, he was freezing his ass off. And tomorrow *was* Thanksgiving. He owed it to Mercy and Hannah to try one last time for work before he headed home empty-handed—again. Taking a fortifying breath, he pulled open the door to the bar and stumbled into the comforting stink.

"What'll it be?" The barkeep—a human Goliath—swiped at a puddle on the bar with a filthy rag and eyed Zeke. He didn't look eager to pour him anything, but that was fine since Zeke wasn't asking.

He took a deep breath and tried to make his voice low. In lockup he'd learned that to talk to a group of hard men in anything less than a growl was a basic invitation for a fist headed straight at him. "You need any help in here? I could sure use a gig right about now." One of the men down at the opposite end of the bar was biting into a Polish sausage covered with mustard and sauerkraut, and Zeke felt his stomach lurch like a dog straining on a rope. He was so hungry he almost wanted to cry, and the sensation was even worse when he thought about what Hannah must be feeling. But Mercy had that job with the sheep now. That was something.

The barkeep put one of his pawlike hands on the counter. "Sorry, but no." He hesitated. "You okay, son?"

"Sure." Zeke shrugged and bobbed his way to the door, though nothing could have been further from the truth. At least he hadn't gotten into a fight, he thought. There was that. At least he hadn't reached across the bar, swiped a bottle, and just gone to town with it, pouring the booze into himself like feed down the gullet of a goose. What he *wanted* to do with himself and what he *could* do were not very often one and the same. He'd learned that lesson the hard way.

On the drive home, the paroxysmal rattling of the truck and the ice forming on the road shaped his thoughts into jagged and disjointed shrapnel. Fragments of suspicions, regrets, and sorrows mingled with other, sharper judgments, scooping out a mental path as slippery and treacherous as the road he was driving. He replayed the scene he'd witnessed with Cal, the woman who obviously wasn't his wife, and the young blond girl. If he were quicker, more like Hannah, Zeke thought, who could twist an argument so fast you forgot which end was which, he would figure out a way to profit from the little get-together he'd seen. But knowing his luck, he'd get busted for extortion or something and thrown right back in the slammer. In the end it would come down to what it always did: his word against everyone else's, and he already knew who would lose that horse race.

It struck him that just as there were two layers of canopy in a forest, the green and tender shoots beginning to come into their own, and the overarching, bigger branches, full of dark and heavy leaves, there were two sets of justice in the world: one for people like Cal McAllister and another for boys like him. As he mulled over the inherent unfairness of this, he wondered how, when presented with interrelated wrongs, a body was supposed to know which one was the worst. He had beaten a man so badly he would never walk straight again—true—but only because that man had hurt Mercy. Zeke had done time, and the other two men had not. When a crime went unpunished, Zeke wondered, did it mean it was any less wrong?

His head knocked against the truck's passenger window as he went around a turn, and he snapped to attention. He hadn't realized he'd been half dozing, lulled into semiconsciousness by his abiding hunger and the crunch of the tires against the dirt and snow. He was nearing the path that led down to the clearing they now called home. Just a few more wide turns and he'd be there, back with Mercy in the warmth of the RV, where things made more sense. He moved his foot on the gas to head into the next bend, but before he could press down, the truck was suddenly skidding, the back wheels digging an independent arc across the road. Zeke spun the steering wheel, but that only worsened matters, throwing the truck onto the narrow shoulder and smashing him full force into a tree.

When he came to, he had glass stuck in his hair and his left shoulder hurt like hell. He wiggled the fingers on that hand, relieved that they all seemed to be working, and eased out from behind the wheel, being careful not to cut himself on any loose shards of metal or what was left of the window. He stood gape-mouthed for a moment, trying to absorb the exact magnitude of this latest of his fuckups, and then gave up and began trudging back to the clearing.

He wasn't really surprised when he heard the cops coming down the path a little while later, their belt hardware jangling, radios squawking. He watched from behind the RV's curtain as the circles of light from their flashlights bobbed, then grew wider and brighter as they neared.

He hadn't done anything wrong, he thought as he gathered his coat, his hat, and laced his boots. On the other hand, he'd done absolutely everything wrong. He'd left the truck smoking on the road. He'd been driving when he was too tired. He didn't have a proper registration for his vehicle. Any number of infractions they could haul him in on. There was just time for him to kiss Hannah and help her into her coat before they both slipped out into the trees. He left Hannah tucked in a copse of prickly holly and set off down the ravine. No doubt the police would try to book him on drunk-driving charges, not caring that he was as dry as a well in summer. Facts weren't going to matter much in a case like his. He knew that the town hadn't liked his father, and they weren't prepared to like him either.

Halfway down the slope of the ravine, he stopped. Something was very wrong. The secret quietude of the forest at night was being ruptured by the distant grind of machinery and the wailing of sirens. Using the river as a guide, Zeke followed the bends of the valley bottom, twisting and turning with the water, the commotion increasing as he approached the scene and saw what looked like a school bus tipped into the water. Keeping to the shadows, he held his breath and thought furiously back to the moments before his own accident. There hadn't been a single soul on that road besides him. He was certain of it. And yet, astoundingly, here a bus had fallen. He watched as a pair of paramedics crawled out of the wreckage bearing a stretcher with a lifeless blond girl on it. Zeke held his breath and looked closer. It was the girl from the movie theater. The one who'd been talking to Cal McAllister, her yellow hair spread around her as if she were swimming.

Slowly he backed away into the vegetation. At his feet the Androscoggin flickered with cold malice, the moonlight on its surface winking at him in mocking flashes. *You're only as good as the story you carry,* it said. *And you aren't fooling anyone. Tell the truth and you'll just get called a liar.* Up above him on the ridge, he heard a dog braying and then the stamping of police boots on the snow, and without hesitation he turned and plunged into the safety of the water, heading for the opposite shore, where the woods grew thicker and the steep hills beckoned. He looked back once at the river, wishing he could go to Mercy and Hannah, but even as he fled, he knew it was going to be quite some time—if ever—before he crossed back to that life again.

Two days after the accident, to Mercy's unending frustration, Zeke was proving as good as his word. Though she knew he wasn't wholly gone from Titan Falls, he also wasn't anywhere she could find him. On the one hand, that was fine news, for if she couldn't hunt him down, surely Abel Goode couldn't either. On the other hand, she had a thousand questions for her brother and no way to answer them.

By now the route home from Hazel's was a path Mercy could have trudged in her sleep. Out of the valley and into town, then past the library, past the general store, with its tempting bins of penny candy and its back aisle of stationery goods, past Lucky's Tavern. That was one place she knew she wouldn't find Zeke. The mill loomed behind everything always, its smokestack as forbidding as any watchtower, like the trick painting of an old-fashioned, bewigged man Mercy had once seen in one of Hannah's library books, whose eyes followed her no matter where she moved.

Today Mercy decided to take the long way home down by the river on a neglected, weedy path. The vegetation was mostly buried by hillocks of snow, but she kept an eye peeled anyhow. Arlene had always finished all her plant and herb gathering well before the first flurries, drying her finds and storing them in glass containers for the winter. Mercy had some of those samples left, but her stores were dwindling and she wished for the thousandth time for her mother. Maybe she would know a plant or a cure for the comatose Fergus. If only he would wake up, he could say what had really happened on the road and the town would believe him. If Zeke was innocent of causing the crash—and Mercy believed he was—then he needed someone else, someone who wasn't a Snow, to stand up and say it.

Mercy felt her throat grow tight. When the population of Titan Falls stared at her brother, she knew, they perceived good looks riding hard on the heels of a rotten reputation, but Mercy saw straight through all that to Zeke's damaged heart. They were so similar, the two of them—halves of an uncertain whole—but he was the boy and slightly older, and growing up he'd always tried to use that to her advantage. Most of the time, he'd gone on to discover all the worst parts of life first and tried to smooth them out for Mercy. The times he couldn't—like when those men had found her in the woods—were times she didn't like to think about.

When she was six and Zeke was almost eight, he'd taken her deep into the woods and made her wring the neck of a rabbit he'd snared so she would get her hands on death first and meet it eye to eye before it took her by surprise. She'd startled when she'd felt the rabbit's heart fluttering so fast against her palms and then had gone ahead and wrenched the neck as Zeke showed her. When it was over, Zeke had her skin the creature to teach her what lay beneath its fur. To this day she still had that pelt, stretched and scraped and gone bald in patches—a souvenir of her primary encounter with the fact that everything in this world was food for something else.

When she was eleven, a boy in one of the campgrounds they were holed up in started teasing her. Mercy had been nothing yet but a tangle of dark hair and sharp elbows and knees, so skinny and jagged that Arlene had called her a human zipper. Every morning the boy would lie in wait for Mercy and buffet her with pebbles when she exited the RV—nothing that would cause any damage, just stones that would blister her skin and hurt. When Zeke found out what was going on, he picked up the biggest rock his fist could hold and went in search of the boy. The whole campground heard the cries coming from behind the washhouse, but no one did anything. The next morning the boy and his family took off before dawn, their vehicle leaving behind a reproachful trail of blue vapor that burned Mercy's lungs when she stepped outside to watch them depart.

But there were other times, when he wanted, that Zeke could pluck a note of gentleness from his belly like a song. The year they didn't have any money for Christmas gifts, for instance, Zeke had astounded them by pulling out a wooden box he'd been keeping hidden, flinging open the lid, and releasing a score of luminously colored butterflies. Hannah, four at the time, had squealed and careened about the tight space of the RV, her plump palms extended to catch the glory rising in circles all around her.

Mercy looked up from the sodden ground to find that she was almost at the mill. Slack winter shadows were creeping along the surface of the river, gathering and separating, oozing ahead with the current of the half-frozen water. She stopped for a moment, trying to reconcile her earlier perspective of the tower and the rectangular factory with this closer, more intimate view. In front of her, the back wall of the mill rose in a monolith of gray, its windows menacing pinpricks. Mercy instinctively hunched in on herself, although if anyone were looking out, they might hardly see her in her mud-spattered work coat and boots.

She stopped. She'd reached the edge of the mill yard now, where machinery was hunkered under layers of tarps for the season and where the men parked their trucks and cars. A small hidden creature—a mouse or perhaps an early bat—squeaked unseen in the shadows. Mercy shivered. She couldn't imagine a more unlovely place. It hadn't snowed for a few days, so the ground was a smear of mud and frozen sludge crisscrossed with a web of tire trails. She picked her way through the vehicles, not entirely sure what she was even looking for. Parked closest to the mill was a splotch of brazen color in the crowd of pickups and four-wheelers, dun-colored and dented, all of them. She stepped closer. Without a doubt, it must be Cal McAllister's car, for no one else in Titan Falls had the luxury of possessing something merely because it pleased him, because it was beautiful, an end in and of itself.

Timidly she reached out and ran a single finger over the hood. The metal was cold to the touch and slickly polished, and her finger left a clouded smear. She quickly retracted her hand, and the mark faded. Inside the car the leather tufts on the upholstery were as plump and taut as bread loaves just pulled from a steaming oven. Mercy wondered what it would be like to crawl into such comfort after a day spent in the cacophony of the mill. Was the transition from clattering gears and whining saws to the insular comfort of leather and gleaming chrome a blessing for Cal, she wondered, or did he have to push away a little pang of guilt as he watched his workers climb into their own battered vehicles and drive back to equally scruffy homes? Mercy had heard that the mill was getting ready to lay off a round of men.

She wondered how they would feel about Cal and his fancy car then.

But beauty always had at least one flaw nicked into it, just as something unredeemably ugly could be its own kind of lovely. Sometimes it took only the blink of an eye to see it. The light dropped a shade, casting the last of the day into formal dusk, and Mercy scanned the sky. In a world of gradations and shadows, of one road blending into the next—the only life she'd ever known—she wondered how she was supposed to winnow out a fixable truth.

When she looked back down to the car, her eye fell on a fine spray of yellow mud filmed on the inner wheel casings. She bent over, the edges of her hair sweeping onto the ground. Upside down, she could see that the undercarriage of the car was clotted with the yellow mud from Devil's Slide Road. She frowned and reached a finger out. It didn't look that old. The color still held its sulfurous tang. The ruin of Zeke's truck was covered in the same dirt, faded to the same shade but not yet so bleached that it had turned an ordinary brown. Not that many people dared to travel Devil's Slide Road—not at this time of year at least.

Mercy bit her lip, trying to construct a timeline of the accident in her mind. What if Zeke had been ahead of the bus the whole time? And what if someone else had come up behind it and tried to go around? It was possible. There'd been several different tire marks in the frozen mud when Mercy had gone to look at the crash site: the wide, swerving ones from the bus; the bald tracks Zeke's truck left, also swooping off the road; the short neat lines of police vehicles; and another set, too, from good tires, Mercy could tell. But either the cops hadn't noticed those or they didn't care. And why should they? They already had their suspect in

Zeke. Mercy straightened up, her mind whirling. Cal's car, she noted, had very fine tires indeed.

She was turning to leave when she felt a prickling along the back of her neck. She lifted her eyes to the windows and spotted, on the very top floor, the figure of Cal staring down at her. Even from this distance, his eyes looked cold and hard. He didn't move as Mercy backed out of the mill yard and returned to the path by the river, her mind working furiously. Common sense said that she and Zeke and Hannah should load up the RV and get out of town while they still could, but she had been altered by that quick change of light and the revelation of the mud on Cal's car. Something wasn't right, she felt in her gut.

The problem was that no one could say what had really happened. The children who'd been on the bus were too addled and probably hadn't been paying attention to the road anyway, and if Zeke came forward, Abel would clap him in cuffs and haul him off before he managed to squeeze out two words in his defense. That left only Fergus, cocooned in his nest of bandages, his sleeping mind tucked up like a nut in a hard shell. But what if he woke? What if *she* could rouse him? Would he remember then? If he did, he could help prove that Zeke was innocent like he said.

No doubt whatever really happened that night had been a terrible mistake, but the problem, Mercy realized as the last of the day's light rolled itself up and curled away, was that no one in Titan Falls seemed prepared to admit that. And why would they, she thought as she stared at the dark geography of the mill, when nothing in their lives was accidental, when they lived and died by design of the mill?

And lately nothing in Titan Falls seemed to be very certain at all. Hazel had told her about the impending mill layoffs. How glad she was, Hazel had said, that Fergus was not a mill man. How fortunate that he had his job driving. As if, Mercy thought now, bad luck could be evaded like a dangerous stretch of river, portaged with your boat on your shoulders and your gear on your back, a shortcut of safety taken on land. She looked at the Androscoggin. In a few more weeks, ice floes would cover its surface completely, but even when those waters looked dead, she suspected that they would still always be swirling down along the bottom, shifting sandbars and submerged logs around so that, come spring, no one would know what they were dealing with exactly. And maybe, Mercy thought, easing back onto the weedy, unused trail that would lead her into town, just maybe, that was exactly what Cal McAllister was counting on.

Chapter Seven

The dead, no matter how long passed, love nothing more than attention and remembrance, to hear their names flitting from living tongue to living tongue. When it comes to that, there is nothing like a good funeral, even if it is not their own. Certainly this was the case with Gert Snow. Reunited with the air, dancing once again on the lips of the townspeople, Gert's newly freed spirit began kicking up mischief. She started with the burial of Suzie Flyte.

The day dawned eerily warm over Titan Falls, slushing up the neat sheets of ice that had formed on the river, making a mess of the path in front of the church. Stella Farnsworth felt the first insinuation of a flutter in her belly. When she went to change into black for the service an hour later, she found a foot-shaped bruise smeared on her skin that would remain there for the rest of her pregnancy. All through town, people's measures of cream curdled in coffee, shower water ran to freezing before scalding, and mice frolicked in pantries.

Cal woke earlier than usual that morning with a pounding headache and the feeling that something heavy and insistent was sitting on his chest. For a moment, groggy with sleep, he thought it was their old cat, Moss, before he remembered that it had been years since the beast had been alive. Groaning a little, he threw the covers aside. June shifted in her sleep, her arm snaking across the bed toward him, but he evaded her and stood.

She cracked an eyelid. "Do you want coffee?"

"No." Cal slid on the pants he'd left draped over the armchair in the corner. "You sleep. I'm going to check on a few things at the mill. I'll see you later at St. Bart's."

June had half hitched herself up on one elbow. "But your suit..."

Cal found the garment bag hanging on the closet door and hooked it over his arm. "I'll change in my office. Go back to sleep."

With a mumble, June complied, burrowing herself back in the covers and rolling onto her side. Cal observed her for a moment, her body so well known to his, even after all its changes. When they'd met, she'd been as narrow and pliable as a ribbon, and then, pregnant with Nate, she'd been plump as a summer pheasant. Lately the angles of her youth seemed to have vanished forever. Her body lacked the pleasing tenderness it had once possessed. Was it the slight weight gain she'd suffered over the past few years? Simply the beginning of the descent into life's second half? Cal didn't know. He missed the girlish June, however, and the way her plaid skirts used to dance just above her knees, though if he were being honest, he knew that this yearning said more about him than it did her. Now when June wore skirts, she wore them longer, if she bothered to wear them at all.

The woman he'd been seeing in Berlin had no such qualms about showing off her legs or anything else. Bryga, her name was. She was a Polish-American girl, a waitress he'd met at the soda fountain, a single mother to a small son. The boy's father had been killed in a logging accident, but she didn't like to talk about him. She didn't like to talk much at all, in fact, and at first that was what Cal thought he wanted. It was enough—to help himself to someone young and maybe a little dumb, to someone so close to home who was nothing like it.

At least he'd thought so before this mess with the bus crash. Now his throat closed up every time he recalled his quick conversation with Suzie outside the movie theater in Berlin. In exchange for the girl's discretion about Bryga, he'd promised to restore her father's mill job. It had seemed such a simple bargain at the time: her silence for his word of honor. Suzie hadn't even needed to point out that Nate was sitting a mere fifty yards away, hunched in the dark of the movie theater. That was obvious. Where Suzie led, Nate followed. It had been like that since they were six damn years old. Cal had just forgotten all about the youth-group trip. He'd glanced uneasily at the theater doors, eager to wrap up the transaction.

When he remembered what happened next, his blood ran cold.

"If I hear one whisper about any of this, your father won't just lose his place at the Titan Mill, he'll lose his chance at any of them. Do you understand? You have to keep your mouth shut."

And Suzie, with the same astonishing sass she'd had as a child, sneered. Displaying the sarcasm that only a teenage girl could produce, she'd looked him straight in the eye and made an X over her heart. "I promise," she said. "Cross my heart and hope to die."

The floor of the mill was blessedly empty when Cal arrived on the morning of the funeral, the machines gone quiet for Sunday, sculptural in their stillness, industrial hunks of oiled metal and gears that lost all meaning unless they were spinning, whirling, spraying. In the storeroom great rolls of paper sat like blank gravestones or monuments, their significance indeterminable, yet to be written.

Cal made his way to the metal staircase leading up to his office and reached to turn on the light, but when he did, sparks jumped out and burned him, leaving an unpleasant ozone flare lingering about his nostrils. He cursed and examined his hand. There was a dusky brown spot burned into the pad of his thumb, staining the whorls of it. He stuck it in his mouth and pulled it out again, but the mark remained. Cursing even more, Cal clattered up the steps and let himself into his office, opening the blinds for light and throwing the garment bag over the back of a chair, rumpling his funeral suit surely, but he had much larger worries.

Below him the river spread its waters in wintry glory. Cal's father, Henry, had deliberately relocated his office to this strategic spot, where he could keep an eye on the comings and goings of traffic to and from the mill. At this time of year, the river was well on its way to being iced to calm, but in spring and summer and all through the autumn the currents bubbled and churned. Once, even forty years ago, floats of logs had still been pushed down in this manner, the wood hauled out, dried, and sawed. Cal had seen old tintypes of jams that had gone on for miles and stood as tall as a three-story building. Now the lumber was trucked in, and, honestly, Cal was glad. It made for a quicker and more efficient delivery all the way around, fewer men hurt and less of the end product damaged.

Not that Cal had a call for half as much wood lately. It was hard to churn out roll after roll of clean white paper without making some kind of mess, and where was he supposed to put it? When Cal was in college in the 1970s, the government passed the Clean Water Act, and in the years since, the state had turned ever more draconian about water quality, fining mills at the drop of a hat, for the least transgression. It was bullshit, Cal thought. Here he was paying through the nose to upgrade the converters and he'd still been nailed three times in the past five years for infractions. And he wasn't alone. The King Mill had closed, he'd heard, and over in Maine the Horne operation was going down faster than a lead fishing lure. When business dropped in a mill, layoffs happened. And when layoffs began, so did union troubles. It was a twin vise that Cal didn't see how to squirm out of.

He surveyed the icy riverbank below the window. Once again he felt the same pressure on his chest that he'd woken with. He stuck a finger under his collar and loosened it. Ever since the accident, he'd been vacillating between feeling like he was about to choke to death and the opposite, more alarming sensation of his entire existence loosening quickly, of a piece, and without his permission. Sweating a little, he sank into his desk chair and opened a book of accounts, the print swimming before his eyes, the awful truth of the accident filling his head.

So help him, but he'd been the one to pass Fergus on Devil's Slide Road. He'd been hoping to beat the bus out of Berlin, but he'd had to drop Bryga off all the way at the other end of town and double back on himself, and by the time he'd reached Devil's Slide Road, there was the old yellow bus wheezing ahead of him, gasping around the icy turns, shuddering along at the pace of a mule.

Cal considered his options. If he stayed behind the bus, he would risk everyone on it seeing him enter into town. June would collect Nate, head to the cabin, and then wonder where the hell he was. Word might get back to her about his late arrival in town, and he'd have to explain. But if he overtook the bus, he could slip into the night, speed down by the mill, and take the road out to the cabin, arriving before June and Nate and leaving himself free of their questions.

He waited for a place where he knew the road stretched straight for a heartbeat and, without any hesitation, gunned his engine and passed the bus, hoping that none of the children—Nate most especially—would recognize his car in the dark. And then he was in front of Fergus. Another curve, more pressure on the accelerator, and he was free, shot into the darkness, the bus headlights having vanished in his rearview mirror.

It was a maneuver he'd done a hundred times before, mostly in the summer, true, and mostly when he was much younger, but never with disastrous consequences. So what had gone wrong? Cal turned a page of the ledger and wondered, his stomach queasy. Had he driven Fergus off the road? Fergus was getting older. His reflexes perhaps weren't what they used to be. What if, startled, he'd wrenched the wheel too far in the wrong direction? Or had it been as simple as Fergus hitting a stray patch of ice on his side of the road, one he might have driven over anyway, with or without Cal zooming around him?

Cal hadn't had any idea of the fact of the accident, not until June had come to the cabin with Nate and told him. His first thought had been an overwhelming horror of what he'd caused, followed by a violent flood of relief that Nate was standing in front of him, shaken and scared but physically fine. He listened, knowing he should confess, that he should say *something*, but before he could, June recounted how Abel had found Zeke Snow's truck smashed into a tree a little way past the crash and how the boy had gone on the run. Cal hesitated, unsure what to make of this information, for he'd seen that, too, the smoking hulk of Zeke's pickup pushed up against a tree, steaming in the dark like a wounded animal, and he still hadn't stopped.

Guilt had overcome him, and he'd been on the verge of doing what he knew he should and confessing everything when June interrupted him and told him about Suzie, sealing his lips forever.

He'd immediately pictured the mitten folded like a lover's note in his overcoat pocket. Beads of sweat pearled along his spine and began to roll down his back, and the blood pounded in his ears with a single thought: *I have to get rid of it. No one can know.* Instead he'd gone up to bed feeling sick, and in the morning, when he'd stuck his hand in his pocket, the mitten had been gone. It had taken just one glance at June to ascertain that she'd been the one to dispose of it. *A hole in your pocket*, she said, her eyes locked on his, the open door she was standing in front of pushing a current of cold air over to him. *I patched it up.* But both he and she knew there'd never been a hole in the first place.

Cal closed the ledger and shoved it aside. It was useless trying to make heads or tails of the mill's failing accounts when his personal affairs were so wildly out of order. He'd brought it all on himself, though, first by messing around with Bryga after he'd sworn up and down to June that no infidelities would ever happen again and then by passing the bus and not stopping when he'd spotted Zeke's wrecked car. He hadn't offered Fred Flyte his job back either. He wondered again what June had done with the mitten, knowing he would never ask her, and he reassured himself that burying Suzie was the first step in putting the whole mess behind him forever.

It didn't feel that way, though. He gazed again out the window at the ice sheets on the river, slipping and bumping against one another. For one thing, in searching the crash site Abel had gone and found goddamn Gert Snow's bones, thereby uncovering a business Cal's father and Cal himself had tried very hard to keep quiet. And then there was the question of Fergus. If he died, Cal would have even more potential blood on his hands, while if he lived, it could be worse yet. He might remember.

The phone rang, shrill as a crow, and Cal jumped. June was still sleeping. Everyone else was off for the day. There was only one person he could think of who might try to call him here on a Sunday, and he'd vowed that he would never let himself so much as look at her again. The phone continued to ring four, five more times, then fell into defeated silence. Cal opened the ledger book, found his place, and took a deep breath. First to order the mill accounts. Then he'd go to St. Bart's and take care of his own.

Holding on to saplings and various trees for support, Mercy made her way early on the morning of Suzie's funeral down what looked like a deer trail to the bottom of the ravine, where the river bent and pooled in a big angry turn, its waters beating back against themselves, putting up a hard fight. With every inch she gained on the river, Mercy stepped more slowly, making sure of her footing. To fall into the maw of the Androscoggin alone out here would be disastrous, she knew. She took off her hat and wiped sweat from her forehead, staring at the churn of the current.

If she followed the bank north a little ways, she'd come to the site of the crash. The bus had since been winched up with no small amount of trouble by a towing crew, snapping branches and uprooting small trees as it went, leaving a long and painful scar gouged into the earth. There were no doubt plenty of things of interest left behind and overlooked, but Mercy wasn't concerned with them. Thus she chose to walk south, doubling back on her route, but lower down now, skirting the river. The tree line thinned as she stepped along the bank, avoiding the water that so terrified her. She walked for several minutes, then paused and let out a three-beat warble of a whistle.

It was the hunting signal Zeke had taught her, the one that just she and her brother knew. Four days she'd waited to try it, only to hear resounding silence. She pursed her lips and blew again, not expecting anything different, but this time she heard a faint rustle and then looked into the trees just in time to see her brother darting out of them. He motioned her to thicker cover, putting a finger to his lips. "We got to make this fast," he whispered, looking around nervously. "They've had dogs out here."

"Hey," Mercy said softly, her eyes widening. One of *his* eyes was swollen, and the other was bloodshot. His left cheek was bruised, and his bottom lip had a cut with dried blood crusted on it. He slid down onto the ground and tried to smile. "Guess I missed Thanksgiving."

Mercy shrugged, then took off the pack she was carrying and sank onto the ground as well. She'd brought some stale bread and the last hunk of the government cheese Zeke had scored in Berlin when they'd arrived. "You didn't miss much." She thought of the green-bean recipe she'd pilfered from Hazel's homemaking magazine, which was still folded in her coat pocket. It seemed like a coded fragment from another life—one to which she'd lost the key.

Zeke took the food gratefully, but to her surprise he didn't immediately begin to devour it. He had to be hungry, though. Four days in the woods. Even if he'd been poaching game, he'd still be starved for bread, for something hot and satisfying.

Zeke regarded Mercy warily. He seemed to be waiting for her to speak, and when she didn't, he went ahead and filled the growing silence. "Did Hazel fire you yet?"

Mercy's head snapped up. This was so typical of her brother. Here she'd been worried sick about him, and he greeted her not with reciprocal concern, or even with thanks for the food, but with an accusation. That was Zeke, though. He was capable of great tenderness, she knew, but only on his terms.

Zeke nudged her. "Well, did she?"

"No. Of course not."

He snorted. "You think she still trusts you?"

Mercy jutted her chin and said nothing.

"It's not bound to last, you know."

Zeke reached over and gently touched her on the shoulder. "When will you and Hannah be ready to leave? I can manage in the woods fine, but I think for all our sakes it'd be better if we hit the road sooner rather than later. They're going to string me up if they find me."

Mercy bent her legs and pressed her lips against the knees of her dirty jeans. Her ass was getting wet from sitting, but that was her own damn fault. She knew better than to plant herself on the bare ground. Zeke had imparted that to her. He'd taught her everything about life in the woods. Which side of trees moss grew on. How to tell when a storm was brewing. Not to dampen your own fool butt by plopping it on the ground. But there was terrain in the world, Mercy was beginning to realize, that only a woman was equipped to navigate.

It wouldn't be difficult to leave. She could have everything ready in less than an hour. The RV had half a tank of gas, enough to get them some distance. Maybe they could try driving south, down to the warm Gulf waters, or out to the Rockies.

They'd have to pick up work on the way, but surely they'd find something. Enough to get by. They were experts in that.

Then Mercy pictured how Hannah's face would crumple when Mercy told her to gather her things and get a move on. Hannah was counting down the days until she started real school, and she loved the little library in town, where, for the first time, she had a card in her own name.

Mercy chewed a thumbnail. They hadn't been in Titan Falls long, but already she could feel the beginnings of strings tying them to the place. It wouldn't be so terribly hard to break them, but Mercy found that she didn't want to. She thought about the Christmas when Zeke had presented Hannah with those butterflies. This year was bound to be just as lean, but surely they could get a tree and decorate it. Mercy could sew some ornaments from rags, and Zeke could carve Hannah something whimsical out of fir or knotty pine—a cat with a moving tail or a bird you could blow into and make it whistle. He was clever enough with his knife to do it, to make a whole menagerie come to life out of the dullest wood. Hannah was getting to an age where she would benefit from a steady home, but Mercy wasn't sure she could do it alone. Without Zeke she could provide shelter, but not a real family. And besides, this land was theirs.

She pushed her knees back down onto the wet earth and regarded her brother. Even separated from him by more than a ravine, she would always be able to see the good streak that ran through him, shiny as a seam of metal in a mine, but it pained her that no one else could perceive that. It was as if there were two Zekes superimposed cockeyed on top of each other: the mute and ill-spoken public version versus the loving brother. All Mercy wanted to do was to twist the lens and bring the two together.

She focused back on the ravine. They didn't have much time if she was going to voice her suspicions about the accident. Ever since she'd seen that mud on Cal McAllister's car, they'd been building in her like a bank of angry storm clouds. This was her chance to let them go. She turned on her brother, fury growing in her. "Look me in the eye and tell me if you were the one who really caused that crash."

Zeke slid his gaze away again to some unidentifiable point in the middle distance. It was an old trick of his—getting lost in time and space. "Does it matter? You know I've done enough bad shit that it was gonna catch up to me sometime."

Mercy put her hands on her thighs. Her palms were sweating. She opened them, her fingers tingling like they'd fallen asleep. The angrier she grew with her brother, the more her hands burned, and she wondered if this is what Arlene had felt when she laid hands on someone to do a healing. Maybe there was a finer line than Mercy had ever imagined between great anger and great love, and without the one you would never be able to feel the other. "Yours aren't the only tire prints on that road. I saw that clear as day."

Zeke clenched his teeth. "Mine are the only ones that matter."

Mercy sighed, frustrated. Ever since Zeke had come out of jail, it was like he was both *here* and *there* all the time, tuned to two channels at once so he never got any kind of clear picture going in his head. One minute he'd be gutting a strung-up deer like he'd done a thousand times before, his jeans sitting low on his hips, a cigarette dangling from his mouth, and the next his eyes would go glassy and gray, as if his soul had been swept away in a fierce current and pulled out to a chaotic sea.

Whenever Mercy asked what it had been like while he was locked up, Zeke just said it was nothing she needed to know about, that it was the landscape of a bad dream—scorching in the summer and chilly in winter, gritty the whole fucking time. But *something* had happened to him, Mercy knew, and she always felt it was all her fault. If Zeke hadn't stumbled into that clearing in the trees, he never would have half killed those two men, who in the end had walked away as free from guilt as newborn fawns, although physically scarred forever. She sighed. "Do you remember *anything* from the crash?"

"There was a bunch of metal meeting wood, tree branches whacking me when I got out, and shitloads of broken glass."

"Didn't you look in the ravine?"

Zeke shrugged. "I don't know." He ran a hand over his bruised face. "Jesus. Don't look at me like that. I've seen enough in my time, okay?"

Mercy wriggled her legs to keep her blood going in the cold. "There must have been noises. Voices. *Something.*" Or maybe there hadn't been. Maybe Zeke had been ahead of the bus all along. Zeke possessed a hunter's walk, Mercy knew. Even in heavy boots or in the wettest of mud, he rolled heel to toe, heel to toe, his breath held tucked in his lungs for later. He owned the timing of a hunter as well—not the discipline of a warrior's rush and charge but the wait-and-see of a stalker followed up with deadly aim. If there was something to be found, Zeke always uncovered it.

Up high above them, Mercy could hear the faint, rattling approach of a vehicle—probably Abel or one of his minions. Because of the complication of Gert's bones, they kept returning. Men like that would last five minutes against her brother in the wild, Mercy thought, but if they caught him, it would be a different matter entirely. She leaned forward. "You know if you don't fight this tooth and nail and come up with some proof that you're innocent, they'll put you up for murder, and that will break my heart."

For a moment her words almost had the intended effect. Zeke's eyes watered, but all too soon he overcame the emotion, clearing his throat and leaning away from Mercy. He stood up, brushing off the seat of his dungarees. Frustrated, she joined him. One jail, she could see, had become much like another for her brother. Innocent, guilty—he didn't seem to care anymore what he got labeled. He was both. He was neither.

Zeke regarded his sister. "So you aren't fixing to leave." It wasn't a question.

Mercy put her hand in her pocket. Inside was the knife with the carved stag's head. She didn't feel like giving it back to Zeke just now, though. "I can't. Hannah wouldn't make it in the cold, with nowhere to go. We have no money, and wherever we go, there'd still be a warrant out for you." But there was another reason, too, one that, once she acknowledged it, resounded in her like a bulging iron bell. *Someone* had to make things right—for Fergus and Hazel, for the Flytes, for her brother—and if Zeke wasn't going to, then Mercy would.

"Then I'm not going anywhere either."

This was exactly what Mercy had been afraid of—Zeke's noble tendencies coming out again in exactly the wrong way. "Zeke, you have to leave. Only for a little while. It's just dumb not to. You'll get caught for sure."

He grinned. "Not if I'm right smart." And with a quick kiss on her cheek, he was gone. As he slipped back into the woods, Mercy felt a tight ball of grief forming in her chest. She'd heard plenty of variations of stupid applied to the Snow name over the years, but "right smart" was one thing none of them had ever gotten called. She was about to begin picking her way back up to their clearing when she heard the rustle of Zeke behind her once again.

He hesitated and then spoke in a rush. "I did see one thing. Something in town, before the crash. I saw Cal McAllister talking to that blond girl who died. Outside the movie theater. She dropped her glove when she went in, and he took it. He was with another woman—someone who wasn't his wife—and that girl, she saw the whole thing. It seemed like he was promising her something, but I don't know what."

Mercy's mind swirled with this information. She almost didn't feel Zeke's lips as he touched them to her numb cheek. The sensation pulled her back to herself. "Wait." She drew the knife out of her pocket. "You forgot this." She eyed him sternly. "If you're going to risk getting caught just to carve necklaces and trinkets for Hannah and leave them in the smokehouse, this blade does a better job."

Zeke colored, then took the knife and folded it into his own pocket. In a quick blink, he was gone, leaving Mercy to head back toward daylight and the deputies, wondering what a man like Cal McAllister was doing holding on to the mitten of a dead girl, not to mention being seen with a lady who wasn't his wife, and what a woman like June McAllister would do if she happened to find those things out.

Tucked alone in the very last pew of St. Bart's, a shabby watchman's cap pulled close around her ears, Mercy shifted uncomfortably, unsure of what to do while she waited for the funeral of Suzie Flyte to begin. Arlene hadn't exactly been a wealth of church etiquette. Up front, Mercy could hear the whispering of the town wives—no doubt wondering how she had the nerve to show her face at this event. In the very foremost pew, she could see the back of the woman she knew to be Suzie's mother. Unlike the other wives, she was sitting with a fierce stillness that was familiar to Mercy. It was the posture of a woman struck so many times with hard luck that she could only wait to see what more the world would throw at her.

The town wives had arrived at St. Bart's with time to spare, fully ready to engage in conversational battle, winter scarves loosened, handbags clutched reverently, lips cocked for a round of whispering. They cast uneasy glances at Mercy, swapped knowing looks, and then set to work trading information. Mercy leaned forward to glean what she could.

"When she's not out with Hazel's sheep, I hear she hangs over Fergus in his hospital bed, like *that's* going to do any good," Alice Lincoln hissed to Dot and her husband in the third pew from the front of the church.

Next to Alice, Margie Wall wore a face clouded with the misgivings of a devout woman. "Those Snows are bad news, mark my words."

Alice nodded. "The boy certainly is. And I don't even need to go into that old business with Pruitt and Gert."

"What did he do anyhow?" Pregnant Stella Farnsworth had slipped into the pew next to Margie, her eyes rounder than usual. Margie licked her lips. When a morsel of gossip was this good, it was best delivered low and slow. "It's not what he did. It's what he supposedly knew."

Stella wrinkled her brow, not understanding where Marge was leading. Dot sighed, exasperated. "Oh, for heaven's sake, Stella. He was always insinuating that Henry McAllister was responsible for Gert's death. Lord knows what Cal was paying Pruitt to keep quiet about his father, truth to the tale or not. Gossip like that's not what you want on a mill floor."

Stella's eyes flickered open even wider. She was far younger than the other women, not even born when Gert disappeared. "Do you really believe Henry McAllister might have killed her? Why would he do that?"

Margie shrugged. "I don't know. No one does. But it's suspicious, don't you think? I'll tell you one thing. Cal's certainly kept the issue hushed. I've always wondered about that."

The women sat back in their pews, hands folded in their laps, and thought about this. They'd been warned by their husbands never to interfere with any of the dealings of the McAllisters, however large or small they might be. Did they want their livelihoods to dry up like the river in a drought year, leaving them bare-bellied and parched? they were warned. Or did they prefer to work together to protect what they had the only way they knew? Mill business wasn't always pretty—no one was trying to say otherwise—but when was anything ever lovely in Titan Falls?

A new pair of footsteps rapped up the center aisle of the church's bare wood floor, and the ladies fell silent at the familiar, authoritative rhythm. Without a word June McAllister took her customary pew up front, her back straight, her arm cradled firmly in her husband's grip.

"Do you think they heard?" Stella Farnsworth whispered loudly, and Margie shushed her, glancing nervously over at June, who didn't twitch but simply bent forward as if in pain or prayer, indicating with her silence that she had indeed heard more of the conversation than she was in a mood to let on.

Apparently now the service could begin. The Reverend

Thomas Giles, eighty if he was a day, Mercy guessed, and so shortsighted he almost had to lick the prayer book to read it, appeared in the front of the church with a meek "Please rise" as Cal and June took their places.

But their son did not sit with them. Instead he lingered at the back of the church near Mercy, hands jammed in his pockets, a heavy scowl gathering on his face, the kind of frown Arlene would have said she could scoop up and slice cold. Mercy glanced out the church window. Today ground and sky, heaven and earth were equally frozen and gray, and none of them looked to be a place she'd want to send a loved one. On the other hand, the same thing stood for the woods Zeke was running in. Mercy startled as Nate began to sit down next to her, bumping her hip. "Sorry," he mumbled, and frowned harder when he recognized her. Mercy produced her own unpleasant expression. *We're all God's children, dirty or clean*, she wanted to point out, but something in Nate's posture—the broken angle of his bowed head, maybe—made her look closer at him, and what she saw tugged at her heart.

She followed his gaze to the back of his mother's head several pews forward. In every town, Mercy had learned over her years of wandering, you could always find a woman just like June McAllister—glossy-haired, fond of pert little scarves, a woman whose front porch was reliably and seasonally decorated. Sometimes she was a schoolteacher. Sometimes she was the preacher's wife. It was the kind of woman who social services would no doubt say Hannah should have as a mother. As a girl, in fact, Mercy used to imagine just what that would be like—to have a pair of feathery hands soothing her forehead before sleep and hot breakfasts waiting when she woke up, to be followed wherever she went with a solicitous gaze. But that was before the men in the woods had gotten hold of her. Now, Mercy was grateful for the absence of such a figure, who would demand to know what had happened that day and, in doing so, would open up the wound fresh again, like shooting a buck twice to kill it once.

Mercy glanced at Nate again. In his looks he resembled his father more, she would have said. He had Cal's wheat-colored hair and blue eyes but June's graceful bearing. Rich *and* handsome. A combination Mercy suspected she was never going to get to experience in this lifetime, not with her mud-puddle bloodlines. But maybe Suzie Flyte had had herself a taste for that kind of life. Mercy leaned a little closer to Nate. She couldn't say what prompted her mouth to spit out what it did next, unless it was the simple fact that she had almost nothing to lose. "Was she your girlfriend?"

Nate clenched his jaw. "She was too smart for that." His blunt reply surprised her. Mercy leaned back a fraction of an inch and stole another peek at him. Maybe the angle of his head wasn't broken after all, she decided. It could simply be bitter. Here was a boy with the weight of a legacy teetering on his shoulders—something Mercy knew nothing about—along with a heap of accounts he was probably going to have to grow up and settle if the rumors she'd heard around town were true. At that moment June turned her head, peering anxiously back at her son. When she spied Mercy, she shot her a nasty look.

Mercy waited until June turned back around and the congregation had risen for the opening hymn. Aside from Hazel, she hadn't had occasion to talk to anyone in town about the accident, never mind someone who'd been a part of it. This was probably neither the time nor the place, but Mercy knew she wasn't going to get another chance. Maybe he'd seen a second car or something. She leaned closer to Nate, careful not to let anyone hear. "Do you remember anything from the crash?"

His answer was quick. "No." The organ crashed and hit an off-key note, and Mercy flinched. Nate turned his full gaze on her. "That land's not any good your family's sitting on, you know. You all should clear out."

Mercy set her chin. "And go where? Some of us don't have a mill to our names."

Nate snorted, but his voice had a little tremor hiding in it. "Believe me, it's not all it's cracked up to be."

The congregation rustled and seated itself, Mercy and Nate included. They didn't speak for the rest of the service, but Mercy couldn't stop thinking about the boy sitting next to her and how, were their fates reversed, the last thing she would want would be to inherit the din of the Titan Paper Mill, just as Nate probably wouldn't relish all the miles she and Zeke and Hannah toted up in a typical year. Surely, she mused, there had to be a middle way of passing through the world, something between the crunch of time clocks and packing up and drifting wherever the wind blew you. But what would that kind of life look like? Mercy had no idea. Whenever she let her mind run along those lines, all she could ever picture was Hannah's small face with the pinch fattened out of it and a burst of laughter lighting up her eyes, and Zeke no longer feeling the need to check over his shoulder before he took a step.

The last trill of the organ warbled into nothingness, leaving a gaping hole in the air of the church that felt to Mercy like possibility—a silence that could be filled with anything at all and folks would choose to believe it—before the moment was swallowed by the rising tide of the townspeople's feet.

All through Suzie's service, June struggled to keep her chin steady and her eyes dry. St. Bartholomew's was packed, and the McAllisters were tardy, so much so that they found themselves having to squeeze in shoulder to shoulder against Archie Lincoln and his wife, Alice. June looked behind her as she settled herself, concerned that there was no room for Nate, and out of the side of her eye she caught him lowering himself into a pew in the back, right next to Mercy Snow. Alarmed, she half rose to go fetch him, to have him sit anywhere except in that one spot, but the Reverend Giles appeared and asked them all to stand, and June knew that her chance to correct the situation had passed. Nate would have to stay where he was.

Across from her, June could see Dena's shoulders shaking, though she wasn't making a sound. Fred Flyte's thick arm girded Dena's waist, and the more she shook, the tighter he squeezed, until June wondered that Dena could breathe anymore at all. June glanced sideways at Cal to see what his reaction was, half of her wishing the guilt of what she suspected he'd done would come spilling out of him right then and there, the other half praying it never would. His face, however, remained a mask betraying nothing. *When did he learn to do that?* she wondered. *And why did I never notice until now?* She cracked a hymnal open in front of her and sang the appointed hymn, rose for the Lord's Prayer, and did not look at any of the faces around her.

When Suzie was younger, she'd been just like the daughter June had always longed for and never been able to have—a blond slip of a child with a gap between her front teeth and eyes that picked things apart. She'd had a bottomless appetite, June recalled, bigger than Nate's, even. Her eyes would light up at the sight of June pulling a fresh tray of sugar cookies from the oven or dishing out a plate of spaghetti and meatballs, and before June knew what she was doing, she'd be laying one extra place at the table.

"I can't seem to keep the child in food," Dena used to apologize over stitchwork during sewing circles, her own cheeks gaunt from years of getting by on beans and bread. "She's got a hollow leg and then some. Next time you send her on back to us."

"Oh, I don't mind having her over here one bit," June always replied, and what could Dena say to that, when she knew about June's inability to have more children? Dena had too many. She was happy to share. After feeding Suzie, sometimes June would offer to comb her hair, braiding the mass of it into two shining plaits and tying their ends with bits of clean satin ribbon she fished out of her sewing bag. She longed to make a dress for the girl—something with a big skirt and smocking—or whip her up a rag doll with yellow hair and blue button eyes, but she knew that Dena wouldn't let her daughter accept such gifts. Mill pride had its limits, and June knew her place. Suzie continued to wear her brothers' old cast-offs, and truth be told, she seemed happy in them.

Or at least she had until a few months ago, when Suzie and Nate suddenly seemed to have become painfully aware of their differences. Nate had grown busier with sports and studying, and Suzie had started hanging out with a crowd of girls who lined their eyes in swaths of hard black kohl, collected boys' class rings as trophies, and drank like thirsty fish at parties in the woods.

"'In the midst of life we are in death; from whom can we seek help?'" intoned Reverend Giles, and a sob escaped from the congregation, floating up among the church's dusty rafters. "'From you alone, O Lord, who by our sins are justly angered.'"

What could Suzie's sins possibly have been? June wondered. Surely nothing more than the usual trespasses of a rambunctious teenage girl. Maybe a case of loving the wrong boy from one of the outlying rival towns. Maybe even something petty, like shoplifting an eye shadow from the drugstore in Berlin or swiping a bottle of rye from the package store. Things Nate had maybe even tried himself, though June didn't think so. Not her son. Not when he had the whole of the McAllister reputation to uphold and the threat of his father's temper looming over him. Unlike Suzie, Nate had something to look forward to and expectations to fill. One day, Cal coached his son again and again, the mill would be his, and he couldn't very well run it with the ghosts of rumors haunting him. "The McAllisters don't have skeletons to hide," he always said. "We're all backbone, pure and simple. Remember that."

June tucked her hands in front of her and recited the Lord's Prayer, considering the constitutions of the two men she loved best in the world. If what Cal said were true—and based on her late father-in-law's rumored behavior, she had her doubts about that—if the McAllisters were all spine up and down, then what place had they left for hearts?

After the service a ragged receiving line formed on the way out of the church, and Mercy Snow stepped up to Dena. At her touch, to June's surprise, Dena quit sobbing and calmed enough for Mercy to press a twist of wool decorated with roughly carved wooden stars into Dena's hand. "This is for you. It's just a little thing my brother once made, so you don't forget to look up at the stars from time to time and remember there's a heaven."

June waited for Dena to up and slap Mercy for such impertinence, to hurl the charm into the pews, perhaps, where it would settle with the day's dust and sorrows, but instead she clutched the dinky string to her breast and whispered, "Thank you."

Whatever next? June wondered as she stepped out of the church, trying to keep her chin steady under the weight of the townswomen's nosy gazes. If the lion was going to lie down with the lamb like that, why, something was clearly afoot. Unbidden, the red flash of Suzie's mitten flitted through her memory. Cal was involved with the wreck somehow. June knew it, but before she could ponder that problem further, she descended the last church step and stumbled. She smoothed her skirt and looked around to see who had noticed, but it seemed no one had. June shivered, relieved but also disturbed. Twenty years in a town, and she still felt like she could trip right off the face of it and no one would notice. Or maybe they would and just wouldn't care, the way they overlooked the random articles of clothing and shoes that were sometimes shunted along in the currents of the Androscoggin, which eventually appeared several miles downstream in a pell-mell of bashed-to-heaven logs and silt, stripped of all identifying traces of their former owners, blank and perfect as fresh sheets of paper ready to receive the press of a strange new hand.

Chapter Eight

Left undirected after a calamity, grief will puddle and flow willy-nilly, finding its own peculiar channels into people's lives, each one a little different than the last. In the days after Suzie's burial, a small but steady stream of townspeople, some of them bearing hastily homemade wreaths of holly and mistletoe, made their way out to Devil's Slide Road to the site of the bus crash to try to gain some perspective and also, if they were being honest, because they were drawn by the sensationally gory lure of Gert's uncovered remains and what they could mean.

Hazel, much to her surprise, turned out to be no better than the rest of the town. It had been a full week since the accident, and there was still no change in Fergus's condition. Hour after hour, Hazel held his hand in the hospital, patted the swollen patch of his cheek, and listened to Mercy's accounts of the activity going on out in the rest of the world. Finally, driven by her own baser instincts and a powerful need for fresh air, Hazel left the side of her husband and went to see what all the fuss on Devil's Slide Road was about.

If finding Gert's long-lost bones was a miracle of sorts, it was Hazel's opinion that it was a purely accidental one. After all, what *didn't* have the potential to startle and amaze when you were in the woods? A den of newborn foxes, their fur still wet, might be uncovered, or a pulsing cloud of fireflies, or a cave so deep it had no bottom. Bones, however, were not rightly unusual. Hazel stumbled across them on her land all the time and in all variations: deer femurs with their sinew still hanging, the rotted fossils of rodents and squirrels, as neat and tidy in the dirt as anatomical models. Once she found a coyote skull thick with bees, life cupped within death, and though she had the urge to pick up the seething mass just to feel that balance for a moment, she knew that she'd be punished with a thousand stings if she did.

Along with a clutch of other curious souls, she stood in a tangle on the side of Devil's Slide Road, not far from where the bus had begun slipping down the ravine, and peeked over the lip of the gorge. Sure enough, the remnants of Gert grinned up at her from a little ways down, as if sharing a cruel joke that had been a long time coming. A low barrier of wire had been erected around the partially uncovered skeleton, but it was an unnecessary precaution. Even a generation later, the people of Titan Falls were inclined to keep their distance from the likes of a Snow. Hazel shuffled closer to the edge of the road and stared harder, unimpressed. *Such a fuss over what's basically a pile of dry sticks*, she thought, and then, picturing the inert form of Fergus, immediately regretted it.

She sniffed and took in the familiar faces around her. There was Margie Wall's husband, Tyler, and behind him stood Frank Billings and Archie Lincoln, Fergus's card buddies. Stella Farnsworth was there, too. And more people had congregated farther down Devil's Slide Road, closer to where Zeke had crashed his truck. Some had brought flowers or ribbons to leave in memory of the Flyte girl and in support of Fergus, too, Hazel guessed. A few folks met her eyes and gave curt nods, and others politely ceded her space, but no one approached her, and Hazel forgave them their lack of manners. Part of it was her own fault, keeping herself apart the way she had since Rory's death, and part of it was simply that in a corner of the world where winter could freeze a man standing and summer could melt him to the heels, it didn't do to let grief get the upper hand. Near her, Tyler Wall and Archie were in the middle of a discussion.

"What are they going to do with her?" Tyler was asking.

That stumped Archie. "Don't know."

Stella spoke up. "They're thinking to cremate the bones, I heard. It was June's idea."

The men nodded. "Any idea what did Gert in?" Archie said.

"Naw." Having grown up near the din of Titan Mill, with a father who manned the paper screens and a husband who oversaw them, Stella had absorbed the lingua franca of hardwood vowels and granite consonants uttered in the shortest sentences possible. In this case, Hazel thought, that conversational style was for the best. There was only so much gossip a body could abide about a dead woman, after all, and, when it came to Gert, Hazel had heard everything. How she'd caught the eye of Henry McAllister before she disappeared under mysterious circumstances. How Pruitt then came along and never paid a penny of the taxes on his property and never worked much either but always had money for booze. What incriminating tidbit about Henry had Pruitt held over Cal? Hazel wondered. It must have been something damning, for Cal McAllister had so far not been recognized as a vast philanthropist in his lifetime.

A flicker of movement in the trees across the road caught Hazel's eye. A small figure was dashing from one pocket of shade to another, shyly approaching the open grave. "Who is that?"

Tyler squinted. "Looks like a kid. I heard there was a little one out here, but no one ever sees it much."

At first it was difficult to tell if the creature was a boy or a girl, but as the child emerged from the forest, Hazel saw that it was female—or on the verge of becoming so. It was tough to tell with the girl bundled in a bulky and stained parka, rubber boots that appeared to be at least a size too large, a scruffy knitted cap in a riot of rainbow colors topped by a pom-pom, and lobster-claw mittens. In odd contrast with her attire, she moved forward with the dainty steps of a ballet dancer.

Hazel realized she must be looking at the youngest Snow. Mercy occasionally spoke of a smaller sister, and once or twice before the accident Hazel had even found herself sending a slice of extra pie or half a loaf of bread home with Mercy. Judging by the gaunt angles of Mercy's cheekbones, food wasn't abundant in the Snow household (such as Hazel imagined it), and it turned out that she still remembered all the things Rory used to love to eat: apple cobbler with extra cinnamon baked in, dill bread spread thick with butter, peanut nougat. After Mercy's employment Hazel had begun baking these old favorites again, filling the kitchen with bittersweet aromas that simultaneously evoked Rory even as they highlighted his long absence.

"Is that pumpkin bread?" Fergus had asked just the day before the wreck, his eyes widening as he'd tentatively sniffed. "Why, Hazel. What's come over you?"

Now Hazel eyed the beneficiary of her cooking with suspicion. Up close the child had none of the innocent charm one would expect from a girl of her size. Instead her dirty little face puckered knowingly as she came to a stop in front of Hazel.

"You're the lady with the sheep," she declared, sizing Hazel up. Hazel remembered Mercy telling her that her sister was a reader, and she could see that now. The youngster squinted as if she were used to poring over pages for long hours in dim conditions. She just *looked* like she'd perused too many stories beyond her years.

Hazel put a hand to her heart. Unbidden, it was flopping and twisting in her chest like a bass pulled to air. How many years had it been since she'd stood nose to nose with an actual child for any length of time? "Yes," she finally exhaled, for what else did one say to a plain fact accurately stated? The girl's ratty coat was a faded shade of bile that offset the rust stains on her filthy jeans. Hazel watched as the child burrowed in one of its pockets, her face screwed up with concentration. The skin of her bared wrist was smudged with dirt, as were her nails. Finally she pulled out a fistful of granite pebbles, shiny with flecks of mica, just the kind of flotsam a child's eye would land on. Solemnly she walked over to the ravine, stared down the slope, and then flung the pebbles onto the bones.

There was an intake of breath from the crowd. Hannah combed the townspeople head to toe and blinked. "The bones wanted them," she explained matter-of-factly. Before anyone could react further, the child made her way back to where Hazel was standing. She planted herself squarely in Hazel's path so that even if Hazel wished to, she wouldn't have been able to avoid the girl. "My sister and I are sorry about your husband," she said, tipping her chin up. "Real sorry." Before Hazel could summon her voice, Hannah surprised her by taking one of her hands in her grubby own. "But don't worry yourself, ma'am. My sister's going to make him all better just like my mama would have. Then you'll all see that Zeke didn't do it."

Hazel watched dumbfounded as the child zipped up her parka and pulled her mitten on again. The girl surveyed the townsfolk, nodded once to them, and stepped her way back into the trees, taking festive hops over the rocks and branches scattered in her path.

"How in Sam Hill is a Snow going to make anything better?" Tyler Wall grunted, and no one replied, for none of them had an answer to a question like that.

"Be quiet, Tyler." Hazel spun on her heel. She knew that the whole damn town thought she was madder than a March hare for letting Mercy pass across her door in the first place, and maybe she was. On the other hand, for the first time since she'd heard the terrible news about Fergus, a small beat of something like hope was pulsing away inside Hazel. She let her gaze wander down the ravine to the sorry pile of bones and then back up again to the muddy mess of the road. It was a hell of a place to try to make a living. Hazel would give the Snows that, but maybe, just maybe, it wasn't the land out here that was cursed. Maybe it was the folks. And folks, as Mercy had pointed out, were always the problem.

June was busy fishing holiday decorations out of the attic and lining up the boxes along the hall, their labels color-coded according to their contents. Every year, on the weekend following Thanksgiving, she liked to do this, but this season, for obvious reasons, she was late with her preparations. They hadn't yet gone out into the woods to cut their tree, and June wondered when they would. It should be soon. She was having her Christmas sewing circle in a week's time and wanted the house to look right. The town needed to get back to its usual rhythms, whether it was ready to or not, and June knew that as Cal's wife she was the one person who could make that happen. Where she led, the other women would follow.

She opened the box closest to her—tagged red for ornaments—and lifted off the tissue paper that covered a layer of delicately blown glass balls, stamped tin soldiers, and an assortment of bells. Tipped in the corner, crumbling with age, was a dough wreath that Nate had made back in kindergarten, the green paint faded and chipped. June plucked it out of the box, cradling the circle in the palm of her hand. Cracks riddled the surface, threatening to shatter the whole into fragments. If she'd had more children, she mused, how many more of these fragile tokens would she have from the past, and would they make the present more palatable? Probably not. Life was just plain fragile, June reflected, laying the ornament back on the tissue paper. How fast it went by.

The front door slammed, and June quickly drew the box flaps back together. Nate was staying at a school friend's for dinner, so it must be Cal, home early from work. She ran her hands through her mussed hair, tucking strands behind her ears, and brushed a spot of dust off her trousers. She wished she had time to swab on some lipstick, but she could already hear Cal's heavy footsteps coming up the stairs, seeking her out.

"Hello. You're home early." Ever since the accident, and since finding Suzie's mitten and seeing that swath of yellow mud on Cal's car, June had kept up a guarded normalcy around Cal and, most especially, around Nate. If she just pretended hard enough, she thought, if she baked loaves of gingerbread and decked the house with tinsel and played all their favorite holiday CDs, everything really would go back to the way it had been before the crash. If she and Cal simply never talked about it, the whole terrible accident would eventually fade to indeterminate shades like an uncomfortable old photograph snapped years ago.

Christmas was June's favorite time in Titan Falls. Her childhood holidays had consisted of a fake Douglas fir leaning in the corner of their living room with its lower needles singed off from an electrical fire, a shrimp dinner, and the majority of the day spent evading her mother's boyfriend du jour. In the twenty years of their marriage, Cal had never once suggested going south for the season, and June had never once complained about his lack of interest, not even when her mother had still been alive. It was one of the things that made their partnership work. Her need to reinvent her life perfectly matched Cal's need for someone to be wholly consumed by his world and his alone. June had no desire to change this dynamic.

Cal glanced toward Nate's closed door. "Is he in or out?"

"He's at Tommy's for dinner."

Cal sighed heavily, and only upon looking at him more closely did June notice the dark circles bruised under his eyes. "June, I need to tell you something." The muscles in his jaw ridged and tensed the way they only ever did when he had bad news to share.

Was it the mill? Had he just laid men off, a threat he'd been faced with for months now? June knew he was trying to wait until after the holidays. But his tone was too soft for that, and there was a tremor in his bottom lip that mill matters had never invoked. Her stomach dropped. *No*, she thought, *just don't*, but Cal kept talking, staring straight at her, still in his overcoat, the same one that had held Suzie's mitten.

"I was in Berlin the night of the accident."

June closed her eyes. Cal's voice rushed at her as if down a long tunnel, gaining velocity.

"I met Suzie that night, June. Outside the movie theater. She begged me for her father's job back. That's when she dropped her mitten."

June opened her eyes.

"The one I know you got rid of."

June knew that Cal wanted her to confirm what he'd just said—to explain what she'd done with the mitten. Instead she asked a question she didn't really desire an answer to. "What were you doing in Berlin?"

Cal hesitated, but that was fine. June could wait. One of the Christmas boxes looked like it had been chewed on by mice, she noticed. She made a mental note to put poison out in the attic. Pests shouldn't be allowed to multiply. "Were you alone in Berlin?"

No reply.

"You said it wouldn't happen again."

"I'm sorry."

And he was. June could hear it in his voice along with... was it uncertainty? She thought back to the time when she'd found the strange bra after his trip to Boston. He'd been contrite then, too, but not anxious. Something else was wrong. June stepped closer to Cal, searching his eyes. In spite of everything, they had a life and a son together. Deep down she still loved him, and that was something. "What is it?" She almost reached out to cup his cheek but refrained, still badly stung by the confession he'd just made.

"I don't know if Zeke really caused the accident."

June sucked in her breath. "What do you mean?"

"I mean, I was on the road that night, too. I..." He trailed off. "I drove by his truck on the side of the road. It wasn't him."

June put a hand over her mouth. She worried she might be sick.

Cal stepped closer to her and lowered his voice, as if what he was going to say next could only be uttered in the most terrible of intimacies. "June, I can't afford to let anyone in this town know, not now with the way things are at the mill, with layoffs coming after Christmas."

June had hoped those wouldn't go ahead for certain. It was just one more dreadful thing to keep secret. "Did anyone see you?"

"No. I'm pretty sure. Or if they did, they didn't know it was me."

"And your... appointment... in Berlin? What about her?" She couldn't bring herself to call it anything else.

Cal clasped June's hands in his. "That's all over with. Please, you have to believe me."

She bit her lip and considered. "Why are you telling me all this now?"

Cal slid his gaze away from hers. "I need you to do something."

June blinked with frustration. Never in his life had he been spurred to action by love or conscience, only necessity. It was the way Titan Paper had operated since time immemorial, and Cal was first and foremost a mill man. She'd known that when she married him, but she hadn't minded then. Of course, that was before the affairs, back when June had thought she still might change him just a little.

Downstairs, their phone started ringing. Cal clenched his jaw and made no move to answer it, and June understood what he was trying to tell her. It might be someone important, or it might not, but he would not jump to see. He meant what he'd said about ending the affair. If Cal's life depended mainly on the operations of the mill, so by extension did hers. She wished now that she'd managed to destroy the mitten wholly and not just hide it, but she could fix all that come spring, when the path to the cabin cleared and she could return. Cal need never know. Until then the item would be safe. No one would ever have any reason to link the likes of the McAllisters to such a business. She swallowed her tears. Funny how good intentions in a marriage could breed deception just as easily as they did intimacy. Maybe that was another one of the late Hetty's lessons that June should have learned before now. She swiped the drops out of her eyes and looked properly at her husband for the first time in a long time. "What do you need me to do?" she asked.

June approached the Snow property with the heel-toe caution of a practiced tracker. Per Cal's instructions she'd waited until it was nearly dusk to be sure no one would see her and had parked her car a little ways down Devil's Slide Road, just before the turnoff to the clearing, not wanting to announce herself before she'd truly arrived. Back at home she'd left her holiday boxes lined down the hall. In the fridge there was a mix of brownie batter, and on the stove the kettle was primed and ready for tea when she returned.

From the road she followed a bumpy pathway to the oval clearing in the woods, the only level patch around here before the world tilted again and dropped to the chaos of the river. On the east side of the clearing, June could see the charred stone foundation of an old house, the chimney long since tumbled, the roof beams burned or, if salvageable, no doubt carried away for other enterprises. Next to it was the splintering hut of the smokehouse, the size and childish shape of a dwarf's dwelling, and across from that a manifestly ugly vehicle of sorts was parked—top-heavy, fenders sagging, kitted out with a smokestack and mismatched windows, and rusted beyond all decent hope. June gawped at it and wondered how they'd managed to drive it down the path she'd just walked, and then she wrapped her coat tighter around her and stepped daintily through a thicket of frozen weeds, wrenching her ankle on a crushed can hidden under the snow. She fought the urge to swear. What kind of people lived like this? she wondered. Dogs wouldn't even.

A noise coming from the smokehouse caught her attention, and when she turned her head, June was surprised to see a child—a small figure swallowed by a huge, dirty parka. The girl seemed equally alarmed to catch sight of June. She stared up at her with the frozen dignity of an owl. In her hand June saw that the girl was carrying a book, marking her place with her thumb, the sign of a veteran reader, though she couldn't have been more than eight, June thought. The girl assessed her and then, deciding it was safe enough, spoke. "Hello." Her breath billowed in a fog around her narrow face.

June blinked. She knew every kid in Titan Falls, down to the babies, but she didn't recognize this girl. Or did she? She looked closer. There was something familiar about the child's greenish face and plain almond eyes. It was a smaller version of the late Pruitt Snow's.

"Are you looking for the ghost?" the girl said.

June put a hand across her chest. "Excuse me?"

The child looked exasperated. "The ghost of the lady that used to live in this spot. She was right here. But when she heard us, she disappeared."

In spite of the cold, June found that she'd begun to sweat. She loosened her scarf. "Ghosts aren't real, you know."

The girl shrugged. "This one was."

"What's your name?"

The girl cocked her head. "Hannah."

The littlest Snow of them all. June took a step closer. "And what are you reading?"

Hannah tipped the book so June could see the laminated cover. "Ovid." She pronounced it OH-vid. June raised her eyebrows in astonishment, but Hannah didn't seem to notice. Instead she smoothed open the volume to the page she'd been marking and ran her hand over the paper. She looked vaguely ashamed. "I stole this out of a library in Maine because it's the kind of book I knew I'd never be through with. I'm on the part now about Phaeton"—she stumbled over the name—"who tries to drive a chariot across the sky, but gets killed by Jupiter. Phaeton's sisters are so sad they turn into amber trees."

Amazed, June looked at the dirty sheen on the girl's coat, the cracked boots one size too big, the pants that only came to her ankles, and remembered that when Suzie had been that age, she'd never wanted to read but was always moving with the casual lope of a wild horse. Just then June noticed a glint of silver nestled in the bulk of the girl's parka. She looked harder. It was a man's silver cuff link, a piece of yarn wound around it like a necklace charm. How odd. Before the child could object, June lifted the bauble and then quickly dropped it as if she'd been scalded, seeing the points of the *M* sharply carved in the metal. She knew this object. She knew it very well, in fact, for Cal had its mate in a box in his top bureau drawer. It had belonged to his father, but he'd only inherited the one.

"What?" The girl looked puzzled.

"Where did you get this?" June's voice came out harsher than she meant it to.

Hannah clasped a protective hand over the cuff link and stuffed it back inside the neck of her parka. She cocked her chin at a stubborn angle. "I found it. Finders keepers."

"In the smokehouse?"

Hannah didn't answer, and June took a step closer, knocking her boot heel against a stone. It was so very easy to trip out here. The footing was uncertain, the land slicked with patches of effluvia, and deep down in the ravine, June knew, the river's current was deceptive.

"The Androscoggin carries away what it wants and then returns what it doesn't," Hetty had warned June before her marriage. "All of us from Titan Falls know this, and those who don't know it deserve whatever comes to them." June had taken the warning for what it was and said nothing, but now she wondered if her mother-in-law had perhaps been trying to get her to make a crucial choice before it was too late: stay or go, flee or return, one or the other, but never both, not in this place.

Down below in the notch of the ravine now, June could hear the river eddies rustling, devious as a covered basket of snakes, some of which would charm and others strike. In her pocket she had a lump of cash. It was more money than she thought she and Cal needed to offer, but no matter. It would cover a fresh start for the family someplace else. Anyplace else.

June thought about the laundry she had waiting back at home, the grocery list she'd hung on the refrigerator, the list of bills piled on her desk, their envelopes flapped open like little parched tongues. The clock on the landing would be ticking like a bone grinding in its socket.

She studied Hannah. There were a million reasons she knew she should just offer the money and then walk away from the girl—more than a million, probably—but they were no match for the sudden and paralyzing stroke of doubt June was suffering. What if Cal was wrong? What if he couldn't just make all this go away? What if he *shouldn't*?

June took a step closer to the child, half expecting her to vanish, but she did not. It was so cold in this hollow, June felt like she might crack. She couldn't imagine a little girl enduring it. She bent down and spoke softly. "Would you like to come with me for some dinner? Also, I have some books you might like to see." She did have them, too—somewhere. Nate's old adventure tomes and her own mythology texts from college. Tales of pirates and gods and knights with shining swords. She could wash Hannah's clothes, June thought, while the brownies plumped in the oven and the child ate a bowl of stew, and then she could give her a hot bath and wrap her in a huge, fluffy towel. Maybe she could even teach her to knit. June could almost feel what it would be like to sit shoulder to shoulder with Hannah on the sofa and cup her delicate hands in the larger nests of her own while she worked the girl's fingers around the yarn, just the way she'd always longed to do with a daughter.

Hannah took an uncertain step sideways, folding her book closed back on her thumb. Her gaze flicked quickly over June's shoulder to the bank of trees behind her, growing black with the late afternoon's shadows. "Thanks, but I'm not supposed to go anywhere. My sister would get hopping mad if I did."

"Where's your sister now?"

"Over at Hazel Bell's. She's looking after the sheep. Soon, if I'm good, she's going to take me to see them." She said it with a measure of pride, the way other children boasted about visits to theme parks or motels with swimming pools. "And I'm starting school soon, too, just like I'm supposed to, so don't you worry." June's eyes narrowed. She had forgotten all about Hazel Bell hiring the Snow girl, but then, before this accident, people often overlooked Hazel. She was as reclusive as a barn owl and twice as canny. June had always found the business with those so-called sugar-baby stones in the trees distasteful in the extreme.

She shook herself back to her senses. Hazel and her sugar babies were excellent reminders of why it didn't do to go digging up secrets in Titan Falls. The nonsense out here with Gert's bones was bad enough. June eyed the string with the cuff link around Hannah's neck again. It was tucked away now under the girl's coat. June sincerely hoped it remained that way. If she got rid of the one Cal had, there would be nothing to tie the family name to this place. Without further ado, all business again, June pulled the envelope containing the cash and written offer out of her pocket. "Here," she said, handing it to Hannah, glad to know that at least one person in the family could read. "Give this to your sister. It's *very* important. Do you understand?" She paused. She was struck with an urge to pass on to the child some kind of benediction or blessing. Instead she found herself proffering a threat. "And tell her she ought to be taking better care of you. Tell her..." June hesitated again. Why was she even getting involved? This child was nothing to do with her and never would be. "Just say that we have standards in this town, and people who aren't afraid to enforce them. Do you understand?"

Hannah took the envelope wide-eyed. "Okay," she breathed, and then she turned and fled, whipping past June like a sprite. June caught a scent of something wild—pine sap, deer musk?—rising up from the girl's clothing and skin, but before she could identify it, Hannah was gone, picking her way into the tangle of trees, a blur of flying hair and spindly limbs, the realest ghost June was sure she'd ever met.

Chapter Nine

Miracles can occur by design or by chance, but in retrospect people usually agree that they happen for a reason. In the case of the unexpected awakening of Fergus Bell, however, the cause was murky at best. Everyone concurred that his reemergence was a marvel, even if not totally successful, but whether it was in the end a blessing or a curse depended on who was doing the deciding. The fact that Mercy Snow was hanging over his bed when it happened only complicated matters, for no one could decide if she was a mere witness of the event or the very source of it—not least of all Mercy herself.

She'd arrived that morning at the hospital later than usual with her face drawn, empty of her usual promises and apologies. It had been one week since the accident, but for Mercy time had begun to unwind like one of Hazel's balls of wool—in no discernible order, one string leading many ways.

"Late night?" Hazel asked, observing the creases grooved into Mercy's forehead and the circles under her eyes. Then she sat up in alarm. "Are the sheep all right? Are you putting the vitamins in their feed like I told you?" Besides the constant fear that Fergus might never arise, Hazel also battled epic bouts of worry over her flock. She'd never before been parted from them, and the heartache was almost as bad as what she was enduring with Fergus.

Mercy absentmindedly chewed on a piece of her hair. "They're fine, Hazel. All tucked up in the barn."

"So why the long face?" Hazel hated herself for asking, but she went days sometimes in this room without talking to anyone except nurses and doctors, and they just yammered at her in their bewildering medical lingo. On the other hand, silence was golden. Hazel had heard enough now about the gentle side of Zeke and Mercy's determination to clear his name. Too late, Hazel put up a palm. "You don't have to tell me. It's okay."

But Mercy had pulled up a chair and was fishing in her jeans pocket for something. She withdrew a crumpled note.

"What is that?" Hazel asked.

Mercy unfolded the note and smoothed it across her knee, then passed it over. "It came with a big lump of cash." Hazel's eyes widened when Mercy told her the amount. *I suppose I'm going to have to find someone else to look after the sheep*, was her first thought, and her second was, *But why would June do this?*

The note supplied the explanation. It offered, in June's schoolmarmish handwriting, a twenty-four-hour period of leniency toward Zeke if the Snows would just get themselves together and get the hell out of Titan Falls for good. Hazel looked at the date. "What are you going to do?"

Mercy accepted the note back. "It's not like I can just go out and find Zeke. He has to come to me. And even if I could, leaving wouldn't solve anything, no matter the amount of money."

Hazel produced a crochet hook and a ball of yarn. She avoided Mercy's gaze. She hadn't said anything, but she'd been having doubts lately about how smart it had been to get involved with these accursed Snows. So far they'd brought nothing but trouble to her door, even if the mother was supposed to have been some kind of backwoods healer. That skill set didn't seem to have rubbed off on Mercy, however. She glanced quickly at the girl. "Do you have to tell your brother? What if you just took the money and went?"

"What, and leave him here?" Even without looking, Hazel could hear how outraged Mercy was. Mercy sighed, and Hazel briefly felt low about her suggestion. For one thing, she really couldn't afford to find anyone else for the sheep right now, and for another, Mercy wasn't a bad sort when it came down to it. But it didn't look good, the two sisters huddled alone out there on Devil's Slide Road like that. It made everyone uneasy.

"So what are you going to do?" Maybe it really was better if they moved on, Hazel thought. Maybe June McAllister had a point.

In reply Mercy ripped the note into tiny pieces and deposited them in the garbage. "That's where this belongs. I put the money back in her mailbox this morning." Then, to Hazel's dismay, Mercy turned her attention to Fergus. "I'm so sorry about all this trouble," she said, stroking his forearm gently. "But I am going to make things right for a change. You'll see. I know I can do it." Hazel watched as she laid her hands on his forehead, cupping his broken skull, and breathed in and out in time with him, like they were dancing. Shocked, Hazel looked away, almost more embarrassed than if she'd interrupted a pair of lovers, though Fergus, she knew, didn't have a single romantic bone in his body. Just a heap of good ones.

The machines hooked to Fergus started going haywire. One of them beeped out an uneven rhythm, another buzzed like a car alarm. Hazel shot her hand out to make Mercy stop, but before she could, Fergus did the unbelievable and opened his eyes. Hazel let out a whoop, and Mercy sank back into a chair, her arms dangling limp as wet strings of wool.

Hazel turned to her, tears dancing in her eyes. She hadn't been one to listen to the malarkey of Mercy's home remedies and claims to folk healing, but it was never too late to change the stripes on a tiger. "God bless you right down to your grubby toes. You really did it. I bet everyone in town changes their tune when they hear about this. Even June McAllister."

Mercy jumped away from Fergus as if she were unwilling to be held accountable for one more thing, marvelous or not. She honestly hadn't expected Fergus to wake up, not really—even though Arlene had possessed some ferocious healing powers—and she wondered if her touch had done it or if Fergus had simply been responding to some mysterious inner clock of his injuries that only he could read. Where did one person's influence on another ever begin or end? Mercy wondered. Was there a way to make manifest the secret ties that bound unlikely souls together in sin, or bliss, or random kindnesses? Or were outer appearances all anyone could go on? If that was the case, she and Zeke were screwed.

She brushed her hair out of her eyes. She didn't look too certain about Hazel's prediction. "Maybe," she finally said, the words sitting in her mouth as sour as unripe apples, "but if you do talk to June, you should remind her I said it's better to give than receive."

At first Hazel was so happy to see Fergus back that she didn't notice he'd been returned touched by the angels. Almost right away, however, it became clear that while a miracle of some sort might have occurred, it was a partial one at best, a gift wrapped in a maze of complicated strings.

After an exhaustive battery of tests, the hospital spent the better half of a morning describing to Hazel all the therapy options available to her: live-in centers, traveling nurses, part-time rehab wards. Some of them were too far away to bother with. Some sounded downright unsavory to Hazel, and all of them cost the blessed earth. "Do I look like I'm spun out of money?" she brayed to the administrator who was trying to help her navigate the mountain of paperwork Fergus now seemed to require. "Next I suppose you're going to hand me a brochure for the goddamned Ritz."

The administrator—a very pink-skinned young woman with a nervous habit of sucking her bottom lip, paled a shade. "Gosh no, ma'am. Nothing of the sort."

Finally it was Mercy who came up with the solution. "Why don't you just bring him home?" she piped up from the room's darkest corner, where she was slumped in a plastic chair fiddling with Hazel's spindle. "I'll help you with him. Heck, I wrangle the sheep every day on my own. Together we can probably handle the likes of Fergus."

And so it was agreed. Hazel signed what seemed like a cartload of documents declaring that she knew what she was doing in bringing her own kin back where he belonged and that no matter what happened, she didn't have plans to hold Heritage Pines Hospital responsible for the outcome. Hazel snorted at that. "You all are the ones who wanted to pull the plug on him in the first place, remember?" To which the pink administrator said nothing, simply bit her lip some more and scurried as far away from Hazel as she could.

Once he got home and put on some weight, Fergus looked

much the same as ever on the outside, from his bulbous chin down to his hammer toes, but his mental faculties were a different matter altogether. It was as if his innards had been scoured clean, leaving just a dry husk of a man smiling at elements he could no longer put together in good faith.

In the bustle and logistical riddles of moving the bedridden Fergus, it was initially easy for Hazel to dismiss the faraway sea that his eyes had become, or the nonsense words he sang to himself like a toddler. She knew very well, of course, the state he was in, but it wasn't until he was home that she truly *felt* it. Hazel was surprised to find that she minded the drool that collected on her husband's chin during mealtimes and that the babyish way he clapped his hands and begged her to sing to him affronted her. "I'm no singer, Fergus, you know that," she told him roughly time and time again, pushing his hands back down by his sides and turning her cheek from his pleading gaze.

But Mercy, it turned out, had a voice like an actual lark. "I'll sing for you, Fergus," she said out of the blue one evening when Fergus started up his frantic jiggling and shaking of Hazel's hand. "What do you want to hear?" And then, without waiting for an answer, she took a deep breath and let out a note so high and pure it seemed snatched from heaven. It was "Amazing Grace," Hazel realized, but sung with such a lilt that it came out like a whole new song. How odd, she thought, watching as some of the light seeped back into Fergus's gaze and his chin took on its familiar sensible set, that a mere chit of a girl would be the one who could bring him back, and not his own wife. That thought was immediately followed by another, more unsettling one. *Why is that?*

Hazel crossed over to her spinning wheel and began fussing with the spindle—her cure for ailments of the soul. She still had some carded wool left over from last spring's shearing. She'd coax out a good long string of yarn, she decided, and go make some color. She'd tucked some dried blue hyacinth blossoms in a jar somewhere in the pantry, she remembered. Blue for constancy, for memory, but also the color of a heart grown cold. Hazel gave herself a shake. What nonsense. Fergus's mind might be in a bit of a pickle at the moment, but his heart was going just fine. It was as steady as ever, red as the day was long—a fist right in the middle of him holding all the loose ends of Hazel in a single bunch. As long as it held fast, so would she. She just didn't like to think about the fact that Mercy might be the glue in that knot.

Hazel and Mercy were walking out to check on the flock when they discovered a web of coyote prints outside the barn—little dots of treachery flecked into the snow. It was the week before Christmas, but out in Hazel's valley you wouldn't know it. There was nothing festive about the woods. Together, Hazel and Mercy stared at the marks, trying to read the pattern, though prints like that screamed only one thing any way you blinked at them. Cursing a blue streak, Hazel flung open the barn door to find her sheep huddled in a panicked clump on the far side of the structure. She crossed over to try to comfort the flock, but they were having none of it. They rustled and bunched away from her. The biggest ram struck out at her with a foreleg and bared its teeth, and Hazel didn't half blame the poor beast, for even with all of Mercy's help things hadn't been what they ought around the place since Fergus had come home, and even the animals knew it.

Mercy settled the beast and returned to the marks, her mouth flattening into a hard line as she studied the divots first from one angle, then from another, as if she were auguring the future. "That's not from a coyote," she finally insisted. "It's from a wolf."

Hazel froze with the bucket of water she was hauling and considered. A rogue wolf creeping around her animals was the last thing she needed to worry about. She sniffed and poured the water into the trough in one smooth motion. "That's ridiculous. There haven't been wolves in these parts for fifty years." But, more and more lately, hadn't there been sightings? Hazel believed she might even have seen one herself not long before the accident—a silvery shadow slipping into the far end of the valley just after dusk, a flicker so quick it had been easy to brush it off as a trick of the light. Coyotes, Hazel knew how to deal with. Foxes, too, and bears, of course, but a wolf was a different creature altogether—smarter, more patient, almost human in its cunning. You could look a wolf in its eyes and see what its opinion of you was, providing it let you get that close and live to tell about it.

Mercy didn't say anything. She never sassed back, Hazel had noticed, or even disagreed when she thought someone else was wrong. She simply stayed silent and let the quiet take its course, which some might have said was good manners but which Hazel was starting to find sneaky for reasons she couldn't articulate.

"Okay, fine," Hazel finally conceded. "I'll rig up another floodlight on the back side of the barn. That ought to do the trick." But still Mercy said nothing. *Does she want the damn beast gone or not?* Hazel wondered. Ever since the accident, things down in her valley were changing—she could feel it. For one thing, Gert Snow's unearthed bones were causing all kinds of controversy all over town, and then there was the news that the mill was going to do a round of layoffs after the holidays, and folks were still up in arms about the accident.

Bringing Fergus back from near death—and the more Hazel replayed the scene in her mind, the more convinced she became that Mercy had been an initiator of the event rather than a simple witness—had not necessarily worked in Mercy's favor the way Hazel had thought it would. Because Fergus remained feeble, he was of absolutely no use in clearing anything up about what had happened with the bus. Not only couldn't he recall the accident, he could barely remember his own name. Several times a day, Mercy tried to jog his memory when Hazel wasn't looking, but Hazel always caught wind of what was going on and broke up those sessions.

"That's enough," she'd declare, waving Mercy out of Fergus's face. "Let the man have his peace." Although, to be honest, Fergus was nothing *but* peaceful these days.

The news of his startling recovery had bitterly divided the town. There was a small contingent, led by the grieving Dena and the addle-brained Stella, who viewed his return as a genuine wonder. As a result, they were inclined to give Mercy, and maybe even her brother, the benefit of the doubt, but most of the town was confused by the apparent act of God and therefore suspicious of it. On one of her rare trips to town, Hazel overheard Stella Farnsworth loudly opining in the bread aisle of the general store, "Why would that Snow girl want Fergus to regain his senses if he was then going to turn around and incriminate her brother? I mean, think about it. That would just be stupid. Maybe it's true that Mercy Snow knows something about that crash that we all don't."

The strenuous rumble of Dottie Billings put Stella in her place. "Once a Snow, always a Snow. Trust me, they're no good. I'll have you think back to Pruitt and how unpleasant *he* was."

Hazel held her breath and listened for anything more, but the two women adjourned to the cash register, unaware of her presence, much to Hazel's relief. Though Hazel would never admit it, she, too, vacillated between amazed gratitude for whatever Mercy had possibly done to wake Fergus and the unsettling worry that if Zeke Snow hadn't caused the accident, maybe it was Fergus who had.

And then there was the business with June McAllister and the money she'd tried to give Mercy to make her leave town. That didn't sit right with Hazel at all. What was it to June, Hazel mused, if Mercy stuck around Titan Falls spouting off her brother's innocence to anyone who would listen? Cal was about to let a fifth of the men go from the mill, so Hazel knew that the McAllisters didn't have money to burn, especially not the kind Mercy had mentioned. She tried to imagine what would make them want the Snows gone so badly, and though she had a hunch, she decided ignorance was bliss. The first thing you learned in a mill town was to keep your nose to the grindstone and out of other people's business, especially when they happened to *own* the damn mill.

I should have hired a boy, Hazel thought. She observed Mercy now in the chilly air of the barn, but the girl was the picture of innocence. "Everything all right?" Hazel asked.

Mercy cracked her knuckles joint by joint, sending tiny little pops into the air, like bubbles breaking. The sheep flicked their ears. "I'm fine."

It was the worst kind of fine Hazel had ever heard, but in spite of all the questions firing inside her head, she wasn't one to pry. She swung the empty watering bucket back and forth. It had a deep dent down near the bottom, but that was okay. Hazel couldn't remember for the life of her how it had gotten there, and she didn't care either. If a thing still worked, why worry yourself sick about the dings and nicks it collected? Spend your time splitting hairs, Hazel knew, and soon you'd be bald. It was a lesson Mercy would do well to heed, Hazel thought, her stomach seizing in a knot of concern for the girl, in spite of all her better efforts.

She saw that Mercy had managed to calm the agitated ram enough to be giving him feed by hand. Hazel narrowed her eyes. That animal normally had so much spitfire in his belly that Hazel was constantly tempted to put an end to him and eat him. Last year, when trying to shear him, Aggie had ended up with a bit thumb and one of his kneecaps knocked blue. But look at the beast now, nuzzling Mercy like he was a puppy. How did the girl do it? Hazel supposed she ought to thank her, but instead she felt a hot flush across her chest. They were *her* sheep, and Fergus was *her* man. A flock could have only one shepherd.

The distant sound of tires crunching over gravel interrupted her thoughts. Hazel frowned. She wasn't in the mood for a visitor, but she was in less of a mood to stay here in the barn with the likes of Mercy. It wasn't anything the girl did, really. It was more all the uncomfortable little truths she made Hazel realize about herself. She put down the pail. "Finish up out here. I'll go see who that is."

Mercy was entranced with the ram and didn't reply, so Hazel stalked back to the house. Wolves, apparently, were the least of her worries.

Hazel had just managed to hang her coat on a peg in the mudroom when the knock arrived on the front door—a woman's hand, Hazel could tell, for a man's raised fist wouldn't arrive with a question hanging in it like that. Hazel sighed deeply and then went to go greet whoever it was, trying to step lively about it. When she saw who was standing on her porch, however, she fought off the urge to slam her door and lock it twice. "June."

As usual, June looked better than Hazel thought she had the right to. Hair dyed in a salon and not from a box, pearls strung around her neck, cashmere-lined gloves so soft and thin that Hazel could practically read June's palm through them. June thrust out a smartly wrapped package. "Afternoon, Hazel. I brought you half a loaf of lemon tea bread. We missed you at Suzie's service, you know." Hazel accepted with reluctance. *Just half the loaf,* she thought sourly. *Isn't that typical?*

It was true that she hadn't gone to the memorial for poor Suzie, but she thought her lack of public piety should be her business and hers alone. Hazel's faith in God had gone straight to the ground with Rory, and she was still waiting for it to return. She couldn't have borne to sit in a hard church pew staring at another child's coffin, and she didn't particularly wish to split words now with the likes of June McAllister. Hazel remembered how much it hurt to talk after Rory's passing and how, when she did, her voice came out broken and raspy, like she didn't have enough air in her to put together two good thoughts. She steeled herself now and, against all her better instincts, opened her door a hair wider. "Come in."

Normally, on the rare occasions when the town wives came out her way to buy their yarn, full of gossip from June's infernal sewing circle, what they really wanted, Hazel was only too aware, was to sniff out how she produced her colors. Hazel happily sold off any and all of her skeins of yarn, but she never gave away any of her other trade secrets—not that they were really hers to give. Any of those women could have figured them out, if they'd really wanted to. The plants she used to dye her yarns were plentiful and free. All a woman needed to add was a little alum to fix the hues and whatever sorrows she happened to hold, and Lord knew there were more than enough of those to go around in Titan Falls.

But today June was after something else entirely. She shuffled inside Hazel's clean hall, dripping rivulets of dirty snow off her fancy boots, craning her neck, peering about her like a prize turkey. She barely had the good grace to wait until they were settled in the parlor to get down to business. "Is that Snow girl here?"

Hazel's eyes narrowed. She'd taken refuge on the stool beside her spinning wheel, but there were no contraptions in the world, she suspected, that could deter June McAllister when she wanted information. "Mercy's in the barn."

June placed a hand on her chest and fluttered her eyelashes. "Oh, *good*." She lowered her voice ominously. "We need to have a little discussion, and it would be best if it were private."

Hazel glanced at her watch. Fergus was napping, but any minute now he'd awaken confused, trapped in the sticky realm between sleep and consciousness, between this world and whatever came after it. Of all the moments that were difficult with him—and there were a host of them—Hazel dreaded these spells the most. It was the futility of sounding the voice of reason into a pair of deafened ears that got to her. She had never been one to perform an action without first identifying a corresponding motive, a fault that Fergus had always begrudged her. "Woman, ease up," he'd pleaded just days before the accident, when Hazel was nagging him about why he still chose to drive the St. Bart's bus—for free, no less—when neither of them attended church anymore. "When the Lord calls on you, he doesn't give you all his reasons."

"No, he certainly doesn't," Hazel had snapped back. That was her whole point.

She patted the worn nap of her corduroy trousers over her knees now and resisted the urge to start fiddling with her spinning wheel. She should probably offer to go cut June a slice of the cake—a measly slice, she'd make sure—but if she went into the kitchen, she wouldn't be able to hear Fergus. June, however, didn't seem to miss the lack of refreshment. She smoothed her wool slacks and assumed an expression of concern. "And how *is* Fergus?"

"Just fine." Hazel would straight up be a monkey's butt if she were going to give the likes of June McAllister ammunition to take back to her sewing circle.

June waited a beat, but when it became apparent that Hazel would be providing no further information, she cleared her throat. "Well, that's wonderful. It's just a marvel, isn't it, how he came back to us."

Hazel didn't like June's use of the plural "us" in that sentence. Did the McAllisters have to lay claim to every damn thing in town, even the miracles? She lowered her eyes. "I guess."

"And it's just amazing how it all came to pass. Although"—she licked her lips—"it's certainly ironic that the Snow girl was standing there when he got his life back while it was her brother who almost killed him in the first place."

Hazel might not be cozy with the Lord, but she wasn't above calling on him to get her out of a tight spot when need be. "Mercy didn't do anything. It was all God's work. She was just standing there." Although was that quite right? Hazel thought back to the moment in the hospital when Fergus first opened his eyes. He'd blinked straight up at Mercy and even smiled a little, too, she remembered, like the two of them were in on the same secret joke.

June crossed her knees and spread one of her hands across

her lap. She was wearing the pale kind of nail polish that barely showed, Hazel noticed, and what was the fool point of that? "That's not what folks in town believe."

Hazel sat up a hair straighter. "What do you mean?"

June's fingers curled tight, as if she were hooking a barb onto a fishing line. "The ladies are beginning to wonder if maybe Fergus is the one who drove the bus off the road and caused the Snow boy to crash. I mean, *I* don't believe such nonsense"—June tapped the spot above her heart—"but you know how gullible some of the women in town can be. After poor Suzie's funeral, Mercy gave Dena Flyte some sort of charm that helped the poor woman through her grief. And I gather she's been brewing some concoction for Fred Flyte on the down low. He's quit drinking, if you can believe it."

Hazel could not. Fred Flyte was as pickled as a barrel of Swedish herring.

But June wasn't finished. "You'll never guess what he's gone and done."

"What?" In spite of herself, Hazel was intrigued.

"He's gone and applied for Fergus's job driving the tow truck and plow."

"What?" Hazel's head snapped upright.

"Yes. And Horton says if Fred stays properly sober another two weeks, he'll take him on. He can't afford to be down a driver during snow season, and he feels sorry for the family."

Hazel sat thinking. Fergus might never recover, or he might take years to do it. Of course Horton wasn't going to hold a job for him, but still. It needled her to think that life was moving on so fast. And it irked her more to think that Mercy might somehow be the one urging it along.

"I think"—June touched the tips of her pink fingers to that

treacherous spot above her heart again—"that perhaps you're being a bit too kind for your own good here, Hazel. I can understand you needing the extra help, especially now with Fergus, but really, I think you should consider that you may have a wolf in sheep's clothing in this girl."

Hazel blinked at June's choice of metaphor, wondering if it was deliberate, but before she could decide, June continued.

"These Snows have brought nothing but trouble since they've arrived. Zeke's *wanted*, you know." She shook her head. "I think it would be best if they left."

Wasn't that just like a McAllister, Hazel thought. Playing with people's lives as if they were dolls in a playhouse. Paper dolls. She folded her arms. "You can't simply up and make them leave town." Was the old Snow homestead even *in* the limits of Titan Falls? Hazel wasn't sure.

These details didn't seem to concern June. "No," she simpered. "Of course not. But neither do we have to give them any reason to stay." She shifted a little, inching closer to the edge of the sofa. The worn cushion buckled and threatened to pitch her headfirst onto the coffee table, but June regained her balance. "Actually, the truth is, Hazel, I came here to ask you an enormous favor. I was wondering if you might take Nate on for some work. I know you were advertising earlier this year, but Nate was so busy with football."

"What about his job in the mill? It's going to be his one day, after all. I'd think he'd want to learn to run it."

June shook her head, her hair falling in a regretful wave along her cheek. "Nate hasn't been himself since the accident. He's angry. He quit the hockey team, he doesn't want to see anyone, and I'm worried about his grades." She hesitated. "I'm not sure working with his father is a good idea right now."

"But working out here is?" Hazel folded her arms.

"I think it could be, yes. Please, Hazel. You don't have to answer now, but think about it." June drew herself together and arose, the wool of her trousers falling as crisp and neat as if it had never been sat upon. Upstairs, Hazel heard the bedsprings squeak and then Fergus cry out. She flinched. June cast her eyes toward the ceiling, then back to the spinning wheel. "Spun anything good lately?"

Hazel stayed on her stool. "It's the wrong season. Shearing's not for a few more months yet. I'm almost out of wool."

"Oh, that's too bad. I imagine with Fergus out like this you must be relying on your sales. I can help with that. Nate and I both. Or"—June stepped out to the little hall where Hazel had hung her coat, leaving Hazel no choice but to follow and hope that Fergus would be fine for a few more moments—"I could make it difficult. It would be terrible if my sewing circle broke up, wouldn't it? We've been such a good source of revenue for you. But I've been thinking lately about taking up something more highbrow. Watercolors, perhaps."

Hazel swung open the front door, letting in the tingling air. In the distance she could see the hunched form of Mercy wending her way back to the house with an armload of firewood, snow dusted all up her legs. From this far she could be anything or anyone—male or female, a friend or a foe, a live soul or the walking dead. Hazel suddenly wasn't sure of anything anymore. "Okay," she said quietly. One thing sheep taught you was when to call a spade a spade. They were not creatures of subtlety. Instead, they brought you straight down to the elements: weather, feed, the values of their skins and wool. Everything with sheep was very basic.

June pulled her fancy gloves on with the alarming grace of a snake slipping back into skin it had shed. "Oh, wonderful! Nate will be so pleased. I can't wait to tell him. Shall we have him begin after the holidays, to give everyone time to get used to the idea? Also, that should give you time to handle your situation." She glanced at the approaching figure of Mercy. "So sad," she said, "but really, what else can we do? Their problems are not ours."

Without further ado she clipped across the porch and picked her way back to her car, leaving Hazel to linger in her front doorway and consider all the ways that statement was not true before giving in to the fact that there wasn't a damned thing she could do about it.

Chapter Ten

In spite of the many headstones that populated it, the little graveyard adjacent to St. Bartholomew's was almost always deserted. That fact was easy enough to ignore during the bursts of autumn foliage and the early buds of spring, but not come winter when the woods around town thickened into streaks of gray and black and there wasn't anything else by way of visual distraction in the village—nothing green or sweet, just a cold so fierce it raised welts on people's cheeks and bit the fingers of those foolish enough to go without gloves. It wasn't, June reflected, that the people of Titan Falls didn't love their departed; it was just that they knew firsthand the futility of commemorating them in such weather. It was one of the many problems of life in a mill town. Like it or not, people were constantly forced to make terrible choices—between food and heat, fixing their cars or patching their roofs, sending their sons or their daughters out to work instead of school—and then had to bear the consequences of those decisions. So no. No one had time to mourn, especially not in winter.

The first layer of snow that fell on Suzie Flyte's grave was a mere sprinkling of the finality yet to come. It landed as light and free as a bridal veil, giving the town time to get used to the idea of her absence. Soon, however, as December lengthened and passed and the bulk of the weather set in, a thicker layer replaced the delicate flakes, and then another and another, until by mid-February even Suzie's granite headstone was nothing more than a blunt white memory. That didn't stop Dena, however, from battling her daily way through the elements to the spot where her daughter lay. Sometimes the townswomen saw Dena hunched over the grave, an ice witch haunting her lair, and though they debated the necessity of going and fetching her, none of them ever dared to. She sat for as long as she could in the cold, the red scrap of Suzie's remaining mitten clutched in her hands—a slap of color that reminded June of things she would rather not face.

Against all odds it was Fred who'd taken up the necessary tasks of the couple's survival—doing the shopping once a week in the Millers' general store, shoveling their short little drive, chopping wood out back with the chawed butt of a cigar clamped between his molars, the very picture of health, and for that he could thank Mercy Snow.

He'd come stumbling home from Lucky's the week before Christmas to find Dena sitting in the darkened kitchen, contemplating a jar of cloudy liquid. "What is it?" he'd slurred, and she'd blinked at him.

"I don't half know. It's for you. I found it in the letter box with a note. Says it's from that Snow girl."

At first Fred had been hesitant to drink the concoction. Any man would be after the load of gossip he'd heard circulating about Mercy down at the tavern.

"Why's she so damn attached to her big brother anyway?" Arch had pondered aloud over his fourth beer. "Seems like they might be just a little *too* close, if you know what I'm saying.

Perhaps that boy's on the run for some other reasons we don't know about."

That produced a salacious chuckle from the other men at the bar.

"Maybe she's got a past, too. Girl that age with no man around to speak of. How do you think she's paying the bills? I bet it ain't all by virtue of Hazel's sheep. Betcha she's got a few rams of her own on the side, if you know what I mean."

Fred had shifted on his stool. He was an irrepressible souse, but deep down he was still a father and a churchgoing man. Even whirling drunk he was uncomfortable with the direction the conversation was taking. He spun his empty glass on the bar. "I don't guess I'll ever get my old job on the mill floor back now, what with the newest round of damn layoffs I hear is coming."

A chilly pause swept over the bar. Fred had just committed the conversational equivalent of poking a branch into a hornet's nest. Mill talk at the bar was generally confined to the terms of the latest betting pool, grisly recaps of past accidents, and snide comments about coworkers' hygiene and sexuality. Len, the barkeep, was in thick with Cal, and the men lived in fear of being accused of cozying up to state river inspectors, courting union organizers, or otherwise plotting against the hand that fed them. When layoffs like the looming ones occurred, half the men in the bar drank with resentment glowing in their bellies and the other half with guilt, but no one ever uttered a word about the cause of all that grief.

Arch quickly did the first thing he could think of to save the situation. "Wonder if that little Snow bitch and her brother are connected to the downturn. First they almost kill our kids, then our jobs hit the dirt. If they don't leave soon, we'll all be going up in flames."

"Don't forget about Gert's bones," Tyler Wall put in, adding to Mercy's perceived crimes. "I tell you. Finding them was no accident. She's up to something out there."

Fred Flyte finished his shot in silence, regretting the shit storm of superstition and bitterness he'd apparently unleashed on what he was increasingly sure was an innocent girl. When he arrived home and found the jar of liquid left by Mercy, along with instructions to drink all the contents at once, he was reluctant to do so, but he also felt he owed it to her.

The drink was far fouler than anything Fred Flyte had ever ingested in a bar, but, amazingly, it provoked in him such a revulsion to alcohol that he would no longer even walk on the same side of the street as Lucky's. Sober enough for real work, but still locked out of the mill, Fred beat all the other men about to lose their jobs to the punch and took over Fergus's routes with the tow-truck company. Maybe it was from spending his days seated after a lifetime of standing up, or maybe it was all the solitary reflection that driving afforded him, but in the weeks that followed the tragedy of the accident, Fred slowly plumped back to life, his cheeks fattening under the flaps of his hunter's cap, the broken tooth cupped in the front of his mouth seemingly whiter if no less snaggled. It was as if he were privy to some forthcoming news that no one in town knew about yet but which, when it arrived, would blind them all with good fortune.

"Honestly," Abel Goode said to June outside the Millers' general store in February. "He's as straight as a preacher now."

June frowned. So far none of her plans to get rid of the Snows were working. Her bribe, generous in the extreme, had been rejected, so she had done the next-best thing and gotten the girl fired, but even the threat of starvation wasn't doing anything. What had Hetty always said? The devil loved idle hands? June hoped she hadn't made a tactical error in giving Mercy more time to get up to mischief, but this latest news about Fred was not encouraging. First the miracle of Fergus and now another one with the hopeless Fred Flyte. June didn't need the town to start turning to Mercy as some kind of saint. The next thing she knew, they'd be clamoring for her to fix the situation at the mill, and then where would June and Cal be?

She pictured the trashy little clearing where the RV stood, or more accurately *leaned*. Anyone could see it was a place past its prime, had it ever even possessed one. And that poor child. Dirty hair. Raggedy fingernails. A little bubble of compassion welled in June's chest. Mercy and her brother, June could scorn, but the child didn't deserve that kind of life. A small part of June thought she should do something about it and call social services on the so-called family, but who was to say the girl would be put anywhere better? The life of a foster child, June knew, was not a happy one, and much as she wished to see the Snows gone, she didn't wish to see them completely ruined. Not Hannah at least.

June shifted her grocery sack on her hip and narrowed her eyes. The only hope was for Abel to catch that criminal Zeke or, better yet, find his lifeless body. With winter set in good and well, he'd freeze to death in the woods if he wasn't careful. "I would have thought you'd be holding that boy in custody by now."

"I agree," Abel said. "He's been gone two-plus months. Damn me if he isn't either an ice cube or coyote food. At this point if we find a scrap of him, it'll be a miracle."

Miracles again. June was getting sick of them. "Well, he's guilty as the day is long." Abel shot her a sour look, and June quickly shut up, for she knew what Abel must be thinking—that if the mill layoffs went on much longer or got much worse, he'd have to deal with trouble far closer to home. June sniffed, offended. It wasn't Cal's fault that competition overseas was getting worse, the jobs shipping off like reverse mail-order brides. No one liked change. That was a fact. Not even Abel, which June saw as an advantage.

She had avoided the accident site, but she wondered now if everything out there was all cleaned up: Gert's remains, and the twinkling bits of smashed windows, and the gouges the bus had left down to the bottom of the ravine where the Androscoggin gurgled and danced under ice, like a bad woman's legs under heavy skirts. "Gert's bones," June suddenly demanded. "What's been done with them?"

Abel pushed his hat back on his fat head. He saw that June's mouth was a drawn bow, and for a moment he felt a stab of pity for her. She was clearly never bred for a life of mill grit, and yet here she was anyway, full in it, half freezing in front of the town's crappy general store, staring down the knowledge that her husband might not be any better than the hard drinkers and lotharios who worked for him. And that wasn't even the worst of what Abel suspected of the McAllister men. He sighed. "Why do you care?"

June considered. She recalled the sound of the river turning around its bend down at the bottom of Devil's Slide Road. Such a place for a woman to live and die, she thought, bathed in the floating filaments of the town, almost completely covered over by them. Almost, but not quite. "It seems like someone should," she finally said.

Abel couldn't argue that. "Someone does. The coroner went ahead and cremated them. The ashes were given back to the Snows. The eldest girl took them, since she was the nearest relative."

June's lips puckered. In the distance there were a gaggle of approaching footsteps and wagging tongues. "I'm having the ladies for a sewing circle, as you can see."

Abel readjusted his hat and turned to leave before he was surrounded and possibly drowned in feminine chatter. Before he could get gone, however, June waylaid him. "Do me a favor. If you see Cal, don't tell him we spoke about Gert. And one other thing. I want those ashes. Promise me you'll bring them."

Inwardly Abel cursed everything from the top of the mill tower to the bottoms of his own two boot soles. The hardest part of his job was never what he found out; it was always what he had to keep quiet. "Don't worry," he said. "I'll get you the remains." Didn't want to but would. The McAllisters kept him in feed and office, after all. Abel had learned the hard way that keeping the peace was the wise course in Titan Falls, even if it meant bending the law a dogleg to do it.

With the ritual care of a medieval monk, June laid seven silver needles out on a tray, along with a selection of brightly colored silken threads. The slivers of metal glinted in the hard afternoon sun—a row of tiny sabers arrayed for inspection before battle. She couldn't be too careful when it came to hosting her group of ladies, June knew. There was no telling what loose threads they might notice, what crumb might have gone uncollected in a darkish corner, and wouldn't they love that, June thought, to find a crack in the McAllister fortress that they could worry and widen?

The women were embroidering a hanging for the children's section of the library in memory of Suzie. It was a scene of an apple tree, its gnarled canopy divided into quadrants, one for each season. June was working on the spring panel, knotting tiny blossoms and flecking them with the merest hint of pale green leaves that widened and unfurled toward summer. She rolled the muslin pieces out now, placing them in order, stark branches, then the same limbs blooming into cautious life before erupting into fiery reds and golds. *Resurrection*, June thought. It was a fitting theme, the simplest mystery of all, even here in Titan Falls. Fergus had come back from the dead. Out of his daughter's passing, Fred Flyte had been brought back to his senses, though whether that was a good thing or not remained to be seen.

Most of the women had arrived, but they were still waiting on Dot, who was bringing Dena. It was her first sewing circle since the funeral. June was about to offer the ladies some tea when there was a knock at the door, and Dot strode into the front hall with her mannish walk, ushering a reluctant Dena into the room like a prisoner.

The ladies began twittering all at once, flapping gums and hands, escorting the grieving woman over to the plushest armchair in the corner—June's customary spot, though no one seemed to care about that now.

June banged eight teacups onto her biggest tray and added the teapot. "Dena, let me serve you first," she said, laying the tray on the sideboard and busying her hands with the service. "We certainly have missed you."

Dena was taking in the half-embroidered panels that the ladies had spread out before her, tracing the fledgling lines of threadwork with a hesitant forefinger, tears swimming in her eyes. "Oh, she would have loved this, I know," she rasped, the finger coming to rest on the spring panel—June's handiwork.

June poured her a cup of tea. "Here you go. I have to say,

you're looking well." A tad thin maybe, and pale, yes, but surprisingly strong underneath the sheen of grief she still carried.

Dena lowered the cup to her lap and licked her lips. "Oh, I can't take the credit. Fred's been feeding and looking after me. He's quite a different man these days, you know, and it's all down to that Snow girl."

The ladies leaned their heads closer at the mention of Mercy. "What's she been giving him?" Stella asked, her pregnant stomach a boulder hunched under her sweater.

Dena shook her head. "I don't know. Some concoction she drops off without a word on the porch. Fred says the stuff tastes worse than two-day-old whiskey coming back up, but it's doing the trick. He can't even wink at a bottle without going green around the gills."

June distributed the rest of the cups. "I hear Fred's taken over Fergus's driving routes. I was out to see Hazel Bell. She's none too happy about that."

Dena's gaze darkened as she jutted her chin. "What are we supposed to do? Her man's not getting any better, and we have to eat. There was a job just sitting empty." Her eyes narrowed. "There's quite a few of those in town these days."

Margie Wall, whose own husband was one of the men most certainly facing a layoff, colored, then placed a warning hand on Dena.

June sank into a chair in the opposite corner. Cal was right. The upstart talk about the state of the mill was getting out of bounds. Something had to be done. She fixed the ladies with her haughtiest gaze, one she'd learned to fake at Smith. "Hazel fired Mercy, you know."

"Oh, that's terrible! Who's going to help her out with her flock?"

June lowered her eyes. "Nate is."

Silence greeted this news. Finally Dot spoke, her words blunt as a pair of fists. "Was that your idea or his?"

"Does it matter? He needs something to occupy him ever since..." She trailed off, not wanting to say the word "accident" in front of Dena. "Well, he's not been himself lately. Cal and I think a bit of working with Hazel's sheep will be just the thing for him. It'll give him a little time and distance from everything. Cal's agreed to let him go."

The ladies slid sidelong glances to one another, but no one dared remark on the irony of the mill owner's son needing to get away from matters of the mill. Alice Lincoln helped herself to one of the shortbread squares on the sideboard. "I can't imagine," she said through a mouthful of crumbs, "what it must be like for those Snows out in that ravine."

"Then they should leave." June gritted her teeth.

"I hear the little one's started school finally," Dot said. "I've seen her in the morning. She has to walk along Devil's Slide Road to town to get to where the bus can pick her up. Poor thing."

At the mention of Hannah, hot pinpricks attacked the back of June's throat, and she couldn't decide if the sensation was guilt—a kind of mild choking—or simple distaste. This bothered her. Ever since her encounter with the child, June had found herself thinking of Hannah more and more often. She hadn't realized how much she missed the press of little fingers inside her palm or the satisfactory moment of wrapping a clean child in a bath towel fresh from the dryer—the hundred simple tasks a day she used to perform and would never again be allowed to do. She, too, had heard about the girl starting school, and this brought to mind packs of fresh yellow pencils, oxford shoes buffed to a shine, and tin lunch boxes. Hannah no doubt had none of these things in her life, but they were things June could provide.

"The Snow men are a bad bunch, I'll give you that." Margie Wall chewed a piece of shortbread. "But maybe those girls deserve some sort of sympathy. There but for the grace of God and all."

The ladies murmured and nodded. June felt a bead of sweat form on her hairline. This was getting completely out of control. She clapped her palms together and then picked up the tray with the needles on it. "Ladies, let's not forget that we have a task to do. Dot, I believe you were working on autumn?" June passed the appropriate muslin panel to her. "Dena, why don't you join Dot?"

A silence fell over the room as the women took their needles, bent their heads, and began to stitch, their needles pricking, prying, and then just as quickly closing the little holes they were making in the fabric of one another's lives.

The woods were always mean in winter, hoarding their bounty under uniform drifts of snow, but this year they seemed to Mercy more sparing than usual. In the weeks since Hazel had asked Mercy to leave her employ, Mercy's frame had gone from sinew down to mere bone, just like the spines of the trees surrounding her. She and Hannah were lower than low on all their stores except cold and hunger. They needed heating oil, money, and food. There were only so many slowpoke rabbits to be snared down the hill and only so many times you could split a can of beans into a week. She worried constantly about Hannah's health and always gave her the lion's share of what was available, even when it wasn't much. Somehow, though, Mercy didn't think any of it would go very far to convince an authority figure that she was a fit guardian for her little sister.

She simply had to keep trudging forward, hoping for the best. She foraged what she could. Sometimes she found a clutch of fossilized berries. Once, in lieu of anything else, she steamed a spray of spruce needles just for their aroma. Sheets of ice sealed the river shut tighter than a rich man's hand. Occasionally Mercy glimpsed dark shapes flitting under the glaze—fish, stupid with the cold—but she had no way of getting at them. Even if she did manage to break through the ice with an ax or the butt of a rifle, she still wouldn't have dared for fear of slipping all the way under. Water was water, even when it was ice. Mercy still didn't trust it.

When she got up the nerve, she haunted the few hoop gardens in town under thick protection of night, pilfering forgotten squashes that were half to rotten on their vines and hothouse tomatoes, little balloons of life in an otherwise monotone world. Each time she savored the suck of humid air underneath the domes of plastic sheeting, wishing she could stay just a moment longer in such a wet and abundant world. She broke into root cellars to spirit away sacks of dusty potatoes and braids of onions, and when she did have the odd dollar to spend in the Millers' general store, she made certain she left with more than she came in for stashed in her enormous parka's pockets. She suspected that Mr. Miller saw, but he didn't say anything, whether out of pity or a broader charity, Mercy didn't know.

If the winter wood was stingy, hoarding its bounty, it wasn't half as sparing as the general population of Titan Falls. After a heavy snowfall, Mercy spent a day lurking with a shovel outside the houses in town, hoping to pile snow for a few coins, but all she got for her trouble were insults tossed at her by a group of little boys and curtains twitching closed. Mercy stared at them with spite. She guessed it didn't matter how many men she appeared to wake from the dead or how many she cured of drink. No one in town wanted to be the first to stick his or her neck out in kindness and risk getting it cut by the McAllisters, who'd made their feelings about Mercy's family plain. Plenty of men in town were sitting around idle now after the mill layoffs had finally gone into effect, but they floated in hopeful bubbles, willing themselves to believe they'd land back where they started sooner rather than later, frantic to keep that illusion from popping.

Mercy looked up from her pacing to find herself in front of the McAllister house. She planted her feet square and regarded the gingerbread trim frosting the front porch, the holiday wreath still tacked to the door, its giant bow ridiculously crisp and festive, even the requisite picket fence. It was the kind of home Hannah should be living in—a place where the rooms smelled like beeswax and lavender, with lots of books and a round kitchen table with a pot of flowers set in the middle. Mercy sniffed in the cold. If only Zeke had been anywhere but on Devil's Slide Road that night. They would have had the real Christmas that Mercy had been planning. She wouldn't have had to give Hannah a sweater of hers that her little sister had always coveted for her only gift. And Zeke surely would have seen to it that Hannah had woken up to something magical and unexpected: a live rabbit popping out of a wooden hat, maybe, or a fairy marionette with delicate movable wings.

Mercy stared at the house's upper windows, wondering which one was Nate's, and mused that if Zeke had been raised as the heir of a paper mill, he might have been better with words. Maybe he would have come to see them the way Hannah did—as portals to whole other worlds—instead of as individual condemnations, black-and-white smudges of proof that he wasn't as good as everyone else.

Mercy blinked, breaking her reverie. In front of her, as if she'd summoned him, she saw that Nate McAllister was approaching her. He must be coming home from school, she realized. It was later than she thought. When he reached her, he lingered, hands in his pockets, toes stubbing at the snow, as if he wanted to speak to her, but his mother hustled out onto the porch, flapping her arms like a bird in distress, cawing about homework and also about some errand his father wanted him to do down at the mill. June waited for Nate to pass indoors before she marched out to confront Mercy.

"It's illegal to solicit people in this town."

It took every little ounce of Mercy's willpower to keep from bending over, gathering a shovelful of dirty snow off the driveway, and flinging it in June's direction. Mercy stared down at her boots—almost worn through and scratched clear to nothing at the heels. They had about another thirty days in them, tops, Mercy was guessing, and she meant good days, not ones full of hard weather like this. She colored and dropped her eyes. "We're hungry."

"You should have thought of that before you began meddling in things that have nothing to do with you."

"Like you did when you told Hazel to fire me?"

June's voice came out as measured as a row of pins. "I'd be careful if I were you. You've lost your father. You've lost your brother. You wouldn't want to see any more family members taken away, would you?"

Mercy felt a flush of panic. "What's that supposed to mean?" Although she knew perfectly well what June was insinuating.

June McAllister was exactly the kind of woman who would rather see a child scrubbed to the raw side of clean and dressed in frills but lonely instead of dirty and loved. It was Mercy's biggest fear—that social services would come and snatch Hannah from her.

"Where's your sister?"

Mercy took a step back. "She's at the library." Where it was warm, and where the chairs were tufted with clean leather and the wooden floor smelled like beeswax, and where the lights worked. All the creature comforts Mercy wanted to provide but couldn't.

A tight smile danced around the corners of June's mouth, as if she had a secret. Well, probably she had lots of them, Mercy thought, what with all those ladies flocking to her parlor every week to gossip and sew, their fingers crawling like fat bugs over corn, so full of themselves. She could see a bunch of them inside now.

But then June's features softened. "She's quite the reader, isn't she?" The hairs on Mercy's forearms stood up. This unexpected gentling frightened the bejesus out of her, far more than any threat. She wouldn't begin to know how to repay the burden of a kindness from the likes of June—not that she believed that the woman was capable of producing one. Why was she so interested in Hannah? And how did she know that she liked to read so much?

Mercy folded her arms. "She's signed up for school now, if that's what you're asking. Just like she ought to be." Hannah was thrilled by that development. Every morning she headed up the path toward Devil's Slide Road, holding Mercy's hand. But clearly she hadn't been as careful as usual about getting friendly with the townspeople. Mercy made a note to have a talk with

Hannah, reminding her that book learning and the dangers of the real world were two very different things.

She looked at the façade of June's house again, with its sparkling windows, and reconsidered all her wistful daydreaming. In reality, if she had to live in such a structure, she'd go stark raving mad. Then an idea occurred to her. In hunting, Zeke had taught her, if you couldn't find any game, you had to flush it out. "Something's always hiding," he said. "Trust me." That's just what Mercy was counting on now.

She licked her lips. "Do you know where your husband was the night of the crash?"

A worried look flickered across June's face, but she quickly recovered. *So she knows*, Mercy thought. Then, just as her brother had taught her, she moved in for the kill. "Because Zeke saw him talking to Suzie in Berlin that night."

Mercy didn't see June's hand until it was too late. The slap bit into her cheek, but the pain felt good.

"You little bitch," June hissed.

Mercy was tempted to point out that Cal's tire prints at the mill looked to her a lot like a set left on Devil's Slide Road the night of the accident, but those marks had long since vanished, and besides, the final lesson of stalking your prey was the art of knowing when to back off and quit. She rubbed the red spot blooming on her cheek and turned to go. "Stay away from us, and I promise I'll do the same."

From the corner of an upstairs window, she caught the pale face of Nate McAllister gazing down on her like a baleful moon. He seemed so alone, and really, he was terribly good-looking. A boy like that deserved some company. She glanced up at him and raised a solitary hand in greeting, a wicked plan beginning to sprout in the wilds of her mind.

When Mercy arrived back at the ravine's clearing, she found Abel Goode waiting for her, hat in hand. He'd come, he announced, to take possession of Gert's ashes. Mercy felt her knees grow weak with relief. *As long as he's not coming for Hannah*, she thought. But it wouldn't do to let Abel know that. She marched up to the RV but didn't open the door. "The ashes? What do you want those for?"

Abel fiddled with his wristwatch. "Turns out there was a mistake made in this matter. They're actually the property of the town." Christ, but he hated this part of the job. Look at these people, camped out here in squalor for no good reason that he could see. Maybe June was right. Maybe it was better for them to move on to someplace that wanted them. On the other hand, that would mean abandoning the search for Zeke, and Abel hated the thought of letting a man get away with murder.

Mercy folded her arms and settled in for a fight. "Nope, sorry. She's our kin. She stays with us."

Abel adjusted his badge. "Not according to town code." He paced over to the smokehouse and peered in through the open door, but there was zero sign of Zeke. Abel scowled and crossed back to Mercy, who was blowing a plume of cold air straight up, like she was testing out the route to heaven.

"Hiding a fugitive will get you time yourself, you know," Abel said.

"Well, then I guess it's lucky I'm not."

Abel cleared his throat, knowing when he was licked. "I'll just take those ashes, then, if you don't mind." It was Friday, his shift was almost over, and there was a barstool with his name on it waiting for him at Lucky's Tavern. At least he could get this matter of Gert off his chest. The damn woman had been trouble when she was alive, and she was twice as much dead. What was it with the Snow family anyway?

Mercy smiled. "Be my guest." She swept her arm out to the steep embankment behind the trailer. "She's scattered right out there."

Abel paled. "You tossed the ashes?"

"Yup." Mercy jigged from one foot to the other, trying to keep warm. "You're going to have a mighty hard time finding any bit of her, but you're sure welcome to try."

Abel hitched his pants up and ground a boot toe in the snow. "I'm better at finding live men," he spit. "You all better watch your back. When I catch Zeke, he's going to pay, and so will you. Guilt by association is the worst kind." He stumped back up the weedy pathway to his squad car, his official hardware rattling around his midsection, a man with the weight of the world hanging on him.

The next morning Mercy woke to find a brace of wild pheasants hanging from a high branch outside the RV, their carcasses neatly bound by the legs, their frozen necks swanned into crooks. Mercy scanned the ground all along the tree line and even into it, but there were no footsteps, no prints of any kind to show that anyone had passed this way. She turned her gaze back to the birds, marveling at the delicate beauty of their plumage. Such loveliness in the cold months was rare. To have it bundled and presented all at once was startling.

Mercy cut the birds down, cursing a little under her breath. If Zeke really wanted to help them, she thought, he'd show his face and come up with some proof of his innocence. She was barely hanging on alone out here. But she wasn't going to turn down the gift of food. She could dry some of the meat into jerky—the smokehouse ought to be put to some use, after all—and roast the rest over an open fire. Her stomach growled as she imagined the birds' juices running down the crisped-up skin and the dark flesh waiting underneath. Or maybe she'd make a stew, pulling out the large dented pot, waiting for the fire to burn down low, and simmering the pheasants, bones and all, in a broth flavored with wild juniper and bay leaves.

One thing was certain: It was too cold to stand outdoors for very long. She'd take the birds into the smokehouse, Mercy decided, and do her plucking there. As she wandered toward it, she noticed a fresh row of logs neatly chopped and stacked along the back wall. She frowned. Those were new, too. But how had Zeke managed to deliver them so soundlessly? Again there were no footprints, just a series of flat patches in the snow where Zeke had probably wiped his trail clean. Mercy glanced around, hoping for one small sign of him, but there was nothing. Suddenly she wished she hadn't given him back his knife. She would have liked to have it now, a little piece of him she could keep ready tabs on.

She banged into the dusty little space, ducking low under the cobwebs dangling from the door lintel. Everything inside seemed untouched. The dented iron cot still sagged in its corner, its mattress stained and lumpy. The trio of rusty hooks still hung from the ceiling like question marks. It wasn't the kind of place you could conceal anything in. If Zeke had rested up here, Mercy certainly couldn't tell. No, most likely he'd done a drop and run, scuttling back into a hidey-hole so dark and distant that only he knew about it.

Mercy lit the kerosene lantern she found near the cot, then

squatted and began plucking the first bird, her fingers pulling off the glorious speckled feathers and scattering them around her. Maybe she'd use the larger quills to make a pair of fairy wings for Hannah—she could try to be whimsical like her brother—and stuff the underfeathers in her quilt as extra batting. It was thin now, after all these years. It could use some shoring up. Mercy frowned. She'd been looking forward to begging for a flawed fleece or two from Hazel come shearing season, but that was a plan gone off the rails now, thanks to that nosy June McAllister.

A shaft of light illuminated the gloom of the smokehouse's interior, and a knife-bladed gust of wind seared Mercy's back, threatening the lantern. She turned around to see Hannah standing in the little doorway, shivering in her nightclothes, parka, and boots, her book of Greek myths clutched under her arm. Mercy patted the spot next to her. "Hello, turtle. Come inside."

Hannah sniffled and let the door slam behind her. "What are those?" She crept closer to the birds.

"Pheasant. You haven't seen Gert's ghost around here lately, have you?"

Hannah shook her head, her ragged curls swaying. "Not since we scattered her ashes. But that doesn't mean she's gone."

Mercy laid one bird down and began on another. She needed to be careful about what she said next. "You know, it's not really a good idea to talk about things like our ghost at school with all your new friends."

Hannah's face darkened, and she looked down at her feet. "That's okay. I don't really have any friends."

Mercy's heart seized with this information, but her fingers kept a steady rhythm as she pulled out feather after feather. "It's not a good idea to talk about what happens out here with *anyone*." Hannah crossed over to the little cot and bounced on it, making the springs squeak. Mercy, busy with her birds, winced at the noise but didn't look up. "Stop that. It's annoying." There was no reply from Hannah, but at least the springs quieted. "You don't ever chat to the mill owner's wife, do you?" Mercy knew Hannah's gregarious ways all too well. The child would converse the ear off a housefly, but she was ominously mute now.

"No," the girl said at last.

Mercy glanced up to see Hannah's bottom sticking up in the air as she peered under the cot on her hands and knees. She clucked her tongue. "Get up off of there. Floor's filthy. And God knows what's living under that cot. Could be spiders or who knows what all." Spiders, Mercy recalled, were one of Hannah's greatest fears, after water. But she didn't seem to care about them now. "Did you hear me? I said get up before you tear your nightdress to shreds and I have to spend the better part of a morning fixing it."

Hannah finally obeyed, wrapping her parka tight around her. Mercy squinted through the dusty air. "What are you looking for?"

Hannah righted herself and blushed. "Nothing."

Mercy remembered the string of carved stars she'd confiscated and given to Dena. Clearly Hannah was hoping for further treasure. "Anything you find out here isn't necessarily yours, do you got that? You tell me if there's anything here that didn't used to be. Do you promise?" Hannah nodded, miserable, and Mercy went back to her work. "You better get your bones inside before they freeze solid. I'll be in soon. And then you best get off to school. Are you going to the library after?"

"Probably."

Mercy knew she should be glad that Hannah was finally settled in a proper school and that she should be grateful, too, for the refuge the little brick library provided for her sister, especially now that the cold was crystallizing ever harder, but there was something about the heaviness of the place and the way the windows fronted the building that reminded Mercy too much of the jail that Zeke had spent time in. Also, June now knew that Hannah spent time there. Mercy turned to her sister. "Remember what I just said. Keep your mouth shut, okay?"

"Okay."

"Okay to what?"

Hannah flung open the rickety door, once again letting in a burst of stabbing cold. "Okay to everything." Stuck in her mess of feathers, Mercy watched her little sister dart back into the gray morning, resisting the urge to run after her and marveling at how only she could make it sound like she was saying both yes and no to everything in the whole world at once.

Chapter Eleven

Hannah had a terrible secret. She wasn't really attending school. That first morning she'd been so excited as Mercy had walked with her down the road into town to catch the bus, but the school's looming hall, with its shiny linoleum floors and the roaming packs of pigtailed, beribboned girls and the slamming of metal lockers had set off a shaking inside her that she'd never known before.

She'd worn her best jeans for the first day, freshly patched by Mercy, and she'd combed her wavy hair smooth, but Hannah could tell that it wasn't enough. Her shirt collar was stained a noxious yellow, her teeth felt scummy, and dirt ringed her cuticles. She clutched the doorframe as more kids pushed their way past her, knocking her with their backpacks.

"Move it, greaseball," a boy with crooked teeth and fat cheeks growled at her, and Hannah obliged, easing herself farther to the side while she tried to work up the courage to thrust her way into a universe she could tell wanted less than nothing to do with her.

The shriek of bells reverberated, and before she knew what she was doing, Hannah was running away from that sterile throat of corridor and back into the wide open air she trusted. At first she lingered in the fields behind the school, amusing herself with making snow angels and a snowman, and then, when the cold started to nibble at her, she set off walking back to Titan Falls, where she would find a warm seat for herself in the little library, which was full of cozy nooks between dark rows of shelves. She could get lost and then lost again in books, trailing her fingers over story after story she had yet to read. And best of all, none of them were her own.

It was easy as peaches to slip by Miss Dinton, the elderly spinster librarian. For one thing, she was half deaf, and for another, sleep overcame her in midmorning after a cup of chamomile and a graham cracker. Hannah waited, peeking through a side window until she spied the old woman's head bobbing forward on her chest, and then she tiptoed past the front desk and made her way to the second floor, where the shelves narrowed and all the best books were hidden.

For a week this strategy was successful. Every morning Hannah walked down Devil's Slide Road swinging a cloth sack into which Mercy had put a nub of crab apple or a rough heel of food-bank bread, pretending she was off to catch the bus. Instead she loitered in the sanctuary of the woods, digging pinecones out of the snow and snapping icy, low-hanging twigs. When she knew that the coast was clear, she skipped into town, taking care to skirt the side of the road in case she needed to make a dash for cover. Hannah's talent wasn't just seeing ghosts, it turned out. She knew how to be one, too.

She discovered the mythology section in the library and happily tore through the *Odyssey* and a book of Norse legends. Then, opposite a shelf of American history, she happened upon a collection of fairy tales, which was where June found her, hunched over an illustrated page, her lip trapped between her front teeth in concentration. June noted this and smiled. Nate used to do the same thing when he was young.

When June first spied the child hopping through the shrubbery opposite her house, she thought she might be seeing things. Panicked, she recalled the rumors going around town that wolves had been spotted in the area, but as her vision focused, she quickly realized she was simply staring at the Snow girl. She watched with fascination as the child disappeared out of her field of view, wondering where she might be headed. Clearly not to school—another violation of the proper upbringing June could see the child was being denied. The next morning she waited at her window at the same time, breathing shallowly against the glass and exhaling when she once again spotted Hannah's small dancing figure. On the fourth day, she followed Hannah, though she had already figured out where she must be going.

She smiled now and stepped closer to Hannah in the library, walking very slowly so as not to startle the girl. "Hello there," she said, squatting down so she was eye level with the child.

Hannah looked up from the illustrated page she was poring over. Her face was filthy, June saw, and her hair looked like it hadn't been brushed in a week. "How long have you been here?" June asked, though she could have answered the question herself. She wanted to see if Hannah would tell her the truth, if the pull she felt toward the child was somehow reciprocal. If it was, she decided, she would give herself permission to interfere just a little—offering the child some food, maybe, or buying her a new hat. She didn't get the answer she was expecting.

Hannah blinked, caught between the dreamworld of her book and the sterner angles of the library. "Only for two pages."

June hid her smile. The child was so thin. She looked like she could blow away in a hard wind. "Have you eaten today?"

Hannah puckered her lips. "I had a bowl of oats at home."

June pictured a soggy mass of grayish grains. Back in

her kitchen, she had half a ginger cake and a round of sugar-powdered cookies smeared with strawberry jam. She leaned closer. "Are you still hungry now?" She pictured fixing a tray of dainty tea sandwiches filled with cucumbers and cress and eggy mayonnaise.

For a split second, Hannah's face turned savage. Her cheeks angled stark as a wolf's, and the sockets of her eyes seemed to darken. "Yes," she whispered.

June held her breath and stretched out an open hand. "Do you want to come with me?" She remembered all the summer afternoons when Suzie and Nate would tear through the front hall in their filthy sneakers, screaming for sandwiches, for cookies and lemonade. While she had been in the thick of them, the sweetness of those moments had been impossible to fully recognize, the way you never knew what your own voice sounded like until you heard it played back on an answering machine or a videotape. Suzie was gone, dead and buried, but against all logic here was another child in front of June, needy in the worst way, ripe for loving. *One girl in the place of another*, June thought. What was wrong with that? It was resurrection at its simplest.

Hannah hesitated, as if she sensed that they were lingering at a dangerous crossroads. If she accepted June's invitation, it would mean betraying the trust of Mercy. How many times had she warned Hannah not to mingle? How many times had she painted the dangers of strangers? Hannah knew that something bad had happened to her sister in the woods with a pair of men and that Zeke had paid the price for it, but surely June, who trailed the sugary scent of vanilla, was different. Surely she couldn't be anything like the disguised stepmother painted on the page of the book Hannah was reading, who hid an apple behind her back and smiled to show teeth that were black and broken. Hannah licked her lips. "Okay," she finally said, unfolding her legs and gathering her coat.

"Do you want to bring your book?" June nodded at the volume Hannah was still holding. "I can help you check it out."

Hannah considered. Up until they'd moved to Titan Falls, all the stories she'd ever read, she had stolen, not borrowed. Then she'd been stuck carrying the guilty weight of them. It had never occurred to her until now to script her own adventure. Solemnly she slid the book into its place on the shelf, squeezing the witch and her apple back into darkness, suspending them in mid-villainy until the next reader came along.

"No," she said, reaching up and taking June's hand, trying not to thrill at the velvet whiteness of it. It was the hand of a queen who could summon magic and spells or keep them hidden in a fold of brocade. It was a hand beautiful enough to tempt fate. "I'm pretty sure I know what happens next."

But June did not end up taking Hannah home. Instead, once they got outside the library and the bright air rushed up through her sinuses, June began to think through all the dangers of letting the likes of Hannah Snow through her front door. For one thing, someone might too easily see them. And then the child might steal something or make notes for her sister to come back and hoist something later, or she might leave something behind that would betray her visit—a stray trinket or wayward footprint from her filthy boots. June frowned. How would she explain her sudden private fondness for the littlest Snow to a mean-eyed jury of townswomen when she could barely begin to account for that affection herself?

Glancing about to make sure no one was watching, June led

Hannah around the shadowed side of the library. She put her hands on Hannah's thin shoulders and leaned down so their two faces were level. She had an idea. "How would you like to go eat in a restaurant?"

Hannah's eyes lit up. "Oh, yes."

June pushed her farther into the shadows. "Wonderful. Why don't you let me go fetch my car? You start walking out of town, back toward Devil's Slide Road, and I'll come along and collect you."

Hannah looked doubtful—she generally avoided Devil's Slide Road during school hours—but the lure of hot food was too great, and she soon agreed to June's plan. To quell the little seed of unease that had begun to sprout in her belly, she reasoned with herself while she trudged the few blocks out of town. She couldn't understand what Mercy's objections to June were. The mill owner's wife seemed lovely to her. She smelled good. Her honey hair was shiny as an otter's and held back with the prettiest pair of tortoiseshell combs, and she always bent down when she was talking to Hannah, as if she were about to share a delicious secret.

In the car, though, they didn't speak much. Hannah fought the urge to duck when they drove by the spot in the woods where their encampment was, but the trailer was tucked well down from the road, she knew. Anyway, Mercy was probably out roaming the woods, searching for food.

They drove to Berlin. It was bigger than most places Hannah ever went. She stared out the car window as June negotiated Main Street, gazing at the graceful façades of the buildings. A good portion of them were abandoned. Others were still inhabited but sinking in on themselves. Hannah wondered if living pressed up so tightly against a bunch of strangers' wishes and dreams changed your own.

June pulled in to a parking slot. "Are you ready?" She smiled down at Hannah. How good it felt to be in charge of a child again. "Do you have your mittens?"

Hannah blushed. "Oh, I forgot them." In truth, she'd lately been wearing a cast-off pair of men's leather work gloves that were comically too big on her and not even very warm.

June didn't seem to be fooled. Her stare turned more probing. "You forgot them or you don't have any?"

Hannah began to squirm in her seat. She had to pee, she realized, but was too shy to ask. For the first time, she felt a small flicker of fear when it came to June. Maybe the woman really did have a poison apple up her sleeve. But before Hannah could explore that thought further, June's expression changed to one of tenderness. She reached up and stroked Hannah's cheek. "Of course you don't have any. No one thinks of you, do they, Hannah? Not really. How about if I knit you a pair? What color do you like?"

Hannah answered straightaway. "Green." It was the color that she knew best, the one she saw vibrating behind her eyelids when she closed them to sleep at night, the hue of acre after acre of trees blurring by the RV windows.

June scrunched up her nose. "Green? Really? For such a pretty girl like you? Wouldn't you like pink?"

Hannah blushed with pleasure. Maybe pink was better.

They browsed up and down the shops on the street, peering in windows at the displays. June bought a tube of lipstick at the chemist and a blue plastic comb with flowers painted on it for Hannah, as well as a package of barrettes. In another store she bought Hannah a watch with a white plastic strap and a picture of Cinderella on its face—an object of such breathtaking beauty that Hannah lost the ability to speak. June wanted to purchase her some new boots, but Hannah demurred. It would be one thing to hide a watch but another thing entirely to try to explain to Mercy where brand-spanking-new footwear had come from. Luckily, her stomach started growling and June took her to eat.

They went to an old-fashioned soda fountain where the booths were covered in soft blue leather and the stools in cherry red vinyl and the floor was a checkerboard of black and white tiles that made Hannah dizzy to look at. She was relieved when June asked for a booth, but soon she was squirming again, the need to pee having returned tenfold now that the excitement of shopping was over.

She cleared her throat, her cheeks reddening. "I really have to go to the bathroom," she whispered, and to her immense gratitude June simply raised her eyebrows and pointed toward the back of the restaurant.

When Hannah returned, a waitress was looming over the table while June perused the menu. Hannah studied the woman. She had snow-blond hair piled up on her head as airy and light as a cream puff and a complexion the color of strawberries and cream. At first glance Hannah thought she must be young, but closer inspection revealed faint purplish smears underneath the woman's heavy-lidded eyes and the kind of broad hips that suggested she'd borne a child. When she spoke, there was the hint of an accent, though her English was perfect. Her name tag said BRYGA.

"We have onion soup on special today. And Reuben sandwiches."

June flicked her menu closed. She didn't look at the woman. "I'll have a chopped salad and an iced tea."

The waitress wrote the order down on her pad. Every now and then, she examined June through the fringe of her thick black eyelashes, as if committing her face to memory. She seemed extremely nervous. "And what would you like?" She turned her gaze on Hannah.

Panicked, Hannah opened her menu upside down, the print swimming before her eyes. The waitress laughed and turned it right side up for her. "So many choices, I know, for a little girl like you. Why aren't you in school today?"

June scowled and interrupted her. "She'll have a grilled cheese with french fries and a chocolate shake."

Chastised, the waitress blushed and snapped her pad closed. "Sure thing." She took one last, deep look at June and then bustled off to place their order. June unfolded her paper napkin onto her lap, then reached across the table and handed Hannah hers. "What do you think about that woman?" she asked, jutting her chin at the disappearing plump hips of the waitress.

"She's pretty. Kind of dainty." *Like one of those fancy pieces of cake in that case on the counter*, Hannah thought.

June pursed her lips in thought. "She's Russian, I bet. Or maybe Polish. Her people are anyway. They have their own church across town, decorated with onion domes and everything. For many years it was closed, but they restored it and opened it again. I bet she attends it." June's eyes followed the waitress as she bustled behind the long counter, watching her almost as if she recognized her from some other context, but not quite.

The North swam with an odd mixture of souls, Hannah knew very well. In the insular world of the backwoods, Acadian loggers still spoke their strange clipped French, bands of Italian-Americans had one another's backs, and Slavs of all kinds muttered away half in English and half in their complicated tongues. What did a person have to do to quit being a stranger? Hannah wondered. What made anyone belong to one spot of earth?

June stabbed at her salad with quick, birdlike movements and ate sparingly. Halfway through she gave up and pushed her dish away, watching as Hannah demolished every last fry on her plate and sucked the dregs of her milk shake through her straw. She waited until Hannah was finished before speaking. "We're friends now, right?"

Hannah glanced down at the Cinderella watch on her wrist. She'd have to remember to take it off before she walked into the RV. She nodded.

June leaned forward. "And friends share stories."

Hannah shrugged. Her stomach was beginning to hurt. She wasn't used to so much rich food at once.

"How about this?" June folded her napkin in a neat square. "I'll tell you one of mine if you will share one of yours. I'll start." June folded the square in half. "Do you know who Anne Hutchinson is?" Hannah shook her head. "She's one of my ancestors. A long time ago, before our country was founded, back in the Puritan days, she was thrown out of the Massachusetts Bay Colony for daring to preach her own thoughts. Women didn't do that back then, you see, and the men in charge didn't like it."

Hannah sat up a little straighter. "What happened to her?"

"Oh, it's a sad tale. She was exiled. Do you know what that means?"

Hannah nodded. Exiled was what she and Mercy were now that Zeke was on the run. Exiled was very bad. It was what happened to traitors, and greedy pirates, and to the wicked in books.

June waited for Hannah to raise her eyes to her again. "She went to found another settlement—in Rhode Island—and she lived there for some time, but in the end she was killed by a band of Siwanoy Indians. Her youngest daughter, Susanna, was kidnapped by them and held hostage." June twisted her napkin into a coil. "She was about your age, I imagine, with very long and beautiful red hair. In fact, that's what turned out to be her saving grace. The tribe ended up adopting her and calling her Autumn Leaf. She lived with them for some years, and when she was finally ransomed back to her family, it's said she didn't want to go."

"That's so sad."

June nodded. As a teenager she'd been quite obsessed with these foremothers, imagining the pregnant and outcast Anne lumbering away from the wooden gates of the Bay Colony before turning to Susanna's terror as a strange, shrieking tribe began murdering her mother and siblings. Or had it perhaps been even worse for the girl to be rescued and returned, banished once again from people she'd grown to love?

June hadn't considered this tale in years and wondered what brought it on now. All the trouble of late with the mill and the business with the accident, probably. Once June had believed that marriage to Cal and life in Titan Falls would be a safe mooring, and truly it had been. Just maybe a little too safe. That was the problem. She sighed. "Now *you* have to tell *me* something." She gestured to the string around Hannah's neck and the cuff link dangling from it. "What do you know about that thing hanging on your necklace?"

Hannah hesitated. She was used to reading stories, not telling them, so she decided to tell the truth. "Nothing."

Her answer seemed to please June, and Hannah was glad. She didn't know why, but she wanted to keep the funny button to herself. She put a hand over it and continued talking. "I can see ghosts, you know. Well, the ones who *want* to be seen anyhow. Like the lady who got found in the ravine after the crash. Gert Snow."

June leaned forward. "And what does she say?"

"Oh, she doesn't *say* nothing. But she isn't happy either."

"Why not?"

"Well..." Hannah trailed off. The dead were not easy to explain to the living. They were *there*, all right, even when they weren't. They might choose to communicate through a blast of wind in the trees, or a rock Hannah stumbled over in her path, or an owl calling out at dusk, and it was up to her to figure out what it all meant. "It's kind of like when you dream. It doesn't always make sense in the mornings when you think about it, but when you're sleeping, it does. It's like that. I don't know *why* that lady's ghost is upset. It just is. Something about the river, I think."

June fiddled with the salt shaker. She kept her eyes pointed at the table. "And how about your brother? He's a kind of ghost, too, isn't he?"

Hannah shifted uneasily. Her stomach was starting to feel tight as a drum. In stories, she remembered too late, treats taken from a witch weren't always so sweet. "We don't know where he is." That was true—most of the time at least. Other times Hannah knew very well that Zeke must be right out in the woods behind their camper, because where else were all those birds and skinned rabbits coming from?

June spun the salt shaker in a slow, hypnotizing circle. "I bet sometimes you really miss him. I bet it's hard not having a man around the place."

Hannah shrugged. "Sometimes." Though, really, Mercy was man enough for anyone.

June craned her neck forward so that her eyes were level with Hannah's. "Don't you ever wish you lived in a nice warm house with a pink canopy bed, and the Sunday comics, and cookies waiting for you when you came home?"

Hannah was beginning to sweat now. Her armpits felt clammy under the boiled wool of the sweater Mercy had given her for Christmas. She squirmed, then thought better of it and held herself still. "No." Though, really, she did ache for those things. Wanted them so bad she could close her eyes and see the flutter of eyelet edging a make-believe canopy, smell warm chocolate chips melting in cookies. For the first time in her life, Hannah realized why stories could be dangerous. They made you crave things that weren't really possible—or weren't possible for you specifically.

June scrabbled in her purse for her wallet. Their lunch was coming to an end. All too soon, Hannah knew, she would find herself back on Devil's Slide Road, where the land went either straight up or straight down, forcing her to choose each time she stepped outside whether she wanted to sink in this world or rise in it. Before she could stop herself, one last word slipped out of her. "Sometimes. Sometimes I want those things."

June sat back against the booth's leather. She smiled. "That's good. Wanting is never bad, my dear." June herself was testimony to that. It was by sheer desire alone that she'd ever left the swamps of Florida behind her. The child was looking quite green around the gills now. Maybe it was all the rich food. June did hope she wouldn't be sick on the drive back. With a click, June snapped her purse closed. "Catch me a ghost, Hannah, and I promise I'll give you whatever you want." And she could do it, too. All it would take would be a well-placed call to the right social worker, and Hannah could be hers. She'd give her a better home than Mercy ever could. After this mess with the bus crash, June brooded, Cal owed her that much. He wouldn't dare make a fuss.

As they slid out of the booth, she noticed that Hannah had left her hat behind. June picked it up and began to call out to the child, but the afternoon light was closing in fast. The day was ending. Soon it would be over, and what would June have to show for it? She desperately wanted a keepsake, some tangible proof of the possibility of second chances in life, and so she opened her handbag and shoved the hat inside. If Cal got to keep the mitten off a dead girl, she didn't see why she couldn't have the hat from a live one. What was good for the goose was good for the gander. June buttoned her coat and walked away from the table, eyeing the blond waitress before she left. She was pretty sure she didn't need to explain why she hadn't left a tip.

Chapter Twelve

Nate rubbed the sleep from his eyes and stretched. It was early on a Saturday, dark still, one of those cold mornings where the sky itself seemed to be undecided between dawn and night, light and shade, so that Nate felt a little like the first, last, and only boy in the world. Outside his bedroom Titan Falls was caught in a bubble of preternatural tranquility, the air barely punctured by the censure of crows, the black guzzle of the river, and the belching needle of the paper mill's brick tower.

His father, he knew, would already have left for his office. Paper, he liked to tell Nate, was seven-dimensional, by which he meant there were no days off in the week, not even for a McAllister man. If the pulper jammed, Nate's father would leave dinner or his bed and go help the foreman deal with it. If the converter broke, he had to write a check to fix it or face everything coming to a grinding halt. All for more paper, which no one seemed to want these days when they could get it cheaper from the mills up in Canada or the plants out west, with their huge trees and bigger orders, or even overseas.

One time, when he'd been about four, Nate's mother had taken him to visit his father at work, and Nate had pulled a stray crayon from his pocket and begun scribbling on one of the pristine new rolls stacked and waiting to be shrink-wrapped. The crayon had been red, he remembered, the same color as his mother's lipstick, a riotous color he associated with hearts and fire trucks and circus tents. Red, he knew, was also the color of the insides of people. As he swiped the crayon across the white roll of paper, he wondered if he was suddenly making all the invisible things inside him perceptible. He'd stepped back to ponder that question and admire his work when he heard his father hissing at his mother.

"A hundred dollars of product he's ruined! Get him out of here, quick."

"He's just a child." His mother's voice was low and reasonable, the way it got when Nate was in trouble. No matter what he did, she was always quick to defend him.

But Cal's voice was sterner. It won. "He's a McAllister. One day all this will be his. He better grow up respecting that."

And so every single Saturday since he was eleven, Nate had spent some part of the day at the mill. Until shortly after the crash, that was, when he'd found something peculiar in his father's office. He'd been at his father's desk, looking for a certain receipt to confirm a shipping order, when he'd found it, along with a photograph of a strange blond woman shoved deep in the middle drawer. Nate was about to pluck the picture out of the drawer when his father came bellowing into the room.

"You don't ever go in my desk without permission! What do you have there?" He ripped the receipt out of Nate's hand.

"N-nothing," Nate stammered, his heart pounding. "I'm helping Mr. Felding square the accounts. I was just looking for that receipt."

Cal's eyes were cool. "Well, now you have it. You'd best leave. Don't let me catch you snooping ever again."

"No, sir." Had he been snooping the night of the accident, when he'd seen his father and Suzie talking in front of the movie theater? Nate didn't think so. He remembered the flash of his father's camel-hair coat disappearing into the darkness, the receding set of his shoulders. All this time he'd kept quiet about what he'd seen, too afraid to say anything.

That evening over dinner, Cal announced that starting after the holidays Nate would be working with Hazel Bell's sheep on the weekends instead of at the mill.

"Sheep?" Nate had sputtered, putting down his spoon. "Hazel Bell?" He pictured the weathered Hazel, with her wiry hair blown all crazy around her face and her stumpy rubber boots. Then he pictured the photograph of the blond woman again. Was this his punishment for what he'd seen? "Dad, I don't know a thing about livestock." Nor did he care to. Leave it to his father, though, to find the one thing in the world sure to be worse than heaving equipment or adding up receipts at the mill.

Cal stabbed a roasted potato. "Your mother thinks it's a good idea. Something to take your mind off—" He stopped. Ever since Suzie's funeral, none of them ever said her name—a silence so dense Nate often questioned if his ears were still working right. Sometimes he wondered if something had happened to dull his senses when the bus plunged off the road. Or maybe some crucial part of his spirit had followed Suzie underground. It sure felt like it—like everything in his life was coming at him slow and black through a six-foot wall of dirt. His father cleared his throat. "Well, a change."

"Won't that be nice?"

His mother's voice was always too bright these days, piping and trilling like a windup bird's. She always got like that when there was trouble with the mill—layoffs or new environmental regulations—as if the sheer force of her domesticity could hold the whole damn operation together. There were moments when Nate wanted to smash her and watch all her gears go flying.

"As the weather gets into spring, I imagine it will be lovely to be out of doors on Hazel's land. And soon you'll be hearing from colleges. You'll be away at Dartmouth before we know it."

Nate pushed his food around his plate. Indoors, outdoors. Dartmouth or Titan Falls. Sheep or paper. Nothing really mattered. It was all the same to him.

The morning the McAllister boy was due to show up to work for the first time, Hazel woke at dawn with a quick jerk. She stuck a hand out and laid it on Fergus's warm flank, relieved when he groaned and stirred. His memory was foggy at best, but he was getting better. He always knew her now. He remembered how to hold a spoon and a fork, how to tie his shoes, didn't lose his way around the house anymore. She could leave him alone for a little while wrapped in blankets at the parlor window and trust that he'd still be there when she returned.

Hazel slipped on a sweater over her nightdress and then padded downstairs, her nerves buzzing. She took her parka off the hook by the door, shimmied on a pair of work pants and then her boots, and let herself out into the cold, her mind crawling with a list of creatures she didn't want to encounter: coyotes, bobcats, moose, wolves. Especially not wolves.

She found the door of the barn unlatched—had she forgotten to lock it?—but the animals were fine, snuggled up against one another, stamping their hooves and nosing around for food like always. When they saw Hazel, they started forward toward her as a single unit, jostling one another for position. Hazel braced herself, her eyes running over the familiar little quirks of each animal. There was the ewe with the eyes too close together and the one with the black spot down by her tail, and there was Ballyhoo, the oldest ram, and Dunkirk, the biggest ram, and... Hazel scanned the flock again. Where was the youngest ram? The feisty one that nipped anyone who tried to come near? Where *was* he?

She pushed into the center of the flock and tapped various animals on their backs as she counted, pushing them to one side. She was short a beast. The ram was definitely missing.

Or taken. It happened sometimes, when folks got desperate, when the mill started shutting out men like it was. Hazel paced the perimeter of the barn, inspecting the walls for any openings, but everything was solid. The outside of the door bore the scratches she'd found weeks earlier with Mercy, but no new marks. Hazel scowled something fierce and squinted. Rams didn't just vanish. Someone had definitely stolen this one. She stomped back into the barn to ready the feed.

"Hello?"

Hazel spun around and saw Nate McAllister's teenage frame filling up the doorway. He hovered in the threshold, hands shoved in his coat pockets, jigging from one foot to the other to keep warm. "You're an hour early." Hazel checked her watch. "I don't guess the sheep mind, but don't think I'm paying you for it."

"Sorry. I couldn't sleep." Instinctively Nate reached up and pulled off his woolen hat, though the cold instantly made his ears tingle. He took this for a hopeful sign. It was the first feeling in a while that he could remember paying even a little attention to.

Hazel stumped over and thrust a rusty metal bucket into his gloved hands. "Save your breath and come on in. Meet your esteemed colleagues."

Nate took a tentative step inside the barn—which was really more of an aerated shed, he saw, with straw bedding and various pens lining the sides. The air steamed with the thick smells of lanolin, wool, sheep shit, and hay, and he was surprised to find that the odor wasn't unpleasant, just rich. And he actually kind of liked how the animals bleated to one another, their lips quivering, their long, alien tongues dancing. It was heartening the way they eventually came over and leaned against him as if he were one of their own. Hazel watched with an assessing eye. "That's something. They feel comfortable around you."

Nate wasn't sure about that. They were sheep, after all. How smart could they be?

"You see how swollen she's getting?" Hazel asked, rubbing one ewe's flank. "I bet she's carrying twins. I'm going to have to call Aggie out here to do the shearing next month. Don't want to leave it too long."

Nate regarded the ewe with her riot of wool. It looked dirty and hard-earned to him, and it seemed like a cruel theft to shave it off the animal's back. "Won't she be cold?"

Hazel waved one of her rough paws, bare to the cold but apparently no worse for it. "Naw. The girls run hotter the nearer their time comes. And we don't want a big mess when they lamb." Now that he was up close to her, Nate could see that not all the lines on Hazel's face came from old age. She was probably a decade younger than he thought, just winded and weathered. Her eyes were a vivacious blue. They watched Nate watching her. "After they're all sheared, I'll turn the rams out and keep the ewes here until they give birth. That's when I really know spring is coming."

Nate patted the pregnant sheep. The ewes seemed so accepting of their impending fates, huddled together in a comfortable little group, their mouths going round and round, as if producing new life were no more complicated than breaking down a mouthful of alfalfa. And maybe it wasn't. What did Nate know about it? He'd never before seen a thing hatched or born. All he knew was paper. "When will it happen?"

Hazel squinted. "Oh, not for a spell yet. End of March, I'd say."

Nate thought about that. March was when the layers of ice on the river finally began to crack just a little. At the mill the men started the month off in hats and thick gloves and ended up in shirtsleeves, still chilly but no longer frozen to the bone. The dull clouds eased up a bit then, not much but enough so that folks started to remember what the color blue looked like and then crave it even harder.

Hazel laid her fingers on Nate's arm. "You ought to see it."

"What?"

"The lambing. Usually it all starts in the middle of the night. I stay out here to clip and clean the cords, and help the twisted lambs come out straight, and make sure the ewes are making milk. It's like Christmas."

Two months ago Nate would have believed in that perfect story, but ever since the crash he'd been wary of happy endings. Accidents happened. Shit went down. So did buses. He folded his arms. "What if something goes wrong?"

Hazel's face grew dark for a moment, and Nate realized how much the crash still must reverberate in her, too. Here she was, dug in this valley with her sheep and Fergus, who he'd seen propped at the bedroom window like he was a bored angel stuck on earth.

She shrugged. "Things go cockamamie sometimes. They do. I've lost girls." She frowned. "And I've lost rams, although that's a different matter entirely. In fact, there's something I need to go sort out now." She picked up a roll of baling wire. "Are you handy?"

Nate took the wire and stared dumbly down at it. Then he looked at Hazel shamefacedly. Two days ago he wouldn't have told her the truth. Two months ago he wouldn't have dared to speak to her in the first place, but his life had been turned upside down in that bus just as Suzie's had ended in it. He felt like he was still tumbling, uncertain about when or where he would land. "No."

To Nate's surprise a tiny smile cracked Hazel's lips. "At least you're honest. I'll tell you what. Why don't you go in and sit a spell with Fergus while I go see about a missing ram?"

Nate picked up the toolbox. He was aware that Hazel was giving him a test of sorts, and he was determined to pass it. "I'll check on Fergus, ma'am, but if it's all the same to you, I'll have a whack at that fence." Out in the field, it occurred to him, there would be nothing to bother him but the raw scrape of wind against his cheeks, the rustling of birds and mice in the frozen undergrowth, and his own two hands, square like his father's and pale as his mother's, but trying for once to figure things out on their own.

The scent of fresh blood greeted Hazel as soon as she stepped into the clearing where the smokehouse stood on the Snow land,

and she knew immediately that her hunch about the missing ram had been correct. Growing up in the Duncan Home for Girls, she'd been made to work half her childhood in the kitchens, transforming whatever kinds of carcasses were thrown their way into food. Sometimes that meant plucking a batch of chickens or carving a side of beef. All these years later, she could still identify the metallic odor of an animal bled and butchered, and that scent was here right now under her nose.

She walked around the smokehouse and then peered inside, but it was empty and dark. She paced around the RV, but the curtains were drawn and there were no signs of life, and then she heard a rhythmic *thwack, thwack* coming from the edge of the ravine.

She was too late. She saw that at once. The ram was tied by his feet and hoisted over a stout pine branch, his thick bluish tongue hanging out of his mouth, his eyes bulging and blind. Mercy was skinning him, but her knife was too dull, and she was having to hack and tug at the skin to get it to slide off.

"A greedy father has thieves for children."

Mercy jumped at the sound of Hazel's voice and spun to face her, the knife still in her hand. In spite of the cold, she'd been sweating. Her hair was damp along her forehead. Hazel was startled to see how thin she'd grown. "Hazel, I didn't hear you."

Hazel folded her arms and pitied the poor beast. He had been a magnificent specimen. Now he was just a raw sack of innards waiting to spill. "You've bloodied the fleece. Anyone with a brain would have shorn the animal first."

Even Mercy's lips were pale, and there was a sore erupting at the corner of her mouth. She looked like she hadn't washed in weeks. "Hazel... I know this looks bad."

"I wouldn't have pegged you for a thief."

Mercy ducked her chin. "I'm not." *But my brother is.* The unspoken words might as well have been shouted. Mercy inched forward a step, the knife no longer a potential weapon, no longer even a tool, just an afterthought dangling from her fingers. "Hazel, let me explain. Zeke found him already dead. Honestly. He would never take from someone who'd once been kind to me."

Was it Hazel's imagination, or did Mercy stress the word "once"?

"Look, I can prove it." She turned the carcass sideways, revealing the half-stripped flank. "See where the fleece is all ragged and torn? Do you really think Zeke would slaughter an animal so carelessly? Hazel, I warned you something was lurking around your barn. Didn't I?"

Hazel bit her lip. She didn't know what to believe. With a lurch she remembered the open latch on the barn door this morning. Maybe a predator really had gotten in, or maybe the ram had slipped out, but how unlikely that was. There had been no signs of a struggle in the barn, and sheep were herd animals. They moved either as one or not at all.

On the other hand, she couldn't imagine that the Snows would be dumb enough to pull more trouble down on their heads. This was it, she decided, the final inch she was going to give any of them.

She took a fortifying breath and pulled her spine as straight as she could get it. "June McAllister was right. The only thing you Snows ever make is trouble." She sighed at the mess in front of her. There was so little of the creature left to salvage, whatever had really happened to him. "I want the fleece, such as it is." That, at least, belonged to her. The ram's wool would go back to his flock.

Mercy bowed her head. "I'll bring it to you. I promise."

"If I see so much as your little toe on my land, I'll have it for my own, followed by your head. You can give the wool to Nate McAllister. He'll get it to me." Hazel drew herself together and prepared to hike back to her car. There was nothing left to do.

Mercy's voice floated up the hillside after her. "Hazel, I'm sorry for it all."

The girl's apology floated and then dropped, heavy and final. Hazel didn't even turn around.

Inside the RV, Mercy cracked the last of their eggs in half and dropped the yolk into a clean jar. Zeke hadn't killed the ram—she was positive. But still, did that make giving it to her and Hannah any less of a crime? Without the animal she and Hannah risked starvation. With it they most certainly wouldn't hunger, but was it worth it, Mercy wondered, to trade the last shred of Hazel's goodwill for something as fleeting as full bellies? Once again Zeke had acted according to his own impeccable moral code—he'd found a dead ram that would have been wasted, and Mercy and Hannah were in desperate need—but in doing so he'd missed the bigger picture. In trying to care for his sisters, he'd threatened to undo any inch of progress Mercy might have made with people's bad opinions in town. She bit her lip in frustration. She would have to ramp up her efforts.

To the mix in the jar, she added a flurry of powdered and dried mushrooms that she'd foraged with her mother on the border of Canada last spring, a pinch of chili flakes, and a measure of vinegar, and then she stirred everything with the blade of a knife. She cleared her throat and turned to Hannah. She loved everything about her little sister, but it was exhausting being her sole guardian. Still, if she didn't take the time to explain the nuances of things to her, Hannah might end up just like Zeke—well-meaning but always somehow in the wrong, no matter what. "Even if he didn't kill it, you know that Zeke still shouldn't have taken that ram, right?"

Hannah yawned and flipped a page in her book. Her stomach was rumbling. She wasn't sorry about Zeke's taking the meat. She couldn't wait to feast. "There's only so many birds in the woods this time of year. Besides, I bet she loses a few animals every season. Or she sells them."

Mercy slammed the jar back on the counter. "That's not the point. How are people going to care about Zeke if they think we're a bunch of thieves?"

"Zeke's looking after us. You should be grateful."

"I'd rather have some answers."

Hannah pursed her lips and quoted Arlene. "Better to let all the dogs lie." She nodded at the jar. "You going into town to drop that off?"

Fred Flyte had been drinking Mercy's remedy steadily, and even though Mercy never asked him to, he always pressed some kind of payment into her hands when she brought him the stuff: a basket of dried apples, a loaf of bread, a pair of striped socks hand-knitted by Dena. "I know it's nothing much," he'd say, "but how do you repay a true miracle?"

Mercy would blush ferociously as she accepted the gifts, uneasy with Fred's accolades. Healing was turning out to be a simple business, really. It was all just a matter of bringing opposites together. To tame a fever, for instance, Mercy cooled it with a paste of rue and mallow. To thin out thick blood, she watered it with cucumber and spirits. Even waking Fergus from his cave of darkness after the accident had been uncomplicated in the end. All it had taken was breath and willpower—his or hers, Mercy still didn't know for sure. But she had held his head in her hands and sent him a message: *Do not go.* That was it. And it had worked, sort of. Fergus had come back, but not the same. Mercy frowned. Thanks to Zeke's gift of the ram, Hazel might well be a stranger now, too.

Mercy looked at the fleece lying on the RV's banquette. She'd trimmed what she could off the animal's skin and had tried to sponge the wool clean, but it was still smeared and dirty. She knew she had to give it back—a promise was a promise—but she longed to hold on to it for a few more days, the last bit she would ever have of Hazel. Lost in thought, she rolled the fleece and tucked it under her mother's old quilt.

What if she could give Fergus back his memory? she mused. Would Hazel forgive her then? But if healing was simply a matter of mending, bringing back a man's memory surely carried further complications, for that involved a wholesale type of retribution—something Mercy wasn't quite sure how to go about in Titan Falls, skinny little lick of a town that it was, full of narrow eyes and narrower minds. She sighed and slid the jar into the palm of her hand. If she was going to put Fergus back right, she was starting to suspect, she was going to have to make some kind of exchange: one soul for another, sister for brother, the damned for the innocent. If only it were so easy to tell which was which anymore.

By Nate's third Saturday at the Bells', the fence didn't really need any further repairs. The ones he'd managed to complete weren't that fail-safe, but Nate didn't tell Hazel that. He suspected she knew it already, and he appreciated her reserve on the matter.

The more he got acquainted with her, the more he liked her. He knew she'd lost her own son sometime back, and he was guessing she must have been a tolerant kind of mother, quite unlike his own, who bustled around him constantly, as annoying as an extra thumb, readjusting his scarf before he left the house, overpacking his school lunches with food he didn't want to eat, and asking him all sorts of questions he didn't feel like answering: Why had he quit the hockey team? What did he want to do after church on Sunday? Who was he going to ask to the winter formal?

When Hazel spoke, it was simply to impart information and nothing more. Most of her conversation wasn't even of the human variety. All her syllables were for or about the sheep. By Nate's third weekend, he'd gotten used to it. One thing he never asked about, however, was the overgrown sugar bush down at the end of the valley, where a profusion of stones stood. The first time Nate stumbled upon it, he almost tripped over one of the boulders, which was half sunk in the snow and rounded. Then, righting himself, he spied all the other rocks set under the trees, and the hair on his arms stood up. He'd backed slowly away, stepping in the footprints he'd made. He couldn't say why he suddenly had such a strong desire to leave the smallest trace possible behind him, but it was so. Even when he and the other high-school kids broke into the abandoned worker cottages down near the river in the spring and summer, he'd never felt such a sense of trespass, but maybe it was because those buildings were, in a roundabout way, his. This place, however, was clearly private. Everything from the low-hanging boughs to the stippled shade in the center of the glen forbade entry. In spite of that—or maybe precisely because of it—the very next week, as soon as Hazel set him free with a set of tools and more wire, Nate found his way back.

When she wanted to, when she really concentrated, Mercy could thread a path through the woods with the easy cunning of a fox. Zeke had taught her this—the way to rock between footsteps, transferring her weight from one heel to the other, rather than pounding her feet into the ground. How to curve her body up against the trunk of a tree, melting into its shadow and musty bark, when to freeze and when to run like a mad dog. The only time these skills had failed her had been in the woods with those two hunters. That was the one thing Zeke had forgotten to impart to her—that there was always someone out there stealthier than you, that hunter could turn prey in the thud of a heartbeat. She thought of Zeke lying hunched in a cold cave or walking in aimless circles around fallen trees. A caged hunter, Zeke had always said, was worse than a downed one.

Mercy folded the ram's fleece she was carrying tighter to her chest and swung her gathering basket over her arm. Out here in Hazel's sugar bush, there was no need to take precautions. It was a deliberately abandoned space, and though Mercy didn't understand who all the stones belonged to, she intuited enough to comprehend that they were to be left undisturbed. In her travels with Arlene, she'd often run across strange totems in the woods: mysterious runes incised into tree trunks, weathered twig crosses half rotted and leaning toward the grave themselves, and, once, a log carved into a fantastical creature, half woman, half bird. These places, her mother had taught her, were often the best for gathering plants. "They breed the unexpected," she'd instructed Mercy. And as proof, under the chimera, she'd found a smattering of tiny orange-capped mushrooms that she wouldn't let Mercy touch but cut with gloved hands at their stems and carefully bagged.

Mercy scanned the low growth in front of her. Occasionally she leaned down and plucked a twig or snapped some rushes into her basket. She was so focused on the particular as she wandered from tree to tree that she was startled to come across Nate McAllister bent over a fence post at the far edge of the space, a ball-peen hammer tossed at his feet. Mercy stifled a cry, and then her panic quickly turned to amusement. She surveyed the mess he'd made—the hole dug too shallow in the snowy mud, the fence post cracked along its bottom, a tangle of wire snared up with a pair of pliers and a hacksaw. Only a fool would try to fence a sugar bush, especially this one. Mercy sidled up on him, pleased with the opportunity to speak freely. "Do you even have a backside idea of what you're doing?"

Nate turned around. He seemed equally startled. "Jesus." He scowled at her. "I thought maybe Hazel would like it if this place was...set apart, I guess. She never talks about it, but it seems like maybe it should be enclosed or something. What are *you* doing out here? Hazel will have your head if she finds you." His eyes fell on the basket Mercy was carrying, filled with all manner of twigs and rushes and roots she'd dug up out of the snow, and then on the fleece still clutched to her chest. "Seriously, what the hell are you doing?"

Mercy decided to take a chance and tell him the truth—or part of it anyway. Ever since she'd run into him outside his house, she had larger plans for the two of them, but she decided to keep those to herself for now. She handed the fleece to Nate, who seemed reluctant to accept it. "Making amends. Give that to Hazel. She's expecting it." She lifted her basket a little. "And making memories. Or at least trying to."

Nate scowled. "I don't understand." Even though it was frosty, he'd worked up a sweat. He wiped his brow. He was just as handsome as she remembered, Mercy was pleased to note.

She bit her lip. Except for Hannah and Hazel, it had been weeks since she'd spoken properly to anyone, much less a strange boy. Her voice came out sounding as scratchy as a bargain-bin sweater. "They're not for me. They're for Fergus."

Nate regarded her, still suspicious. To hear his parents talk, Mercy was a she-devil who was responsible for everything from the exhumation of Gert Snow to the crappy downturn in the paper business. Nate thought his parents were full of shit. "Does Hazel know?"

"Not yet."

Mercy watched him weigh this information. Everything depended on how he reacted to her right now. He picked up the hammer and swung it from one hand to the other. Finally he laid it back down. "You're the one who's making that stuff Mr. Flyte drinks to keep him off the sauce. I heard my parents talking about it. They say it's illegal peddling and that if you're not careful, you're going to poison him, not that they would care. My mom's put Abel Goode on the case."

Mercy paled. If Abel stopped Fred from giving her his small trade, she wasn't sure she and Hannah would finish pulling through the winter, even with the ram meat, a situation that would no doubt suit June McAllister just fine.

Nate screwed up his face. "What do you put in that stuff anyway?"

Mercy shrugged and shifted the basket. "To dry a man out, sometimes you just need to keep his insides watered proper, that's all."

Nate's gaze slid into the distance. "I wish you'd been around to see Mr. Flyte before the accident."

Mercy bowed her own head, remembering what Nate had said to her the day of the funeral when she'd asked if Suzie had been his girlfriend. *She was too smart for that.* At the time she'd thought he'd meant Suzie wouldn't have him, but now that Mercy had tangled a bit with June McAllister, she wondered if maybe Nate wasn't correct after all. It wasn't that Suzie hadn't loved Nate back. She'd just known her place, and it hadn't been at the right hand of the mill owner's son. Neither was Mercy's, but she didn't plan to let that stop her.

Nate turned his gaze back to her. "It's like ever since she died, nothing matters that much anymore, you know?"

Mercy pictured the way her brother's back had hunched like a cautious beetle's as he'd disappeared down the throat of the prison hallway after each visitation, then again as he'd vanished into the ravine's woods. There was more than one way to lose a person. "I know."

Nate made a divot in the snow with his boot toe. "I wish *I* could heal people." He swept his arm out at the defunct fence post. "I can't even do this right. Instead all I'm ever going to do is make more stupid paper."

That in itself was something, Mercy thought, to take the wilds around them, grind it all up, smooth it out, and churn it clean and flat. She tried to think of anything pristine in the texture of her life and failed. All her edges were splintered and torn, all her pages written on. She tightened her grip on her basket. If she couldn't sow, she could at least gather. She stepped closer to Nate. "You know, there's a difference between healing and saving. Only one of them is God's work." It was an Arlene phrase.

Nate looked up. "Which one?"

Mercy gazed up at the tangle of branches above her. "I don't know." It was frustrating standing here among so much untapped sweetness, so much richness she'd never get at. Mercy's mouth watered, and then, suddenly, with the quick brutality of an arrow striking flesh, she knew exactly what would bring Fergus back. She regarded Nate. He was an unlikely accomplice, with his patrician looks and bluer bloodline, and he certainly wasn't dexterous when it came to handiwork, but he was here in front of her, and that was worth something. Mercy ran a hand down one of the trees. "Do you want to start?"

"Start what?"

"Healing. Or saving. Maybe both. I'm not sure yet. If I give you a list, can you meet me here next week with some special tools?"

Nate looked at her suspiciously. "Are you planning on tapping the maples?"

Mercy gave the tree a solid thump. Memory was supposed to begin and end with the body, but didn't always. Maybe you could drain it like the sap from a tree, and what then? She pictured the bare scar of earth at the bottom of the ravine where the bus had come to rest and the sliver of a grave where Gert's bones had been found. The hole was gone—filled—and yet every time a crow clacked out a call from a tree, every time the wind snapped and rattled twigs, Mercy wondered if it was Gert, or maybe the equally disembodied Pruitt, materializing out of thin air to haunt her. She stood up. "I'm going to try to give Fergus back his roots the only way I know."

And maybe, if all went well, she might even find some of her own.

Chapter Thirteen

You never knew what early spring was going to bring you in Titan Falls, but you could always bet it would never be anything good. The season was a fickle one, in which muddy runoff might freeze overnight into treacherous brown slicks, ravenous field mice invaded basements and kitchens with a boldness disproportionate to their size, and the river, replenished with snowmelt and a winter's worth of illegally dumped sulfites, started flowing with a faster urgency. It was not a period of public congenialities, heartfelt exchanges, or much gossip. Even the men in Lucky's Tavern were more subdued than usual come early spring, resting their fists in heavy knots on the bar, hesitant to start something when they weren't sure how it would likely finish, especially in the face of continued layoffs. More accidents happened on the mill floor at the tail end of winter than during any other time, and the men, knowing this, figured they'd rather not bother killing one another when they could just as easily kill themselves.

It was with some trepidation, then, that in the middle of March the entire population of the town woke to find a most unusual gift waiting on its collective stoops. Alice Lincoln was the first one to discover the jar half filled with an amber-colored liquid deposited outside her front door, but she soon determined that she hadn't been the only one favored. Up and down the village, each and every household had the same concoction waiting for it in a motley collection of glass containers. Some families found jam jars perched on top of their mailboxes, others plucked glass vials used to hold spices off benches on their front porches, and some received what looked like old ketchup bottles, their labels soaked and scraped away.

"What do you think it could be?" Margie Wall asked at the emergency sewing circle convened in June's front parlor. She tilted what might have been a cola bottle first one way and then the other, making the mysterious substance slosh.

"It smells sweetish." Alice wrinkled her nostrils and then took another whiff. "Familiar, even."

Dot was the only one brave enough to taste it. She dipped the tip of a meaty pinkie into what was clearly a recycled mustard jar.

"Oh, Dot, don't!" the expectant Stella cried, her belly plumper than ever. She had only a few weeks to go in her pregnancy, and she lumbered now with the uncomfortable swayback of an old milk cow. "What if it's poison?"

Dot waved off the objections, raised her finger to her lips, and then smiled triumphantly. "Why, it's maple sap!"

This set off a tizzy of proclamations and questions. "Sap, not syrup?" Stella asked, cautiously dipping her own forefinger into the liquid.

"Who put it out?"

"It reminds me of what Mercy Snow gives to Fred." All eyes turned to Dena. A hush fell over the room. Several of the ladies put their jars down with loud rattles.

"Is she trying to kill us or cure us?" Alice asked.

"Maybe she's trying to make amends." Margie always did see the good side of a situation.

June watched the proceedings with tight lips. She had neither opened the lid of the canning jar she'd received nor deigned to bring it indoors.

"Look, there's some kind of message on the bottom," Stella suddenly declared, peering at the tiny piece of paper taped underneath her jar. "I think mine says '*forgive.*'"

"So does mine," said Dot, squinting at her own pot. Alice and Margie confirmed that the same thing was written under theirs.

Dena was staring at June. "What does yours say?"

Grimly June went outside to fetch the jar. Against all her better instincts, she tipped it over, a bad feeling beginning to burn in her stomach. Plain as day, a message was indeed scribbled, but it wasn't the same as everyone else's. June's simply said "*forget.*"

All week Hazel had been preparing for the shearing. She'd blocked off two pens inside the barn, made sure the outlet for Aggie's clippers worked and that she still knew where the extra-long extension cord was, and stocked herself with a roll of plastic sacks into which to stuff the fleeces. Always, shearing seemed to her to be an act of theft, capped off with the hasty inspection and bagging of the wool, though the flock never seemed to mind. To the contrary, the animals mostly submitted peacefully to their fate once Aggie wrestled them onto their backs. They lolled like narcoleptic lapdogs, their heads angled to one side, their front legs crooked at the knee, and when it was over, they shook themselves, spun around, and got straight back to the business of looking for feed with the rest of the flock. Who knew? Hazel thought. Maybe the animals were glad to shed the burden of their wool and start collectively anew.

This year the sheep seemed to guess it was coming. They bleated and milled around one another in the barn with more vigor than usual, waking out of their winter torpor, the pregnant ewes proudly trotting and showing off their burgeoning bellies and teats, the rams feisty as all get-out. They startled when they heard the clacking of Aggie's truck and hustled themselves into a protective knot, their eyes and tongues darting.

"Hi-ho, lady-o." Everything about Aggie's annual visit was always the same, down to his greeting, but this year, Hazel saw, he was holding the hand of a small girl who looked to be about ten or eleven. "My daughter, Ivy," he proclaimed, removing his hat per usual and scratching at his thinning hair, a little sparser than it was the year before. Aggie was a widower. Hazel wondered about the toll it would take on a man to raise a girl all alone, and then she debated which was worse: losing your child or the mother of that child. It was a question she didn't think there was a very satisfactory answer to. "She's learning the ropes and lending me a hand this year, aren't you, sweetie?" Aggie tousled the girl's hair, but the child didn't break rank. She folded her arms in imitation of her father's habitual stance and glared at Hazel.

"She's a fierce one," Hazel remarked.

"Aye." Aggie paused. "How's Fergus?" Hazel saw Aggie once a year, but word traveled up and down the narrow neck of the New Hampshire woods. Hazel wasn't a bit surprised that Aggie had heard about Fergus's condition, but she was startled that she minded so much.

Sometimes, in the contented blur between sleep and day, Hazel would forget everything that had happened. In the morning she'd wake with her legs tangled against Fergus's and his hands wrapped in her loose hair. She'd reach for his torso, as if to pull him over her, but he'd make a confused sound and she would jerk fully awake, returned to the fact that the warm-blooded man she'd married was gone for good, or at least for now.

Sometimes Fergus would lift one of his gnarled hands and stroke Hazel's cheek or smile at her with the lopsided portion of his face that still worked, but other times she would notice his eyes darting around the parlor in frantic zigzags, landing on her spinning wheel, on the old chesterfield or the antique phonograph, like a man in a dream trying to wake himself. Hazel would have to soothe him then, unfurling his clenched fingers and massaging the ligaments, wrapping his knees in a blanket and tucking it tight. She worried about him when she left him alone to see to the sheep, but what could she do?

It reminded her of the time when she'd first started husbandry and her flock had gotten stranded out in an autumn storm. No matter which way she'd moved, the animals had turned away from her, paying no mind when she tried to herd them.

"Get on!" she'd shouted, rain running down her face, but the beasts were deaf and stubborn with fear. Hazel had been tempted to give up then. She'd been cold to the marrow and wet through, one woman raging against the whole wide world. And then something in her had snapped. She remembered the way Rory's head had lolled against her shoulder at the end and how, in that moment, he'd seemed to grow lighter and not heavier in her arms, and she knew with savage certainty that she had stayed on the earth for a reason. She was damned if she would lose another living thing on her watch. Ten minutes later the sheep were rounded up and locked in the barn, just as miserable as they'd been before.

Hazel felt that way about Fergus, like she'd rescued him from the elements, but in doing so had only managed to deliver him into a fresh state of confusion. She snapped herself back to Aggie's inquiry about Fergus. "He's in the parlor." Hazel tipped her head in the direction of the house. "All alone."

Aggie's eyes flickered in understanding. He was a man of few words and deep comprehension. "Ah. Then let's make this quick. You got the bags ready?" Hazel nodded. "Which one do you want me to do first?"

She fetched one of the younger ewes, a small specimen with particularly lovely eyes, and soon the air of the barn was filled with the electric buzz of Aggie's clippers and the loud protestations of the flock.

Ivy crouched quietly in a corner, hands folded across her knees, her little face puckered in concentration as she watched her father work. Hazel's heart contracted into a painful knot as she observed her. Her coloring was much the same as Rory's had been, and she possessed the frank and curious gaze he'd had. It was like witnessing a ghost in reverse, Hazel thought—an apparition of an unrealized future instead of a curtailed past. Had Rory lived, would he have sat watching Aggie shear? For the first time in years, Hazel had the sudden urge to go see Rory's stone out in the old sugar bush, but she pushed that thought aside. Her son had gotten sick, and she'd buried him. End of story. Hanging over his bones wouldn't bring him back.

At some point, nearly halfway through the process, Aggie noticed Hazel staring at Ivy. His eyes went back and forth between the two of them before he announced that the girl must be hungry and sent her out to wait in the truck. "There's jam sandwiches and a thermos waiting," he said, gruff, before shooing his daughter out into the gray cold. "Go on."

"I have cake in the house—" Hazel started to offer, but Aggie flipped another ewe at his feet and turned the clippers on, filling the barn with the same purposeful sound a hive of angry bees would make.

"This ewe's having twins," Aggie announced as he finished the last girl, palpating her belly with one of his gnarled hands. The sheep rolled her eyes up at Aggie in helpless surrender. She opened her mouth and panted. Hazel fetched her paint. She daubed each twin-bearing ewe with a dot of red spray paint. The girls with single lambs got blue, and the occasional sheep with triplets received a smear of yellow. Aggie's practiced fingers probed and rubbed. "But there could be trouble. One lamb feels bigger than the other." He frowned. "Probably only the one will live. Just so you're prepared." Aggie flipped the ewe back onto her feet so quickly she was stunned by it. It took her a moment to catch up with herself, and then she clattered away, all newly trimmed hooves and pink skin. The sheep looked like different beasts after they were sheared. All their flaws were visible—their legs just a hair too long for their bodies, their square flanks bloated over their skinny knees, their floppy ears halfway to looking like donkey ears.

Hazel finished stuffing the last fleece into the plastic sack. Like the others, it was of excellent quality. The wool was supple with lanolin and free of too much filth. As soon as the weather cleared a little and after the business of lambing, she'd wash the fleeces and lay them out to dry in the sun, letting nature bleach what soap couldn't clean. Hazel liked to use the stretch of lawn just off her porch for this job. She'd putter around indoors while the wool dried, glancing out the windows from time to time to make sure birds didn't come down and try to steal or foul her bounty.

"It looks like you massacred a passel of angels and took their wings," Fergus remarked the first year Hazel had shorn her sheep. Horrified, she had flown to the upstairs bedroom window and looked down on the tufts dotting the lawn.

"No it doesn't." But it kind of did, providing that angels could ever be caught. Hazel wondered if Fergus would remember that quip when he saw the fleeces this year or if, after his brush with death, he carried a different image of angels altogether. Maybe instead of the ephemeral beings everyone conjured, the angels were really as hard-shelled and shiny as beetles. Perhaps instead of arriving with a face of human mercy, they came down with articulated legs, wriggling antennae, and multifaceted eyes that could see not just your side of the story but all the versions necessary to produce the honest truth. That would be useful, Hazel thought, when it came to the whole mess of the crash. Ever since June's visit, Hazel hadn't been able to get rid of the tiny germ of doubt settled deep inside her. What if Fergus *had* made a mistake? What if Zeke really *was* innocent? In that case maybe it was better Fergus didn't remember.

Aggie was cleaning out his clippers and rolling up the rest of his gear. He packed everything—the hoof clippers, the file, his gloves—into a single neat canvas bag and then surveyed the naked flock with satisfaction. "I remember when you just had the one, way back when. Remember how you sang to him the first time I did the shearing?"

Hazel nodded. She still occasionally sang to her animals, especially during lambing season, but she didn't tell Aggie that. He would think it was ridiculous—and it was. Sometimes, though, a song was really meant for the singer. Back when Hazel still attended St. Bart's, belting out the hymns had always been her favorite part of a Sunday. At those moments, listening to the town's combined voices trilling up to the rafters, she used to think that folks had it all wrong when they talked about going to church to invite God in. Surely, Hazel thought, it was the other way around. You went to let him out.

"You going to be okay?" Aggie had jammed his hat back on his head and was peering at her with concern, the way he would inspect a sheep with infected udders or a split hoof. "I heard you fired that Snow girl, but she's still out there on Devil's Slide Road, isn't she? I hear the McAllisters are hopping mad about it. Abel Goode says June pesters him at least once a week with new plans to roust them out of there. I hear she's talking about calling child protective services on them, though I'm not sure starting on the little kid is the right way to go. Still, you must miss a pair of helping hands around here."

Hazel drew her shoulders back and shook herself out of her fog. "Don't be a stooge, Aggie. I'm strong enough to corral one of the rams when it's in a mood. I think I can handle the flock on my own. Besides, I've got the McAllister boy on weekends now." She didn't say a word about Mercy, though she'd certainly been on Hazel's mind ever since the gory incident with the ram. Now she was glad as a ten-dollar bill that June had talked her into getting rid of the girl, although it bothered Hazel to remember the hollow angles of Mercy's cheeks and the obvious thinness under the bulk of her jacket. But no. Hazel ought to have trusted her instincts from the get-go. The Snows were good for nothing but trouble. Always had been and always would be. By holding her door open wide to Mercy and inviting her to step across her threshold, Hazel had done nothing but curse her own fool self.

They strolled out of the barn and latched the door. Aggie took in the scratches on the wood with a critical eye. "Coyotes? They're getting worse every year." His forehead wrinkled. "Wait. Where's that young ram of yours? I thought we were one short. Oh, Hazel—"

She cut him off. "Margie Wall claims she saw a wolf in these parts, but that woman's got an imagination." She couldn't say why she didn't want Aggie to know the truth about the ram, and this bothered her almost as much as the crime itself.

Aggie was concerned. "A wolf is a worry with lambing season around the corner."

"I'd take a lone wolf over a pack of coyotes." Hazel shrugged.

"Can't argue that." Aggie shook his head. "This town's falling apart. First there was the accident, then that business with those old Snow bones. Now we've got wolves. Next they'll be closing the mill down one hundred percent. I hear another operation over in Maine is shutting next month. There's only Titan Paper and one other left around here."

Hazel double-checked the barn door. "That's exactly why I'm in sheep. If worst comes to worst, I can always eat them."

Aggie waved his hat at Ivy to signal her to start up the truck, and the girl obeyed, a delighted grin on her face. Hazel's heart hurt just looking at her. Aggie turned back to her. "I'm serious. Take care out here, Hazel. And if you need anything when the lambing starts, call me." He grinned. "I can lend you Ivy."

If I had her, I might not give her back, Hazel thought. She knew what the women in town said about her and her sugar-baby stones. Well, half the women anyway. The other half had lost children just as Hazel had. Still, it was easier to mock Hazel for her grief than try to confront the reasons for their own sadness, but in the end it all boiled down to the mill and the river, she suspected. Gert and her family had allegedly always been complaining about the noxious water, and look where it had gotten them. In the ground, was where. Snows and McAllisters, Hazel suspected, went way, way back.

Not that Hazel, or anyone else in town, was one to go bringing any of that up in polite company. Hurt was something you buried once and for all in Titan Falls—bones and everything. Hazel discovered early on in the Duncan Home for Girls that sorrow was as common as brickwork. There was nothing special about hers. Once an orphan, always an orphan. Or so she'd always told herself, until the day she accidentally learned that she might be less of a stray than she believed. There was a reason Hazel had moved to Titan Falls, but it was one she almost never dared admit to herself, much less anyone else.

Now, as she trudged from the barn back to the house in the early spring twilight, she heard the distant sound of an owl calling in the trees and once again felt the stab of Mercy's betrayal. In spite of all that, she still missed the girl. Having Nate around wasn't the same, but it was an improvement over no one. Better the devil you knew, Hazel supposed, although it didn't answer the question of what you were supposed to do when the devils you knew included absolutely everyone.

On June's wedding day, Hetty McAllister had sent her down the aisle with a warning and a curse. If June wasn't careful, Hetty had hissed, fussing with her veil and handing her the bouquet, she would be driven to distraction by life in this town. Any number of things could do it: the vapors that fouled the place to high heaven in the warmer months, the constant noise, the calamity of a fall of logs jamming the Androscoggin, and the inevitable limbs that were fatally crushed in the act of freeing them.

"Are you sure you want to do this?" Hetty had asked, and June, struck mute by love and wedding nerves, had nodded furiously. At the time what she'd loved best about Cal was how he wasn't just from Titan Falls but actually *of* it. Every day she looked forward to his coming home from a day at the mill with the heavy odor of pulp hanging in his hair and wood shavings stuck in his trouser cuffs. It seemed the most natural thing in the world to June, as if, when it came to Cal, wood and flesh were one substance.

But sprouting roots, it turned out, was a far more painful business than June had anticipated. Now, as the early spring shuddered forward, the days thawing and the nights still freezing, a vague malaise draped itself over her, worse than anything she'd felt before at this time of year, swathing her in perpetual ill will. The sewing circle was finishing up the wall hanging in Suzie's memory, embroidering the tiniest buds on the apple tree's branches with green silk thread the color of dragonflies, basting over their previous stitches again and again to make the bark rough.

As the project neared completion, the women gathered more frequently in June's parlor. Normally June relished such company, but now she felt smothered by it. For one thing, the mill was operating at half staff. After the first round of layoffs, Cal had let go another group of men, including Alice's husband, and June could feel the unspoken resentment of the wives buzzing in the room like a ball of riled hornets. It made her careful in the extreme. Cal had promised that orders would pick up again with better weather, but June didn't say that to the women sitting around her. She simply kept her head down and stitched, hoping to set an example of patient industry the rest of them would follow.

She was beginning to regret the memorial panels for Suzie. The work was fussy, painstaking, and required the press of too many hands too close to June's own. She sensed, in the women's tense shoulders and tight lips, the same impatience from the other wives. Suzie was buried. The business with the accident should have been, too, but here they all were, led by June, pricking it over and over with their needles. How stupid she'd been, June thought. Knowing what Cal had done should have made her cautious. Instead what had she done but invite rumination over the incident? She took comfort in the fact that in another month or so the road out to the lake cabin would be passable enough for her to go find the cursed mitten and destroy it once and for all. After that she would feel better. Nothing would be able to touch her family.

In the meantime June never wanted to see another needle in her life. The thought of hosting one more sewing circle made her want to tear her hair out and trample it like a woman lit on fire. The pricks of pins sliding along a hem were tantamount to someone performing voodoo on her nerves. She would glare at the townswomen she knew so well—at Dot's face, bland as a winter tomato, and Alice's double chin and widow's peak—and wonder what she'd done to herself to end up trapped in a stuffy parlor with a bunch of ladies she knew almost everything about and yet cared so little for. She thought back to her student days at Smith and wondered what would have happened if she hadn't married. Would she be an English professor as she'd planned? Perhaps. Or maybe she would have ended up back with her addle-brained mother in Florida as she feared, turning into a younger version of her. No. Cal had saved her. If nothing else, he had made that particular scenario impossible, and for that grace alone June felt she owed him more than she could ever give.

The women in the sewing circle were blissfully unaware of June's glum mind-set—a fact she was grateful for until she realized why. Somehow, without her noticing, they'd fallen into a tizzy of enthusiasm for the maple sap that Mercy was providing them. Even stalwart Dot was converted. "Look, my arthritis is gone," she chirped, fluttering her thick fingers like they were butterflies.

"My ulcers haven't bothered me in a week now," Alice chimed in, and Margie added that she'd dropped five pounds without even trying. Stella said she was waiting until her child arrived before she sampled her portion of sap, but there was rampant speculation about that decision.

"Maybe you want to take it now," Margie gently prodded. "I mean, look at all the good things it's done for us. Maybe it will..." She hesitated, looking for the right words without bringing up the sugar babies buried out at Hazel's. "Make your babe strong."

Stella chewed her bottom lip and appeared to consider what Margie was saying. She had a point. As Stella's due date grew closer and the Androscoggin began to quicken under its thinning patches of ice, she had been thinking more often about those stones planted on Hazel's land. They were touchstones in the realest sense of the word. When a woman had a healthy child, people said it had "come through just fine," and when a woman bore a babe disfigured or dead—a sugar baby—folks just pressed their lips together and eyed the river uneasily.

But what if there was a way around all that? What if Mercy Snow had found an antidote to the years of poison and sorrow that swirled in the currents of the Androscoggin? Politicians and river inspectors had famously tried to clean the waters up, but she suspected that getting the river to run pure was going to require more than a bunch of government men's signatures, or even the reluctant efforts of Cal and the other mill owners. It was going to take the tongues of women and the stories of the children they'd loved and lost. Maybe change in Titan Falls was going to take someone like Mercy Snow.

"Ow!" June had pricked her finger. A rosette of blood unfurled on her fingertip. The ladies watched it bloom.

"Let me get you something for that." Dot stood up.

"No, it's fine." June stuck her finger into her mouth, savoring the metallic tang. "Leave it." She pressed on the wound and held her breath, determined to keep the balance of the world—her world—in check, a dominion of steel pinpoints and paper edges, where the splinter of a log could pierce a man's heart, a mitten of red wool could undo the years of a careful marriage, and a drop of sap could turn blood to honey.

Cal was furious when he found out about the fondness the townswomen had developed for Mercy's jars of sap. "You promised months ago that you were going to see to it that the Snows left," he hissed as he sat himself down to dinner. "The whole mill floor is buzzing with talk about this girl's so-called cures. Now some of the men are even questioning if her brother really caused the crash. I can't have it, June. That family has to go."

"I've been trying." June untied her apron and took her place at the table, set with lace and her wedding china, but really, she knew, she would be heartbroken if she woke tomorrow and found Hannah disappeared. She had a constant tug-of-war going on in her soul. On the one hand, she wanted nothing more than to snatch the girl out of the filth of her life and be the mother she'd clearly never had; on the other, she couldn't bear the idea of the pain such a move would no doubt cause Hannah. "Shall we say grace?"

Tonight she'd made beef en croute and green beans amandine, followed by Swiss rolls, the delicate chocolate sponge cake rolled oh so carefully around brandy-infused cream. Nate came down and silently took his place, and he and Cal stared at it all glumly, their napkins laid on their laps in predetermined defeat, neither one of them looking at the other. The food was too rich and too much, June knew, but these past few days she hadn't been able to help herself. She'd been edgy and nervous and had to direct her energy somewhere.

She hadn't told Cal that Mercy had given her a jar of sap or about the message on it. Instead she'd hidden it deep in the bowels of the pantry, behind expired tins of anchovies and a jar of suspect-looking chutney that Dot had gifted her at Christmas. Even tucked away in the gloom, however, the substance asserted itself, calling out to her with its treacle thickness, its amber warmth, the scrawl of the word "forget" still a faint smudge on the bottom of the glass. Once or twice June took it out of the cupboard, intending to throw it away, but each time her hands hesitated over the bin and she ended up putting the jar back on the shelf, then closing the door to the pantry with uncharacteristic firmness.

She'd begun craving sweets: hard sugar candies in lollipop colors, squares of dark chocolate that coated her tongue in oily cocoa, the fluff of cake stuffed against the lining of her cheek. Normally so careful about her diet, June nibbled and snacked her way through her days, filling her pockets with peppermint rounds for the times when she had to stand in line at the post office or the general store. She wondered if the raw sap in the jar was working on her even though she refused to test it. Maybe, just as it cured those who consumed it, the substance also affected those who refused it. Perhaps, June speculated, Mercy was working a spell on her in reverse. Instead of having her needs met, instead of rows upon rows of the neatest stitches, she was suddenly left with gaping holes in her life.

"'Bless us, O Lord, for these, Thy gifts, which we are about to receive from Thy bounty,'" Cal muttered.

June closed her eyes and let her mind wander to the prospect of Easter lunch. They were halfway through Lent already. Should she serve ham or lamb? Maybe an entire ham would be too much. After all, it was just the three of them, and she should be mindful that many tables in town were going to be light on substance this season. In years past they'd shared the holiday with the mill foreman, Tom Plimpton, and his family, and even once or twice with her entire sewing circle. There had been years when June had had to set up a children's table in the kitchen, when the ham almost wasn't enough, when there'd been so many side dishes brought by the wives that they'd run out of room on the sideboard.

This year June was hatching a secret plan. She was going to prepare an Easter basket for Hannah, trimming it with fake grass, marshmallow chicks, and candy eggs wrapped in pastel foil. Nate was far too old for such fancies, a fact that pained June. She longed to hear the shrieking of him and Suzie as they tore through the backyard with their baskets slung over their skinny arms, poking in the bushes for hidden treasures. Life flowed along as fast as any river, it turned out, and though June had no idea where it was taking her, she was nonetheless determined not to sink in it, not to be swallowed whole by the currents of time. Hannah could help her turn back the clock and start over again, and June would do better this time around.

Cal sawed at his beef. "The Loomer account is four months past due, but what am I supposed to do? Go over there myself and shake the change out of their empty pockets? They're in the same boat as us. Broke as thieves. And the Blakes have started buying from an outfit overseas with fewer restrictions."

He sopped up his sauce with his bread. "How am I supposed to compete?"

June bit her lip. Since the holidays Cal had been pulling longer hours than ever before, trying to cope with the precipitous slide of the mill. New lines stood out around his eyes, and his face looked thinner. But even though he was working late, June was confident he was right where he said he was—hunched over his desk in his office and not in the arms of that waitress in Berlin.

She knew it had been wrong to seek her out, especially with Hannah of all people in tow, but she'd wanted to assure herself that the woman was really no one special, that she was someone whom Cal really could snip out of his life as easily as a stray thread hanging off a shirt cuff. Face-to-face with her, June had been totally satisfied. The downcast expression the waitress had borne was proof enough of recent heartbreak, and June had detected something more in the woman's gaze as well—a flash of recognition. Maybe she'd seen June's photograph in Cal's wallet or recognized her from an article in the local paper about June's charity work, but it didn't bother June, this tacit acknowledgment. If anything it made the groundwork clearer.

June was trying. She really was, but everything still felt wrong between her and Cal. Part of it, she knew, was his confession about his responsibility for the accident. He'd almost killed their son, not to mention many of the other town's children, and he *had* killed Suzie, and June could only watch as the guilt ate him alive from the inside out. At night he tossed and turned, muttering and sweating, and he'd taken to driving at a stately speed, rounding corners with his knuckles gripping the steering wheel. Last week he'd changed the sedan's tires, and June had to confess she'd been glad. If she could have gotten rid of the whole car, she would have.

If it weren't for the accident, she wondered, where would they be in their marriage? Nate would be leaving for Dartmouth in the fall, and June was having trouble imagining just her and Cal sitting across the table from each other. Although it galled her to admit it, maybe waitresses in Berlin weren't the problem. Maybe the two of them were. She regretted having only one child, not that it had been her fault. *It's just bad luck*, Cal had always insisted each time she lost a baby. *The very worst*, she'd agree, tearfully nodding, but inside she always secretly wondered if she weren't being punished for escaping the childhood she'd so hated, for trying to trick fate into somehow granting her a better deal.

June spooned a portion of beans onto her dish and reached for the gravy boat, but when she tipped it, she got an uneven drizzle of glaze across her plate and a spot of sauce on her blouse cuff. She swore under her breath and dabbed at the stain with the corner of her napkin, but then she looked closer and saw that the dish was chipped, right on its spout. For a moment she fought a wave of rage. She could order a new one, but that wasn't the point. Some things couldn't be replaced. Some things *shouldn't* be.

Cal had filled his wineglass a little too full. The bottle sat close to his left elbow. Nate was slouching in his chair, his head bent over his meal, but this had been his manner ever since the accident. He slinked through his days with the silent concentration of a feral cat, avoiding his mother's eyes and most especially her conversation.

June turned to him now. "How's Hazel? Are you getting on all right with her sheep?"

Nate provided a noncommittal shrug.

"How's poor Fergus? Is he getting any better? Any memory yet of..." June trailed off awkwardly. "Well. Is he improving?"

Another shrug.

Cal poured himself more wine. "Abel said he found what looks like a camp spot in the woods out near her place. Rumor has it one of her rams went missing. You know about that?"

This time Nate didn't even twitch.

Cal's face grew dangerously red. He turned back to June. "You know where I'm going with this, June. Those lowlifes are causing all kinds of trouble. Do I need to handle this?"

Oh, I think you've done enough, June thought sourly. She twisted her napkin in her lap. "What if Abel cites them for illegal peddling? Surely that sap that Mercy is handing out must violate just about every health code on the books."

"It's not peddling if it's a gift." Nate was suddenly sitting up straight in his chair, his eyes alert. "She's not selling the maple sap. She's just giving it away. Don't you see? She's trying to do something good."

Cal ignored him. "I still say the key is Zeke. Flush him out and his sisters will follow."

"Jesus, Dad." Nate was on his feet, his food untouched on his dish. "They're not rodents."

Cal's eyes flashed. "Are you sure about that? Son, for the better part of a century, our family has been entrusted with keeping the balance of this town. There wouldn't even *be* a Titan Falls if it weren't for the foresight of the McAllisters setting down roots here and building from the ground up. One day the mill and all its responsibilities are going to fall to you, and I'd like to hear you say then what you think about a bunch of freeloading no-goods feeding off your honest day's work." The last bit of his message was shouted up the stairs after Nate's rapidly disappearing back. "And you." He turned to June. "I don't think you've been trying too hard at all to get rid of the Snows. I heard you spent an afternoon parading that little one around Berlin."

June paled and began to gather the plates together. "Why, whoever told you that?"

Cal leaned forward and caught her narrow wrist in his hand. "You know how small these parts are. I'm surprised at you." He squeezed, compressing her tendons, her veins. "Suzie's gone, June. Another girl can't take her place."

The way another woman almost took mine? she thought. The chip in the gravy boat caught her eye again, and she frowned. One wrong move and the whole thing would fall to pieces right in front of her. She lifted her gaze to Cal. "And whose fault is that?"

"What do you mean?"

If she'd had the mitten then and there, June swore she would have done it—fetched it from its hiding place and slapped him right across the face with it, demanding to know just what he saw in a floozy waitress in Berlin.

June freed her arm from Cal's fingers. "Nothing." The urge for truth was fickle, and June had lived in Titan Falls for far too long. She'd been trained by the rhythms of the river to know that there was a price for every gift bestowed by nature. Things required careful management. A full river could sweep over its banks, destroying everything in its path.

On her way to the sink, June tossed the gravy dish into the trash.

Chapter Fourteen

"Do you think there's much more in there?" Nate was looking at the three taps he and Mercy had driven into the biggest sugar maple. Mercy removed the buckets and poured the accumulated sap into one of them.

"Doesn't matter. I have what I need. We can take the taps out now." As the days had been heating up, the sap had been running faster. The bucket was half full. Soon sugaring season would be over. It was time for Mercy to cook some of the sap for Fergus. Any leftovers she'd somehow try to get to Zeke. Her brother needed some sweetness in his life, a reminder that not everything in the world carried with it the cold threat of metal on metal.

"What did you put in that stuff anyway?" Nate peered into the bucket. "The whole town's talking about it. My dad's freaking out. He's really pissed."

"Nothing that wasn't already there." That was the beauty of it. The townspeople were simply getting a taste of what had been around them all along.

Nate unwound the brown-and-yellow scarf twisted around his neck. It had been made from the wool of Hazel's sheep, the earthy colors steeped out of plants gathered from this very valley. He had never thought about that process before, but ever since he'd been working with Hazel, he'd been seeing all kinds of things in a new light.

The lambs had finally come, for one thing. Nate had never witnessed anything like it. He'd arrived last Saturday to find twelve new creatures gamboling about on rubber-band legs and an exhausted Hazel trying to keep up with them all. "When did it happen?" he asked, spinning around and taking in the scene.

"Started on Tuesday. Most of them came by Friday. But we've still got one to go." Hazel patted a ewe with a red spot near her tail. She'd been marked to indicate that she was bearing twins. "I'm worried about this one. Aggie said something might be off with the pair, but we'll have to see. If she doesn't go into labor soon, I'll have to call out Dr. Hemmings."

But Hazel needn't have worried. That afternoon, as Nate laid down fresh bedding in the birthing pens, the ewe began to paw the ground and groan—a low, persistent sound, almost human.

"Oh, Lord, here we go." Hazel hurried around the barn, collecting her birthing kit. Nate spied gloves, surgical scissors, iodine, and a thick, soft rope. "What's the rope for?"

"Sometimes you have to shift a lamb if it's coming out wrong, but it's hard to keep a grip on the legs. You don't want to lose them."

Nate winced. "Doesn't that hurt the ewe?"

Hazel regarded him. "You really are your daddy's boy, aren't you? All you've ever known is the belly of that mill. Trust me, when a lamb is coming, the worst thing you can do is hesitate. Once a birth is set in motion, your job is to keep that momentum going. You can't undo nature once it gets rolling, son."

Nate thought about that. In the mill there was always a prevailing threat that things could come to a grinding halt at any moment. The men punched their cards every evening as they left the building for Lucky's Tavern, their time briefly their own again, but they always jumped at the chance for overtime, and they grew edgy that if they screwed up badly enough, they wouldn't get any more hours ever again.

But you couldn't control time by stamping holes in a card, Nate was beginning to suspect, and you couldn't stack it up either, like so many reams of paper waiting to be trucked. You could only grab it by the slippery leg and yank.

The last pair of lambs came quicker than even Hazel had been expecting. The first one birthed easily, a limp sack of a creature with impossibly tiny hooves. It was a good size, Hazel said, for a twin. Nate watched, fascinated, as she rubbed the side of the lamb gently with some straw and cleaned its broken umbilical cord with a solution of iodine and alcohol. Stirred to life, the lamb began wriggling.

"Don't worry about it now," Hazel barked as she slid the creature up to let the ewe lick it off. "We've got problems here." She rubbed her hand with lubricant and inserted it again into the ewe. "The legs are back."

Nate held the bleating ewe on its side as Hazel, elbow-deep, ran her hands over the unborn lamb, feeling and trying to position it. Eventually her fist emerged holding the tiny branch of a leg. Hazel slid the noose of the rope up past the first joints and tightened the loop. "Come here," she ordered. "You do the next one. Rub your hands with that." She indicated the lubricant. "And be gentle."

The inside of the ewe was shockingly warm. Nate gasped as his hand was swallowed into its uterus, and he exhaled again when he felt the slick mass of the lamb. He fumbled over what he guessed was the bulb of the head and then encountered the delicate stick of the other leg. As Hazel instructed him, he eased it forward out of the ewe, his heart pounding.

Hazel was pleased. "Good. Now let's see what we're dealing with here." She attached another loop of rope to the lamb's second leg and pulled both cords as the ewe contracted. Just as before, the lamb slipped out in a floppy mass. Just like its mother, it had a black dot on its coat down by the tail, Nate saw. "It's so small," he said, and he was right. Compared to its sibling, this lamb was minuscule, almost as if it were a different breed entirely. Hazel rubbed its flank and cleared its nasal passages, but the lamb seemed reluctant to breathe. She patted it a little harder, and finally the lamb took a shuddering breath. Hazel brought it up to its mother to let the ewe lick at it, but the animal refused. Hazel's face darkened.

"What's the matter?" Nate asked.

"This doesn't bode well." The ewe, relieved to be finished with the business of birthing, gave a lurch and heaved herself to her feet, ambling a few steps away. The first lamb wobbled after her. The second one remained where it was in the straw. "That's no good at all."

Nate was surprised to find himself panicked. He gazed down at the helpless lamb, fighting an urge to scoop it up. "Doesn't the mother want it?" He swallowed hard against the lump in his throat.

Hazel went to fetch a tube of colostrum for the lamb. She seemed remarkably calm to Nate. "Sometimes it happens this way. I'll put it with another one of the ewes and hope for the best."

"You can do that?"

Hazel's eyes were steady on Nate. "I'm raising a flock, not a hundred individual animals. They're all part of the same family. What one doesn't want, another will take. Didn't anyone ever teach you that?"

Nate blushed. "No."

Hazel pressed her lips together and said nothing, but it was clear what her opinion of that was. Nate watched as she carried the tiny spotted lamb over to one of the pens where a ewe was contentedly nursing a single lamb. "I think she'll do nicely," Hazel said, and dropped the orphan in. Immediately the ewe began to nuzzle the new lamb and lick it. Hazel smacked her hands together, pleased. "See?"

As Nate stood under the maples with Mercy a week later, he still wasn't sure what to think about everything he had seen that afternoon. It was only seven days on from the lambing, but the pair had bonded just like a natural mother and her offspring. Only Nate and Hazel knew the truth, and this bothered him. He had a sudden urge to share what he knew. He realized he was taking a risk, but he couldn't help it. He turned to Mercy. "The lambs are here. Do you want to see them?"

Mercy cocked her head. "And have Hazel shoot me with a double-gauge? No thanks."

Nate smiled. "She went into town for the afternoon. I'm keeping an eye on Fergus. Hazel won't be back for hours."

Mercy hesitated, the bucket of sap hanging heavy in her hand. She still felt guilty about the ram that Zeke had taken for them, but she missed Hazel with an ache so hard it sometimes made her teeth hurt. She knew she shouldn't go anywhere near the sheep, but the temptation was too great. Also, if she wanted to move things along between her and Nate like she'd planned, she had better get a move on it. She put the bucket down. "Let's go."

In the barn Nate led Mercy to the tiny lamb, telling her the story of how he'd helped it be born. "It's funny. I kind of feel like it's mine in a weird way. Did you ever help birth anything?"

Mercy shook her head. "I'm only there for the other end of things. When we shoot a deer, for instance, or trap rabbit. I don't think it's the same."

Nate didn't reply. Unlike most of the boys in town, he hadn't grown up hunting, and he'd never been curious about it. But there was something he wanted to ask Mercy. Gently he slid his elbow closer to hers on the railing of the lambing pen, relieved that she didn't pull away. When she stood still and really stared hard at something, he'd noticed, her features softened and she became very pretty. Each time that happened, his pulse always sped up a little. "Speaking of hunting and all that..." He trailed off, trying to pick his words carefully, afraid he would send her temper flaring and scare her away. "Well, what was the deal with Hazel's ram? Did you or your brother take it?"

She flinched. For a moment he thought she might swing at him, but she took a deep breath and looked him straight in the eye instead. "A coyote or a wolf or something got it first. I know it wasn't right, but it was too late for it anyway." She didn't bother to point out that hunger made its own rules. Nate wasn't the kind of boy who would understand that.

"So Zeke's still around?"

Mercy shrugged. She wasn't dumb enough to give up information like that to Nate McAllister. He'd helped her in the sugar bush, but she still wasn't sure how much she could trust him. It didn't matter, though, just as long as he fell for her. That was her plan—to conquer June's son, the person June loved best, and then see what she had to say about things. Only problem was, Mercy was surprised to find out how much she really liked Nate. She inched her arm away from his, immediately missing the pressure that had been building between them. "I better go."

"Wait." Nate grabbed her by the shoulder. Mercy tensed, the memory of what had happened to her in the woods filling her with panic, but Nate's eyes were kind. He relaxed his grip but didn't take his hand off her shoulder, and Mercy found that she didn't want him to. "Are you in contact with him? You can tell me. I promise I won't say anything."

Mercy shook her head. "Sometimes I think I see a flash of him in the trees, but he's never really there. Or maybe he always is. I don't know. I feel him around me all the time but never spot him." Except for the once, when they'd spoken down by the river and Zeke told her that Cal McAllister might very well be a murderer.

"That sounds familiar. Sometimes I think my father's a kind of ghost, too. He's always working." Nate had never thought of it before, but what did he really know about the man he came from? Mostly that he ran the mill with an iron fist and that one day he expected Nate to do the same. And Nate always thought he would. Here in the barn with Mercy, however, feeling her warm skin underneath his nervous fingers—so like Suzie's—Nate was starting to wonder if maybe he'd been a kind of ghost, too, for most of his life. He didn't want to be one anymore. Without saying anything else, he leaned forward and kissed Mercy, gentle at first and then with more passion, letting the heady mixture of the scent of fresh straw and the rush of maple sap from Mercy's tongue and the tingle of cold spring air mix inside him until he thought he might burst. *I'm alive*, he thought as he drew Mercy closer, *and I want to stay this way.*

As Mercy relaxed into Nate's embrace, the little orphan sheep danced into the corner of her vision. Her eyes focused on the fleck of black down near its tail, and it gave her hope. *This is all a game*, she reminded herself as she wrapped her arms around Nate and returned the kiss, but for a moment it was nice to believe that everything in the world, even the most flawed creature in a flock, found a home for itself eventually.

Hazel rarely came into Titan Falls if she could help it. Even before Rory's birth and his unexpected death, she had her reasons for keeping herself separate, just on the edge of things. It had never been Hazel's intention to weave the strands of her own life into the warp of the community—or at least not to let anyone know that's what she was doing. Before Rory passed, she used to attend church, switch out her week's library books, and grab an occasional bite at the diner, but after Rory's death, and now with all the distractions of her sheep and the burden of caring for Fergus, Hazel could honestly say that she craved town company about as much as a bucket of ice come the middle of winter.

Still, she couldn't totally avoid society if she wanted to keep her small amount of business humming. At the beginning of each wool season, just as she was ready to start combing and spinning her fleeces into different weights and textures of yarn, she reluctantly made her single annual appearance in June McAllister's sewing circle, and this year she couldn't afford to skip it.

Hazel thought of the appointment purely as a fact-gathering mission. She had no idea what the ladies termed the visit behind her back—and didn't care to know either. She tended to keep the hour in June's parlor businesslike, inquiring about upcoming projects the ladies thought they might be undertaking and advising what weight wool they might want to use, learning which colors they fancied and how much and how soon they could pay. It was rarely an extravagant sum. Hazel made most of her money selling surplus sheep—the ewes who were too old to breed anymore, the male lambs—and sometimes, if she really needed money, one of her better specimens.

This year she had seven male lambs she could part with,

including the bitty one with the smudge at his tail, not that he would fetch much. It hurt Hazel a little to think of auctioning him. For a split second, she was tempted not to, remembering that first lamb Fergus had ever brought her—it had been an orphan, too—but she gave herself a shake and put a quick stop to silly thoughts. Necessity called, especially with Fergus in his current state. She didn't know if they'd ever see another paycheck out of him, and his pension was smaller than she'd been counting on.

The tow-truck company had tried to insinuate that the reduction in his pension was due to the accident, but Hazel had given them a solid piece of her mind. "First of all, you're stacking apples up against oranges. Fergus wasn't even *in* one of your vehicles. And you know as well as I do that he was in no way responsible. Why, I bet if he hadn't been driving, everyone on that bus with him would have been killed instead of just the Flyte girl, and if he was wholly himself, *he'd* be telling you this instead of *me*." Of course, if Fergus were himself, Hazel wouldn't have been having the conversation in the first place.

She patted the loose ends of her frizzy hair back into the knot she wore at the nape of her neck and took a deep breath. June McAllister's front porch was not the place for entertaining self-doubts. Behind the door she could hear the buzz of the town ladies as they waited, their gossip punctuated by the clatter of teacups and then, cutting through the convivial hum, the authoritative ring of June's voice, encouraging them to take their customary seats.

"Hazel! Welcome!" June threw the door open without warning, catching her off guard and putting her in an even worse mood. "We're all already gathered and waiting. Please, come in."

Every time Hazel stepped into June's home, it occurred to her that the woman really did live a paper life. Everything that Hazel could see was swept clean and was as squared as a fresh sheet of parchment. All the rooms were decorated with antique patterns of wallpaper—intricate swirls and paisleys in clashing colors that made Hazel's head ache. Meekly she followed June to the parlor.

The ladies stopped their chatter when she entered. Alice Lincoln half rose, but Dot shot her arm out and stopped her. "She's not royalty, you damn fool," Dot hissed, and Alice plopped back down on her ample bottom.

Hazel was surprised to find Dena Flyte hunched in the far corner of the parlor, her chair a little out of kilter with the rest of the other women's, her eyes hooded so that Hazel couldn't easily read her expression. Certainly she was much thinner than the last time Hazel had seen her, but grief could swallow the flesh right off you. Hazel knew that from experience. After Rory she'd dropped a dress size and never gotten it back. Though Fergus had always sworn he never minded, Hazel rather suspected that he sometimes missed the old curve of her hips, the bounty of better days.

Hazel took her seat in front of the semicircle, a little uncomfortable as always with being so exposed, but that was the damn problem convening with a bunch of women. They left you no choice but to either join them like a mindless lemming or stick out like an infected thumb. Hazel smoothed her skirt and sniffed. At least a thumb had its uses.

"Well," she began, "this year I had a real bumper crop of fleeces, so I imagine—"

"Hazel," June cut in, "before you get started, please allow me to speak on behalf of us all when I say that we sincerely hope Fergus is coming around."

Hazel blushed, half in anger and half in embarrassment. "He's fine."

"And we also want to say how brave you've been all this time, taking care of him out there on your own." The women murmured and bobbed their heads. Hazel smashed her lips together to keep herself from saying anything she'd later regret. June made it sound like she was some kind of martyr, when what else was she supposed to do with little money and a broken husband? Hazel eyed the ladies. Any one of them would have done the same. Heck, many of them had.

She put up a hand. "Thank you. Now let's talk yarn."

The next half hour passed in a blessed blur. Stella was in a dither about baby blankets and booties and caps. She was already a week late and so put out she could almost not form a sentence whole, either backward or forward. Alice thought she might like to crochet some table runners this summer, and Dot had her heart set on a new coverlet for her bed. "Something in a nice, relaxing purple," she instructed, and Hazel immediately pictured the delicate hanging bloom of a foxglove. She nodded and made a mental note that come July she should gather an extra armload of the flowers.

Tea was drunk and pineapple upside-down cake consumed on June's basketweave china. Per usual, Hazel refused all offers of refreshment. For one thing, she was there to conduct business, not eat like a show horse, but the real reason was that it gave her pleasure to know she wasn't beholden by even a single crumb to the likes of June McAllister. "Don't be contrary," Fergus had once said when she explained this reasoning to him. "The woman's just being polite."

Hazel had snorted. "Do you really believe that? June McAllister counts the flies that buzz in and out of her life, mark my words. She doesn't do anything without a reason." Neither did the McAllister men, Hazel more than suspected, though she couldn't solidly prove her misgivings. But she knew she wasn't alone in that suspicion. The town had whispered for years about

Pruitt being on the low-down and dirty payroll of Cal McAllister, though for what, no one really knew.

As Hazel rose to leave, gathering up her gloves and her good handbag, it occurred to her that of all the women, only Dena hadn't mentioned what she would be making come the warmer months. She hadn't said anything at all, as a matter of fact. Well, that was understandable. She would put a stone in the sugar bush for Suzie, Hazel decided, even though she wasn't technically a child. Hazel nodded a final time at the ladies, busy now with second servings of cake and more cups of tea, and let herself out.

"Hazel, wait!" She was halfway down the porch steps. She turned in confusion, expecting June but finding Dena instead.

Hazel clomped back up the steps. "Don't worry. I haven't put a stone out for Suzie, but if you'd like, I will."

Dena looked surprised. "I would. Thank you." Hazel wasn't sure if she should apologize for the whole mess with the bus or commiserate. It was possible that Dena blamed Fergus for what happened or, at the very least, begrudged Hazel her luck in still having him with her. Hazel knew that if she were in Dena's place, *she* would have.

She put a sympathetic hand on Dena's forearm. "Maybe this year isn't the year to set out on any new projects. I understand." A period of grief was never the right time to start on a fresh endeavor, Hazel knew, for the heart couldn't look both forward and back. Once unraveled, a length of thread took time to wind back up again.

"I know." Dena wrapped her arms around herself. She was only in a light sweater, and although spring had brightened up the air, it was still chilly enough. "I just wanted to thank you."

Hazel was straddling two steps. At Dena's declaration she wobbled, then regained her footing. Wrath she would understand, but a show of gratitude unbalanced her. She frowned. "Whatever for? I haven't put the stone out yet."

"For letting Mercy tap your maples. Everyone is talking about how the sap's working wonders on them. Fred's a new man." She paused, her cheeks reddening. "I hope you don't mind."

Hazel could feel the blood draining from her face. She clutched the porch railing.

Dena hesitated, her expression uncertain all of a sudden. "Didn't you know?"

"Did Mercy tap the trees in my sugar bush?" Hazel's voice sounded as if it were coming from some other woman's body.

Dena stared at her feet again.

How dare the girl? Hazel thought. It was bad enough living with whatever mumbo jumbo she might have bragged that she worked on Fergus, but it was utterly unbearable to think that she'd brought the sugar bush back to life when Hazel had deliberately kept it fallow. She gripped the wooden railing harder, ignoring the splinters digging into the fine leather of her one nice pair of gloves.

"Didn't anyone tell you?" Dena put a hand over her mouth. "But I guess how would they, right? You don't come into town all that often. Still, I thought you might have got some."

"No."

"Well. Everyone in town got a little. And it's done great things, Hazel. You should be proud."

"Hazel, you're still here." June's front door opened, and she appeared on the threshold like an avenging household angel. Her shrewd eyes flitted from Hazel to Dena and back again. "Dena," she said carefully, "I think Hazel's probably had her fill of us now. Isn't that right?"

Dena opened her mouth to reply, but nothing came out, and

wasn't that perfect? Hazel thought as she stumped down the rest of the porch steps to her car. There really was nothing left to say on the matter, she supposed, for when it came to getting her fill, June McAllister was already the hands-down local expert.

Once home, Hazel flew into her kitchen with the ire of a bull. She ignored Fergus, who was in the parlor, stationed contentedly at his spot by the window. She set her handbag down on the table and looked around, and then she began her search. She opened the flour drawer, but it was empty. The cupboard under the sink was dark as always, and there was nothing in the back of the fridge but the usual half-empty containers of mustard and pickles, a quart of milk, the butter dish, and leftover scraps from last night's dinner.

Then her eye fell on the closet where she kept her cleaning supplies. Inside, there was the mop and broom, stalwart as a pair of soldiers, a stack of stained buckets she sometimes used for dyeing, a jumble of cans of cleanser, bottles of window cleaner, and finally, as she suspected there would be, a trio of glass jars tucked in the darkest corner. Nate no doubt had snuck in and put them there, waiting until he could slip the contents to Fergus. Hazel should have known he'd fall under the spell of that Snow girl. She should have seen that coming two days down the road.

She pulled the vessels out and inspected the contents. The color was richer than anything she'd ever managed to get from the sap the few times she'd tapped the trees—an amber so full it looked unearthly. Hazel scowled something furious and uncapped one of the containers, taking a cautious whiff. The stuff smelled slightly different, too, like juniper, and bay, and something else a little suspect that Hazel couldn't put her finger on. Camphor, possibly. Checking over her shoulder to make sure she was still alone, she stabbed her forefinger into the mixture and waited for a second. She half expected her flesh to burst into boils then and there, but nothing happened, and so, mustering up the same enthusiasm she would use for a spoonful of cod-liver oil, she took a taste.

It was sweet, like maple syrup always was, but there was a spicy kick she wasn't expecting. It wasn't unpleasant. In fact, it immediately made her greedy for more. She scooped up another drip with her finger and swallowed again, this time tasting the bittersweet tang of cinnamon and the comforting zest of nutmeg and the earthy undertone of clove. She'd just closed her eyes to concentrate on that flavor when the most startling thing happened: Rory's face appeared to her as clear as a bell, sharper than any of the photographs she possessed of him, as real as he'd been in life. She gasped and opened her eyes, but everything about Rory was with her, the familiar weight of him against her chest as an infant, the loose web his fingers had made around hers as he lay dying in the hospital, the particular flaxen color of his hair. How had she forgotten those things? And how long had she been missing them? She flew to the silverware drawer and fetched a spoon.

"Fergus!" she cried, scooping up a napkin. "Fergus! I have a treat for you. I have something I want you to try." If Mercy Snow could somehow manage to give her back her husband and son, Hazel figured, then maybe, just maybe, she could see to it in her soul to cancel out the price of a single gutless ram.

Chapter Fifteen

For a child who knew where to look, the world was chockfull of treasure. The smooth pebbles, stray pennies, and empty folds of foil gum wrappers that Hannah collected from ditches and plucked off curbsides weren't worth a king's ransom by any stretch of the imagination, but she loved her gewgaws nonetheless—maybe even all the more because no one else did.

Like a crow feathering its nest with bits of shine, she tucked all her finds on the shelf in the smokehouse, adding to her trove. There was the jar she'd filled with quartz and mica and another that contained pennies and coins. There were her books of fairy tales and myths stacked so carefully, their covers laminated in the clear plastic wrappers of libraries, their pages worn to the luxurious texture of kid. She wasn't sure what she would ever do if she lost those. Around her neck she still wore the button on a string, which June had told her was really called a cuff link and which men apparently wore to hold together their shirtsleeves.

Lately instead of Hannah being the one to go out and find treasure, it had been coming to her. Over the past few weeks, she'd stumbled upon a variety of surprising objects tailored to catch her eye. There was a poppet sewn from skinned hide and prettied with smudges of what looked like berry juice for eyes and a mouth. There was a bangle twisted out of birch bark and a crown made from a spray of brown-and-white-spotted feathers. Each time Hannah received another gift, she ran like a wild thing through the woods and down the ravine, calling her brother's name, until she reached the bottom, where the deep bend of the river glittered and swirled. There his trail always ended, and she met with silence.

Hannah would crouch by the water and keen after Zeke. Nothing, not even curiosity, could compel her to tiptoe any closer, for just like Mercy, Hannah had a great fear of anything larger than a puddle. She would stand on the bank, breathing hard, and listen to the wind, the birds, and the sound of water wearing down rock, and always, just under all the usual chatter of the woods, there was another sound, too, a lower register of fury that only she could hear, and this voice knew her by name.

Hannah had seen Mercy fling Gert's ashes somewhere else in the hollow, but she couldn't remember the exact spot. She wanted to, though, for although Gert was returned once again to the earth, she wasn't at peace. Far from it.

It was Gert, Hannah was sure, who was causing all the troubles that she and Mercy had been having lately. The more minor things were easy to shrug off. Mercy cut her finger on the lid of a creamed-corn can, and it wouldn't heal, no matter what she did. Squirrels or mice had chewed through the hose on the propane tank, and they were out of duct tape to fix it. The sole on Hannah's left boot was coming loose, letting in the wet and snow, but she knew better than to ask for a new pair.

Harder to ignore were the threats June McAllister had once again started sending their way. Those were more serious than a smashed plate or the windows in the RV sticking. Mercy said

June was mad about all the maple sap she'd given away to everyone in town.

"You'd think folks would be a bit more touched with gratitude," she grumbled. "They should be standing up to the likes of June McAllister. Instead what's that snake of a woman doing but plotting our downfall? I swear she's more persistent than the devil."

Hannah chewed her lip and said nothing. In the smokehouse she'd also hidden the spoils of her day with June in Berlin: the Cinderella watch, the blue comb, and the barrettes. Unlike Hannah's other trinkets, these weren't in plain sight. She'd stuffed them in the rusted old coffee can and tossed it in a shadowed corner under the three iron hooks, where even Mercy wouldn't be tempted to snoop.

Hannah had lost count of the number of times the sheriff had been out to see them. He'd come to try to take possession of Gert's ashes. He'd come to give them a citation for fire danger because of their leaky propane tank. Mercy had ripped that up in front of him, and he'd sighed and just written her a new one. He'd come to check Mercy's license, and to inspect for flood risk, and, most ridiculously of all, because he said he'd been receiving complaints about noise.

It had gotten so bad that Hannah even considered going back to school, but before she could, a new visitor arrived. This one was a lady. She said she was from state social services, and she was most interested in speaking to Hannah, who had just hiked up from the bottom of the ravine and was about to burst into the clearing when she heard Mercy murmuring in an unusually subdued manner. Hannah had crept as close as she dared to the open trailer door and hidden herself behind a thick tree trunk.

"I understand your confusion," Mercy was saying, "but there's no children here. No, ma'am."

Hannah couldn't hear what the lady said back to her sister, but she didn't like the frosty tone of her voice.

Mercy spoke a little louder, her clear vowels floating out into the thick of the forest. "I don't know why there's a girl enrolled in school by the name of Snow. It's a coincidence, I'll grant you that."

The woman's voice bubbled up again, cold and very sure of itself. Hannah closed her eyes and leaned her forehead against the tree trunk. She could guess what the woman was telling her sister.

When she opened her eyes, everything had gone quiet and she saw that the woman was retreating back up the little pathway to Devil's Slide Road, where she must have left her car. Hannah waited an extra four heartbeats before she crept out from behind her tree and made her way to the camper.

Mercy wheeled on her with fury. "Where the holy hell have you been?" She put up the palm of her hand to stop Hannah before she could even answer. "Never you mind. It's lucky your little behind wasn't anywhere nearby. We've had an unpleasant visitor, and she shared a very interesting story." Hannah worked her toe on the filthy carpet of the camper while Mercy eyeballed her. Her voice gentled. "Why don't you tell me?"

Hannah broke down then and confessed everything—how school had not been the paradise she'd been imagining and how she'd been spending her days secreted in the library in town, or tucked up cozy in the wreck of a worker's cabin she'd discovered behind the mill, or even, sometimes, right here in their own woods, climbing up and down the steep hillsides like a little goat until she grew too tired for words and snuck into the smokehouse for a nap on the rusty cot, being careful not to squeak the springs and give herself away.

Mercy sighed with relief that it wasn't June who'd made good on her threat to call social services after all. "No wonder you're always so filthy!" Mercy exclaimed, drawing Hannah close to her and wrapping her thin arms around Hannah's even skinnier shoulders. Tangled up together, the two of them were all sinew and bone, but the living kind, with the blood still running something fierce inside.

"You should have told me," Mercy scolded, letting Hannah out of her embrace. "I wouldn't have been mad, honest. But listen, Hannah, this isn't over yet by a long shot. You need to be careful from now on. You need to make sure no one catches you, least of all that McAllister woman."

Hannah's heart thumped like a gong in her tiny chest, sending bad vibrations ringing all over her body. She blushed and hung her head, trying to conceal the shaking that had started up in her hands. "Okay."

Mercy shooed her from the camper into the last of the hard season's daylight. "Go on and fetch me some kindling. We're going to have to make a campfire tonight. We're out of propane again."

Hannah scampered away, grateful to be set free but troubled by what she hadn't told Mercy—specifically about her afternoon with June in Berlin and about what June had said to her when they parted, all that nonsense about canopy beds and cookies. Hannah crept into the smokehouse, found the coffee can, and gazed on the gifts June had bought for her. The watch no longer seemed so magical. Hannah saw that the white plastic wristband was grimy and already laced with tiny cracks, and the metal on the clasp wasn't hefty silver, just some cheap shiny coating that was flaking off. Cinderella's gloved arms were twisted awkwardly into inhuman angles. She looked like an octopus.

Sniffling, she took the items outside and tossed everything into the wilds of the trees. She couldn't undo the afternoon she'd spent with June, but she could throw it far away and leave it there cold. She took the can, a vessel she had no use for anymore, inside again and chucked it back under the hooks, which hung in the gloom and pointed at it, like teeth in the mouth of an all-seeing wolf.

More than anything Hannah missed the library. She'd read all her books so many times she knew half the words by heart, but it wasn't safe to go into town now, Mercy warned her time and time again.

"What if someone reports you? What if June gets her hands on you and this time she really does send social services out here?" Mercy crouched down to peer into Hannah's eyes. "They might try to take you away, do you understand? They might say I'm not a fit guardian." And when Hannah nodded mutely, Mercy sighed and ruffled her younger sister's hair. "You're a Snow, little monkey. We can't help that, but we *can* help keep it that way."

Hannah longed for the life in town. Even though she knew she couldn't trust June, she still thrilled to remember her visit to the soda fountain in Berlin, where the nice blond waitress had scurried around, bringing them food. Stuck in the ravine all day, Hannah grew more skittish, jumping when she heard a chickadee break into song or the crack of an icicle thawing in the noon sun.

It was almost as if she had two sets of eyes—one for the ordinary world of laundry being hung out to dry and dishes stacked in the sink and another pair that saw wonders that most other folks overlooked: a bird's nest wedged in the fork of a tree and lined with what looked like the papery wings of moths, a fox curled up in the snow with a bushy-tailed squirrel, an ice patch frozen on the river in the shape of a heart. They were messages from Gert, Hannah knew. *Pay attention*, they said. *I'm trying to talk to you.*

Today there was a set of very faint indentations in the mud—so light that Hannah had trouble seeing them. She wondered if they were even real. They wound from Gert's old gravesite down through the trees and headed first toward the river, then away from it, and then back down again, growing softer all the while. Hannah was alone. Mercy had refused to say where she was going. "Never you mind," she'd snapped when Hannah had asked, but it must have been somewhere good, because her cheeks had been all lit up like a Christmas tree and she'd twisted her hair into a pretty knot at the back of her neck and smudged some gloss on her lips from an old pot of color. After she left, Hannah had taken the rouge and put some on her own face and mouth, then inspected the results in a cracked hand mirror. It was no use. She still looked like what she was: a child who was knobby to a fault and skinny everywhere else.

In the empty bowl of the ravine, it was easy to feel as if the world had gone on ahead without her. As she followed the mysterious marks, she thought about Zeke disappearing the night after the accident and wondered what would happen if she vanished like that, too. Would Mercy know how to read the signs she left behind?

She paced back to the clearing, having lost the trail of prints and her interest in them. Maybe she'd just been seeing things. The geography of the Snow land was simple to a fault—up or down, in the trees or out of them, above the river or straight into it. It was the kind of landscape that could almost be a hundred better places but never quite was.

Inside the smokehouse Hannah was met with the usual gloom and meaty odor, but straightaway she felt that something was different. She looked around, the hairs on her arms prickling. There was the rusty cot, angled just the same, and there were the three hooks, hanging like barbarous tongues, but the coffee can underneath them was gone. Shivering, Hannah stepped farther into the shadows and saw that someone had moved it over to the shelf with all her other riches. Her heart skipped a beat as she considered the implications of this. Had it been Mercy? If so, Hannah was glad she'd thrown away her loot, otherwise she'd be in for a whipping and a question-and-answer session when her sister got back.

But what if Zeke had left her another present? Maybe the footprints had been realer than Hannah had thought. She raced forward to peek inside the can and was both disappointed and relieved to find nothing there. She frowned and put it back on the shelf.

Standing under the maple trees in the sugar bush after a late-April morning's work with the sheep, Nate couldn't understand how a spot so filled with sadness could make him feel so alive, but he was guessing it was all to do with Mercy. He couldn't stop thinking about her. The way her hands felt cupped inside his, the way her lips pressed against his own mouth until he felt as though the two of them were one person.

Which was crazy, really, because she was nothing like him. In fact, she would have been the last girl he would have looked at twice. She was scruffy around her edges, not even really that pretty. Striking, yes, with her tangled mess of dark hair and unexpected angles, but it wasn't a beauty that set out to please. Instead it hit Nate like a fist square between the eyes, completely unapologetic, in the world whether he liked it or not. Sometimes he wondered if his sudden infatuation with her was deliberately cultivated on her part, orchestrated to irritate his mother, but then he decided he didn't care. He was young, alive, and in love. He closed his eyes and inhaled the intoxicating scents of fresh mud and bluebells and a whiff of something like molasses that evaporated before he could enjoy it.

He heard a noise. Expecting Mercy, Nate leaped up off the stone he'd been sitting on, but his face quickly reddened. He squinted. "Mrs. Flyte?"

Dena Flyte drifted into the clearing, past the skeleton of a fence he'd never finished putting up around the maples. "Hello, dear."

Nate wasn't quite sure what to say. Ever since Suzie's death, except for church on Sundays, he'd had minimal contact with the Flytes. His parents thought it was better that way. He glanced around nervously. Moments ago he could barely wait for Mercy to arrive. Now he sincerely hoped she wouldn't. "What are you doing out here?"

"I'm visiting Suzie's stone. Hazel said she set one out for her."

Nate looked around him in horror. "She was out here?" His mind began racing. Hazel must have seen the taps. They were hard to miss. She must know what he was up to. Maybe she'd even found the sap he'd hidden in the broom cupboard. He'd promised Mercy he would give it to Fergus, but he was still waiting for the perfect moment. He swallowed, trying not to panic. "I thought these stones were only for babies."

Dena drew herself up. "Suzie *was* my baby."

Nate didn't know what to say to that. He'd never seen a single townswoman out here. Normally they avoided this place like the plague, taking to heart the maxim that once planted, sorrow was best left to sprout roots in solitude. The only thing he could do for himself right now, Nate figured, was leave—and quick. Besides, it was awkward standing in front of Suzie's mother when his head was now full of Mercy. "I better be going." He turned to start sauntering back toward the barn. If he was lucky, he'd be able to catch Mercy before she neared the sugar bush.

"Wait." Dena put out an uncertain hand. "How have you been?"

Nate shifted, uneasy. For him to admit that the accident had changed everything for him, that he was not the same boy he used to be, seemed like it might pain Mrs. Flyte. But to lie and say he was fine also seemed like a sin. He shoved his hands in his pockets and mumbled, "Okay."

"I hear you've been working out here with Hazel and her sheep. Imagine, a McAllister man freed from the mill."

Nate wouldn't have put it that way, but it wasn't an inaccurate description of his situation. Freed was exactly how he felt. "It's only until I go to college in the fall. My parents thought I could use a break."

Dena didn't say anything to this, and Nate remembered how furious she'd been when his father had fired Fred and how Mr. Flyte had gone on a bender worse than any of his others. Suzie had later appeared at church with red-rimmed eyes and a bruise on the side of her cheek, and when he'd asked her about it, she'd told him that what happened within the four walls of her family's home was her business and hers alone. Then she'd asked him to get her father's job back.

"It doesn't work like that," he'd tried explaining. Similarly to what went down in the Flyte house, what happened in the head office of the mill was no one's business but his father's. And one day Nate's. Suzie had never forgiven him for pointing that truth out, and that, in retrospect, might have been the last straw that drove them apart before the accident.

"It can't last too much longer." Dena had crossed over to what must have been Suzie's stone. Nate hadn't noticed it, but it was glaringly obvious now. The dirt around it looked raw and newly dug, and unlike the others it hadn't had time to collect any lichen. Dena rested one hand flat on it, as if she were feeling for a heartbeat.

"I'm sorry?"

Dena's gaze was hard. "The mill. All the layoffs. Your father won't survive too many more rounds of those. Thank goodness Fred's found new work."

At that moment Nate heard Mercy sneak up behind him. She'd put some kind of rouge on her lips, he noticed, and the stain of red made her skin seem even whiter. Dena's eyes flickered from Nate to Mercy and back to Nate again. "I wasn't aware you two knew each other."

"We don't," Mercy said. She wouldn't look at Nate. "Not really." Her voice was high and nervous. "I should go. I'm not really supposed to be here."

"No, I'm leaving." Dena came over to Nate and raised her hand. For a split second, he thought she was going to slap him, but she simply put her palm up to his cheek. "Don't worry," she said. "Your secret is safe with me, my dear boy." Her touch was surprisingly gentle. Before Nate could try to deny what she was implying, or maybe justify it, she was gone, leaving a vibration of sadness lingering in the air behind her.

"She knows about us," Mercy said, watching her go.

"Yes." But how much? Nate wondered. Did she know that he'd loved Suzie right up until the moment she died, for instance? Did she know that he still missed her now? And could she tell as she passed out of the wood and into the sun that his heart was as pocked as the skin of the tapped maples around him?

Mercy came up and captured his hand. "It'll be okay."

"Maybe," Nate answered. Or it wouldn't be. Somewhere in

the middle, there had to be a balance between smothering normalcy and catastrophe, he thought. He just had to find it, and he was beginning to suspect he would never do it in Titan Falls.

As an early graduation present, Nate's parents had bought him a car. Nate wondered how his father managed to swing it with business so bad, but Cal boasted that he'd gotten such a good deal on the two-year-old coupe that he couldn't pass it up. "Bill Tyne at the dealership in Gorham owed me a favor. Besides, you'll need a car for college." And then, in typical fashion, like a careless dog trampling a field of perfectly blooming flowers, Cal went and ruined the moment. "It's a gift, but it's not free. This summer, I expect you to work for it in the mill until it's paid off—with ample interest."

Nate was tempted to throw the keys back at his father and tell him to go to hell, but he refrained. A car would get him a lot farther from Titan Falls a lot faster than his own two feet. How perfect, Nate thought, if Cal ended up being responsible for helping his only son skip town.

Now, on the deserted road that led to Hazel's farm, he held the door open for Mercy. "Please," he said, sweeping his arm out. "You're the first person to go for a ride in it with me."

Mercy crept into the passenger seat and ran her hands over the fine leather seats. "Where are we going?"

Nate slid behind the steering wheel and grinned. It pleased him no end that his first traveling companion was someone whom his parents so reviled but he was so crazy about. "You'll see."

They drove out of town in the opposite direction from Hazel's place and Devil's Slide Road, which gave Mercy a measure of relief. She didn't think it would do to have anyone from Titan Falls spot them together. As they bumped along a quiet road, sheltered on either side by tall stands of trees, Mercy leaned against the glass and let the cool of it soothe her aching forehead. She knew that being with Nate was a bad idea—maybe the worst—but there was something so irresistible about being taken for a ride like this, where she could prop her head on the seat and just let her mind drift. Normally when she was traveling, there were a million things to think about: whether or not she was too tired to see the blacktop straight, if Hannah was getting motion sickness, what they would find when they got to a new camp.

She hadn't even realized until this moment how exhausting it was trying to steer fate like that. And could you really do it anyway? Suddenly she felt completely drained. The winter had taken its toll. When was the last time she'd eaten a full meal, or bathed her whole body all at once in water hot enough to scald her, or worn anything that didn't itch or hang off her in unflattering rumples? She couldn't remember. What would it hurt to let herself have this one afternoon with Nate, whose hands and mouth were so gentle they felt like a prayer unfolding along her own flesh? No one would ever have to know, and when the day was over, Mercy promised, she would give him up and let things go back to their natural order. She would return to the ravine, haunted by the silent shadow of her brother, and Nate would finish the summer at Hazel's and then be gone into the wider world. And because she was starting to care for him, she would let him.

She drifted off to sleep, and when she woke, Nate was turning the car down a dirt road. He drove a little way into the woods, the wet spring trees hanging over them like concerned giants, and then pulled off the path. He grinned as if he knew a secret. "We have to walk from here. It's about a mile. But it's worth it, I promise. Come on." He stepped around the car, opened Mercy's door, and held out his hand, and she hesitated for only about a half a second before she took it.

Mercy could feel the lake before they came to it. Just like Arlene, she could sniff a hidden spring out of a forest in high summer with the same ease of a thirsty hound or find the smallest thread of a creek, no matter how twisted and shaded its path. Truth be told, she preferred those kinds of waterways. Rivers and lakes made her nervous. They were too much of one element in one place. A body didn't stand a chance against them. As for the sea, Mercy didn't even like to think about it.

The road was muddy, so they stuck to the woods, where the ground was cushioned by a thick layer of pine needles and rotten leaves. When they came upon the cabin, Mercy blinked in surprise to find a building so well hidden in the trees, despite its size. Nate pulled her in for a kiss, then scrabbled under a rock by the door for the key. "No one will bother us here," he promised. "We can be alone."

Inside, the air smelled of the previous autumn and dust. Nate flicked on the kitchen light, sparking the fixture, and pulled sheets off the couches. He felt suddenly shy around Mercy, aware of the dissonance her presence caused in a place that he associated with his parents. She must have felt the same, for rather than settling on the sofa next to him, she wandered through the room, touching the knickknacks on the bookshelves and picking up framed photographs, smiling at each image of Nate frozen in different stages of development. He blushed. No one in his family ever looked at those pictures. They were just props, like the ancient pair of snowshoes mounted on the wall above the door out to the porch or the stuffed prize bass his grandfather had caught a million years ago.

Mercy came to a standstill at a window that overlooked the porch and the lake. "Do you want to go down to it?" Nate asked. The water would still be frigid—it always was until July—but they could sit on the dock and dip their feet in.

She shivered. "No. I hate the water. I can't swim."

He came up behind her and put his hands on her shoulders. "One day maybe I'll teach you. It's okay, we can stay inside. We don't have to do anything. We can just talk."

Mercy surprised him then by turning around and kissing him. "That's not what I'm thinking about."

"Then what? Your brother?" Nate nosed the side of her neck. Mercy smelled like spruce and fresh grass. Green scents.

She twitched her shoulders. "Maybe. And Hannah. Everything. Also about what will happen in the fall."

Nate silenced her with another kiss. Was this how it would have been with Suzie? he wondered. Would his heart have flopped around in his chest like a tricky fish and his hands sweated? Or had he and Suzie known each other too well ever to make the leap to being lovers? Maybe, if she'd lived and they'd tried, they would have been disappointed in each other and then they would have had to go on with that knowledge souring in them as they aged.

Everything about Mercy was strange to him, but the strangest thing of all was that ultimately she felt like home. Nate remembered playing tag as a little boy and the relief he'd always feel as his palm brushed whatever was base: a tree, somebody's porch railing, the flagpole on the side of the school yard. Twisting himself up with Mercy felt the same way. He was flooded with a mixture of relief and triumph.

Without saying anything more, he led her upstairs to the loft, where the beds were narrow and the ceiling sloped like that of the tree house Nate used to have. Together they tumbled onto the mattress and, shivering, began to peel the layers of clothing away from each other. Mercy hid her face against Nate's shoulder. The skin on her belly was hot beneath his hands, but her fingers were cold. "Have you... I mean, is this the first time...?"

"No." She cut him off but didn't add anything more, and Nate didn't have the guts to ask. He'd been with two girls before, both cheerleaders, both times at parties when he'd been drunk, but this felt different. Mercy didn't desire him because he was Nate McAllister, heir to the Titan Paper Mill. She wanted him in spite of it. And maybe, he thought, pulling Mercy's frail body down onto his as he rose up to meet her, that's what true love was—not the affirmation of everything he knew himself to be but the absolute erasure of it. Without that, he suspected, he'd never be granted a chance to change.

Afterward they lay together, watching through the tiny hatch of the window as high noon mellowed and the sun sank a few inches lower in the sky, the light easing from yellow to a watery gold. Mercy sat up, clutching the sheet to her breasts. Outside, she could hear the lapping of the lake, and the noise shivered up her spine, filling her with a familiar dread. For months she'd been carrying a passel of burdens, and she realized she was tired of that weight. Nate wrapped a lazy arm around her waist and drew her back down to him. His skin was warm and his breathing easy. Mercy let herself relax against him. His breath tickled her shoulder, a Morse code of stops and starts that gave her chills. He traced a line down her arm with his thumb. "Let's leave," he said.

Mercy gathered the sheets back together and began to sit up. Well, what had she expected? Nate was his mother's son, after all. He was in a whole different league from her. He came from a world of such plenty that he probably didn't think twice about throwing out something as simple as an old plastic bag. She should have known he'd be done with her quickly. Just maybe not this soon. She bowed her head so that her hair fell like a curtain between them. "Okay. Will you let me get dressed again in private?"

Nate scowled, confused, and then spoke in a rush, parting her hair so he could stare straight into her eyes. "No, I mean let's leave Titan Falls. Together."

Mercy caught her breath. Part of her being with Nate had to do with her plan to try to trap him, it was true, but this was even better than she expected. For a moment she could see it, the two of them slid together in the front of the car, the windows rolled down, squealing away from Titan Falls. Then she frowned. It could never happen, of course. She had Hannah to look after and Zeke's name to clear. She was a Snow, and he was a McAllister. They were paper and rock. One was going to cancel out the other. She turned her cheek. "Don't be ridiculous."

"I'm dead serious. I've been thinking about it. After I graduate, let's just leave. I'll be eighteen in a few weeks. I have a car. And I'll be getting some money then, too."

Mercy gawped at him. "But what about college? I thought you were all signed up to go off to some fancy one."

Nate's face grew dark. "Dartmouth. It's where my father went, and his father before him. I hate it. It's the last place I want to go."

Mercy was silent. Unexpectedly, here was this boy she was starting to love, who treated her so kindly she was able to forget for a moment that she was damaged goods. Her life was already full enough of busted things. The sound of the lake pulled her back to reality so hard it was almost like someone yanking on her hair. "I'm thirsty," she said, slipping out of Nate's grasp and winding the sheet around her. "How about I get us some water?"

The stairs were cold under her bare feet and the kitchen floorboards even chillier. She opened cupboards, looking for a pair of glasses, and then random drawers, curious about the flotsam and jetsam of the McAllisters' lives. She found the summer silverware, mismatched and dented, and another drawer full of battered spatulas and nicked wooden spoons, and then what she surmised was the junk drawer. Idly she flicked through its contents: matches, random lengths of dirty string, coupons years expired. And then her hand touched something soft. With a little difficulty, Mercy reached back into the overly full drawer and made contact with the object again. She twisted and tugged, pulling the thing out into the light, intent in her curiosity.

"What are you doing?" Nate padded into the kitchen just as Mercy lifted the scarlet mitten up to her face, gasping as she recognized it. Nate's voice cracked her back to her senses. "Where did you get that?"

Mercy indicated the open drawer. "I found it. Right here. It was right here all along."

Nate snatched the glove out of her hand, balling it up. "That's impossible. How did it get there?" His face was pale.

"I don't know." Mercy was shaking a little. Maybe Hannah was right about all the ghosts she was always saying she saw. "I just reached my hand in the drawer, and there it was."

"Do you know whose this is?"

Mercy didn't take her eyes from his. She remembered the sight of Suzie being brought into the hospital, a single mitten just like this one balanced on her chest. "Yes."

Nate put a fist to his forehead, the crushed wool red as any wound. "Fuck. She was wearing these the night of the accident. She left the movie theater in the middle of the movie for a smoke, and when she came back, I noticed she'd lost one. Her mother made them."

"With Hazel's wool."

"Yes."

Without taking her eyes off the mitten, Mercy sidled over to Nate. She didn't know what he might do with it, but she knew that without it she might never be able to prove there was another side to the story of the crash. She put a hand to Nate's cheek, but he wouldn't look at her. She kissed him and sent her words sliding into his ear, slow and sure, like a drizzle of honey. "Let me prove my brother didn't do this."

Nate closed his eyes and exhaled, retreating into the silent core of himself where Mercy couldn't reach. He thought about the night of the crash, when Suzie had come bustling back into the theater lobby surprised and irritated to find him there. He thought of the familiar figure he'd seen retreating with his hands stuffed in the pockets of a camel-hair coat. Slowly Nate unfolded his palm and gave the mitten to Mercy. "We better head back to town."

She exhaled and tucked the mitten into her pocket. "What should we do?"

"I don't know." It didn't matter so much to Nate now. By opening up the cabin early, he'd broken the rules of time, bringing the past crashing into the present, mixing up his future with Mercy's. Mrs. Flyte's words from the sugar bush echoed in his memory: *It can't last too much longer.* Maybe she was right, but not for the reasons she thought, and that didn't give Nate any comfort either.

Somehow he'd always thought it would feel better than this to ruin his father.

Chapter Sixteen

It was beginning to occur to June that Cal was stone-cold right. She absolutely wasn't the correct person to go and banish the Snows. After all, a body wouldn't use a hammer to push a tack into a board or a torch when the flick of a match would do just fine. Likewise she was beginning to figure that she'd been going about the business with the Snows all wrong, but what else could she do? The situation had become untenable. They had to go.

"I'll be honest, June," Abel confessed from behind the mess of his desk. Half-empty coffee cups were stacked on manila files. His hat sat on top of the filing cabinet. If the mill was the beating heart of the town, Abel's office was its growling belly. "We don't have much to go on here. We're still looking high and low for that boy, but unless we find him, there isn't anything we can do."

"What about the little girl?" June couldn't bring herself to use Hannah's name these days. When all this was over, she had decided that she would definitely apply for custody of the child. Cal owed her that much, and she owed it to Hannah—a whole chain of obligation and guilt and misplaced responsibility that only June could straighten out, link by link.

Abel picked up one of the coffee cups, inspected it, and then quickly put it back down. "She's about as impossible to spot these days as her older brother."

When June had finally worked up the nerve to call social services, she'd gotten nowhere with them. She was astonished to hear that they'd made one visit to the Snow property already, which hadn't yielded any evidence of a child. June had blown her hair out of her face with exasperation. "But she's registered at the school! I've seen her myself. We spent an entire afternoon together. Sometimes she hides right here in the library, in plain sight."

Abel shook his head now, pulling June back to the present. "There's no real proof she really exists. She registered for school but never showed. The kid's just not in the system, June."

June huffed an impatient breath into the office's stale air. "You know, I don't mind the Snows per se. Why, I feel nothing but sorry for that poor child, forced to squat in those kinds of sorry conditions. It's Cal who really wants them gone." Cal, who more or less paid the entirety of Abel's salary, when it came down to it. June let that subtext hang and then leaned forward. "And what about you? Don't you care about justice? Don't you want to catch Zeke Snow and make him pay for all the grief and pain he caused when he ran Fergus off the road?"

Abel's face grew sorrowful. "I've been in the law a long time now, June. Justice doesn't always come around the way you expect. Sometimes it doesn't come at all."

June stood up. "In that case it sounds like one of us better go looking for it."

Abel rose to see her to the door, wishing Hetty were still around to clamp her daughter-in-law firmly back under her wing. *She* never would have gotten her neck bent out of shape over the likes of the Snows. Hadn't even done so when it came to the whole matter of Gert, although the less said about *that* the better, in Abel's opinion. He helped June into her coat. She wasn't a born-and-bred mill girl. She might not know that the river had current and depths no man in his right mind would want to rile. He wrapped a hand around her elbow. "Be careful what you get up to. You might not find what you're expecting."

June shook him off. "Oh, I expect I will."

And that, thought Abel, watching her walk through the door, was exactly what had him worried.

June left Abel's office fuming. She drove to the mill and jammed her car into park, then sat for a moment to cool down her temper. It wouldn't do to approach Cal in a huff. But really, she steamed, Abel should have known better than to dismiss her efforts. In the entire twenty years of her marriage, June had always prided herself on not being one to pull rank in the small circle of the town, but now Abel had left her no choice.

"June, what are you doing here?" Cal jumped to his feet as his secretary showed June into his office, quickly hiding the paperwork he'd been reading. More bad news.

"Hello, darling." June offered her cheek to be kissed. "What are you working on?"

Cal loosened his tie. "Just wrestling with some accounts." An understatement if he'd ever made one.

June draped herself over the visitor's chair in front of his desk. It was deliberately hard-backed, she knew, to discourage anyone from getting too comfortable. "I've just come from Abel."

"Oh?" Cal cocked an eyebrow.

"Well, he was absolutely no help. I tried to explain that it's a matter of vital importance to you that the Snows leave town, but he just doesn't seem to be *doing* anything."

Cal's jaw grew tight. "I thought we'd agreed to handle this ourselves, June. Why have you gone and gotten Abel all mixed up in it?"

June gaped at him. "Because he's the *sheriff,* Cal. He's already mixed up in it, what with the manhunt for Zeke and all. He *should* be doing more."

Cal moved so quickly June didn't see him coming until it was too late. He came around the desk swinging, and whether he meant to strike her or simply intended to scare her by swatting the air near her, she never really knew. His hand nevertheless struck her cheek, leaving a stinging streak of red. She gasped and blinked at him. Cal stood frozen for a moment, staring at his hand with a look of bewildered horror, and then he glanced out the glass-paneled door of his office to check if his secretary had seen. When he spoke, his jaw was tighter than a bobbin, but his eyes were rueful. "I've got it handled."

"But I thought you wanted—"

"I said you and I will handle it. We'll do it today."

June put a hand up to her cheek, hoping the rash of the slap would fade before she had to walk out of the mill. The last thing she needed was fifty pairs of eyes trained on that one single mark. Outside, she could see the river, full with the melt from spring, its peaceful surface so deceptive.

Cal reached out to June and stroked the spot he'd just hit. He looked almost as shocked as she did. "Jesus. I'm sorry. It's just that everything is coming down on me now. I swear, once everything is sorted out with the mill, you and I will make a fresh start. Maybe we could go to Europe for a few weeks. Wouldn't you like that? You could poke around in dusty old churches and libraries to your heart's content. Everything will go back to the way it was."

June wasn't buying it. *Time here only flows in one direction*, she thought as Cal put his arm around her. *Just like the damn river.* In Titan Falls there was no such thing as going back. That was the whole point of everything. Cal ought to have known that better than anyone.

Hazel was hanging the first dyed yarn of the season on her porch railing when June McAllister arrived. The wet loops were dripping in bright streaks. Hazel was working with the color green—a lovely, grassy hue with an undertint of cheery yellow. If ever there was a true color of spring, June thought, Hazel had just captured it. Later, after everything, June mused, maybe she would return to buy some. She slid her sunglasses off. "Is Nate in the barn?"

Hazel shook her head. "I let him go early. It's such a beautiful day, and I figured maybe he wanted to go spend it with some friends. Won't be too long now before he's off to college, will it?"

Maybe it was the change of season, or maybe it was the old scarf she'd tied in a loop around her hair or the swinging of her dyeing smock, but Hazel looked younger than her years to June, almost girlish. Her hands were stained the same green as the wool. June wondered how long it took for the dye to wear off and why Hazel didn't wear gloves. Maybe she liked being physically marked by the labor, June figured. Maybe she needed proof that she still had some weight in the world. June could understand that. There were days when she, too, felt like she was swimming around in thin air.

June put on a pout of disappointment. "Oh. I was hoping to catch him." In truth, she was glad Nate wasn't here. It would make Cal's plan run so much smoother. Already he was out in the grazing meadow, she knew, inching toward the sheep.

"Just keep Hazel talking," Cal had told her on the drive out to

Hazel's. "If you have to, find a reason to go lure Nate away from the sheep. Let me do everything else." At the mill he'd changed into old work clothes and a pair of heavy gloves, then shoved a battered cap on his head, but to no avail. He still looked exactly like himself. Then he'd gone to borrow a truck.

June slid her sunglasses back on her nose now. Her cheekbone was still tender from where Cal had lashed out at her. She winced when the plastic frames brushed the spot. Hazel squinted at her. "How'd you get that bruise on your cheek?"

"Oh, it's silly." June fluttered a hand up to her face.

Hazel turned back to her wool. *Please just shut up about it*, June prayed, but Hazel was never one to take other people's suggestions, especially not subliminal ones. "His father had a mean streak, too. You never knew him well, of course, but I saw what he was like back in the day. The whole town did. Especially Gert Snow."

Suddenly the bruise on June's face didn't hurt anymore. Her whole body had gone cold. "What do you mean?"

Hazel fiddled with the green wool. *Green for go*, June thought. "The Snows and the McAllisters have...a history. But surely you know."

The flash of an initialed cuff link tied up tight on a piece of yarn and hung around Hannah's neck winked in June's memory. Men didn't just lose cuff links. They removed them. There was really only one reason Hannah would have found that particular item out in the old smokehouse. Henry must have left it there.

Just how well had Hazel known Henry McAllister, June suddenly wondered, and wasn't it odd that Hazel's husband, of all the men in town, should be the only one never to have set foot in the mill? It was downright peculiar that a woman who kept herself so apart for all these years would turn out to be such a font of local knowledge.

Hazel smiled, but the gesture wasn't a bridge of friendliness, a reaching-out from one soul to another. It was more of a bludgeon. June took a surprised step away, a stumble quite out of character for her. *She's not even a little afraid of me*, June realized as Hazel looked her in the eye and spoke as if she knew the secret of a lifetime.

"No one else would say this to your face, my dear, but you are in far, far over your pretty little head. Go ask your husband who Gert Snow was to his father, but don't blame me if you don't like the answer. Now, get the hell off my porch."

Sheep were so stupid, June thought as she skirted the edge of the sugar bush, looking for Cal. And she wasn't much better, it seemed. All this time she'd thought she could keep the McAllister secrets as boxed and neatly categorized as her Christmas ornaments, but that was pure folly. She had the terrible feeling that her life was snarling into an unholy mess, knotting its way into fearsome and unexpected shapes she would have no hope of ever untangling.

In the meadow out in front of her, Hazel's flock was grazing. Unlike the prehistoric, tropical creatures June had grown up around—alligators and sharks, snakes and terrapins—sheep were herd animals to a fault. If one of the members bolted, the others would do the same, bleating as if already caught. On the other hand, gain one beast's interest and you'd soon have them all eating out of the palm of your hand, just as her roommates in college were always trying to do with men. She pictured the party where she'd met Cal, her in a plaid old maid's skirt, him telling a joke to a group of doll-like blond girls with ruby lips and dollar signs in their eyes. He'd been drawn to her because she was different, because she was nothing like those brash, glittering specimens, but what he didn't know—what she'd never told him—was that she'd wanted to be exactly the same as them.

From her place in the trees, June watched as the man she'd married, borne a child with, and was starting to grow old with pulled an apple chunk from his pocket and held his palm flat until one of the ewes approached and snuffled at the fruit. The rest of the sheep bleated and crowded closer.

Maybe it was the discrepancy of sun versus shadow or the distance from which she was viewing him, but June suddenly saw her husband the way another woman might—his mistress, maybe, or even, long ago, June herself. He was still adamantly good-looking. Bushy-haired and muscular, his jaw pleasingly square. His hands were tender along the palms and tough on the knuckles. His wrists were solid, and he walked like he wasn't afraid of anything in the world, this husband of hers, this adored only son, heir to a paper fortune. But hadn't he also proved himself to be a cheater and a liar? He'd caused a bus crash that had almost killed his son and did kill his son's best friend, and, like June, he was hell-bent on covering it up.

June felt a wave of sickness wash over her. Her mouth flooded, and she bent at the waist, afraid she might vomit. She thought of what Cal had said to her in his office—that he could make everything go back to the way it used to be, but that was the worst idea in the world. Ever since Smith, going back to her old life had always been June's biggest fear. Now, for the first time, she wondered if it had to be. Could it perhaps be possible to return to a place without also reverting to the person you used to be there? June had never thought so, but she wasn't so sure anymore.

When she straightened up again, she saw that Cal was closing in on a tiny lamb with a black spot down near its tail, gamboling a little bit apart from its mother. A wild animal would never let a stranger approach its babe, June thought as she watched Cal. She wouldn't have. But it was okay, she reassured herself. In a few hours, the lamb would be returned, reunited with the ewe, its displacement forgotten. She and Cal just needed to borrow it.

What happened next was not part of the plan. Cal was supposed to catch the lamb and quickly take it to the truck. He would tie it up near Devil's Slide Road, making it look as if Mercy or Zeke had poached it. Instead June watched with helpless dismay as Cal drew a hunting knife out of his pocket. *Where did that come from*? she wondered as he straddled the lamb's tiny back, yanked its neck up, and drew the blade hard across its windpipe, releasing a shockingly dark flow of blood. The lamb shrieked once, then crumpled between Cal's legs as the other sheep ran away in confused panic. The mother ewe went with them but came trotting back halfway, torn between the close safety of the flock and the loss of her offspring. Trying not to be sick, June watched as Cal wiped the blade in the grass and then reached into his pocket and withdrew a bright child's hat with a pom-pom on it. It was the same one Hannah had left behind during her lunch with June. This last detail had been June's idea. Sometimes, she'd explained to Cal as she handed over the hat, it took the sacrifice of an innocent to bring about a right. Abel had seen Hannah wearing this very hat. He might not want to hear June's complaints about the Snows, but after Hazel started haranguing him with physical evidence, he'd have to listen.

June covered her face with her hands. *Hannah*, she thought. What would happen to her? June had only meant to imply thieving, not a slaying, but Cal had gone and changed the story on her, upping the stakes without asking her permission. The Snows would be blamed, and this time, maybe, Hannah really would be removed from her sister's care. And no one would ever want a girl like that. *I have to go get her*, June thought. *I have to try to fix what's just been done.*

A soft voice came floating out of the trees. "He's not here."

Sweating, June turned and saw Dena Flyte drifting toward her through the dappled shadow of the wood, squinting in the sudden light. Quickly June stepped farther into the shade of the sugar bush, trying to block Dena's view of the meadow. "What?"

Dena's gaze was probing. "Nate. He's not here."

"Oh. I see." June's heart was racing. Had Dena heard the death bleat of the lamb? Had she seen Cal bending over it? She prayed that he went straight to the truck he'd parked on the road instead of seeking her out. How could she explain his presence to Dena? She swallowed and tried to calm her nerves. "I... didn't expect to run into anyone out here."

Dena offered no explanation. She must have put a stone in the sugar bush, June reasoned, although Suzie was neither an infant nor a victim of the river's ills.

Dena smiled. "If you want, I could tell you where he is."

For a moment June was tempted to snap that it wasn't necessary, she could find her own son, but she didn't want to antagonize Dena. She wriggled her sweating hands in her pockets and tried to look patient. "That would be very kind of you."

"You're not going to like the answer."

"Dena, for heaven's sake."

Dena's gaze turned canny. "You bought him a new car."

"Yes."

"Well, he went spinning off in it today, happy as a lark, but he wasn't alone. Not hardly."

"Who was he with?" Nate hadn't been close to any of his old friends in months now, but June's heart skipped a beat to think that he might be coming out of his shell at long last. Maybe things were going to be fine in the end.

A cold smile June hadn't known Dena was capable of spread across her face as she looked June straight in the eye. *She saw everything*, June realized just as Dena spoke.

"He was with Mercy Snow."

June fled. Things were so far from fine they were in a different realm.

Hazel knew immediately that something was terribly wrong in the meadow. Sheep didn't lie. They couldn't, and that was the best and worst single element about them. They were naked in their needs, bald in their dependence, and if she thought about that fact too much, it always broke Hazel's heart just a little, for who was she to be given the charge of such splendid and simple creatures?

Normally the sheep rushed her when she came at them with a bucket full of extra feed, but today something had them spooked. Hazel paced across the field, enjoying the late-afternoon sun against her bare arms and the squeak of damp grass underneath her boots. Just that morning Fergus had said her name clearly for the first time since his homecoming, and the sound of it still rang in her heart hopeful and fierce. Spring was finally here. The lambs had been born, the frozen fields had thawed, and Fergus was coming back to her—maybe not the same as before, maybe not all of him ever again, but enough so that life could go reasonably on.

She was so lost in gratitude that she almost didn't spot the scrap of Hannah's hat. The rough breeze had caught the woolen strands of the pom-pom and was playing with them lazily. Frowning, Hazel stepped closer and then froze at the abomination stretched out at her boots. She crouched down over the dead lamb's still body and pressed a thumb into the blood spilled in the grass. It was cool, but not yet congealed. Hazel rose and glanced around, a rage building so fast inside her that it reminded her of the moment when the ice plates cracked on the river and spun to life in the spring current.

She dragged the lamb to the edge of the field as the sheep watched from a wary distance. How much misfortune was one woman supposed to bear in the course of a single year? Hazel wondered, then pushed that thought out of her mind. This was a time not for self-pity but action. First she would bury the poor lamb, and then, when she was done, so help her God, she was going to get to the bottom of this mess.

A man set loose in the Great North Woods quickly discovered that he had two immediate choices on his hands. He could go mad from the vast quiet surrounding him or he could learn to use all that silence to his advantage. Over the past few months, Zeke hadn't stuck as close to Titan Falls as Mercy probably believed. Most of the time, it was true, he was right there in close proximity to his sisters, watching them with the stony stare of a hawk, noting everything going on before him but giving away nothing. He knew, for example, that Mercy had begun meeting Nate in the sugar bush and how she really felt about him. He'd observed Mercy wending her way back to Devil's Slide Road after time spent with Nate, her elbows cocked jauntily, a tickle of a smile dancing on her lips, and the feeling had struck him in the gut like a drunk's sloppy fist—that Mercy *wasn't* all alone, that one day she might move on, leaving him stuck permanently alone out here in the trees. So as not to be forgotten, he tried to remind her of himself. He left trinkets for Hannah, deposited game at the RV step, chopped wood in the dead of night, but none of it was enough. Over the course of the winter, his sisters had grown thin, then truly frail, until Zeke worried they really would disappear. When he'd found that downed ram out at Hazel Bell's, the temptation had been too great and he'd taken it, ashamed that his own hunting skills hadn't been enough to keep his sisters in feed.

Zeke didn't mind hunger for himself. In prison he'd dropped down to the bone and hadn't gained much back since his release. In fact, he rather thought deprivation might be his new permanent condition, and he was fine with that. It made life on the run so much easier, but it pained him to watch that process devour Mercy and Hannah. For what it was worth, Zeke was still the man of their family such as it was, and it began to occur to him that he ought to be doing more than just causing trouble.

And so, for the first time in his life, he'd started to listen—to the erstwhile advice of his dead mother, to his own lousy conscience, to the scolding of the winter wind through the bare branches. And he began to hear what he had never bothered to before in any of his travels: the long narrative threads of a specific place that made it more than just a series of random bar fronts, convenience stores, food pantries, and a quick road out.

Moreover, Zeke found to his surprise that *he* was part of the story. At least he was as of dawn today when he'd snuck out to the ravine. He knew he shouldn't have lingered, but he'd whittled a little twig angel for Hannah, and he wanted to leave it for her in the smokehouse. He smiled when he saw all her battered treasures lined up on the old shelf: her pilfered library books with titles he couldn't even pronounce, curling scraps of wire, stray buttons, and, tossed under the three iron hooks, a dented coffee can. Idly he looked inside, first thinking it was empty, but then he spotted something Hannah had never bothered with or maybe just never noticed—some sepia pieces of paper wound to the inner curve of the tin like a second skin.

He pulled them out eagerly. The ink was faded and the type smeared on the first piece of paper, but the seals looked official enough and there was no mistaking the name printed across the top: *"The Duncan Home for Girls."* Zeke peered closer at the writing. It seemed to be some type of record of admittance from fifty or so years ago—no names, just the circumstances and dates of children deposited. The second paper was an invoice. Zeke didn't think too much of it until he read the name Henry McAllister next to a surprisingly sizable amount.

Zeke folded the pages and slipped them into his back pocket, his mind going into hunting mode, stalking and creeping, following the trail. Mercy had mentioned early on that Hazel was an orphan, raised nearby in an institution that had shut its doors for good some years earlier. It had to be the same place. What if, he mused, there was some kind of connection between Hazel and the McAllisters, and what if that connection was a blood one? It might explain why Hazel had chosen to linger for all these years on the outskirts of Titan Falls, an oddity with her sheep and her wool when the rest of the village was paper to its core. Maybe she really did love the quiet scoop of her valley and the art of husbandry, or perhaps she had reasons for staying that were more complicated than anyone knew.

Zeke cracked the smokehouse door and put an eye up to the slit, checking for an all-clear before he made for the trees again, but this time he had a solid destination in mind. He was many things, but he wasn't a common thief. Ever since he'd stolen it, that damn ram had been weighing on his conscience. Now he thought he might finally have a way to pay it back.

As Nate drove down Devil's Slide Road, Mercy once again considered his suggestion to run away together. He had some money coming to him, he'd said. How much could he mean? She had no intention of really going through with the scheme yet couldn't help but think: What if they really did take Hannah and just flee? They could be a little family somewhere far away from the likes of rivers and trees. Hannah could finally go to a decent school. She could have a whole shelf of brand-new books to her name.

Suzie's scarlet mitten lay on the seat next to Mercy, its frantic color an insult against the dull leather. Nate seemed to have aged in the hour since they'd found the mitten and closed up the cabin. He'd left Titan Falls a mere boy, Mercy thought, and here he was returning almost as embittered as she was. It was a transformation even the bus crash and the trauma of losing Suzie hadn't accomplished, and Mercy was more than a little sorry for it. Even Nate's voice seemed to have deepened, ripened by the shock of what he now knew. "Do you have any idea where your brother is?" he asked, grim.

Mercy stared down into the ravine as they sped along. "No." Zeke was everywhere and nowhere all at once. That was the problem. He could be standing right behind the closest tree and you would never even know unless he chose to let you.

There was something else, too. Mercy wasn't sure she wanted Zeke anywhere near Nate. Nate was nothing like those two men in the woods had been—nowhere even close—but Zeke wouldn't have cause to know that. And if her brother found out that Mercy had a fantasy of running away with Nate...well, there was no telling what he might be tempted to do. "You can take apart a whole," he always said, referring to their bond, "but you can't undo it." Words Mercy used to find comforting but which chafed now. She turned to Nate. "I need to handle this my way. Give me an hour and I'll see if I can track down any trace of him. If not, then we'll go to Abel. Agreed?"

She held her breath. For a moment she was afraid Nate would keep driving into town, but when they arrived at the pull-off that led to the path to the clearing, he suddenly stepped on the brakes hard, throwing Mercy off balance. She gasped as the seat belt cut across her chest, knocking the wind out of her, and when she looked up, she saw June McAllister's car pulled to the side of the road just ahead of them.

"Isn't that your mother's car?"

Nate's voice was wooden. "It is."

"What is she doing out here?"

"I don't know."

Mercy bit her thumbnail. "This is bad." She pocketed the mitten.

"I know." From the way Nate said it, Mercy knew that all bets with Zeke were off.

The clearing was too quiet. The RV door was open, Mercy found, but inside, it was empty. The place stank of stale upholstery and trash. Mercy blushed to have Nate see the conditions in which she lived. She wanted to reassure him that she knew perfectly well that garbage needed to go out and that food speckled with green was no good, but the prickle of unease she was feeling was too strong for her to worry about anyone's good opinion now.

"Hannah?" she called, but there was no answer from the

sleeping loft. "Hannah?" Mercy climbed the ladder only to find the mattress empty.

"Follow me," she barked, flying out of the RV to the smokehouse and flinging its door open, but it, too, was vacant. Hannah's trinkets sat on their shelf—the poppet that Zeke had made her, a carved angel, the jar of coins, and an old coffee can dented to hell and scorched on its bottom. Mercy peered inside and then stuck her hand in. Nothing.

"Hannah?" she called again, louder this time. *Please don't let June have her,* she prayed, but her stomach flip-flopped as her mind formed the words.

From down in the ravine, so faint she might not have heard it at all had it not been for her heightened concern, Mercy heard a cry. She cocked her head, willing it to come again, and it did, fainter this time, as if the sound were traveling away from her. That wasn't good.

"Come on." She ran out of the smokehouse, grabbed Nate, and headed into the forest, past Gert's erstwhile grave, where the earth suddenly gave way and plunged down to the river. Mercy moved with a lithe surety, hopping between the trees as Nate slid and stumbled after her, trying to keep up.

Mercy heard her little sister before she saw her. "No!" Hannah was protesting. "Get *away* from me. I don't want to go with you! Help!"

Mercy burst out of the trees to see June McAllister advancing toward Hannah, who was trapped between her and the river. She took a panicked step backward, her heel only a few inches away from the water now, but June kept coming toward the child. "If you don't come with me, they'll put you in a home," June was pleading. "You don't want that, do you?"

Mercy started running to save her little sister, but before she could reach her, Hannah turned and did something desperate.

She plunged into the river—knees, then hips, then finally her birdlike shoulders slipping under the water.

"Hannah!" Mercy screamed, hovering on the bank. Every cell in her body wanted to fish the child out of the river, but her feet were paralyzed.

"Get her!" June wheeled on Mercy. She seemed to be saying something about Abel arriving soon. "You need to get her out of here!" One of Hannah's arms shot from the water, and then her head slipped under. This time Mercy didn't think twice. She dived straight into the icy water.

Under the surface it was black and cold. Mercy had no breath and no blood anymore to move her limbs. Frantic, she tried to paddle her arms and legs, but they were numbed from the frosty water and wouldn't comply. Her foot briefly slid along the bottom, but that dropped away again as the current pulled at her. Where was Hannah? Water flooded Mercy's mouth, then spilled down her throat. Where was the bank?

Just then she felt a pair of arms squeezing her waist and tugging her to shore. Her head lolled forward as blackness closed in around her. *Nate*, she thought as she felt mud touch her cheek, but when she opened her eyes, she saw the hilt of a knife carved with a stag. Not Nate.

She looked up and saw Nate pulling Hannah from the river, her body limp, her lips blue, but her chest heaving, thank God. Mercy tried to say her sister's name, as if uttering it would be enough to make her dry, but before she could, there was a loud gun crack, and then Mercy's nerves exploded. She tried to pull Zeke's arms away from her, to run back to Hannah and the river, but there was an almighty stinging weight in her chest, an anchor she couldn't escape. She looked down and watched as a bloom of blood spread across the front of her with alarming speed. Her vision tunneled, and she heard someone crying her name, but whether it was Nate or her brother, she couldn't figure. She tried to sit up, but the pain grew too intense. There was so much she wanted to say and couldn't. Her time for talking, it seemed, was over. Others would have to take up the thread. She arched back into the wet mud, her eyes rolling to Zeke, and he, as if he finally understood what she'd been trying to tell him all along, bent over her, his bony ribs making a cage over hers, heart to heart, his weight indeed the other half of her as she floated from this life to the next.

Hazel wouldn't have gone and pulled a rifle on Zeke Snow, but Abel was a lawman with a jumpy trigger finger and a job to do. Hazel realized that nothing good was about to happen as soon as Abel had gotten Zeke in his sights, and in that regard she'd proved absolutely correct. Abel had missed and shot Mercy instead, and then all hell had broken as loose as a cave of rabid bats.

The minute she'd found the lamb and Hannah's hat lying next to it, Hazel had deduced that something was fishy. The Snows were unfortunate and bad to the bone, but they were not wastrels. They ate what they took from the world, maybe not always fairly or entirely legally but regularly enough that their violence had a sound logic operating behind it. If Hazel knew anything, it was that no Snow would leave a perfectly good meal to bleed to death on the ground, and she could say that with confidence because she wouldn't do it either.

She picked up the hat thinking that maybe Zeke had dropped it on his way back across her valley. He'd come to her door just after daybreak, and though her first impulse had been to fetch her double-gauge, turn it on him, and advise him to start running, she'd chucked that idea like a hot coal as soon as he started talking.

Plenty of men could worm their way into a woman's heart with a smooth line of chat, but in a paper town it was only words drawn in ink that carried weight. And the words Zeke had come to show her, Hazel quickly saw, were as heavy as they came. "Where did you say you found these?" she asked again, the documents from the Duncan Home for Girls clutched in her fist like a pair of winning lottery tickets. But they were even better than that, for lottery tickets only cemented the perfect happiness of your present and future, while these two chits of paper confirmed everything Hazel had ever suspected about her past.

Like hundreds of other poor souls up and down rivers in these parts, she'd been born and left an orphan, but unlike them she possessed a curious paper trail. During her last year at the Duncan Home for Girls, she'd assisted the head, Miss Blenheim, in the office, learning to type, take dictation, and file. It was during one of Hazel's clandestine forays into the bowels of the Duncan Home's records that she first found the list of annual donations from the Titan Paper Mill, all of them signed by Henry McAllister, all of them made in August, on the very same day as her admittance.

Hazel's decision to settle in Titan Falls hadn't been accidental—not by a long shot. She and Fergus had found their perfect valley, yes, but Hazel also couldn't resist the chance to live directly in the shadow of the mill, right under the gaze of Henry McAllister himself, so proud with his haughty wife and young son, surrounded by shifting currents of gossip that might tell her who her mother had been.

She'd never wanted it to be Gert Snow, but now that Zeke had come to her and told her where he'd found the papers, she couldn't deny her theory any longer. No wonder no one in town had ever mourned Gert's loss. She must have died soon after giving birth, maybe even by taking her own life. Had Hazel really been left by the river as an infant, she wondered, or was she perhaps stolen in the night and left somewhere Gert could never get her back? Pruitt must have figured it all out somehow when he took up residence out in the clearing—and Lord only knew by what nefarious means he'd gotten his hands on these papers—and that's why Cal McAllister had never tried to run him out of town. Hazel lifted the wrinkled pads of her fingers up to her lips in careful thought. She looked at the ragged-haired boy standing in front of her, his eyes sunk too far in his head to be good for anyone, his nerves as jittery as hers. Hell, his nerves *were* hers. He was a Snow, and so, in a roundabout way, was she. They were kin, and kin could tell each other anything. "Did you cause that bus crash?"

Zeke didn't blink. "No, ma'am, but I think I know who did. I just can't prove it."

Hazel believed him. Mercy had been right all along. She jerked her chin toward the trees. "You best hightail it out of here. Don't let yourself be seen. I'm going to go talk to Abel, see what he can do. Hannah didn't kill that lamb, and you didn't push Fergus off the road. Something's not right about any of this." She looked again down at the papers crumpled in her fists. Something hadn't been right for quite some time.

Abel was a man of action first and talk later. When Hazel arrived at his office with the story of the sheep, Hannah's hat in her pocket, she barely had time to follow him to his squad car, much less school him on fifty years of back history. Against her better judgment, she shut up and went along, staying silent on the drive to Devil's Slide Road. They could sort out one problem at a time, she decided. When they got to the Snow turnoff, however, they found a pair of cars parked on the side of the road.

"What the holy hell is June McAllister doing out this way?" Abel muttered, slamming his door and adjusting his belt.

"Do you hear that?" Hazel put out a hand. From down in the ravine, they could hear the cries of Hannah. They slipped and stumbled their way down to the river, where they found an ashen-faced June pleading with Hannah and the frightened girl running as fast as her skinny legs would take her straight in the direction of the river. Hazel hung back along the bank, watching with horror as Hannah tore into the river and sank, and then as Mercy followed. *They can't swim*, she remembered, but just as she began moving forward to point this out, Abel raised his gun and a dark figure burst out of the trees from the opposite bank and plunged in after Mercy. There wasn't time to protest that Zeke Snow was doing a good thing, to tell Abel everything she now knew about the crash, to beg him to lay off his fool weapon and stand down. Abel aimed and fired. Mercy fell.

Across the river Nate lay drenched and shivering on the bank, Hannah in his arms. At first Hazel was worried that the girl had drowned, but soon she saw tiny signs of movement. The child rolled onto her side and began throwing up river water. June stood near them, frozen to the root with guilt, her mouth moving but producing no sound. *Someone please do something*, her gaze said, and though Hazel wanted nothing more than the power to turn her back on the whole sorry scene, stump her way up the ravine, and reenter the peace of her valley, she knew she never could, not after seeing what was on those two papers Zeke had given her. The image of the first lamb that Fergus ever brought her arose, the poor thing wrapped in a sodden blanket, bleating for its life. Once sheep had been her salvation. Now it was her turn to do some saving, and she guessed that was going to start with another little girl orphaned on the banks of a river, only this one would grow up knowing exactly who she was. Hazel would see to it, and if that wasn't a promise, Hazel thought, already stepping forward into the wet mud, then the sky wasn't blue, sheep didn't flock, and the only thing people could do with the innocence they'd lost was to remember it and weep.

"Hush, now." She reached Hannah and threw her coat over the shivering girl. No weeping allowed on her watch. Not now. Not ever. Or so help her, Hazel vowed, sweeping back Hannah's dark hair so she could give her a kiss, she'd be a monkey's butt straight up, and that's all there was to it.

Chapter Seventeen

Every Tuesday at a quarter to three, in the very tiniest of Florida branches, the local librarian began the children's story hour word for word with the same chapter and verse. *Pity the sinned against, but pity more the sinner.* If the twenty-odd children settled cross-legged on the floor—some of them swiping at runny noses, some sleepy-eyed in pigtails, some twiddling strands of the ancient carpet in between their chubby fingers—found this homily strange, they never showed it. But then they were used to the librarian, comfortable with her scratchy voice, hard in its vowels the way northerners' voices sometimes tended to be, even though she'd been born in this very town. Today, however, for the first time in her tenure, instead of launching straight into one of her stories, the librarian paused, fixed the children with a quizzical stare, and posed a question: *But how do you know which is which?*

Startled at this violation, the children blinked up at her. One boy, redheaded and freckled to kingdom come, lifted a thumb to his mouth and began to suck in thought. The librarian fought the urge to pry the boy's digit gently from his lips, the way she used to with her own son when he had been small. A spasm rippled across her chest, coming to rest in between the tender muscles of her ribs, but whether the pain originated from the rickety valves of her heart or from the memory of her long-missed son, she could no longer say. Absence, it turned out, had worn this organ down to a blood-filled rag beating in her chest, and not necessarily filled it with fondness.

Finally a small girl in the back raised a tentative hand. "A sinner does bad things."

The librarian nodded. "Yes. But what happens if he also saves someone?"

The girl considered. "Then he's not a sinner anymore?"

"That ain't right." The toothless boy with curls furrowed his brow. "He's still a sinner."

"So once a sinner always a sinner, is that it?" The librarian's gaze drifted over the heads of the children and landed on an embroidered wall hanging framed next to the window. It depicted a single tree and the four seasons. The yarn was faded and frayed with age, but the stitches were still sturdy and even, and the librarian would know because her fingers had made many of them.

"Ma'am?" The shyest boy in the group, a little older than the others, raised his hand. He was almost too old for the story hour, but the librarian had always liked him. "Would the story help us figure your question out?"

"Perhaps." The librarian nodded. The children were clever. She would give them that, but they were innocent still. They knew only the panoramic and exaggerated villains of cartoons and video games: horned creatures with scales and spindly fingers, pneumatic men with oversize guns and black visors, aliens with blasting, menacing ships. But real badness wasn't like that. It masked itself in the faces of the people you loved, arrived in the form of accidents and misunderstandings, paraded through your life on quiet wheels before it exploded everything all at once.

Yet here she was doing it, too—speaking of evil in sweeping generalities when the problem with it was that it was always very, very specific. One bad choice even though you knew better. A decision to keep quiet when a word was required. Sometimes your own face reflected in the mirror, an accusing echo.

These poor children, she thought, spreading her skirt across her knees. They had no idea what kinds of things lay ahead of them. The shine would start rubbing off them soon enough. In the meantime they still had so many lessons to learn and disappointments to suffer, not least of which was the fact that although June was sitting right here, plain as a sunny day, not one of them seemed to recognize the sinner in their midst.

In a buttery puddle of light, under a row of neat square windows in the library of Smith College, a young woman sat reading. Her lips moved slightly as she scanned the page, uttering the complicated syllables of a language not quite lost although certainly no longer in general circulation. But that was exactly why Hannah liked ancient Greek. Every time she uttered a line of epic poetry or quoted a stanza of a drama, she marveled that a world long since disappeared could be brought back to instant life. Hannah had always had an affinity for ghosts.

Sometimes, when a rattle of wind shook the fiery-leaved trees on the quad as Hannah walked back to her dormitory or the moon rose and filled her windowpanes like a curious face, she would smile and remember Mercy, wishing that her sister could see her now. The Greeks, Hannah knew, were excellent interpreters of auguries and omens, but after Mercy's death Hannah had quit believing in the power of the dead to send signs and signals. Instead, she thought, it was enough just to remember.

Hazel had been concerned when the time had come for Hannah to make a decision about college. She had several offers. "Are you sure you want to go to Smith?" Hazel had fretted. "*She* went there, you know." She being June McAllister, of course, a name none of them ever invoked unless they could help it. But June was the whole reason Hannah was attending college in the first place, Hannah pointed out. She was providing the money for it, and anyway, Hannah argued, just because one woman walked in the path of another didn't mean their journeys would be the same. For one thing, Hannah wasn't running away from anything. When she thought of June, Hannah recalled afternoons in the Titan Falls library, and her first time at a restaurant, and a Cinderella watch. But she also remembered rushing into the river and the frigid shock of going under, then waking up and finding out that Mercy was gone. When June had offered to pay for Hannah's tuition and all her needs, Hannah had thought long and hard and then accepted. This apple was an offering of peace, she determined, not poisoned. In the end June was just a woman with much to atone for—not so wicked as a queen written down on paper, but not so easily categorized either.

The real reason Hazel was worried about her going to college, Hannah knew, was that she thought Hannah would forget them. "Things are changing so fast around here you won't know tops or tails when you come back," Hazel fretted, packing a trunk for Hannah the week before she was due to depart. She had a point. After Cal's arrest and sentencing, the mill had stuttered along at half capacity for almost a decade, but it had just been sold to a Canadian outfit that was promising to overhaul the whole place. They were the lucky ones, Hannah thought. All up and down the river, mills sat empty-eyed and shut. On the other hand, without the extra pollution, the Androscoggin was running cleaner than it had in years. Fish jumped in the summers, and people even dared to wade out in some spots, laughing with their pants rolled over their knees. But who knew how long that would last? Change was the one thing you could always count on in a river town.

When she thought Hannah wasn't looking, Hazel stuck a jar of maple sap into the corner of the trunk. Hannah watched her do it and smiled to herself. Then she went over to Hazel and embraced her, feeling how thin her shoulders were growing. "Don't worry," she whispered. "I might be leaving, but how could I possibly turn my back on Titan Falls? Everyone I've ever loved is right here."

All Hannah had to do to prove that point was walk past the sheep out into the sugar bush. Fergus's stone—two years old now—lay in a dapple of sunlight under the biggest maple, and Mercy's sat next to it, covered in a feathery moss the color of green apples. Every winter Hazel tapped the maples herself and distributed the sap to everyone in town. The people who remembered the accident and the terrible events in the ravine received their portions with a nod and a solemn murmur of *"Mercy,"* both a name and a blessing, for Mercy had taught them that sorrow flowed in this life, but so did sweetness in equal measure, perfect halves of a whole, and that you couldn't dam them up. Better to let them run, the town had decided, like color into wool.

The college library had darkened. It was ten minutes to closing. Hannah rummaged in her bag and pulled out her current bookmark. She liked to use photographs so she always felt close to home. This one was of Zeke and Ivy's new baby girl. Zeke had settled down with Hazel, and last spring he'd married Aggie the shearer's daughter. Zeke had a way with animals, it turned out, maybe from his years of stalking and hunting them. But these days Zeke didn't kill so much as a fly. Instead he waited openhanded and let creatures come to him.

In the snapshot the child lay on her back in her crib, her face tipped up to the camera, her hands extended like pink starfish, her mouth bubbling into a smile. Suspended over the crib, a flurry of wooden butterflies hung on invisible strings, a constellation of complicated beauty. Hannah remembered the box of butterflies of her own that she'd opened for Christmas one year and the way their powdery wings had brushed her cheeks and hair, but these, she thought, were even better. They would never fly away. These were carved to last, their bodies and wings shellacked, their antennae and legs minutely jointed. No matter what happened, these specimens would live forever.

When the letters arrived, it was always spring, the sticky Florida air heating into a furnace of salt and swamp grass, the sky swarming with jeweled insects and migrating birds. The envelopes appeared as if by magic, the paper battered and waterstained, decorated with the delicate and upright calligraphy of foreign characters. The marks were indecipherable in their stark beauty, an alphabet of mystery, often embossed with stamps of flowers or animals painted in startling colors.

Once there was a vermilion dragonfly smeared like a seal across the lip of the envelope so that to open it June had to tear the creature's wings. Another time the postal stamp bore the image of a red star with a golden crescent moon nestled in its belly. Sometimes June wondered if these symbols were secret messages to her, a code she was supposed to know somehow. Other times she accepted them as simple accidents of communication, a one-sided burst of a language that she was only just now, for the first time in her life, learning to speak.

One year Nate's letter informed her that he was giving

vaccinations in East Africa, where, he said, the earth was the color of rust. The next he was tending an outbreak of cholera in India, where the cows were so sacred they could lie for hours in the road and be perfectly safe. Security, June knew, was all-consuming for her son. After the terrible events in the ravine and the death of Mercy, Nate had left Titan Falls as soon as he could. He wandered for a year, then attended university and medical school in Arizona, where the land didn't hold the burdens of either many rivers or many trees. And then, because that wasn't far enough away from the memory of Mercy, he'd left the country for good, doing clinic work in the places that called to him, permanently unfixed.

But could you ever really leave behind the people you'd loved? June didn't think so. The past was not a distant country, a spot to be marked on a map with a pushpin, a touch point for miles traveled. It was more of a continuum, a river. Even now, after all the terrible things Cal had done, for instance, after he was almost through serving time for vehicular manslaughter, June still sometimes remembered him as he'd been when she'd first met him: a young man with the strength of wood in his bones and paper in his blood. If she could go back, she asked herself again and again, would she make all the same choices once more? Would she have married Cal? Maybe, she realized. Probably she would.

But that didn't mean she would do everything identically. When it came to her own culpability in the death of Mercy and the cover-up of the bus accident, June was still coming to terms with what she'd done and, worse, with what she hadn't. Cal had insisted when Abel came for him that June knew nothing. When she'd tried to contradict him, he'd shot her a look and June had fallen silent, understanding that with a glance her husband had given her the only thing he could. Her marriage, it turned out, had been no more difficult to unravel than Suzie's mitten. All it had taken was finding the right thread and giving it one hard yank.

She'd known immediately what she had to do—not just leave Titan Falls but leave it absolutely, unwinding herself all the way back to her beginning, past Cal, past her years at Smith, down to the bobbin. As tempted as she was to say that she couldn't believe what she'd done to protect Cal and all the appearances she once thought mattered, as much as she wanted to plead that they were the actions of a different woman in a different lifetime, she knew that would be the worst crime of all.

And so she did the most painful thing she could think of. She went back. She rented a cottage just three doors down from the childhood wreck where she'd grown up and, purely by accident, lucked into a job at the library. Mrs. Tumbridge, the ancient librarian from June's childhood, hadn't cared that she didn't have a degree in library science or any, for that matter. She was, it turned out, a Wellesley girl.

"What? How did I never know?" June asked.

"You were too hell-bent on getting out of here. You barely ever gave a fish time to fry. I know because once I used to be just like you."

June colored. "Well, time is *all* I have now."

Mrs. Tumbridge patted her hand. "I know that, too, dear."

Every now and then, on an evening when the sky was bleeding out its most glorious sunset colors or during an afternoon thunderstorm, June would sit down and attempt to compose a letter to Nate.

"More than anything, I regret. If I could take it all back, I would.

I know I did wrong." Incomplete phrases, half sentences and false starts. None of them told the whole story, not even close. She always ended up crumpling the pages and throwing them out, telling herself she didn't have Nate's return address anyway. Sometimes she ran water over the words first to make the ink blur and encourage the stationery to break into flakes of pulp. After being married to a paper man for most of her adult life, June was only too aware that it was a substance that lent itself just as easily to outright lies as it did to the fiction she so loved. But how could you know which was which? It was the one question she should have been asking all along. Were stories a pack of lies disguised as veracity, or was it the other way around? Had all the things she'd told herself about Titan Falls over the years been the truth or just her version of it?

In answer, every Tuesday, she gathered the town children together at her feet and spun a tale full of wicked queens and noble princes who'd lost their power to fight and princesses trapped under sheets of river ice. She turned Mercy into an empress of winter, daubing her lips with frost and crowning her hair with icicles, and Hannah into a cherub of spring. Zeke was a hunter who could carve an animal out of wood and breathe life into it, and Hazel was a woman who could see both the past and the future alike. Far from being stuck in one, June had the ability to shape stories, she was beginning to realize. Once she had not thought much of that bequest. She had misused it and ignored it, denied it to herself, but now she was coming to comprehend that it meant absolutely everything. It was the only thing, really. She'd been given the gift of the last word. The very least she could do was make sure it was a good one.

Acknowledgments

The Androscoggin River is a waterway that tells a version of American history that I feel is in danger of being lost—a story of gumption, ingenuity, and technology, but also one of displacement, irresponsibility, and loss. In researching this book, I came across so many evocative photographs of old mills and learned so much about the passage of the Clean Water Act that I heartily recommend the curious to explore the subject. An excellent starting point is the Bethel Historical Society, which has an excellent Web page dedicated to the fascinating history of this region. Bates College students, in collaboration with the Androscoggin Land Trust, also put together a detailed regional timeline of the river broken into sections. Finally, Bowdoin College offers a fascinating "living history" page of the Androscoggin, complete with original documents about the paper industry and probing questions.

It takes a small village to put out a book. First thanks go to my lovely editor, Helen Atsma, for her good sense and divine ability to know what a story needs and for her calm faith and patience. And thanks to my agent, Dan Lazar, for being a mentor, an advocate, and a friend. I am so appreciative of the entire operation at Grand Central Publishing, from Caitlin Mulrooney-Lyski and

Kirsten Reach and the art department (who makes such gorgeous covers), and Maureen Sugden for copyediting, all the way up to Jamie Raab, who runs the whole place with impeccable style.

I owe a heap of thanks to all the people in my daily life who see me working at home in my pajamas, listen to me wail about deadlines and plotlines, and who are always standing at the ready with champagne when it's all done: Pam, Andrea, Chantel, Lynn, Jack and Nancy, Lala, and Bella. Thank you to the whole Drever clan.

Thank you to Books, Inc., and to Book Passage for being so supportive of my novels over the years. A special thanks to Calvin Crosby for his wonderful humor and support, and to Elaine Petrocelli for creating a magical emporium packed with the best books, writers, and readers.

Finally, thanks to the people who make me who I am: Willow, Raine, Auden, and Ned. Here is another story for you.

About the Author

Tiffany Baker is the author of *The Gilly Salt Sisters* and *The Little Giant of Aberdeen County*, which was a *New York Times* and *San Francisco Chronicle* bestseller. She holds an M.F.A. (creative writing) and a Ph.D. (Victorian literature) from UC Irvine and lives in the San Francisco Bay Area with her husband and three children.

Reading Group Guide

Questions for Discussion

1. June McAllister is, in some ways, an outsider in Titan Falls. What does her outsider status mean to her? Is it always a detriment? Is June a sympathetic character?
2. Cal McAllister's mother tells June, when she's a new bride, "In Titan Falls...everything begins and ends with the damn river." What do you think the river might symbolize for June? For Cal? For Mercy? What about the treacherous yellow mud that lines Devil's Slide Road?
3. How do you feel about the women of Titan Falls? Would you want to live among them? Is the way they band together a comfort or a menace?
4. What does MERCY SNOW have to say about fathers and sons? Mothers and daughters? How is Mercy similar to Arlene? Do you agree that Nate is, as a few characters claim, so much more than his father, Cal? Does Zeke ever escape from Pruitt's shadow?
5. Many of the characters in this book feel burdened by fate. Do you believe in fate or destiny? Can you escape what you were born into?
6. Do you believe Mercy healed Fergus? Or that her cures—for alcoholism and for the smaller ills of the women in June's sewing circle—truly work?

7. Toward the middle of the book, June McAllister offers the Snows a large amount of money to leave Titan Falls—Mercy refuses the check. Would you have taken the money?
8. The dead hold quite a sway on the residents of Titan Falls—June frequently recalls her mother-in-law, Hetty, and the advice she gave; Suzie Flyte and her tragic death hover over the McAllisters and Snows; and the bones of Gert Snow speak to Hannah and seem to hold the town itself in their thrall. How do June's recollections of Hetty differ from the memories of Gert Snow? Do you believe the departed influence your life?
9. Zeke believes there are "two sets of justice in the world: one for people like Cal McAllister, and another for boys like him." Do you agree?
10. The residents of Titan Falls all seem to operate under similar, but unarguably different, moral codes. What differences do you see between the characters' ideas about right and wrong? Is any character more right, or perfectly right?
11. The story of MERCY SNOW rarely leaves the confines of Titan Falls. What is the significance of setting in this story? How does Titan Falls compare to your own hometown? Is it like anywhere you've ever been or visited?
12. Were you surprised by the book's conclusion, and by where June ends up? Do you believe stories have the power to help us address rights and wrongs?

A Conversation with Tiffany Baker

Q: The mill town of Titan Falls feels vivid, almost claustrophobically real. Is there a real-world Titan Falls somewhere that inspired the fictional version? Why did you decide to set this novel in a failing mill town?

A: The novel is set along the Androscoggin River during the 1990s, and while Titan Falls is a fictional creation, I did draw heavily from the history of that area, reaching back to the days before the Clean Water Act, when the river was quite horribly polluted. In the 1990s, the industry began to experience booms and busts, and it was really the last gasp before globalization swept in and changed things forever. I deliberately chose a paper mill town because the setting is so claustrophobic. The economies of those towns or small cities were mostly based on a single industry, and therefore the threat of the mill closing provided an instant make-or-break situation. Even the geography is closed-in and tight. There's the river and mountains, and nowhere else to go. As a result, the social structure becomes quite rigid. People have their roles and places. But what happens when that order changes, shifts, and starts to break apart? Our country has undergone an epic reorganization in the last twenty years in terms of our workforce and manufacturing, and Titan Falls is a microcosmic example of that. I wanted to convey the anxiety and stakes that are associated with such a major economic upheaval, but I wanted to do it in purely human terms. I think of Titan Falls as a Petri dish of reluctant social flux.

Q: Do you have a favorite character in MERCY SNOW? If not, is there one you identify most closely with?

A: I am quite fond of Hazel Bell. I love her strength and her pragmatic nature. Her down-to-business voice was so much fun to write. She is a woman with a tough exterior, but a soft heart. I like that through her sheep she is in touch with the entirety of the life cycle, from birth to death. I think of her as kind of an earth-mother—someone who has been through love and loss, and who has some perspective on the nature of the world. Hazel also seems like the kind of woman whose good opinion and loyalty are difficult to gain, but once obtained are yours for life. I felt like I had to earn the right to put her on the page.

The character I perhaps identify with most closely, however, is June, in spite of all her failings. It's not that I see myself as June, and I certainly don't like all the choices she makes in the novel, but I understand her completely and have sympathy for her. She is a woman who has always been made to pay for things in her life. She goes to college on a scholarship and marries into a social circle above her own, but that seeming step up has a price for her. She constantly gives up her own will in order to benefit from what she perceives as desirable. Except, once she gets the husband, the house, and the life she thinks she's supposed to have, she discovers that there are cobwebs lurking in the corners of it. I think of her not as scheming, but as naïve. She is a woman who loves her son and husband more than anything, and who commits the ultimate sin of not letting anything stop her from protecting them—even the strict social mores she has so benefited from. And once she crosses that line, the whole house of cards she's so carefully built for herself collapses.

Finally, I think I channeled a bit of myself as a child into Hannah. I lived a somewhat peripatetic life for a bit as a girl, and I, too, used to haunt the library. The Cinderella watch that June buys for Hannah, by the way, was based on one I actually owned. I have no idea what happened to it.

Q: You've written on your blog about being a woman writer and telling women's stories. Do you believe MERCY SNOW is a woman's story? Why or why not?

A: MERCY SNOW is absolutely a woman's story, and I think that's a really important point. Vital, in fact. The women in the book live in a very male universe. For the most part, the men in town all work at the mill, and while history has amply recorded the rise and falls of the paper mills along that river, it hasn't really chronicled the stories of the women who've lived in the shadows of those mills. Early on in the book, June reflects that in Titan Falls, "sorrow usually ended up being women's work," and I think this is exactly right. At the risk of being called a generalist, it's been my experience that women live quite differently from men. We have the capability of giving birth, for one thing. We have a primal, physical relationship with our children, and we often rely on our sisters and our female friends to pull us through grief in a way that I think is very different from men—especially men in a place like Titan Falls, where gender roles are more codified. I'm not saying this is always the case, but there is something about a group of women swapping stories in a kitchen, or sitting around sewing, or gathered together as they collect children from school that is quite powerful and familiar to me, and which transcends class, race, and nationalities.

Q: There has been so much debate lately about the value and place of "women's fiction" in the marketplace, and I find the whole issue fascinating. To me, it makes perfect sense that the majority of fiction writers and readers would be women. For most of recorded history, women have stood outside the official narrative, but novels give that state of affairs a voice. The phrase "women's fiction" peeves me to no end, however, especially when it's used as a sales category. What does that even mean? If *The Brothers Karamasov* was *The Sisters Karamazov*, would it be given a pink cover and not reviewed?

A: In fiction, I think women writers and readers have the freedom to experience the world in emotional, familial, and linguistic ways that resonate with us, and I think that's ultimately the whole point of reading and writing novels. The novel as a form allows me to voice all the things that go unsaid in life but shouldn't. It's my way of sitting around a kitchen table, passing around a story, and hoping I make a connection.

Q: The characters in MERCY SNOW—Hannah and June in particular—invoke fairy tales and Greek mythology often. Were there any stories or books in particular that inspired you as you wrote this novel, from mythology or otherwise? What books might you recommend for fans of MERCY SNOW?

A: MERCY SNOW is very loosely based on the Antigone myth from the Greek, where Antigone, the daughter of Oedipus, goes up against the king of Thebes in order to bury her disgraced older brother. Ultimately, it's a story about the struggle of individual moral authority versus state conventions, and one that questions the idea of absolute truth. Mercy is meant to be an Antigone figure—an outsider with ties to the town, and disenfranchised by virtue of her sex, her socioeconomic status, and her family history. She's a girl who shakes things up. In one version of Antigone, the king's wife spends her time in the story spinning, and I had fun incorporating that element into the book. Knitting and spinning, in Greek mythology, are significant, for fate is a thread that can be cut at any time. It's a terrifying idea, really, that life is as fragile as a simple string, and that the quick and brutal snipping of it is not up to us.

Hannah is also influenced by Greek mythology in the novel. The pilfered book she so loves is based on D'Aulaire's book of mythology for children, which I have spent the past decade reading to my own kids, and which will always have a permanent, dog-eared place on my bookshelf alongside *Grimm's Fairy Tales*—the only version that should ever be read.

In the novel, June is a former student of literature, and through her, I was re-inspired by all the American literature I read in high school and college, which I think of as the foundation of much of my character: Emerson, Thoreau, Hawthorne, Dickinson, Whitman, even Louisa May Alcott. In short, the Transcendentalists and their kin, who believed that man can be the master of himself and have a personal and soulful relationship with God and nature. It's a very idealistic and American idea, I think, and one that June struggles to live up to in the novel.

Finally, if you find yourself reluctant to leave the world of Titan Falls, I would say to go and read Elizabeth Strout, who writes so amazingly and beautifully sparely about women and New England, and who is the master of making a difficult character someone you love anyway—which seems to me to be one of the aims not just of fiction, but maybe of life in general.